ORPHANS OF WAR

Leah Fleming was born in Lancashire of Scottish parents, and is married with four grown-up children and five grandchildren. She writes full-time from a haunted farmhouse in the Yorkshire Dales and from the slopes of an olive grove in Crete.

Find out more about Leah at www.leahfleming.co.uk and visit www.AuthorTracker.co.uk for exclusive updates on Leah Fleming.

By the same author:

The Girl From World's End
The War Widows

LEAH FLEMING

Orphans of War

AVON

This novel is entirely a work of fiction.
The names, characters and incidents portrayed in it are the work of the author's imagination. Any resemblance to actual persons, living or dead, events or localities is entirely coincidental.

AVON

A division of HarperCollins*Publishers*
77–85 Fulham Palace Road,
London W6 8JB

www.harpercollins.co.uk

A Paperback Original 2008

1

A catalogue record for this book is available from the British Library

ISBN 978-0-00787-960-1

Set in Minion by Palimpsest Book Production Ltd,
Grangemouth, Stirlingshire

Printed and bound in Great Britain by
Clays Ltd, St Ives plc

FSC is a non-profit international organisation established to promote the responsible management of the world's forests. Products carrying the FSC label are independently certified to assure consumers that they come from forests that are managed to meet the social, economic and ecological needs of present and future generations.

Find out more about HarperCollins and the environment at
www.harpercollins.co.uk/green

Acknowledgements

Once again I've borrowed the beautiful landscape of the North Craven Dales for the location of Sowerthwaite, Brooklyn Hall and the Old Vic. I was privileged to meet the late Mrs Frances Capstick of Hellifield who, a few years before her death, gave a wonderful account to our local history group of her extraordinary time in charge of the evacuee hostel, Mount Pleasant, near Settle during the war. Her life and stories inspired the beginning of this novel but Aunt Plum and all my evacuees and their adventures are fictitious. Thank you all my local friends who passed on anecdotes about their own experiences of evacuation. I also found *Evacuation: The True Story*, broadcast by BBC Radio 4 in August 1999 another moving source of information for this book.

Some of the details of the fashion industry in the 1950s were gleaned from Eric Newby's *Something Wholesale: My Life in the Rag Trade*, published by Picador, and Ginette Spanier's *It Isn't All Mink*, published by Robert Hale in 1972.

Thank you, Maxine Hitchcock and Keshini Naidoo, for editing my script with such care and making some thoughtful suggestions. Thanks, also to the 'Flying Ducks', Northern Chapter of the RNA, always there to encourage and enthuse when the going gets tough.

Alasdair, Hannah, Ruari and Josh
This one's for you!

October 1999

The storm in the night takes everyone by surprise: ripping tiles into domino falls, battering down doors, plucking out power lines and cables, hurling dustbins and chimney stacks through fences and down the streets of Sowerthwaite, past the sturdy stone cottages whose walls have stood firm against these onslaughts for hundreds of years.

Showers of rolling timbers hurtle into parked vans, flinging in fury against shutters and barricades. In the back ginnels of the market town, the brown rats newly installed in their winter homes burrow deep into crevices as the wind flattens larch fences, blows out cracked greenhouse glass, twisting through gaps on its rampage.

The old tree at the top of the garden of the Old Vic public house is not so lucky, swaying and lurching, groaning in one last gasp of protest. It's too old, too brittle and hollowed out with age to put up much resistance; leaves and beech mast scattering like confetti, branches snapping off as the gale finds its weakness, punching around the divided trunk, lifting it out of its shallow base, tearing up rotten roots as it crashes sideways onto the roof of the stone wash house; this last barrier down before the storm races over the fields towards the woods.

In the morning bleary-eyed residents open their doors on to the High Street to assess the damage: overturned benches flung into the churchyard, gravestones toppled, roofs laid bare and trees blocking the market square, smashed chimney cowls denting cars, gaping holes everywhere. What a to-do!

The BBC news tells of far worst devastation in the south, but swathes of woodland have been flattened in the Lake District and here in the Craven Dales, so the town must wait its turn for cables to be raised and power to come back on and mop-up troops to clear the debris. Candles, Gaz burners and oil lamps are brought out from under stairs for just such emergencies. Coal fires are lit. Yorkshire homes know the autumn weather can turn on a sixpence.

The tree surgeons come to assess the damage to the Old Vic and inspect the upended beech that's stove in the wash house roof. The pub lost its licence decades ago but the name still sticks.

The young tree surgeon, in his yellow helmet and padded dungarees, eyes the fallen monster with interest. 'Not much left of that, then . . . Better tell them up at the Hall that it's being sawn up. They'll want it logged quickly.'

His boss stares down, a portly man in his middle years. 'She were a good old tree . . . I played up there many a time in the war when it were a hostel, after it were a pub, like. They had a tree house, as I recall. Kissed me first girl up there,' he laughs. 'This beech must be two hundred year old, look at the size of that trunk.'

'It's seen itself out then,' replies the young man, unimpressed. 'We can sort this out easy enough.' They put on goggles and make for their chainsaws.

'Shame to see her lying on her side, though. Happen she'd had a few more years yet if the storm hadn't done its worst,' mutters Alf Brindle, running his metal detector over the corpse. He's broken too many blades on hidden bits of iron stuck into trunks over the centuries, wrapped over by growth and lifted high: crowbars and nails, bullets and even heavy stones hidden in the bark.

'Who are you kidding? It's rotten at the core. Look, you could ride a bike down there and it'll be full of rubbish.' The young man ferrets down into the divided hollow to make his point. There's the usual detritus: tin cans, rotting balls. Then they begin stripping the branches, sawing the trunk into rings.

'What the heck . . . ?' he shouts, seeing something stuck deep into the ring growth. 'Switch off, Alf!'

'What've you got there then?' The older man pauses. 'It always amazes me how a tree can grow itself round objects and lift them up as it grows.'

'Dunno . . . I've never seen owt like this afore,' his mate says, examining the rings, loosening what looks like a leather pouch, the size of a briefcase, from its secret cocoon. Curiously he begins to unwrap the cracked layers of rotten fabric. 'Somebody's stuffed summat right down here. It's like trying to unpeel onion skins.'

As he loosens the parcel he reaches the remains of a tea cloth; its pale chequered pattern still visible. 'Bloody hell!' He jumps back and crosses himself. 'How did that get there?'

The men stand silent, stunned, not knowing what to do. Alf fingers the cloth with shaking hands. 'Well, I never . . . All these years and we never knew . . .'

'Happen it's been here for donkey's years,' offers the lad, shaking his head. 'I can count the ring growth . . . must be over fifty years.'

'Aye, must be . . . You OK? Look, that cloths's got a utility mark in the corner. We had them on everything in our house after t'war,' says Alf, shaking his head in disbelief.

The lad is already making for his mobile in the truck. 'This is a job for the local constabulary, Alf. We don't do owt until they've sorted this out, but better fetch someone from the Hall. It's their property. I need a fag. Let's go for a pint . . . Who'd've thowt it, bones buried in a tree? Happen it's just a pet cat.'

Neither of them speaks as they stare at their discovery but both of them sense that these aren't animal remains.

A tall woman in jeans and a scruffy Barbour paces round the tree trunk in silence, kicking the beech mast with her boot. She is youthful in her late middle age;

the sort of classy woman who ages well and has never lost her cheekbones or girlish figure. Her hands are stuffed in her pockets whilst behind her a red setter bounds over the branches, sniffing everything with interest.

The woman looks down the path to the old stone house that fronts on to the High Street, its wavy roofline evidence of rotting roof timbers bowed under the weight of huge sandstone flag tiles. The tree has crashed through the outhouse at the side, leaving a gaping hole. It's a good job they'd not begun any renovations, she sighs.

The scene of the discovery is cordoned off but soon it'll be all round Sowerthwaite that remains have been found in the Victory Tree, human remains. It will be headlines in the local *Gazette* on Friday. There's not been a mystery like this since the vicar disappeared one weekend and turned up a month later as a woman.

''Fraid it's made a right mess of your wash house, Maddy,' says Alf Brindle, not standing on ceremony with her ladyship. He's known her since she was in ankle socks.

'Don't worry, Alf. We'd plans to pull it down and extend. Our daughter's hoping to set up her own business here: architectural reclamations, selling antique garden furniture and masonry. She wants to use all of the garden for storage. The storm's done us a favour,' she replies, knowing it's better to give the word straight before the locals twist it.

'She's up for good then, up from London to stay?' he fishes.

Let them guess the rest; Maddy smiles, nodding politely. With a messy divorce and two distressed children in tow, the poor girl's fled back north, back to the familiar territory of the Yorkshire Dales.

Sowerthwaite is used to wanderers returning and the Old Victory pub is a good place in which to lick your wounds. It's always been a refuge in the past. She should know, looking down to where they found the hidden bundle, now in police custody.

How strange that all this time, the tree has kept a secret and none of them guessed. How strange after all these years . . . Fifty years is a lifetime ago. How can any of these young ones know how it was then or understand why she mourns this special tree; all the memories, happy and sad and the friends she's loved and lost under it?

There are precious few left, like Alf Brindle, who'll remember that skinny kid in the gaberdine mac and eye patch arriving with just a suitcase and a panda for company with that gang of offcomers who climbed up the beech tree to the wooden lookout post to spot Spitfires.

Maddy stares down at the fallen giant, now cut into chunks, choking with emotion.

I thought you'd last for ever, see my grandchildren out, even, but no, your time is over. Could it possibly be that deep within those rings, in those circles of life, you've left us one more puzzle, one more revelation, one more reminder?

Maddy's heart thumps, knowing that to explain any of it she must go right back to the very beginning, to that fateful day when her own world was blown to smithereens. Sitting on the nearest log, sipping from her hip flask for courage, she remembers.

Part One

1

Chadley, September 1940

'I'm not going back to school!' announced Maddy Belfield in the kitchen of The Feathers pub, in her gas mask peeling onions while Grandma was busy poring over their account books and morning mail.

Better to come clean before term started. Perhaps it wasn't the best time to announce she'd been expelled from St Hilda's again. Or maybe it was . . . Surely no one would worry about that when the whole country was waiting for the invasion to come.

How could they expect her to behave in a cloistered quad full of mean girls when there were young men staggering off the beaches of Dunkirk and getting blown out of the sky above their heads? She'd seen the *Pathé News*. She was nearly ten, old enough to know that they were in real danger but not old enough to do anything about it yet.

'Are you sure?' said Uncle George Mills, whose name was over the door as the licensee. 'If it's the fees you're worried about,' he offered, but she could see the relief in his eyes. Her parents were touring abroad with a

Variety Bandbox review, entertaining the troops, and were last heard of in a show in South Africa. The singing duo were looking further afield for work and heading into danger en route to Cairo.

Dolly and Arthur Belfield worked a double act, Mummy singing and Daddy on the piano: 'The Bellaires' was their stage name and they filled in for the famous Anne Ziegler and Webster Booth, singing duo in some of the concerts, to great acclaim.

Maddy was staying with Grandma Mills, who helped Uncle George run The Feathers, just off the East Lancs Road in Chadley. They were her guardians now that Mummy and Daddy were abroad.

'Take no notice of her, George. She'll soon change her tune when she sees what's in store at Broad Street Junior School.' Grandma's gruff northern voice soon poured cold water on Maddy's plans. 'I'm more interested in what's come in the morning post, Madeleine.' Grandma paused as if delivering bad news on stage, shoving a letter in front of her young granddaughter. 'What have you to say about this, young lady? It appears there are new orders to evacuate your school to the countryside, but not for you.'

There was the dreaded handwritten note from Miss Connaught, the Head of Junior School attached to her school report.

> It is with regret that I am forced to write again to express my displeasure at the continuing misbehaviour of your daughter, Madeleine Angela Belfield. At a time of National Emergency,

my staff must put the safety of hundreds of girls foremost, not spend valuable prep evenings searching for one ambulatory child, only to find her hiding up a tree, making a nuisance of herself again.

We cannot take responsibility for her continuing disobedience and therefore suggest that she be withdrawn from this school forthwith. Perhaps she is more suited to a local authority school.

Millicent Mills leaned across the table and threw the letter in Maddy's direction, her eyes fixed on the child, who sat with her head bent. She looked like butter wouldn't melt but the effect was spoiled by those lips twitching with mischief. 'What have you to say for yourself? And why aren't you wearing your eye patch?'

It wasn't Maddy's fault that she was always in trouble at school. It wasn't that she was mean or careless or dull even but somehow she didn't fit into the strait-jacket that St Hilda's liked to wrap around their pupils. Perhaps it was something to do with having to wear an eye patch on her good eye and glasses to correct her lazy left eye.

If there was one word that summed up her problem it was disobedience. Tell her to do one thing and she did the opposite, always had and always would.

'You can take that grin off your face!' yelled Granny in her drama queen voice. 'George, you tell her,' she sighed, deferring to her son, though everyone knew he was a soft touch and couldn't squash a flea. 'What will your mother say when she hears you've been expelled? They've been footing the bills for months. Is this our reward?'

That wasn't strictly true, as her parents' money came in dribs and drabs and never on time. Her school fees were coming out of the pub profits and it was a struggle.

'Don't worry, it'll save you money if I stay here,' Maddy offered, sensing a storm was brewing up fast. 'I'll get a job.'

'No granddaughter of mine gets expelled! You've got to be fourteen to get work. After all we've sacrificed for your education. I promised yer mam . . .'

When Granny was worked up her vowels flattened and the gruffness of her Yorkshire upbringing rose to the fore. She puffed up her chest into a heaving bosom of indignation. 'I've not forked out all these years for you to let us down like this . . . I'm so disappointed in you.'

'But I hate school,' whined Maddy. 'It's so boring. I'm not good at anything and I'll never be a prefect. Anyway, I don't want to be vacuated. I like it in The Feathers. I want to stay here.'

'What you like or don't like is of no consequence. In my day children were seen and not heard,' Grandma continued. 'Where's your eye patch? You'll never straighten that eye if you take it off.'

'I hate wearing it. They keep calling me one of Long John Silver's pirates, the Black Spot, at school and I hate the stupid uniform. How would you like to wear donkey-brown serge and a winceyette shirt with baggy knickers every day? They itch me. I hate the scratchy stockings, and Sandra Bowles pings my garters on the back of my knees and calls my shoes coal barges. Everything is second-hand and too big for me and they call me names. It's a stupid school.'

'St Hilda's is the best girls' school in the district. Think yourself lucky to have clothes to wear. Some little East End kiddies haven't a stitch to their backs after the blitz. There's a war on,' Granny replied with her usual explanation for everything horrid going on in Maddy's life.

'Those gymslips look scratchy to me, Mother, and she is a bit small for some of that old stuff you bought,' offered Uncle George in her defence. He was busy stocktaking but he looked up at his niece with concern.

'Everyone has to make sacrifices, and school uniforms will have to last for the duration.' Grandma Mills was riding on her high horse now. 'I don't stand on my feet for twelve hours a day to have her gadding off where she pleases. It's bad enough having Arthur and Dolly so far away—'

'Enough, Mother,' Uncle George interrupted. 'My sister'll always be grateful for you taking in the girl. Now come on, we've a business to run and stock to count, and Maddy can see that the air-raid precautions are in place. All hands to the stirrup pump, eh?'

Mother's brother was kindness itself, and all the rules and regulations never seemed to get him down: the petrol rationing and food restrictions. He found ways to get round them. There were always pear drops in his pocket to share when her sweets were gone. He was even busy renovating the old pony trap so they could trot off to town in style, and the droppings would feed the vegetable plot outside. Nothing must be wasted.

The subject of the war was banned in the bar, though. It was as if there was a notice hanging from the ceiling: 'Don't talk about the war in here.' Maddy knew Uncle George pored over the *Telegraph* each day with a glum face before opening time and then pinned on his cheery grin to those boys in airforce blue. He had wanted to join up but with no toes from an old war wound, and a limp, he failed his medical. Maddy was secretly glad. She loved Uncle George.

Daddy was gassed in the last war too and his chest was too weak for battle. Touring and entertaining the troops was his way of making an effort.

Now everyone followed events over the Channel with dismay, waiting for the worst. England was on alert and evacuation was starting in earnest. It was Maddy's job to check that the Anderson shelter was stocked with flasks and blankets and that the planks weren't slippy for the customers and the curtain closed. She helped put the blackout shutters over the windows at dusk every night and made sure the torch was handy if it was a rush to the shelter in the night across what once was the bowling green.

The Feathers was one of five old inns strung along the corners of two main roads between Liverpool and Manchester on the edge of the city in Chadley. It was the only one left with a quaint thatched roof, courtyard and stable block, where their car was bricked up for want of petrol coupons There was a bar for the locals and a snug for married couples and commercial tradesmen.

The bowling green at the back had been turned into an allotment with a shelter hidden away in a pit with turf over the corrugated roof. It was damp and smelly but Maddy felt safe in there.

Maddy had her own bedroom in the eaves of the thatched pub. They were close to a new RAF aerodrome, and men from the station came crowding into the bar, singing and fooling around until all hours. It was a war-free cocoon of smoke and noise and rowdy games. She wasn't allowed in the bar but sometimes she caught a glimpse of the pilots jumping over the chairs and leapfrogging over one another. It looked like PE in the playground.

She often counted the planes out and in during the small hours when the noise of bombs in the distance kept her awake. They'd heard about the terrible fires over London and listened to the ack-ack guns blasting into the night sky to protect Liverpool and Manchester from raiders. She wished her parents were back in the country entertaining the troops and factory workers close by, not out of reach on the other side of the world and their letters coming all in a rush.

She was glad her parents were together but it seemed years since they had been a proper family and most of that time they'd all lived out of a theatrical trunk. No wonder she balked at leaving the only place she called home, to be evacuated. That was why she'd pushed her luck in class, even though she was on her final warning

Being small, though, meant she felt useless – too

young to help in the bar, too old for silly games – and not sure when she'd be old enough to join up and do something herself. There had to be something she could do besides look after Bertie, the cocker spaniel.

When her chores were done Maddy raced to the apple tree at the far end of the field. It was stripped of fruit and the leaves were curling up. It was her lookout post where she did plane spotting. She could tell the Jerries' from the Spitfires blindfolded by now. The enemy planes had a slow throb, throb on its engine but the home planes were one continuous drone. She liked to watch the planes taking off from the distant runway and dreamed of flying off across the world to see Mummy and Daddy. It wasn't fair. They had each other and she had no one.

Granny was OK, in a bossy no-nonsense sort of way, but she was always hovering behind her, making her do boring prep and home reading. It wasn't as if Maddy planned anything naughty, it just sort of happened – like last week in assembly in the parish church when she sat behind Sandra Bowles.

Sandra had the thickest long ropes of plaits reaching down to her waist and she was always tossing them over her shoulder to show how thick and glossy they were. Her ribbons were crisp and made of gold satin to match the stripes on their blazers.

Maddy's own plaits were weedy little wiry things because she had curly black hair that didn't grow very fast and it was a struggle to stop bits spilling out.

Sandy was showing off as usual, and Maddy couldn't resist clasping the two ropes in a vice grip as they dangled into her thick hymn book, so that when they all rose to sing 'Lord dismiss us with thy blessing', Sandra yelped and her head was yanked back.

Maddy didn't know where to hide her satisfaction, but Miss Connaught saw the dirty deed and it was the last straw after a list of detentions and lines. Nobody listened to her side of the tale – how she'd been the object of Sandra's tormenting for months. No, she would not miss St Hilda's one bit.

It wasn't her fault she was born with a funny eye that didn't follow her other. Mummy explained that she must wait until she was older and fully grown before the surgeon would be able to correct it properly but that was years away. There'd been one operation when she was younger but it hadn't worked. Being pretty in the first place would have helped but when Mummy looked at her she always sighed and said she must come from the horsy side of the Belfield family, being good at sport, with long legs.

They never talked much about Daddy's family, the Belfields, and never visited them. They lived in Yorkshire somewhere. There were no cards or presents exchanged at Christmas either.

Daddy met Mummy when he was recovering after the Great War and she was a singer and dancer in a troupe. He was musical too and spent hours playing the piano in the hospital. They'd fallen in love when Mummy went to sing to them. It was all very romantic.

Maddy's first memories were of singing and laughter and dancing when they visited Granny and Grandpa's pub near Preston. She'd stayed with them when the

Bellaires were on tour. Grandpa died and Granny came to work with George when Auntie Kath ran away with the cellar man.

Now everything was changed because of this war and everyone was on the move here and there. She just wanted to sit in the tree with Bertie, the cocker spaniel, sitting guard at the base. He was her best friend and keeper of all her secrets.

When it was getting dusk it was time to do her evening chores, closing curtains and making sure that Bertie and the hens got fed for the evening. Now that she'd been expelled, Maddy wasn't so sure about going to a new school after all. What if it was worse than St Hilda's?

'Go and get us some fish and chips,' yelled Granny from the doorway. 'I'm too whacked to make tea tonight. The books are making my eyes ache. Here's my purse. The one in Entwistle Street will be open tonight. And no vinegar on mine . . .'

Maddy jumped down and shot off for her mac. There was no time to call Bertie in from the field. Fish and chips were always a treat. St Hilda's would call them 'common' but she didn't care.

She heard Moaning Minnie, the siren, cranking up the air-raid warning as the queue for fish and chips shuffled slowly through the door. Maddy looked up at the night sky, leaning on the gleaming chrome and black and green façade of the fish bar.

Outside, little torches flickered in an arc of light on the pavements as people scurried by.

'Looks as if Manchester is getting another pasting

tonight!' sighed an old man as he sprinkled salt all over his battered fish.

'Go easy with that, Stan. There's a war on,' shouted the fish fryer.

Maddy could feel her stomach rumbling. The smell of the batter, salt and pea broth was tempting. This was a rare treat as Gran liked to cook her own dishes. If only the sirens would stop screaming.

Chadley was getting off lightly in the recent air raids as there was nothing but a few mills and shops and an aviation supply factory. The Jerries preferred the docks. As she looked up into the sky she saw dark droning shapes and knew she'd have to find shelter – but not before she got their supper wrapped in newspaper. There was something brave about queuing in an air raid.

Gran would be getting herself down to 'The Pit', and Uncle George would be sorting out all the air-raid precautions before he went down to the cellar.

When she was fed up Maddy liked to hide with Bertie in the Anderson shelter away from everyone, and sulk. She knew four big swear words: Bugger, Blast, Damnation and Shit, and could say them all out loud there and not get told off. There was another she'd heard but not even dared speak it aloud in case it brought doom on her head.

The whistle was blasting in her ears as she clutched her parcel, making for home, when an arm pulled her roughly into a doorway.

'Madeleine Belfield, get yourself under cover. Can't

you see the bombs are dropping!' shouted Mr Pye, the Air-Raid Warden as he dragged her down the steps to a makeshift communal shelter in a basement. She could just make out a clutch of women and children crouching down, clutching cats and budgies in cages, and she wished she'd brought Bertie on his lead. The planes were getting closer and closer to the airfield. This was a real raid, not a pretend one.

Last year it was quiet, nothing much had happened, but since the summer, night after night the raiders came. Her school, once thought far enough out to be safe, was now in the firing line, which was why the pupils were being rushed away to a house in the deepest country.

Perhaps she ought to go and apologise to Miss Connaught and promise to be well behaved . . . perhaps not. The thought of sharing a dorm with Sandra Bowles and her pinching cronies filled her with horror.

Oh Bertie . . . Where was her bloody dog! Now she'd thought about the terrible word.

It seemed ages sitting, waiting, the smell of damp and cigarette smoke up her nose. She wished she was down in the cellar with Uncle George.

Uncle George always smiled and said, 'At least we won't die of thirst down there, folks,' coming out with his usual joke before he went into the night-time routine of turning off gas and water taps, evacuating the first few thirsty customers outside, across the bowling green to the official Anderson shelter they called 'The Pit'. He would be checking that the stirrup pumps were ready for any incendiaries. They all had the drill off pat by now. Everyone had a job.

Now the sirens were screaming, distracting Maddy.

'They're early tonight,' said old Mr Godber, sitting across on the bench with a miserable face. He was one of the regulars who usually came early to The Feathers for his cup of tea and a two penny 'nip', but now he was tucking into his chips with relish. There was old Lily who came in for jugs of stout and who once whispered that she'd been stolen by gypsies in the night but Maddy didn't believe her. There was Mrs Cooper from the bakery, and her three little children trailing blankets and teddies, one of them was plugged into a rubber dummy. He kept staring at Maddy's eye patch and her bag of chips with longing. There was the wife of the fish-and-chip man, and two old men Maddy didn't know, who filled the small place with tobacco from their pipes. It was such a smelly crush in the shelter.

'Where's yer little dog?' said Lily. The racket was getting louder. 'If she's got any sense she'll've run a mile away from this hellhole. Dogs can sense danger . . . Don't fret, love, she'll be safe.'

'But he doesn't like Moaning Minnie.' Maddy wanted to cry, and clutched the warm newspaper to her, looking anxious. She hoped Gran had taken her hat box down there. It contained her jewellery, their documents, her insurance certificates and the licences, and their identity papers, and it was Maddy's job to make sure it got put in a safe place. Tonight the box would have to stay under the bed and take its chance.

The sky was still humming with droning black insects hovering ahead. There was a harvest moon tonight, torching the bombers' path through the dark sky, just the night for Liverpool to be the target. There were planks on the basement floor but it was still claggy and damp, smelling of must.

'Maddy! Thank goodness you're here! Good girl, to stay put in the High Street shelter.' Down the steps came Ivy Sangster, all of a do. 'Yer Gran was worried so she sent me out to look for you. I said I'd keep you company down here,' said the barmaid, who helped them on busy nights. 'I'm glad I found you,' she said, plonking herself down with a flask. 'You'd better eat your chips before they go cold.'

'Did they bring in Bertie? Is he in the cellar?'

'Not sure, love. Your uncle George's gone down as usual. You know he can't stand small spaces . . . not since the trench collapsed on him,' whispered Ivy, who was very fond of her boss and blushed every time he spoke to her. 'Yer gran says it hurts her back bending in the Anderson. They'll be fine down in the cellar.'

They all squatted on benches either side, waiting for the all clear, but the racket outside just got worse. Maddy was trembling at the noise but clung on to her chips. Ivy ferreted for her mouth organ to pass the time. They always had a singsong to drown out the bangs.

None of them felt like singing this time, though. Maddy started to whimper, 'I don't like it!'

It hadn't been this bad for ages. Maddy was glad it wasn't opening time and the pub was crowded or the shelter would be squashed. It would soon be over and they could go home and heat up the supper.

It was dark in the basement shelter so when someone flashed a torch Maddy inspected the walls for spiders and creepy crawlies to put in her matchbox zoo. Everyone was trying to put on cheery faces for her but she could see they were worried and nervous. They were the 'We can take it' faces that smiled on a poster at the bus station.

She tried to distract herself by thinking of good memories. When her parents were 'resting' between jobs, Mummy was all of a dazzle behind the bar, with her hair piled up in curls, earrings dangling and a blouse that showed off her magnificent bust, wearing just enough pan stick and lipstick to look cheerful even when she was tired. The aircrews flocked to her end of the bar while Daddy played tunes on the piano. Sometimes Maddy was allowed to peep through the door and watch Mummy singing.

Mummy's voice had three volumes: piano, forte, and bellow – what she called her front stalls, gallery and the gods. When she started up everyone fell silent until she let them join in the choruses. Every bar night was a performance and the regulars loved her. Daddy just pulled the pints and smiled as the till rang. He sometimes sat down and played alongside her. Singing was thirsty work and good for The Feathers.

'I want my mummy,' whimpered Maddy. 'She always comes and sings to me. I don't like it in here any more.'

'I know, love, but it won't be long now,' said Ivy smiling.

'I want her now and I want Daddy. It's not fair . . . I want Bertie,' she screamed, suddenly feeling very afraid.

'Now then, nipper, don't make a fuss. We can't work miracles. It won't be long now. Let's have some of your chips. Sing and eat and take no notice, that's the way to show Hitler who's boss,' said Mr Godber. 'Eat your chips.'

'I'm not hungry. Why are they making such big bangs?'

'I don't know. It must be the airfield they're after tonight,' he said, shrugging his shoulders.

The whiz-bangs were the closest to them for a long time and Maddy was trembling. She felt suffocated with all these strangers. What if they had a direct hit? What about their neighbours down the road? Were they all quaking in their shoes too?

Was the whole of Chadley trembling at this pounding? They huddled together, listening to every explosion, and then it fell quiet and Maddy wanted to rush out and breathe the clean air.

'I'll just open up and see what's what,' said the warden. 'They're passing over. The all clear'll be sounding soon. Perhaps we'll get a night's kip in our own beds, for a change,' he laughed, opening the curtain and the door.

Maddy felt the whoosh of hot air as soon as the door was opened, a flash of light and a terrific bang. It was like daylight outside.

'What's that noise and that fire? Oh Gawd, that was close! Stay back!' the warden screamed.

Then the droning ceased, and when the all clear sounded everyone cheered.

Ivy and Maddy stumbled out into the darkness, hands clutching each other for support.

There were sounds of running feet and a strange heat and light, crackling and whistling, bells going off. Men were shouting orders. As they left Entwistle Street for the main road, lined with familiar houses and shops, the light got brighter and the smoke was blinding, the smells of cordite and burning rubber choking Maddy's nostrils. As they turned towards home they saw everything was ablaze, houses gaped open, the rubble alive with dark figures crawling over bricks, shouting.

'No further, sorry, lass,' said a voice.

'But we live here,' said Ivy. 'The Feathers down there.'

'No further, love. It took a direct hit. We're still digging them out. Better get some tea.'

That last bang had been The Feathers. Its timbers were alight, turning it into a roaring inferno. The heat of it seared their faces and Maddy began to shake. Granny and Uncle George were down in that cellar . . .

'What's going on? Why can't we see The Feathers? We've got to get to them . . . My granny . . . Granny . . . Ivy, Mr Godber, do something!'

She saw the looks on their stricken faces. No one could survive in that furnace, and Maddy sank back, terrified, feeling small and helpless and stunned by the inferno. She began to sob and Ivy did her best to comfort her. They couldn't do anything but watch the fire rage. Maddy felt sick at the sight of their home going up in smoke and the thought that the two best people in the world, who'd done no harm to anyone, were trapped in that fire.

They all stumbled backwards, recoiling from the furnace before them. There were sounds of fire bells and shouting voices, more whistles blowing. She could hear someone shouting orders and the heat forced her back on her heels, the smoke blinding her, choking her throat with the smell of burning wood like some giant bonfire. The stench was making her feel sick.

The pub was ablaze from end to end. There were fires raging across the road. The garage exploded as the oil caught fire, sending fumes into the air. All she could think about was poor Granny and Uncle George as Ivy rushed forward screaming. 'Two of them in the cellar . . . George and Millie Mills! They're inside in the cellar . . . There's a trap door. Oh God! Get them out, please!' Her voice was squeaky.

'Sorry, miss, no further, not near the fire. We've got to get it under control. Just the two of you outside then?'

'I only went to Entwistle Street for chips, see, for their supper . . . I live here.' Maddy pointed to the fire, not understanding.

'Not now you don't, love. All that timber and thatch, gone up like tinder. I'm sorry. We're digging them out across the road. It's not safe if the petrol tank goes up . . . The airfield got it bad tonight,' said the blackened-faced fireman, trying to be kind, but she didn't want to hear his words.

Another man in uniform was talking to a woman in a uniform.

'Two survivors for you, Mavis,' he said, pointing them out. 'Take them for some tea.'

'We've had our supper, thank you,' Maddy said. 'What about my dog, Bertie? You've got to look for him too.'

'Bertie'll be fine, love. Let the men get on with their jobs. I don't think he went in the cellar. He'll be hiding until it's safe. We can look for him later,' Ivy offered, putting her arm round her, but Maddy shook it off. She must find Bertie.

Maddy could see Mr Finlay from the garage across the road, standing in a daze with a shawl around his shoulders and the children from the house up the lane, clutching teddy bears and whimpering. But when she turned to see if anyone was coming out of the pub she saw only smoke and firemen and burning wood. It was a terrible smell and she started to shake.

Someone led them away but her legs were all wobbly. This was all a bad dream . . . but why could she feel the heat searing her face and still she didn't wake up?

Later they stood wrapped in blankets sipping tea, feeling sick after inhaling the choking smoke, as the sky turned orange. The fire brigade did their best to quell the flames but it was all too late and the whole town seemed to be on fire.

Maddy would never forget the smell of burning timbers and the flashes and explosions as the bottles cracked and kegs exploded as the poor pub went up in smoke. Nothing would be safe in the world after this. She was shaking, too shocked to take in the enormity of what was happening as they were led shivering, covered in black dust, to the Miner's Arms, to be given a makeshift bed in the bar, along with all the other victims of the blitz.

They drank sweet tea until they were choking with

the stuff. Only then did someone prise the newspaper package out of Maddy's hand.

On that September night, the whole area was brought to rubble by stray bombs offloaded on a raid. Nothing would ever be the same again. Suddenly Maddy felt all floaty and strange as if she was watching things from on top of the church tower.

In the days that followed the blitz she roamed over the ruins and the back roads of Chadley, calling out for Bertie. How could her poor old dog try to dodge fire, run for shelter, scavenge around or fight off mangy waifs and strays? She called and called until she was hoarse but he never appeared and she knew Bertie was gone.

Then it was as if her throat closed over and no sound could come out. Miss Connaught came and offered her place back in the school – but with no money to her name, she bowed her head and refused to budge from her makeshift billet in the Miner's.

Ivy took her home to the cottage down the street where she had to share a bed with Ivy's little sister, Carol. All Maddy wanted to do was sit by the scorched apple tree and wait for Bertie, but the sight of the ruined timbers was so terrible she couldn't bear to stay for more than a few minutes. If she could find him then she would have someone in the world to hug for comfort while the authorities decided what to do with her.

Telegrams were cabled to the Bellaires in Durban. Maddy had to sign forms in her best joined-up handwriting to register for immediate housing and papers.

The funeral arrangements were taken out of Maddy's

hands by the vicar and his wife. He suggested a joint service for all the bomb victims in Chadley parish church. She overheard Ivy whispering that the coffins would be filled with sand because no trace of Granny and George had been found. The thought of them burned up gave her nightmares and she screamed and woke up all the Sangsters.

Ration books were granted, and coupons for mourning clothes, but everything just floated past her as if in some silent dream. She shed no tears at the service. Maddy stood up straight and looked ahead. They weren't in those boxes by the chancel steps. There were other boxes, and two little ones: the children from the garage, who had died in the explosion. The family clung together, sobbing.

Why weren't Mummy and Daddy here? Why were they off out of it all? All Maddy felt was a burning heat where her heart was. Everything was destroyed – her home, her family – and just the comfort of strangers for company. Where would she go? To an orphanage or back to St Hilda's?

Then a telegram appeared from an address in Yorkshire.

> YOUR FATHER HAS INSTRUCTED YOU TO COME NORTH. WILL MEET YOU ON LEEDS STATION. WEDNESDAY. PRUNELLA BELFIELD. LETTER. MONEY ORDER TO FOLLOW. REPLY.

Maddy stared at this turn-up, puzzled, and pushed it over for Ivy to read.

'Who's Prunella Belfield? What a funny name,' she smiled.

'She must be a relation I don't know,' said Maddy. 'My grandma Belfield, I expect.'

Whoever she was, this relative expected a reply by return and there was nothing to stop her from going north. At least it would be far away from all terrors of the past weeks. There was nothing for her in Chadley now.

2

Sowerthwaite

'They must be picked fast before the frost Devil gets them!' yelled Prunella Belfield, burying her head into the blackberry bushes, while shouting instructions to her line of charges to fill their bowls to the brim.

It was a beautiful autumn afternoon and the new evacuees needed airing and tiring out before Matron began the evening bed routine in earnest.

'But they sting, miss!' moaned Betty Potts, the eldest of the evacuees, who never liked getting her fingers mucked up.

'Don't be a big girl's blouse,' laughed Bryan Partridge, who'd climbed over the stone wall to reach a better cluster of bushes, unaware that Hamish, the Aberdeen Angus bull, was eyeing him with interest from across the meadow.

'Stay on this side, Bryan,' Prunella warned, to no avail. This boy was as deaf as a post when it suited him. He had runaway from four billets so far and was in danger of tearing the only pair of short trousers that fitted him.

'Miss . . .' whined bandy-legged Ruby Sharpe, 'why are the biggestest ones always too high to reach?'

Why indeed? What could she say to this philosophical question? Life was full of challenges and just when you thought you had it all sorted out, along came another bigger challenge to make you stretch up even further or dig deeper into your reserves.

Just when she and Gerald had settled down after another sticky patch in their marriage, along came the war to separate them. Just when she thought she was pregnant at long last, along came a second miscarriage and haemorrhage to put paid to that hope for ever.

Just when she thought they could leave Sowerthwaite and her mother-in-law's iron grip, along came the war to keep her tied to Brooklyn Hall and grounds as a glorified housekeeper.

If anyone had told her twelve months ago she would be running a hostel for 'Awkward Evacuees', most of whom had never seen a cow, sheep or blackberry bush in their lives before, she'd have laughed with derision. But the war was changing everything.

When the young Scottish billeting officer turned up at Pleasance Belfield's house, he stared up at the Elizabethan stone portico, the mullioned windows and the damson hues of the Virginia creeper stretched over the walls, and demanded they take in at least eight evacuees immediately.

Mother-in-law refused point-blank and pointed to the line of walking sticks in the hallstand under the large oak staircase.

‘I have my own refugees, thank you,’ she announced in her patrician, ‘don’t mess with me’ tones that usually shrunk minor officials into grovelling apologies. But this young man was well seasoned and countered her argument with a sniff.

‘But there is the dower house down the lane, I gather that belongs to you?’

He was talking about the empty house by the green. It was once the the Victory Tree public house, but had been shuttered up for months after some fracas with the last tenant. It had lain empty, undisturbed, the subject of much conjecture by the Parish Council of Sowerthwaite in Craven, tucked away by the gates to the old Elizabethan manor. Not even Pleasance could wriggle out of this.

‘I have plans for that property,’ Mother countered. ‘In due course it will be rented out.’

‘With respect, madam, this is an emergency. With the blitz we need homes for city children immediately. Your plans can wait.’

No one talked to Pleasance Belfield like that. He deserved an award for conspicuous bravery. Her cheeks flushed with indignation and her bolster bosom heaved with disapproval at this inconvenient conversation. If ever a woman belied her name, it was Gerald’s mama, Pleasance. She ruled the town as if it was her feudal domain. She sat on every committee, checked that the vicar preached the right sermons and kept everyone in their proper places as if the twentieth century hadn’t even started.

The war was an inconvenience she wanted to ignore

but it was impossible. There was not a flag or a poster or any recruitment drive without her approval, and now she was being faced with an influx of strangers and officials who didn't know their place.

'My dear fellow, anyone can see that place's not suitable for children. It was a public house with no suitable accommodation for children. Who would take responsibility? I can't have city ruffians racing round the streets disturbing the peace. Let them all be put up in tents somewhere out of the way.'

'Oh, yes, and when a bomb drops on hundreds of them, will you take the responsibility of telling their poor mothers?' he replied, ignoring her fury at his insolence. 'We're hoping young Mrs Belfield would see to things.' The officer looked straight at Plum, giving her a look of desperation but also just the escape she needed from the tyranny of life with Mother-in-law and her gang.

'But I don't know anything about children,' Plum was quick to add. Gerald and she had not managed to take a child to term and now that she was nearly forty, her chances of conceiving were very slim.

'You'll soon learn,' said the billeting officer. 'We'll provide a proper nurse and domestic help. I see you have dogs,' he smiled, pointing to her red setters, Sukie and Blaze, tearing round the paths like mad things. 'Puppies and kiddies, there's not much difference, is there? The ones we have in mind are a bit wayward, you see, runaways from their billets mostly. You look just the type to lick them into shape.' The man winked at her and she blushed.

It was time she did some war work, and a house full of geriatric relatives hoping to sit out the war in comfort was not her idea of keeping the home fires burning.

'My daughter-in-law has other responsibilities. There's the house to run, and with so few servants I shall need her services,' Pleasance countered quickly, sensing danger.

'With respect, madam, I have checked, and Mrs Belfield is registered for war work, being of age, available and without children. It is her duty—'

'How dare you come here and demand such sacrifices from a married woman? In my day, men like you . . . This is unacceptable to me—'

'Mother, he's got a point. I would like to help where I can,' Plum interrupted. 'We all have to make sacrifices. Gerald is doing his bit and now I must do mine. I shall only be down the lane.'

'Who will make up the four for bridge?' Mother sighed. 'I don't know what the world is coming to . . . I shall write to the West Riding and complain about your attitude, young man.'

'You can do that, madam, but I have powers to insist that the stable block and servants quarters' be utilised if needed. Would you prefer to have the kiddies on your doorstep or in your house?'

Plum almost choked at this obvious blackmail. It was good to see her bullying mother-in-law cornered for once.

'Oh, do what you must, but I insist that Mrs Belfield returns each night. Who is there left to do the shutters for the blackout? None of my guests can stretch that far.'

'I'm sure we can find a young lad from amongst the hostel to help you out.'

'I want nothing to do with any of them, thank you,' Pleasance sighed, patting her heart. 'This'll be the death of me, Prunella.'

'She looks a gey tough old bird to me,' muttered the billeting officer under his breath in his strong Scottish accent. The crafty blighters at the town hall had sent a stranger. No one in Sowerthwaite would have dared address her ladyship with such disrespect.

Plum grinned to herself. There were some changes already in this war that were long overdue. Mama was trying to sit out the war as if it didn't exist. She refused to have a wireless in the house or a newspaper or any alteration to her regime, but one by one her maids and groundsmen, chauffeur and handymen had joined up, and they were having to make do in the kitchen with two refugees from Poland.

Why shouldn't town children have fresh air and peace and quiet after all they'd been through? Why shouldn't they romp through the fields and have rosy cheeks and strong limbs, fresh food? Her illusions were soon to be shattered by the first arrivals to the hostel three weeks later: ill-clad children in plimsolls, with scabby chins and nits.

'Is this it?' Plum said, staring in at the Victory Tree with disbelief. She'd never been inside the place before. It was a rough old stone building, little more than a long farmhouse, shuttered up and unwelcoming. 'It needs a lick of paint.'

'It needs more than that,' said Miss Blunt, the new matron, sniffing the air haughtily. 'I can still smell stale ale and urinals: very unhygienic. I thought we'd be using the big house . . . I'm not used to this sort of squalor. How will we ever get it ready in time? The children are due in a few days. Where will we get distemper, Mrs Belfield?'

'That's for the Town Hall to provide, or we can use lime wash; farmers always have lime wash.' Plum refused to be defeated by the size of the task. 'Everything else is ordered. At least they've got plenty of grounds to play in at the back, and there's a wash house and stables for storage. The bar's already been ripped out. This will make a good playroom for them to make a rumpus.' She pointed to the large taproom.

'This will be my sitting room,' announced Miss Blunt with another sniff, eyeing the coal fireplace and the windows overlooking the green. 'You'll be up at the big house. I need somewhere to retire to . . .'

'Why not make your room in the snug? It's warmer and quieter in there. If we can give these children some space to let off steam,' Plum added, thinking of ways to keep them out of mischief.

'I'll be the judge of that. They're not dogs off the leash, Mrs Belfield. These are naughty girls and boys who don't know how lucky they are to be housed. They must learn to run a home and stay in their place. Keep them busy and teach them domestic skills. Make them useful citizens and stand no nonsense.' Miss Blunt was busy making her lists. 'I shall need locks on all the doors. You can't trust common children. They're like wild animals.'

In the end they compromised by making the taproom the dining hall, with chairs and a bench by the fireplace. Old furniture from the servants' quarters was brought down from Brooklyn Hall on a cart. The Town Hall sent two old men to whitewash throughout the building so it smelled fresh and clean and looked brighter. To everyone's amazement, they installed a big bath and flushing toilet at the top end of the staircase. Most of the residents of the village had to make do with outside brick privvies in the yard and zinc tubs.

'It's a right rum do giving strangers fancy plumbing. The Owd Vic's gone up in the world. It were allus a spit'n'sawdust place afore,' laughed one of the decorators as he sloshed the distemper over the bumpy walls. 'Ah could tell you some right tales about this . . . but not for ladies' ears, happen . . . There was a murder here once in the olden days. One of them navvies building the railway line threw some gelignite on the fire and near on blew the place up! They say there's a ghost as—'

'But why's it called the Victory Tree?' Plum was curious.

The old man shook his head. 'Summat to do with the army recruits. Happen they mustered them up here,' he said. 'Before the last war, though. The Sowerthwaite Pals, they were called. Fifty bonny lads went out but you can count on yer hand the ones as came back. I was a farmer's lad and never got to go . . . Lost a lot of my school mates. Her ladyship took it bad with losing Captain Julian, and then Arthur Belfield got a blighty . . . Never see him up here, do we?'

Old man Handby was fishing for information to take back to his cronies in the Black Horse but Plum's lips were sealed. Even she didn't know the full story of why Pleasance had dismissed her son with such venom.

'Where's the Victory Tree then?' asked Miss Blunt, looking across the green to the stocks and the duck pond, expecting to see some big elm commemorating Waterloo or Balaclava.

'Now there you've got me, lady. The only trees we have are those up the lane to Brooklyn planted by her ladyship in her grief. The big one at the top of the yard has allus been there . . . Dunno why it's called the Victory Tree.'

Plum spotted some local children peeping through the windows to see what was going on. Once word got round the town that the evacuees were coming, she wondered just what reception the new arrivals would get when they turned up at the local school.

The world of children was a mystery to her. She hoped the man from the town hall was right and it was just a matter of training, obedience and praise. So far she'd been more a tennis court sort of gal, she smiled, driving a fast car with her dogs hanging out, a deb with not enough education and experience to be doing what she was doing now.

It had been a baptism of fire, sorting out beds and linen and fresh clothes for some of the sad little tykes who turned up at the station with their escort. Some, like Ruby, were pinched and cowed and eager to please; others, like Betty and Bryan, could be cocky and defiant, with wary eyes. There were still six more to arrive.

These were the rejects from other billets, each with a case history in a file, some nervy and sickly so perhaps it would be like running a kennels for the sort of puppies that were disobedient and poorly trained. In her book there was no such thing as a bad horse or hound, just a poor owner, so perhaps her experience might come handy after all.

Plum was to be in charge of ordering provisions, book-keeping and returning a full account to the Town Hall in Sowerthwaite, who were overseeing the evacuation and footing the bills.

Miss Blunt was a former school matron at a boy's preparatory school near York, specially selected to control unruly children, and she wore a nurse's uniform at all times to remind her charges that she would stand no nonsense. It was unfortunate that, to cover her thinning hair, she had chosen a rust-coloured wig, which shifted up and down when she was agitated. Plum could see trouble ahead for the poor soul if she kept up the pretence.

As the children picked bowls of blackberries in the autumn sunshine, Plum saw to her horror that their cotton shirts and dresses were stained purple and lips were dyed blue. There'd not been a peep out of any of them when she told them that every berry they picked was one in the eye for Hitler!

‘Miss, miss, the cow with handle bars’s got Bryan!’ yelled Ruby and Betty in unison, pointing to the boy who was pinned against the stone wall. For once, all his bravado had crumpled.

‘Don’t scream and don’t move. He’s just an old softie really,’ she lied. ‘He’s just curious.’

‘What if he tosses ’m over his head and kills ’im, miss?’

‘Look him in the eye, Bryan, and just hold out your bowl, let him sniff the berries and place it out of reach. Then run like the wind!’ she whispered. Hamish was a glutton for titbits and sniffed the bowl with interest, giving the lad the chance to make for the gate. She’d never seen a boy run faster, and he flung himself over the bars, tearing his shorts in the process. ‘It’s like the cowboys in the Wild West, miss, this country lark,’ he panted. ‘Sorry about the berries. The Rug’ll give me hell for tearing me pants,’ he added. ‘Sorry, miss.’

‘The Rug?’ She looked up as the children giggled. Then she realised it was a nickname – no guesses who the name belonged to. She had to stifle a smile. ‘I’ll say it was an accident in the cause of duty. I reckon we’ve got enough for ten jars of jelly out of this.’

When they returned Matron was waiting at the door, grim-faced. ‘Look at the state of them! Oh, and there’s a message from the Hall. You’ve to go at once, Mrs Belfield says, at once.’

Why did Avis Blunt make her feel like a naughty schoolgirl? It was probably nothing but just in case there was news from Gerald Plum scurried up the line of poplars along the avenue, each one in memory of one of the fallen in Sowerthwaite in the Great War. The war to end all wars had robbed the Belfields of their eldest son, Julian, and injured their second son, Arthur.

Ilsa, the refugee cook, stood in the hallway looking worried. 'Madam's not well. Come.'

Pleasance was sitting in the drawing room with her feet up sipping brandy, flourishing a telegram, and Plum went cold and faint.

'No, it's not Gerry. It's from Arthur . . . the one abroad . . . I thought I told him never to contact me again . . . He made his choice. Now he begs me to take in his brat, blitzed somewhere near Manchester, would you believe. Dolly's mother got herself killed. Nowhere else to go and he asks me to come to the rescue. The cheek of it, after all these years. As if I care what happens . . .'

'Mother, he's abroad. He can't get to his child . . . You have to do your duty, it's your granddaughter.'

Plum was shocked by the coldness of this selfish spoiled woman, who had cut herself off from her second son just because he had defied her and married a showgirl for love. Why, the very aristocracy of England was strengthened by the blood of many a Gibson girl and film starlet.

Gerald was the baby of the family and indulged as such. He dismissed his older brother as a fool. 'He could have kept Dolly as a mistress and kept Mama happy,' which was what he himself had done until recently. Sometimes Plum feared he'd only married her for her wider connections in the County, while keeping his Lillie Langtry in town, until the poor girl made a fuss and demanded he marry her. That's when she disappeared and he came home repentant, bearing expensive gifts. Life was good when they were posted abroad for a while, but on leaving the army Gerald had grown restless back in Yorkshire, running the small estate. They'd meant to buy something for themselves but it seemed sensible to live at Brooklyn with his widowed mother.

Plum's parents were dead and her brother, Tim, was in the air force, stationed in Singapore. They weren't close and she'd never told him much about her marriage. She'd just gone along with the idea, thinking she'd fill the big house with children and life, but it hadn't turned out that way. Now things were strained. However, divorce was out of the question – even Gerald knew that. He had no plans to be disinherited.

Plum had stayed up in the country, hurt and ready to make her own plans, then war had broken out and Gerald was called back into the regiment, and they sort of made things up again. Now the thought of one of their own abandoned in all that terror just like the evacuees troubled her.

'She can't stay here. There's no room,' Pleasance whined.

'Of course there is. I've got more children arriving on Wednesday. If I can meet her then we'll manage somehow. It will be good to meet Arthur's girl.'

'Arthur's street urchin, more like. Brought up in a pub, I ask you, while they cavort themselves on a public stage. I am sick of this dratted war upsetting everything. Where's it all going to end?'

'As far as I can see the world *has* ended for Madeleine; bombed out, her granny dead and parents stuck halfway across the world. Just think of someone else, for a change . . . or would you prefer life under Herr Hitler?'

'Don't be facetious, Prunella. You forget yourself. This hostel thing has gone to your head and coarsened you. I'm too old to look after children.' Mother looked up, her mouth pursed into a mean straight line. She was being unreasonable as usual. Time to butter her up with compliments. It always worked.

'Rubbish! You'll rise to the challenge, you always do. Look how you've provided a house for children already, made a home for Great-uncle Algie and Great-aunt Julia and her companion, and employed refugees. You try to set an example in the community. "By your fruits are ye known" – you keep quoting at me. We'll manage, and I can see to Madeleine.'

'But I said I'd never speak to him again.'

'She's Arthur's child. She's no quarrel with you. The girl never asked to be born or be part of this estrangement. Where's your heart? Do we take in strangers but not our own just because of a silly quarrel?' Plum lit a cigarette from her silver case, drew a deep breath as if it were an oxygen mask. Suddenly she felt so weary.

Pleasance Belfield was the daughter of a cotton magnate who had married into another successful business family. How quickly she'd forgotten her own roots. The Belfields weren't old money but new money made in the cotton trade in Lancashire in the last century. They only bought the manor house when the ancient Coldicote family died out. Why did Mother have to behave as if she was queen of all she surveyed?

This poor mite might be the only grandchild she would ever have. How could she dismiss her so lightly?

'Your grandchild needs a home, Mother. Think about it, at least,' Plum pleaded.

'I don't know what's got into you, young lady. You used to be so compliant and now you're smoking like a chimney,' Pleasance replied, ignoring her request, ready to criticise as usual.

'I'm nearly forty years old. I'll smoke if I like, but for your enlightenment, here are just a few reasons why I do. I wasn't trained for anything but marriage and I have a husband who doesn't love me. I have no children of my own to cherish. I have a brother risking his neck in the skies halfway across the world to keep us safe, so don't call me "young lady". I feel as old as the hills but I would never turn a child of this family from the door, so if you don't like any of this then I'll pack my bags and stay down in the Vic and take Madeleine with me.'

Plum stood up to beat a retreat to her room. It was the only place in the house where she could think her own thoughts. She was in no mood for any more arguments. This rebellion had been coming for months. She was sick of pandering to Pleasance's whims and fancies. She could go to hell!

'Prunella! I suppose you'd better send a telegram at once and meet her in Leeds with the others – but I don't like it one bit,' Pleasance sighed with a look of martydom on her face.

'I'm sure you don't, but you were never one to shirk your duty. Sowerthwaite expects you to lead by example, and what better than to take in a victim of the blitz? I shall need the car to collect them all from the station.'

Plum smiled to herself with relief. Round one to Arthur and his girl. Round one to her, for once.

3

Victoria Station, Manchester, September 1940

Gloria Conley tugged her little brother along the platform, trying to keep up with her mother, who was rushing through the crowds on Victoria Station, dodging kitbags slung over shoulders. Sid kept tripping over men sitting on the platform. The place smelled of steam and smoke and smelly armpits, but it was so exciting to be up close to those big iron monsters. There'd been so much to see since they got off the Kearsley bus into town. It was the longest journey she'd ever had, but Sid was whining about his ear hurting. Where were they going? Gloria hoped it was a trip to the seaside.

'Now you stay put, while I get you some sweeties,' smiled Mam, who was all dolled up in a short jacket and summer frock with a silly little beret with a feather stuck on the side. The soldiers wolf-whistled when she passed and shouted, 'Give us a kiss, Rita Hayworth!' Mam wiggled her bum, enjoying every minute of the attention, for she looked so pretty with her shoulder-length red hair and kiss curls.

Gloria was gripping Sid's wrist for dear life in case they got swept away in the rush. As the carriage doors opened, bodies poured out with suitcases and parcels, and porters rushed around with trolleys. Gloria could hear whistles blowing and the smell of soot went up her nose.

Mam soon came back with Fry's chocolate bars and fizzy pop in a bottle. They were going on a journey, that's all Gloria had been told, and they had to be good.

Since the telegram came last week, Mam had been acting funny. There'd been tears, and the usual aunties sitting round smoking and drinking stout. Something bad had happened: not the coppers banging on the door of their two up and two down in Elijah Street, looking for Uncle Sam, who had run away from the war: not the welfare man coming to see why she'd missed school again: not that nosy parker from two doors down who didn't like the gentlemen callers banging the door at all hours. It was all to do with the 'war on'.

'His dad's copped it good and proper this time and won't be coming back. What'm I going to do with you two now?' Mam sighed with a funny look in her eye while they were on the platform. 'You'll have to be a big girl and take charge of Sidney. I want more for you than I've got here, do you hear? This is no life for kiddies.' Mam was snivelling and rabbiting on, shoving a letter in her pocket, a letter Gloria couldn't read because she was still stuck with baby reading and had missed a lot of schooling looking after Sid while Mam slept in.

'Give this to the policeman on the train, or one of them teachers down there, look . . . with the children. It'll explain, but no telling fibs, Gloria. Be a good girl. Don't lose yer gas masks. You'll be the better without me, love. I'm doing this for your own good.'

Mam was crying and Gloria just wanted to cling on tight to her cotton frock, suddenly afraid. Something terrible was about to happen at this station. 'Where're we going?' she sobbed. For a girl of well over ten she was the size of a nine-year-old, her face framed in her pixie hood.

'Now, none of that! It's for the best. I've got to do right by you . . . I'm going to join up and do my bit.' Mam shoved a clean hanky in her face. 'Blow!'

Gloria didn't understand what she was getting at but Sid was crying and holding his ear. He always had sore ears. He was her half-brother. Not that she knew who her own dad was. His name was never mentioned. The one that got killed was Uncle Jim, Sid's dad, but he was too young to understand. He could be a right mardy baby when he got one of his earaches.

Mam shoved them down the platform following the party of school children with little cases and gas masks, but they went into a full carriage. The train was packed, so she hung back suddenly. 'Damn! We'll happen wait for the next one coming,' she said. 'You'd better go to the lav, Glory. No one wants a kiddie with wet knickers.'

What was going on? Her life was full of mysteries, Gloria thought, sitting on the big wooden toilet seat in the ladies. There was the mystery of the customers who came to Elijah Street, the aunties who were always popping in, the men who went upstairs day and night to buy.

What Mam sold was another mystery, but it meant lots of jumping up and down on the bed and sometimes the plaster came down from the living-room ceiling where Gloria had to keep Sid amused.

She knew Mr Cummings, who came regular as clockwork on Sunday afternoons. When they set off for Clarendon Street Sunday school, he gave them cough drops out of his pocket with fluff on them and told them to hop it. There were others she didn't like who came for a 'seeing to'.

Lily Davidson's mum was a hairdresser and saw her customers at the kitchen sink. Freda Pointer across the road went with her mam round the doors selling magazines. They were religious.

Sometimes when Gloria went upstairs, Mam's bed was all rumpled and messy and smelled of perfume and sweat. 'What do you do up there?' she once asked.

'Nothing you would understand, love. I make them better,' she explained with a smile.

'Like Dr Phipps?' she asked.

'Sort of. I give them treatments to help their sore backs and aches and pains,' Mam said, and Gloria felt better after that.

In the playground of Clarendon Street Juniors she told Freda Pointer that her mother was a doctor and everyone started to laugh.

'My mam says your mam's a tuppenny tart, a lady of the night and she'll go to Hell!'

'No, she's not! She never goes out at night,' Gloria

shouted, knowing it wasn't exactly true as sometimes she woke up and found the door unlocked and no one in the house but her and Sid. If there was a raid she had to drag him out of bed and under the stairs to the cubbyhole and wait for the all clear. Sometimes she took him to Auntie Elsie's shelter down the road.

'Hark at 'er, ginger nut. You're so stupid, anyone can see she's a tart!' Freda made everyone laugh and this made Gloria angry. With all that mass of copper curls, just like her mam, she did have a temper on her. She yanked at Freda's plaits until she screamed blue murder and they punched each other and kicked shins until they both got the cane for fighting in the yard.

That was when she bunked off school again and went round the shops until it was home time. The welfare man called round and she got a clout from Mam for bringing trouble to the door.

'We're as good as any up this street and don't you forget it. I give a service like anyone else. I'm doing war work, in my own way. Them across the road don't even hold with fighting. You've only got one life, Glory. Make the most of it – grab it while you can before you end up like poor Jim, fifty fathoms deep among the fishes, God rest his soul.'

When Gloria got back on the platform Mam was begging cigs off a soldier.

'That took a long time,' she laughed. 'Your skirt's still tucked in yer knicks! Aren't you a sight . . . Now you look after Sid while I just take a stroll with this nice man.' She winked. 'I'll not be long'.

'Mam!' Gloria called, suddenly afraid as the feathers

on the beret disappeared into the crowd. Would Mam come back to them? Gloria felt sick and clung on to her brother.

Was she nearly there, thought Maddy for the umpteenth time. It was hard to see just where they were on that long grimy train heading east, with its damp sooty carriages and brown sauce upholstery. It had taken hours and hours, and the train kept stopping in the middle of nowhere. She peered through the oval hole in the centre of the window, the bit that wasn't plastered up in case there was a blast. All she could see were embankments black with burned undergrowth.

She'd eaten her sandwiches up ages ago and now she was down to the last dregs of the medicine bottle of milk, but there was one bit of chocolate stuck to the pocket lining of her gaberdine school mac. Ivy had shoved the bar in her hand when she saw her off at the station and made sure the guard knew she must be put off at Leeds.

She felt stupid with a label tied round her button and pulled it off, not wanting to be a parcel to be delivered to Brooklyn Hall, Sowerthwaite. What sort of village hall was that: a tin shack with corrugated roof?

The carriages were packed with troops straight off the docks, who slept in the corridors and played cards, the blue cigarette smoke in the carriage like thick fog.

In her pocket was a telegram from Mummy promising they'd get back as soon as they could and asking her to be polite to Grandma Belfield and Aunt Prunella until they came to collect her. She had slept with that letter under her pillow. She could smell Mummy's perfume on the paper and it gave her such comfort.

If only she'd met her aunt before and if only she knew where she'd be sleeping tonight. If only Mummy and Daddy could fly back at once – but they would have to go by sea and round the Cape into the Atlantic, which were dangerous water.

Maddy kept feeling so tired and sad inside since that terrible night, it was as if her feet were being dragged through heavy mud. Every little thing was an effort – brushing her teeth, washing out her clothes. Now she was wetting the bed every night and it was so embarrassing to wake up and find her pyjamas all sodden. Ivy tried hard not to be cross with her but she got so upset. Mrs Sangster would be glad to see the back of her after that.

Now this train was taking her to live with strangers in Yorkshire; a place full of chimneys and mills and cobblestones and grime. She'd seen it on the pictures. The industrial north was near where the famous Gracie Fields lived and made her films. There were terrible towns full of misery, poor children in shawls who crawled barefoot under the weaving looms. The factories belched out smoke that blackened all the houses and it rained every day like in 'the dark satanic mills' of Blake's poem.

No wonder Daddy ran away from such terrible surroundings. Now that towns and cities were being blitzed, other children were being evacuated out to the country. There were lines of them on each platform with labels on their coats, all of them carrying brown parcels, with stern-faced teachers ordering them up and down and ticking off lists.

Maddy sat in her school hat and coat, trying to be patient, but she could hear the noise outside the corridors of teachers telling their charges to hurry up and keep in line. She was squashed like a sardine in a tin, hoping the guard would remember to tell her when they reached Leeds Station, as all the signs had been taken from the platforms as a precaution in case the enemy invaded.

Peering out of her porthole only confirmed her worst fears as she saw rows of brick houses and chimneys poking up everywhere – no green fields and forests in view.

Beggars can't be choosers, she sighed, trying to put on a brave face. She clutched Panda as if her life depended on it, her black curls poking from under her school panama hat. At least she was wearing her glasses and the eye patch was switched over to her bad eye so no one would see her squint. Her jaw was stiff and sometimes she kept shivering for no reason. She wished Mummy was here to cuddle her.

If she shut her eyes she could see Dolly Bellaire dressed for a concert in a midnight-blue sequined gown with her little fur shoulder shrug. She could almost smell the rich perfume of roses and the taste of Mummy's lipstick when she kissed her good night. Her hair smelled of setting lotion and her fingernails were crimson. She always looked so glamorous.

At this moment, though, Maddy would have given

up her new ration books just to have an ordinary mother in a tweed suit and jacket, with a headscarf and wicker basket, going off to the shops, and a dad who worked in an office and went on the eight ten each morning into Piccadilly. But it was not to be, and she must be strong for both of them.

I need the bathroom she thought, but didn't want the soldiers to know she was dying to pee.

'Will you show me where the wash room is?' she whispered to a woman sitting opposite, who smiled but shook her head.

'We'll both lose our seats if I do. It's down the corridor at the end. Ask the guard.' The thought of asking a man horrified Maddy. 'I won't bother,' she snapped back. She didn't like pushing past all those rough uniforms sitting behind the door but she didn't want to wet herself again.

'Will you save my seat then?' she asked the woman, who nodded.

There was a queue when she got there and the smell of the toilet made her feel sick, but then the train stopped at a big station. Men jumped off, others clambered aboard and a woman in a funny hat shoved two children up the steps. She hugged them tightly, big tears rolling down her face.

'Now you be good, do you hear? This big girl will take you to her teacher and look after you. This is Gloria and this is Sid. There's a letter in her pocket. She don't read yet.' The lady was crying and when the whistle screeched she jumped down and ran down the platform away from the train.

The two children started to howl. The little boy was screaming for his mummy. The woman was sobbing and ran down the platform again, waving to the train as they started to chug away. The children were making an almighty racket. Maddy didn't know what to do.

'Shush!' she said to the boy in the balaclava and the girl in the pixie hood. 'You can come with me. Take my hand.' They stared up at her with snot running down their noses. 'What's your name?'

'Gloria Conley . . . and he's Sid,' said the little girl. She looked to be about eight or nine, with the brightest red hair Maddy had ever seen.

It had all happened so quickly she wondered if she'd dreamed it up. The little boy was the size of one of the tiny tots in the Sunday school class and Maddy was cross they'd been left alone. She would have to find the teacher they belonged to and get them sorted out. Perhaps the others had got on at the other end of the train and in the rush they'd got separated. It was all very strange.

Sid began to howl, 'I want my mam!' Gloria was trying to be brave and Maddy knew just how that felt, not having a mummy to hold on to. There was something in the look on that mother's face that worried her. Granny Mills would've known what to do. She would have to take them back with her first and then get them sorted out.

Maddy sat with Sid on her knee and Gloria snuggled up to her, squashing the soldier almost out of his seat. He was not amused. She counted every stop in her head so that she could tell the teacher just where they had got on. There were no signs on the station to help her.

Why had their mother not come with them? They were awfully small to be on their own but then she herself was not yet ten, and travelling unaccompanied. At St Hilda's they never went anywhere without a chaperone. School seemed so far away now, another lifetime ago.

The children were neatly dressed in short woolly coats. They had gym shoes on their feet but their hair smelled of dried-up pee and boiled vegetables. Maddy tried not to wrinkle up her nose and hoped it wasn't long to Leeds.

'Where're you going to?' she asked.

'Dunno,' said Gloria. Maddy decided Gloria was a lovely name and she had a mop of glorious red ringlets even curlier than her own. There were freckles on her nose and cheeks and she had the greenest eyes, like a cat. Sid was just the same, only smaller.

'You've got funny glasses,' said Gloria, pointing at her patch.

'What's your other name again?' Maddy said, ignoring her comment.

'Burryl.'

'No, your surname, Beryl what? I'm Madeleine Angela Belfield but you can call me Maddy.'

'Just Gloria Burryl Conley.'

'Where do you live?'

'Dunno . . .'

'You must have an address. What town . . . what street?'

'Elijah Street, by the cut. Dunno owt else,' Gloria shrugged.

This was hopeless. The stupid girl didn't even know her address or anything. Perhaps she was simple-minded like Ivy's cousin, Eddy, who went to a special school.

'Well, Gloria, when the train stops at Leeds I'll ask the guard to find your teacher,' she offered, feeling very grown up.

'What teacher? I'm not going to school,' Gloria replied.

'But you must go to school, everyone does,' Maddy argued.

'I don't. Mam don't believe in it . . . I look after our Sid for her,' she said proudly. Maddy was horrified. 'What's your mummy's name?'

'Marge.'

'And your daddy?'

'Dain't got none.' Gloria pierced her with her green eyes. 'You ask a lot of questions. Where are you going to then?'

Maddy told them at great length her own sad story. Sid had nodded off on her knee but Gloria was taking it all in. Then the train began to slow down and a whisper went through the carriage. 'Leeds . . . next station.'

The soldier helped to pull down Maddy's little brown suitcase from the rack. She roused the sleeping boy and clutched hold of Gloria's hand. 'You'd better come with me. Aunt Prunella will know what to do. Where's your case?'

Gloria shrugged, pointing to a brown parcel tied up with string and her gas mask. 'Come on, Sid, time to go with her.'

Maddy waited by the carriage door until it was opened for them and lifted Sid out and then Gloria. The platform was packed with soldiers and children milling around. She pushed her way as best she could, with Gloria clinging on to her sleeve, clutching Sid's hand. How would she find Mrs Belfield in all this throng?

Gregory Byrne eyed the line-up of other kids and the welfare officer waiting to hand them over like parcels on the foyer of Leeds Station. It was not going to be easy. This one knew all the tricks and was watching him like a hawk, making him walk in front. Greg had a reputation to keep up. He wasn't called 'Houdini' for nothing at his last billet; the escape merchant.

Any open window, convenient drainpipe, and he was off on the run, living rough, stealing from market stalls, a proper Artful Dodger, but his last escape had gone wrong and now he wasn't as quick after doing that stupid dare.

If only the warden hadn't been such a cow and teased little Alfie about his dirty pants. 'What's this stinking mess?' she accused, shaming him before the gang.

'He can't help it, miss,' Greg had gone to Alfie's rescue. 'Maybe if you stopped picking on him so much . . .' He squared up to the old dragon. He was growing so fast, he towered over her.

'You'll speak when you're spoken to, Byrne. Any more cheek from you and you'll be on your way again. How many billets have you gone through? No wonder your mother ditched you in an orphanage as soon as she cast eyes on you. Not much of a specimen to behold, are you?'

She was eyeing him with contempt but he was not going to be bullied like the others.

'Shut your mouth, you old bag. At least I don't have to look in the mirror and see that frightening gob looking back at me!' he shouted, and the others stood back in horror at his cheek. He was for it now but he didn't care. He'd stopped caring about anything but cars and bikes, years ago.

She'd insulted his mother, who'd died when he was born. How dare the old dragon try it on with him? He was hardened by years of playground abuse. He wasn't going to take no more stick from the likes of her.

'Go to your room, Byrne. I'll not be insulted by a scruff who has the brain of a flea and the brawn of an ox. I am sick of taking in riffraff like you. No one wants you – get out of my sight.'

'Don't worry, I'm not stopping in this miserable dump!' he replied. There was no holding him in a place where he was not wanted. He was out of the window and into the fields as fast as his legs could carry him, to join the other evacuees. They were kept outside all day until it was dark so that they didn't mess up the house. It was a miserable hole but no worse than some of the others he'd been expelled from.

Greg led his gang away from their usual path down to the riverbank, making instead towards the mainline railway line.

'We're not supposed to come down here,' said little Alfie, looking up at him. 'What's going on?'

'I'm off. I've had enough of the old cow,' sneered Greg, his face set with determination. His penknife was tucked in his pocket along with the Saturday spends that he'd been saving up.

'But you've no money.' Alfie was running after him.

'You don't need money; I've done it before,' he said as he made his way to the footbridge, and the others were running to keep up with him. The iron footbridge linked two meadows over the main line going north and south. They were on pain of death not to come train spotting too close to the track.

The others were standing in awe as he prepared for his escape.

'You're not going to jump?' Alfie croaked. 'They go too fast down here.'

'Gertcha! I bet he daren't,' sneered Arnie, who was growing into a bully himself.

'You just watch. I'm waiting for a coal wagon or freight, easy peasy. You can watch. I've been practising for ages,' Greg bragged, but that was a lie. He'd only just thought of the idea.

'Houdini does it again!' His admirers crowded round.

'Where'll you go?' said the little boy.

‘Dunno . . . join up and see some action, runaway to sea,’ Greg replied, lifting his legs over the iron railings, dangling them. They were out of sight and half a mile from the hostel. He was hanging ready to drop as soon as the sound of a train came rattling down the track.

‘Anyone coming to join me?’ he laughed, knowing none of them would. ‘One drop onto an open wagon and we can be miles from here by teatime.’

‘Summat’s coming round the bend,’ yelled Alfie, ‘and it’s a slow one.’

‘Just you watch me . . . I’ll give the old bat a wave when I pass the kitchen.’ Greg was hanging from the bars now. The noise of the train and the steam filled the gully and stung his eyes.

Alfie tried to stop him. ‘Don’t do it!’

‘Get off me, the train’s coming now,’ Greg yelled, pushing him away. They were all consumed in a blind cloud of soot and steam and fire, his ears bursting with the noise as the engine roared past and the wheels clanked.

‘Geronimo!’ he yelled as he jumped, but his timing was up the spout and he banged and ricocheted off the wagon side with a crash. He landed not on the coal but on the track gravel, and heard something crack.

He heard someone say, ‘Fetch the pram! Quick . . . run back for help. Greg’s done for!’

The voices faded and then there was nothing.

He came to in hospital with a leg in plaster, broken ribs and arm, and got no sympathy or visits from anyone. He was treated like a prisoner under guard, but his legs hurt too much to be thinking of escape.

They would move him on again but he had plans. He would get himself fit and then join up before it was all over. No one could keep Gregory Byrne tied up for long.

4

Leeds Station, Five p.m.

The train station foyer was crowded as Plum rushed through the barrier onto the platform, clutching her list of names. The trains were running late and she was overdue at the rendezvous by the drinks kiosk. A queue of dishevelled soldiers eyed her up and down. Perhaps it was a mistake to put on her big cartwheel hat but she thought it might give the children something to follow if there was a crush. Maybe it did look a bit grand for the occasion. She felt overdressed, like Lady Bountiful at Ascot.

All she could think of was collecting the six children on the list from their escort and waiting for the Transpennine Express to pick up little Madeleine. They would catch the connection through Scarperton Junction that would get them back to the hostel for tea, but everything was running late.

Peggy Bickerstaffe, Gregory Byrne, Joseph Ridley, Enid Cartwright, Nancy Shadlow and Mitchell Brown – she knew the names off by heart. With relief she saw them lined up in place with the school welfare officer, who handed them over with scarcely a nod. He shoved a file into her hands. 'Over to you now,' he said, and eyed her hat with surprise. 'Can't stop, don't want to miss my connection. We'll come on a visit next week to see them settled in. Good Luck!'

If she'd hoped for a line-up of compliant little infants to shepherd, then she was in for a big disappointment. This lot were older, scruffier, and two of the lads were taller than she was. Don't show your fear or your ignorance, she primed herself. Dogs and kids could sense weakness, so she beamed with false confidence.

'We connect at last. Sorry to be late but the train was held up for a troop train.' No one spoke but they eyed her hat and her gloves. 'Look, we've just one more to pick up from the Manchester train.'

'Can I be excused?' said one of the bigger girls.

'And me too,' said the other.

'Not yet,' Plum said, quick off the mark. That was the oldest ruse in the book. They were going to have to wait now on the platform. There were whistles blowing, loudspeakers going off and a crush of passengers pushing and shoving for a long train heading north. This bunch could not be trusted to sit while she went in search of information. One blink and they'd scarper to the four corners – time to divide and rule.

'Peggy, Joseph, Mitchell?'

'Yes, miss.'

'I'm Mrs Belfield. I want you to be our scouts and get us the best carriage on the train to Scarperton Junction, just over there. Spread out and make sure there's room for all of us. I've brought a picnic,' she smiled, tempting them with titbits in her basket: bribery and corruption, but just for once she needed them to be on her side. They were eyeing her shopping basket with interest now.

'Nancy Shadlow, Enid Cartwright, Gregory Byrne . . . come with me to find out if the Manchester train has come in. I want you to search out a little girl standing on her own. She's called Madeleine.'

'Yes, miss,' they replied in unison.

Could she trust them to behave? The big boy with the blue eyes brimming with mischief towered over the girls, all teeth and knees, but there was something about him she felt she could trust – call it an instinct for a pack leader. In a litter of puppies there was always one that was confident and friendly and up for good training.

Then she turned round and saw that one of the girls was heading towards the station buffet to a group of soldiers, to beg sweets no doubt.

What did she expect from strange children who were being sent packing into the deepest country just because they had been labelled as troublemakers? But if they thought her a soft touch they were in for a shock.

It was like chasing a naughty dog. It must be brought to heel and admonished on the spot or it would get the upper hand. At least she was fleet of foot and weaved in and out of the crowd. She saw the girl pocket the familiar green and gold packet of Woodbines, sharpish. Looking up, the minx beamed at her in defiance.

'This child is not yet thirteen and underage, so if you're looking for any favours . . .' Plum snapped at the soldiers. 'Just walk in front of me, young lady. Do you think I've nothing better to do than chase after you? I thought I could trust a pretty girl like you but I'm mistaken, you're just a silly little kid. Give those cigs to me. I'm old enough to smoke them.' She threw them back to the soldier and shook her head.

She grabbed hold of Enid's arm and half dragged her back to the other children who were restlessly shuffling about. 'I see that I'll have to escort you myself.'

She turned to the biggest boy. 'I'm relying on you now to find Madeleine across there, Gregory. Tell her Mrs Belfield has sent you and bring her down here as fast as you can.' She was torn between leaving the whole damn lot of them and collecting her niece but what could she do? Miss Blunt had made excuses why she was too busy to come. Who would think six children needed two escorts? Armed guards would be more appropriate. They were not coming to Sowerthwaite for their health, and she was not going to fail her first big test.

He was free! What a turn-up! Greg could scarper off and no one would know where he was – hide on a train, find the nearest port and join up. No one would guess his age or ask. His limp was not so bad now. The funny lady in the cartwheel hat had given him the perfect opportunity, silly cow!

No, that wasn't fair. She was OK, as posh biddies went. He'd seen a fair few of those at the orphanage open days, billeting halls and WVS. They didn't scare him.

She'd picked him out and given him a job to do, asked him to meet another kid and trusted him. That was a change! He was so used to being called 'a bad 'un'.

Greg had no memories of any home but Marston Lodge. When the orphanage was right in the firing line off the Sussex coast, they were moved lock, stock up north, and he'd been picked for farm work, on account of his size.

The farmer near York had treated him worse than his animals, and that was saying much. When he fell sick, he'd been picked up and sent to live with the vicar as a 'special case'.

They'd kept him in a room over the stables and they sent him to a posh school where he got in fights and got beaten up just for being a 'vaccy'. That was when he learned a thing or two in the boxing ring.

Just when he was settling down, having bashed in a few heads of his own, along came that curate creep with the funny stare who had tried to touch his privates. He'd punched him a right hook and been sent to the correctional hostel for being 'out of control'. Here he'd lost his southern accent for good. Now Greg was on the move again and he was sick of fighting his corner, sick of being labelled by the panel as 'delinquent' and a 'dunce'.

Well, he wasn't stupid. He could read and write as well as anyone else, but he just didn't hold with school any more. If only he was fourteen and could leave. He wanted to be where there was danger and bullets and excitement, not to be sent on an errand like some 'trusty'.

As he walked out of sight, the 'trust' word hung heavy. Mrs Belfield had picked him out and chosen him specially. Perhaps it would do no harm to fetch the kid and then bunk off, as these were orders, not punishment for a change.

Then he saw her, the kid in the white school hat with glasses, looking lost and trying to be brave. It was a look he knew so well. Blast it, he couldn't leave her standing there – even if she wasn't on her own.

Maddy stood clutching her charges, feeling suddenly abandoned. There was nobody waiting to meet her on the platform. She had checked this was Leeds Station and she daren't move. Sometimes they made announcements over the Tannoy but no one called her name. She stood frozen to the spot.

Where were the teachers who should've gathered up Gloria and her brother? Now she was stuck with them too and it was cold, damp and sooty, the trains like smoking black dragons on huge iron wheels.

Maddy had her ticket but did they have theirs? What if the guard didn't let them through the barrier? How horrid was Aunt Prunella to abandon her like this?

Then she saw a boy limping down the platform, a big string bean of a boy who looked her up and down.

'Are you Madlin? Mrs Belfield sent me. She's on the other platform with me mates,' he smiled, pointing across the platforms.

'And who're you?' Maddy eyed him with suspicion. He wore shorts to his knees, and plimsolls, his socks were dirty and his straw-coloured hair stuck up at the back.

'Greg Byrne. Who are these two?' he asked. 'I thought you were here on your own?'

'Gloria and her brother . . . they got lost. I have to find someone to take them.'

'Bring them along then. Her in charge seems to be on top of the job, she'll sort 'em out. Did they chuck you out of your hostel?'

'I was bombed out. I've got to go to my granny's.'

'You're not one of us then?' he said. 'These two look like a right pair of book ends. Where did you find them?'

Maddy tried to explain to him as he shepherded them back towards another platform.

'Hurry up or we'll miss the train. Wait till you see her hat, the missus they sent . . . looks like a dartboard.' Greg was racing them down the platform and Sid was half carried between them.

Gloria said nothing but gazed up at him as if he was a creature from another planet. 'Where you taking us? Don't leave us, will you?'

'There's a picnic on the train. Just get them on the train and say nowt. It'll be all right. I think her in charge's a toff,' Greg explained.

'Mrs Belfield is my granny,' Maddy announced proudly to put him in his place.

'Blimey! She's the youngest gran I've ever seen then.'

There was this pretty woman in a big hat standing

outside the carriage, waving to her. She rushed up and held out her hand. 'Madeleine, at last . . . I'm sorry I wasn't there to meet you but I had to collect a few others and I was late, but I knew Gregory would find you.'

'Are you Aunt Prunella?' Maddy asked, suddenly overwhelmed by the smiling face, those dark blue eyes and that amazing hat with the net hanging down.

'Call me Plum, dear, Aunt Plum. I hate Prunella – it sounds more like a box of dried fruit.' She laughed and her eyes creased into a grin. 'Thank you, Gregory.'

Gregory had sneaked into the carriage behind Aunt Plum's back with Gloria and Sid.

'Oh, I was so sorry to hear your bad news. Your daddy has rung but the line was terrible. They'll be on their way home, darling, but it's going to take an age. What a rotten time you've had, but you'll have a home with us for as long as you like. Come on, we've grabbed a whole carriage to ourselves and you can meet the other evacuees. They're going to live in a hostel in the village. Won't it be fun!'

Plum was so relieved to have them all safely gathered in as the train chugged out of the station. It was getting dark and the covered lamps flickered; all she could see were legs tangled up. There was a plump boy in shorts with a grimy bandage half hanging off his knee, full of grit and raw skin. He smelled of Germolene.

Then came Gregory, his strong calves covered in yellowing bruises, wearing plimsolls with holes in the sides and carrying the overwhelming stench of sweaty socks. The next set of knees were bony like door knobs, with raised weals, looking as if they'd been leathered with a strap. Across the seat were Enid's long thin legs in grubby ankle socks, and she wore a pair of patent ankle-strapped shoes that looked two sizes too small.

The next pair of plimsolls were very small indeed. There was a small girl huddled in the corner with another little boy. Their knees looked scrubbed clean but they smelled of wet knickers. Then Plum glanced over at her niece in her brogue shoes and woollen stockings, her school uniform two sizes too large for her and those awful round glasses that hid her big grey eyes.

Why did she think of a tin of broken biscuits when she looked at her charges? They were a bunch of misshapes indeed. Broken biscuits were sold by the pound and thrown together in bags, they got crushed and splintered but they tasted just as good once you sorted them out: Abernethy, Nice, Bourbons, Custard Creams and Garibaldis.

But these were children, not broken biscuits, tired, lost, wretched-looking children. Even Madeleine looked haunted and exhausted.

These were not first-timers, full of excitement at being evacuated to the countryside. No, this lot knew the score. Each had a story to tell and had been labelled as a delinquent, a runaway. A quick flip through their files would yield a catalogue of misdemeanours and black marks.

This was their last chance to settle down and behave. There should be six evacuees and her niece, but when she counted them Plum realised to her horror that there were two extras huddled behind Gregory.

'Who are those?' she asked, her heart pounding at the implication. 'Gregory?'

'Dunno, miss. The girl brought them with her off the train. We couldn't leave them,' he said.

'Madeleine, who are they?' Plum was trying to keep the panic out of her voice.

'Their mother put them on the train and told me to look after them. I couldn't find their teacher. No one came to collect them so we brought them to you,' she said, and Plum could hear the others giggling at her refined accent.

''Er don't half talk posh, miss,' said Enid.

'No, I don't,' the girl snapped. 'Did I do wrong, Aunt Plum?'

More guffaws as they heard her nickname.

'Shush! Have you found out their names?'

'The lady called them Glory and Sidney, but she says she's Gloria Conley and they don't go to school, and it was six stops before Leeds when they got on . . . Manchester, I think. I'm sorry but I didn't know what to do,' whispered her niece. 'Oh, the lady said there was a letter in her pocket and "she don't read".'

'Well done, darling, you did what any of us would've done. Just check her pocket but don't wake her yet,' Plum whispered.

'Shall I pull the cord and stop the train?' offered Peggy.

'No!' Plum snapped, the panic rising within her. What if someone was searching the station for them?

What if worried relatives had called out the police? Oh, why had Miss Blunt not come with her?

'Here, miss, in her pocket, a letter . . .' Gregory leaned over and shoved a paper into Plum's hand. The note was written in pencil on the back half of a torn envelope.

> To whom it concerns.
>
> I am sending them away for good. My fella got killed and I can't take no more. I have no proper home for them and am going away so don't come looking. Tell them they is better off. You can call them what ever name but they will answer to Gloria Beryl and Sidney Leonard. She is ten but don't look it and he is five. I cannot take them with me but they will be ever in my heart. Tell them they deserve better than me.

Plum went cold when she read the contents of the note. In desperation the poor mother had just thrown them on the train to the mercy of strangers. How grief-stricken and depressed must she have been to have done such a wicked thing? She must be traced and found, and made to face her responsibilities, but first they would have to take these children to Sowerthwaite for the night, inform the police and authorities and find a home for the mites.

How was she going to explain all this to Matron, and what would Pleasance make of her granddaughter? At least she showed initiative, and Gregory had sneaked them on behind her back. He was a natural leader and they were going to have to watch him.

Perhaps sometimes things just happened and you had to respond as best you could. She had wanted a challenge and, by God, she'd got one now.

Maddy could see Aunt Plum was upset as she read the letter over and over again. It was all her fault but the lady had told her to look after them and for once she'd been obedient. Now she would be in trouble for letting them get on this train, but Gloria was still sticking like gum to her side. The other girls were staring at her now with interest 'cos she'd done something naughty in their eyes.

'Child snatcher!' whispered the biggest one. 'You'll be for it!'

'Shut up, stick insect,' said Gregory in her defence. 'She done what she had to do. She's been bombed out.'

'What's it like? Did you see any stiffs?' asked another of the boys.

'It was horrid and my dog ran away,' Maddy answered.

'We had to have ours put down. Uncle said as we couldn't feed it proper and the cat too. He put them in a sack and threw them in the dock.'

'I know a lad as put his kittens through the mangle,' boasted the fat boy with the bandage.

'That's enough,' said Aunt Plum, in such a sharp voice that everyone listened. 'We're going to have to be kind to Gloria and Sid. It won't be long before our station so get all your parcels and cases and follow me.

You're in the Yorkshire Dales now – it's wild and dark, and if you jump ship you'll get lost on the moors and get swallowed up in a bog and never found. Do I make myself clear?' she ordered, but there was a smile in her voice.

'Yes, Mrs Plum,' said a lone voice, and everyone giggled.

'I rather like that, Peggy, so you can call me Mrs Plum if it helps you remember what I say.'

Greg stared out into the darkness, wondering what he'd let himself in for. Why hadn't he scarpered when he got the chance? Now he was stuck with this lot and miles away from civilisation, just like before.

They all clambered off the train and stood on the blacked-out station. The air was damp and chilly, but it felt fresh and Greg sniffed the scents of wood smoke and steam. There was a crisp wind that rattled round them as they made their way over the steep footbridge and out through a gate to the waiting black saloon, with pull-down extra seats and a luggage rack on the back.

'Madam says to cover the seats in case these vaccies bring anything with them,' said the chauffeur in leather boots and a peaked cap, eyeing them all with suspicion.

Greg took one look at the car and sighed . . . That's more like it, a whopping big Daimler saloon.

Everyone had to crush in and Sid woke and started to cry so the Plum woman put him on her knee. The man in the black jerkin drove them ever so slowly up a long steep hill with only pinpricks for lights, and Greg couldn't see a thing for Enid's bottom in his face. Where were they going now, miles from anywhere? It was pitch-dark outside and eerie.

All he could see were miles of stonewalls on either side of them. It was like driving through a stone maze. It had been such a strange day and he had almost forgotten why he was here. There was no sound of gunfire or planes overhead. How could this place be so quiet and peaceful and hidden away, and where were the smoking chimneys and factories of Yorkshire?

They stopped outside a long stone house and went inside. He smelled the familiar whiff of Lysol and polish. A woman in a starched apron and a funny helmet and uniform stood with her arms folded, inspecting them as they came through the door.

'Girls to the left, boys to the right. What's this, two extras? They're not on my list, Mrs Belfield.'

Here we go again, Greg sighed. There was always one of these tough old birds waiting to lick them into shape. He should've run while the going was good but it was late and he fancied another butchers at that Daimler.

Mrs Plum was for it too and tried to explain, but everyone started talking at once and pointing at Madlin and the little ones and she blushed. Gloria started to snivel and Sid screamed and said his ear was hurting. Matron felt his forehead and said he was burning up and he couldn't stay there.

'Now look here, you can't just pick up any waif or stray and bring them here. They haven't a scrap of identification on them and no ration books. We'll have to call in the constable. What did you think you were doing?' she spat out a spray of spit in his face.

'Don't be cross with him,' said Madlin, the thin one with the squint. 'I told him not to leave us.'

Greg was touched that someone was sticking up for him, even if it was only a girl, but he could look after himself. He was about to launch into the old bat when Mrs Plum caught his arm, as if reading his mind.

'Matron, I think we should discuss this in private after we've settled the children,' she said, quick to jump to his defence. 'They're all tired and hungry and need to get their bearings, and I need to take Madeleine to the Hall.'

'Well, she can take her two charges with her until I'm told otherwise. We aren't geared up for extras. The bedrooms are full as it is, Mrs Belfield. Though heaven knows what her ladyship will say to these two scruffs. He'll need the doctor, by the look of him.'

'Then I'll leave you to your duties,' said Mrs Plum with a sniff and blazing eyes. 'Come on, you three, time for one last trip to the lavatory and then bed.'

The lads were taken into the attic. There was a row of beds with large jam jars by the side. 'What's these for, ashtrays?' Greg joked.

'Just a trick the doctor thought up to stop any bedwetting, but aim straight!' came the order. 'The lavatory is a long way off and I know how lazy boys can be. Unpack your bags and supper is in the kitchen.'

Greg bounced on his bed. So far so good: clean sheets – a good sign – and a locker for his stuff. It would do for a few nights until he got his bearings and then he'd make a run for it again. They'd gone north and west from Leeds. He knew his geography. They couldn't be that far from a seaport but he fancied another ride in that Daimler.

Gloria was so tired she could hardly keep her eyes open as they drove up a long path with tall trees, and then a great white owl flew across in front of them.

'What's that?' she whispered to Maddy. 'I don't like this place.'

'Just a barn owl and it's not far to Brooklyn Hall,' said Mrs Plum. 'But you'll have to be very quiet when we arrive. Mrs Belfield is not used to little children so let me explain what's happened first.'

'My ear hurts,' moaned little Sid, whimpering.

'I know, darling. I'll find some cotton wool and warm oil for it.'

'Is this it?' Gloria looked up at the huge stone house with a square tower in the middle and windows like a castle. It was bigger than all of Elijah Street put together. It was all shuttered up and unwelcoming. There was a huge oak door at the top of some wide stone steps.

'The windows have got their eyes shut. It looks as if it's sleeping,' she said, making Mrs Plum smile.

They pulled the bell and a young woman in a pinafore came to the door. They were ushered inside and the driver took the car around the back. Maddy thought there must be some mistake. Were they being taken into a school?

A woman came down the stairs with a stick, a tall

woman in a long black dress with a shawl around her arms, her smoky-grey hair piled up high. She smelled of flowers.

'At long last, Prunella . . . Oh, what a pretty child,' she said, grasping hold of Gloria, eyeing her carefully. 'This is not the Belfield golden hair. Where did such extravagant curls come from? So small for her age . . . Come here, child and let me see you. We can do something with you.'

'That's Gloria, an evacuee,' spluttered Mrs Plum. 'Madeleine, your granddaughter, is over here,' pointing in the other direction to where Maddy hung back in the shadows.

'Oh, I see . . . Take off your glasses, girl, let the dog see the rabbit.' The lady eyed her up and down. 'Oh dear, how unfortunate . . . Not our side of the family at all, is she? She's like a horse with a wall eye, not to be trusted. Ah well, it was to be expected.'

Gloria's eyes were on stalks. She'd never seen such a grand room except in the pictures. She'd seen *Little Lord Fauntleroy* and Shirley Temple at the fleapit on Saturday mornings. She was living in fairyland in the middle of the pictures and this was going to be her new home. Then the old lady saw Sid whining. He was going to spoil everything.

'Just shut up and behave or we'll get chucked out,' Gloria whispered in his ear. Didn't he know when he was well off? He was looking queer again.

'This is Gloria and her brother, Sidney, who's not very well. They need a bed for the night and some medical attention, I'm afraid,' Mrs Plum said.

'This is impossible, Prunella. It was bad enough having the one but now you're asking me to put up three and to call out poor Dr David at this time of night. Can't it wait?' The two women were trying to argue quietly but Maddy could hear their angry mutters.

'It's like the pictures, innit?' whispered Gloria, looking around with wonderment. 'I keep pinching myself. If Mam could see us here . . .'

'Where's she gone to?' said Maddy, hoping to catch Gloria off guard.

'Dunno,' came the guarded reply. She was too tired to think what Mam was doing now. She'd just left them on the train to fend for themselves and she didn't understand why, but Gloria was still preening herself for having been picked out as the Belfield girl.

Sid was looking funny again.

'Miss, miss, he's fitting! He allus does this when he's sick,' she yelled.

The old lady looked on with concern as he was laid down, rigid with tremors. Perhaps Sid could be useful after all. If he was sick they couldn't move him and she could stay the night in a palace. She was curious now and wanted to see what it all looked like in the morning light.

'Shall I put something over his tongue? Miss Connaught does that when Veronica Rogers has a fit,' offered Maddy. Her grandmother looked surprised to hear her speaking the King's English in her best elocution voice. At least she wasn't being ignored now in favour of Gloria's pretty looks. That had hurt more than anything.

'Now look what you've brought to our door . . . Send Ilse to The Vicarage and he can phone for Dr David. These lower classes don't know how to look after themselves properly, letting children loose in this state. Those children look half starved and *such* coarse accents. I don't want Madeleine picking it up. Arthur's taught her some manners, I see.'

'I can speak French too,' Maddy added. 'We did French and Latin at St Hilda's but I hate Latin.'

'Speak when you're spoken to, girl,' said the old woman. 'Go and find Ilse and send her off with a torch. This is most inconvenient!'

Maddy wondered if they were expected to bob a curtsy like the maids did, but decided against it. She raced across through the baize door into a warren of passages, Gloria clinging on to her, into the kitchen where they found two women sipping tea.

'We need the doctor for a little boy. Please can someone go to the nearest phone?'

The women jumped up and put on their coats.

'Just the one of you, I think,' Maddy ordered, but the girls shook their heads.

'I not go in the dark. There be ghosts in the lane and soldiers. We go in twos together, please,' pleaded the brown-eyed girl with her hair all scraped into a plait around her head.

What sort of place was this house, where servants were afraid and Mrs Belfield lived all alone? No wonder Daddy never spoke of it and his horrid mother, who was a snob. Why had no one told her that the Belfields lived in a castle with big sweeping stairs and stone floors that smelled of old smoke?

Tomorrow she would ask Aunt Plum if she could join the evacuees in the village. Gloria could stay here with Sid and be petted, but she didn't want to spend another night in this horrible place where she wasn't wanted.

Later, when the doctor came to examine Sidney and pronounced that he'd burst his eardrum and needed bed rest and medicine, the two girls were tucked up in a huge four-poster bed with curtains round the posts. The room smelled of lavender and damp.

Ilse had warmed the sheets with a big copper warming pan and made a fuss of the pair. Gloria was made to stand in a tub and be sponged down by Aunt Plum to see if she had fleas. Her underclothes were thin, clean and she wasn't wrapped in brown paper like some of the vaccies were supposed to be. She was enjoying every minute of the fuss.

Maddy had never undressed for bed with a stranger before. She wanted to be on her own, but not in this barn of a bedroom. She wondered about all the people who'd died in that bed. Were their ghosts still haunting the place?

What a strange day! The only nice thing about it was meeting Aunt Plum, but they never got time on their own to talk over what had happened. Everyone expected Maddy to look after the other two.

She wished she'd never gone to the washroom on the train, never seen the mother shove those two into her hands, but she had. Then she thought of her relief when Greg had limped down the platform to rescue them. Perhaps there was one friend after all who would look out for her – even if he were a boy.

5

December 1940

'Can you pick up my knitting, dear?' gasped Great-aunt Julia as she struggled with her two sticks across the hallway of Brooklyn Hall. Maddy wasn't used to going at tortoise pace but she loved being useful to the old ladies in the drawing room who, wrapped in ancient fur wraps and shawls to keep out the draughts, were busy knitting for the Sowerthwaite Comforts fund. Everyone took it in turns to sit up close to Uncle Algie's battery-operated wireless to catch the news as best they could.

Maddy couldn't believe it was nearly Christmas, nearly three whole months since that arrival at Brooklyn Hall, when Sid had had his fit and Grandma had eyed her up and down with disappointment.

'It's hotting up in Greece,' shouted Great-uncle Algernon across the room, resting his half a leg on a leather buffet as he strained to catch the bulletin. 'Metaxas has said "No" to Mussolini and there'll be trouble in the Balkans, mark my words . . . Oh, and Liverpool and Manchester had another visit from the Luftwaffe last night. Three of our planes are missing.'

'Don't believe a word of it, girls,' shouted Grandma, looking up from her letter writing. 'It's all lies and propaganda. I don't know why you want to depress us with such news.'

Maddy was glued to the six o'clock news every night. She had heard enemy bombers droning overhead at night on their deadly route across the moors, hoping that the searchlight on the field battery would be torching their path for the ack-ack guns.

Her parents were on their way back from Egypt, hinting in their letter that they were going the long route round Africa and there was fighting in the Mediterranean. They were coming home for Christmas, but Maddy would rather they stayed put if there was danger.

It was such an age since she'd seen them and so much had happened, so much to tell them about her new school and friends. How the Brooklyn seemed like a hotel full of shuffling old people, who played endless games of patience and bridge, who quarrelled and fussed over Ilse's cooking and fought to get the best corner by the huge fireplace.

Besides Uncle Algie and Aunt Julia and her companion, Miss Betts, there was a distant cousin Rhoda Rennison and her sister, Flo. It was easy to lump them all together somehow in their grey cardigans and baggy skirts, darned lisle stockings and tweed slippers. Around them wafted a tincture of eau de cologne that almost masked a more acidic smell. The oldies melted into the walls of the Brooklyn between meals along with their ear trumpets, stringy knitting in carpet bags and shawls. Then when the dinner gong rang they appeared from the far recesses of the house, back to the table like clucking hens at the trough, pecking at their plates, too busy to talk to Maddy.

Aunt Plum was worried about Uncle Gerald, who was waiting in barracks down south to be sent abroad soon. When she was upset she smiled with sad eyes and went for long walks over the hills with her dogs, when she wasn't on duty at the Old Vic Hostel.

Maddy walked to the village school each morning with the two Conleys, who now lived in Huntsman's Cottage with Mr and Mrs Batty. It was a funny arrangement: normal school lessons in the morning, mixing with the local children at St Peter's C of E School, and then lessons in the village hall, crushed in with a gang of evacuee kids from Leeds, who were living the other side of Sowerthwaite. It was all very noisy and they didn't do much work, just copying from the board until hometime. There weren't enough teachers to go round.

It was not like St Hilda's at all, and the first thing she'd done was to lose her elocution accent in favour of a Yorkshire one, flattening her 'a's so she didn't get teased, though it made Grandma Belfield furious if she said bath instead of baath.

'The sooner Arthur comes and puts you in a half-decent school . . . You're turning into a right little Yorkshire tyke. It's no good Plum letting you mix so much with that village lot. They're teaching you nothing but bad habits. I hear they've been up to their old tricks again on the High Street,' Grandma sighed, looking up at Maddy's glasses and then turning back to her letter writing.

Maddy smiled to herself as she sat with her arms out so Aunt Julia could unravel a jumper that smelled of mothballs. Peggy, Greg and Enid knew all the best wheezes. It was Enid's idea to fill the cig packet with dirt and worms and then box it up as if it was new and toss it on the pavement. They hid in the little alleyway while the passer-by spotted the cigs and pounced only to jump back in horror. They filled blue sugar bags with horse droppings and left them in the middle of the road so the carters stopped, hoping for a present to give their wives, only for the smelly muck to spill out while the gang had to look, duck and vanish like the Local Defence Volunteers down the ginnel.

Everyone got a telling-off from the constable, and poor Enid was grounded for being the ringleader by Miss Blunt, but she complained they'd all helped so all of them missed the Saturday film show as a punishment except Maddy. Going on her own was not much fun.

Greg was out cleaning the Daimler and helping Mr Batty, and begging old wheels to make a go-kart from the salvage cart. There was always something happening at the Old Vic even though Miss Blunt was strict and didn't like mess. They were busy making Christmas presents out of cocoa tins, painting them and putting holes in the lids to pull a ball of string through. String was very precious now. Aunt Plum took her down to the hostel to join in the crafts after school. They were turning dishcloths into pretty dolls and sewing dusters into knickerbockers with frills on to sell at the bazaar for War Comforts. Soon it would be time to make Christmas paper chains and tree decorations.

The Brooklyn was fine in its own way, but since Gloria and Sid had moved in with the Battys, Maddy felt lonely at night, the draughts whistling round the house like banshees. Aunt Plum and Grandma were always out at committee meetings; the Comforts fund, the WVS, the Women's Institute and the Church Council, so she sat with the oldies listening to the wireless while they dosed after supper. Uncle Algie let her listen to the Light Programme, and the music that reminded her of Mummy.

Mummy's letters were full of interesting places that Maddy dutifully looked up in the atlas with Uncle Algie's help. They had sung in concerts in the desert under the moon and stars.

> We're so looking forward to Christmas and to being a proper family once more. We should never have left you behind, but we thought it was for the best. You have had to suffer because of us doing our duty but be strong and brave. Not long now, darling.

It was a funny war here, nothing much happened at all. There was a gun battery up behind Sowerthwaite, and the Local Defence Volunteers paraded in church. The town was bursting with kids from all over the place but no bombs and no big factories belching smoke were to be seen. It was a relief to wake up each morning to silence and the bleat of sheep but she still felt sad. In her dreams she went back to Chadley, chasing Bertie, singing round the piano with Uncle George, playing with the button tin, making corkscrew coils of knitting with Granny Mills. If only they were here with her for Christmas too.

Her biggest surprise was that the Yorkshire of her *Jane Eyre* heroine was so beautiful and wild, with hills and stone walls creeping in all directions, green grass and hundreds of sheep, cows and pigs in makeshift arks, chicken coops and duck ponds, horses ploughing up the fields by the river and gardens crammed full of vegetables and apple trees.

They were making an allotment behind the Old Vic and Mr Batty was helping the big children plant vegetables. None of them had known a fork from a spade before they started but they did now. Enid and Peggy complained their hands were getting blisters. It was all so peaceful and safe, as if she'd moved to another world, but at what a cost? Why couldn't they all have come before the war to enjoy the scenery?

Maddy's favourite spot was high up in the big beech tree that was planted right at the back of the Old Vic in the corner where the garden became a field. There was a swing rope up to a little wooden den in its branches. The tree was very old.

From their hide-out they could spy on German

planes and hide if the enemy invaded. There was a password to climb up that changed every week.

Aunt Plum said the tree was planted long ago by subscription after some famous victory. No one could remember which battle it was but it had to be hundreds of years old. It must have been in honour of the men of Sowerthwaite who took part; a bit like Grandma's line of Lombardy poplars on the lane up to Brooklyn Hall, which Maddy always felt were sad trees. She called them the Avenue of Tears.

One of those trees was for her Uncle Julian – no wonder Grandma hated anything to do with the war. She did her duty on her committees but her lips were always set in a thin line and she had no smile wrinkles round her eyes like Aunt Plum.

Maddy lay across a branch of the tree daydreaming, her arms dangling down, hidden by a curtain of rusting leaves. It reminded her of the apple tree near The Feathers, but that made her think of Bertie and Gran and the terrible blitz that haunted her dreams. She hoped her little dog had found a new home.

Aunt Plum's dogs were big and bouncy, not the same as her own special friend.

Everything was so different here, she thought, hiding under the canopy whilst she watched for spies. There had to be spies in the district if there was going to be an invasion soon, she thought. She knew the fire drill by heart. Now she was supposed to be collecting beech mast to feed Horace the pig in the shed.

It was fun going on salvaging trips down the cobbled alleyways and lanes, staring in through the doors of stone houses with slate rooftops like fish scales. Sowerthwaite was full of secret lanes that opened out onto the wide marketplace. Its shops lined the streets with arched doorways and bow windows straight out of her fairy-tale book. There were banners across the town hall urging the townfolk to buy Savings Bonds, posters in the shop windows warning of 'Careless Talk', but no bomb sites or proper air-raid shelters in sight, not like Chadley.

Peggy, Gloria and she were in Greg's team, collecting newspapers and jam jars for salvage. Peggy was very round, always puffing, and didn't like pushing the hand-cart; Gloria was always sneaking off looking through shop windows, so Maddy and Greg did most of the hard work, dodging dogs, knocking on doors and trying to beat the other gang for the team to collect most. Big Bryan Partridge's gang cheated by hanging round the back of shops, sneaking cardboard boxes while Mitch Brown and Enid hung round the Three Tuns to cadge bottles, but Miss Blunt liked to have them out of the Vic all day being useful, come rain or shine.

Maddy loved practising for the school Christmas concert in church, making secret presents for the oldies, and now with Mummy and Daddy coming home it was going to be just perfect. Only one thing was spoiling everything now.

Last night her dreams were disturbed by bangs and flashes and the flames burning the pub, and she was running to save them but she couldn't reach them in time and then she woke and her bed was wet again.

Aunt Plum had put a rubber sheet on her mattress when she first came and told her not to worry, but she woke crying from the dream and crying with shame as she sneaked her sheet and her pyjamas down to the scullery to soak in the sink. She was making extra work and there was a war on and it worried her. Then she'd had to creep back in the dark, feeling up the oak banister rail and curl up with Panda, trying to be brave.

The silence outside was scary at first but she strained to hear the night sounds, the bleating sheep, the owl hooting, the drone of a night plane or the rattle of the night express in the distance. She was lucky to be safe and warm in this hidy-hole, but until Mummy and Daddy returned it could never be home.

The old house was friendly in its own way, cluttered with walking sticks and cushions and doggy smells. There were rooms boarded off and shuttered to save on heating. The sun shone through dusty windows, but it gave off little heat now.

Sometimes she walked up from school, up the Avenue of Tears, wondering if Daddy did the same dawdle with his satchel all those years ago. Why had he never come back here?

It was something to do with Mummy and the Millses being ordinary and saying 'bath' in the wrong way, but Mummy was beautiful and sang like a 'storm cock'. When Maddy grew up she would marry someone she loved, however poor he was, if he was handsome and kind. He wouldn't mind that she was leggy and plain with a turn in her eye that never seemed to get any better. She didn't want another operation to straighten it out. The last one in Chadley hadn't worked for long.

Aunt Plum promised when things were less hectic they would take her to see a specialist in Leeds who might sort out her eye once and for all. With the war on, though, Aunt Plum said all the best surgeons were at the front so they might have to wait until peace came again.

It was so peaceful here. The war hadn't bothered Sowerthwaite, and it wouldn't if Grandma had anything to do with it. Maddy touched the bark of Uncle Julian's poplar for luck.

Gloria Conley skipped round the playground singing 'Little Sir Echo, how do you do . . .', her bunches bobbing behind her. She'd just been chosen to sing a solo in the school concert and Miss Bryce said she had lovely voice. She couldn't wait for it to be Christmas now.

She didn't mind being moved out of the Hall because now Sid and she had their own special auntie and uncle of their own and all because of Sid's ear.

It had gone septic and now he couldn't hear in it at all. Miss Plum had explained how ill he was when the Welfare came to take them away, and that he couldn't be moved. Then Mrs Batty asked Mrs Plum if they'd like to come and stay with them. It was such a relief. How Gloria'd prayed not to be taken back to Elijah Street. She hoped that the Lord understood why she had to fib like mad about how Uncle Sam, God rest his soul, had beat them and poor Mam had shoved them on the train out of harm's way. In her heart she knew it was all lies but it made a better story than the truth – that nobody wanted them.

She woke up on that first morning in Brooklyn Hall and thought she'd died and gone to heaven, snug in clean sheets and pyjamas, with thick checked shirts and corduroy dungarees to play out in. There was yucky porridge for breakfast but hot toast and real butter and jam for afters.

Everyone had fussed over Sid until he was better She wished they could stay in the big house for ever but then they'd been allowed to stay on in the grounds at the Battys' cottage, which would have to do.

Mrs Batty did all the washing for the Hall and the ironing. She had a big copper boiler in its own shed and an iron mangle that she turned with strong arms. She made big stews out of rabbits and stuff that Mr Batty 'found' in the woods. Huntsman's Cottage was small but clean, and the old couple let them run wild in the woods and play with the other vaccies after school.

Even school was turning out better than she dared hoped. Her reading and writing were coming on and Maddy sometimes let her practise the difficult words in the reading book. She was getting quite good now but would never catch up the Belfield girl.

The only worry was that Constable Burton was sending someone to find Mam. She was in big trouble now. Gloria prayed that Mam'd take her time to fetch them back or come and live with them up here. She still couldn't believe that she'd just shoved them on that train . . . It didn't make any sense. Gloria never wanted to go back to the cobbled streets and dark corners of the city again, now she'd seen Brooklyn Hall.

It was Miss Plum who explained that Mam was no longer living in Elijah Street. In fact no one knew where she had gone. 'Gone orff, I'm afraid,' she said. 'Not to worry, Gloria, she'll come looking for you soon enough.'

How could Gloria explain that she wasn't worried, she was relieved to be staying put? Old Mrs Belfield said they ought to be put in an orphanage, so she cried and hollered and made herself so sick that Maddy's gran relented, saying that they could stay 'for the duration but in somewhere more suitable', whatever that meant.

It didn't take a numbskull to work out that old Mrs Belfield thought she wasn't good enough to share a room with Maddy. She was not family, but Miss Plum explained that she could come and play with Maddy any time she liked. Try and stop me, Gloria thought.

She loved the Brooklyn, with its wide curving staircase, the pictures up the walls in gold curly frames and the smell of wet dogs and lavender polish. Every shelf was covered in china Bo-Peeps and silver trinket boxes, statuettes and ornaments.

Why must she be banished just because she wasn't born rich and petted with pretty dresses? There were no dancing lessons for her, or ponies to ride. The

Belfields lived in another world, in a big space with fields to play out in, not cramped in a bricked back yard with noisy neighbours, barking dogs and horrible smells.

Yet this war had done something wonderful in transporting the two of them from the town into the country. There would be no budging her now. She and Sid might live in a humble cottage but she was going to stick close to the Big House like glue. Maddy would be her best friend and where she went Gloria would not be far behind, she smiled to herself.

Huntsman's Cottage would do for now but when Gloria Conley grew up she was going to find her own rich man with a house with a hundred rooms and servants so she could live the life of a film star. She loved going to the Saturday pictures with the other vaccies to see Mickey Mouse and Charlie Chaplin, and Shirley Temple in *Poor Little Rich Girl.*

If being rich meant learning to read and write proper . . . no elbows on the table and no slurping her soup, sucking up to her betters, then she was up for it. She was prettier than Maddy any day. That must count for something, *and* she could sing the best in her class. When they saw her on stage in the school show, then they would see she was as good as any of them.

Greg Byrne took the corner fast. He'd borrowed some pram wheels off the salvage lorry, just three to make his racing cart. It was low to the ground with ropes to guide the steering. This was the fastest he'd made

– if only he could control the damn thing. There was a touch of black ice on the tarmac ahead that was going to be tricky but skidding would be even better, he grinned to himself.

It was worth weeks of cleaning and polishing the Daimler, fetching and carrying empties, to have the money to build this racer.

There was something about going faster and faster that made his head spin with excitement. There was nothing to beat it. The trudge up the steep hill track onto the moors, with its five sharp bends, made it all worth it, scaring horses and carts, making tramps dive into the walls out of his way when he careered down pell-mell.

The best thing of all was to cadge a ride on the back of one of the soldier's motor bikes up to the battery field, towing 'Flash Gordon' behind him.

One push and the cart flew downhill all the way with the soldiers' shopping list for the village stores. All he could think of when he trudged back up the hill was the loose change he'd earned and the day when he would be old enough to own a racing bike himself. Even a two-wheeler would be a start but the old 'sit up and beg' two-wheeler bike in the Vic belonged to The Rug; an ancient black metal affair with a basket up front, that made Miss Blunt look even more like the Wicked Witch of the West in *The Wizard of Oz*. She rode it to Scarperton on market day and no one was allowed to borrow it.

She ran the hostel like HMS *Bounty*, with her rules for wayward evacuees, a strict rota for chores, curfew hours, punishment meted out for bed-wetting and lateness, so once or twice he'd let her tyres down just to get even. One of these days he'd do a bunk but not yet.

There was something about the Old Vic that he'd taken to. It wasn't a bad billet. He'd been in far worse, and something Miss Plum had said about him being 'officer material and a born leader' pleased him, even if he did lead the gang into mischief. He was the one that started them off giggling when Miss Blunt's wig went all of a quiver, which made it wobble even more. The others looked up to him as their boss, and Enid had offered to show him her thingy for a ride on Flash Gordon.

Sowerthwaite wasn't that bad a place. There were always summat going on, hills to climb, foraging for mushrooms and sticks, salvaging trips. School was pretty basic. He was marking time for his fourteenth birthday when he could get apprenticed.

As long as he was working on wheels with oil he was happy, and Mr Batty had showed him all the ins and outs of the Belfields' saloon. He taught him to do rough work, taking engine bits apart and putting them back together again. He watched how to decoke the engine and change the oil and tyres. 'You've got engine oil in your veins, me laddo,' Mr Batty laughed.

And once, only once, the chauffeur'd let him sit in the driving seat, showing him the stick gears and letting him drive a few yards. This was sufficient to keep him behaving enough to stay put and not draw too much attention to his madcap schemes.

There was a big garage on the main road out of Sowerthwaite that might take him on as an apprentice mechanic if he kept out of trouble and if Miss Plum put in a good word.

Greg liked walking up into the Dales to the battery field. It was manned by a group of old soldiers. He wasn't supposed to trespass but there was a geezer there called Binns who knew all about birds of prey: buzzards, merlins, peregrines and harriers. Now he could tell a sparrowhawk from a kestrel by its tail.

Mr Batty was a bit of a stargazer and showed him directions by the stars and how to find true north. Greg had never seen so many stars in a sky before, all with different names.

It was a man's world up here, a train-spotter's paradise, perches on rocky cliffs to climb in search of dead eggs, waterfalls with deep ledges to jump into pools when the weather warmed up . . . if he stayed that long.

There weren't enough hours in the day for Plum to finish getting ready for Arthur and Dolly's return.

'I don't know why you're making such a fuss, Prunella,' sniffed her mother-in-law. 'They can stay in the Black Horse. It's what they're used to, after all.'

'Of course they won't! They're family. I don't understand you sometimes; your own flesh and blood . . . It's Christmas, Mother, the season of goodwill. Those two have risked life and limb to get back to Maddy, the least we can do is let bygones be forgotten and give them a proper homecoming. Heaven knows what dangers they've faced *en route*.'

'Please yourself but don't expect me to roast the fatted calf for them. Not a word from either of them in years.'

'Do you blame them? When did you last write to Arthur?' Plum argued, but Pleasance stormed off out of earshot. How could families quarrel over trivia when the country was in such danger?

Her recent visit to London to see Gerald off into the unknown after what was obviously embarkation leave gave Plum a good idea what London was going through. There were raids every night and total devastation in some parts of the town. It had been a bittersweet reunion: going to parties held in smoky basement flats, trying to get last-minute tickets for a show, spending the night in a public shelter when they were caught in a raid, and a twelve-hour journey back on the train. She felt so guilty to be living so peacefully out in the sticks away from such terrors. Their parting had been rushed and fraught and very public.

Gerald listened to all her news of the hostel and her new job politely.

'I must tell you what Peggy said to me the other day,' she prattled on, hoping to amuse him. 'We were running the vacuum cleaner over the drugget in the Vic. Peggy Bickerstaffe, the little pug-faced one who steals biscuits when no one is looking, was supposed to be helping. She just stood there looking at it puzzled. "Am I one of them?" She pointed down to the machine.

'"A Hoover?" I replied. "It's a vacuum cleaner, dear."'

'"That's right, miss, a vac . . . and we're vaccies. We're sent out all day picking up other people's rubbish." It brought me up sharpish, I tell you. You never know what goes on in the mind of a child, do you?'

'I wouldn't know . . .' Gerald replied, obviously not interested, but she wanted him to know what sort of children she was billeting.

'Enid shocked me the other night too when we were making cocoa in the kitchen. She was talking to Nancy and Ruby bragging, almost. "At the last house I was in, I got sixpence for doing cartwheels. The old man used to give me extra if I did it wi' no knickers on," she sniggered.

'"That's enough," I said, trying to change the subject. 'No wonder that girl is boy mad. Makes me think what other things went on and she's still only a child. What do you think?'

Gerald shook his head. 'Let's go to bed.'

They made love on that last night in the hope of conceiving another baby but somehow their very desperation spoiled it for her. She just couldn't relax into it. Part of her was still smarting from his earlier betrayal and wondering if his affair was really over. Was he just humouring his wife to keep her sweet and still seeing Daisy behind her back? Did it suit him that she was stuck up north with his mother, out of sight? Was she just a glorified housekeeper? He knew she and Pleasance didn't get on, but her own parents were dead.

Loyalty would always keep her at her post. That was a given. She'd been raised to value service to others as the duty of anyone brought up in comfort, wealth and security. What she was doing for those unfortunate evacuee children was important. She just wished he would be more interested in his niece, Maddy.

There'd been just time before her return to trawl through the shops to find gifts for her charges. She had clothing coupons from the local authorities to spend on Greg and the Conleys. There were still materials hidden away in shops that could make winter dresses and trousers. She found toys for Sid and Gloria in Hamleys, and a present for Maddy that was a bit extravagant.

If only Pleasance would spend more time with the girl and get to know her, Plum sighed, looking out of the sooty train, but she seemed to avoid the child. It was so unfair. In fact, Pleasance avoided all the evacuee children, claiming she was too busy doing her war work. Sometimes this consisted of little more than endless tea parties with ladies in smart hats bemoaning the lack of decent domestic servants while they knitted balaclavas and scarves. Their comfortable world was being turned upside down by this war and Mother was struggling to adjust to not having her usual creature comforts to hand: their car was doubling up for one of the town ambulances, the bedrooms were filled with aged relatives, and now Maddy had children traipsing up and down the stairs making a racket that got on her nerves. Her son's visit was playing on her nerves too.

How strange to meet a brother- and sister-in-law for the first time. Would Arthur remind her of Gerald or the photo of Julian in the drawing room? Gerald looked so dashing in his uniform with his thin moustache hovering above his upper lip like Robert Donat, the film star. If only he wasn't so handsome.

Men like him didn't have to work to charm the girls, they just turned up, all tight trousers and teeth, and the doves fluttered in the cote around them. She should know – she'd felt the power of his charm beaming in her direction. Theirs had been a whirlwind romance. She'd come out in London and Yorkshire, done the round of debutante parties and balls, been thrown in the path of suitable partners, and Gerald had been the most handsome, persistent and debonair. The fact that she was an heiress of sorts with a good pedigree made his wooing all the more ardent, she realised with hindsight.

The Templetons fought with King Charles, lost their lands under Cromwell and then got them back under Charles II. The estate near Richmond now belonged to her brother, Tim, but there was a generous settlement on her; not a fortune but enough to give her independence.

She was young, naïve, taking all Gerald's flattering attention at face value. He did love her in his own way, as a desired object, a pretty face and the future mother of his children. The miscarriages had changed all that, made her wary, and he'd lost patience and found other pretty faces. His mother was disappointed with them both for not coming up to scratch in the heir department. She didn't like weakness.

Was that why Pleasance distanced herself from

Arthur's child – because she was plain? Was it her roving eye and spectacles, her bony frame and gawky gait that disappointed her? Maddy was growing fast. All the newcomers had blossomed on fresh air, good food and quiet nights' rest.

It was just as she first thought, these children were like a kennel of puppies. She smiled thinking of roly-poly Peggy, who stuck to Enid Cartwright. Both were at the awkward age of fourteen, being too old for dolls and too young for boys.

Little Mitch Brown was a serious chap, old for his years, with a hunted look on his face like a nervous terrier. Bryan Partridge was like one of those lolloping mongrels, willing, shambolic and always racing into mischief. Nancy Shadlow was so quiet she was like a timid sheepdog cowering in a barn yard, silent and wary. She cried for her mam and sisters, and wasn't settling at all. Gloria was a bouncing red setter, impossible to keep still but she tagged along with Maddy, who had the knack of reining her in somehow.

Gregory was the one coming on better than she'd dared hope, the pack leader, handsome in a rough sort of way and proud; a bit of an Alsatian about him. She'd already asked at Brigg's Garage if he could be taken on as a mechanic.

It was promising to be a great Christmas – if only Herr Hitler would give his bombers a holiday over the festive season so everyone in the country could have a good night's rest. Just a lull for a few days would do.

As the towns turned into villages and hills, grey into

green, Plum peered out at the beauty of her surroundings, relieved and guilty to be leaving the nightly raids behind. Her war work was of a different kind from that of the women in the city: trying to give these lost children some fun, hope, and discipline. She tried to temper Avis Blunt's coldness with some warmth and understanding.

Matron was always banging on about them needing a firm hand but Plum had always got more from her dogs with praise and titbits than with sticks and a beating. Too much yelling and punishment made them anxious and confused, and that set them off in the wrong direction. Surely the children needed firm consistency but also praise when they deserved it?

They had hidden the latest food parcel sent as goodwill gifts from the American people. It was bulging with treats and clothing, and so precious. With all the terrible submarine attacks on convoys in the Atlantic, who knew when they might receive another one? There were more tough clothes for playing in, warm nighties, tins of syrup, lovely quilted bedspreads, milk powder, sweets and magazines. Christmas at the Old Vic was going to be fun.

The hostel's Christmas turkey was provided by the Town Council and the Christmas puddings were ready in Mrs Batty's scullery. The children would lunch after morning service and the Belfields, along with their elderly houseguests, would dine later and dress for the occasion.

Plum had used her own coupons to buy Maddy a turquoise velvet dress with long sleeves from Harrods.

It was outrageously extravagant but she wanted the child to have something pretty to wear for her parents. Pleasance would have to go halves with her whether she liked this present or not. The other gift had been hidden at Brigg's Garage for weeks, out of sight of peering eyes.

Everyone was doing their best to be cheerful and festive, but the shops were struggling to keep up with demand. All the factories were up to speed and turned to war production: curtain mills turned into shirt factories, woollen mills turning out uniform cloth, silk mills churning out parachute silk, engineering works pumping out machine tools and spares for aircraft and tanks.

The streets of Scarperton were filled with older men and women with baskets, nipping out in their lunch break to catch up on shopping. The farms were full of land girls. Plum wondered what it was doing to the babies and children, not having fathers around the house and mothers on shift work.

Then she smiled, thinking of her own childhood, when Nanny dressed her to take tea with Mummy and Daddy, if he was home. Sometimes she hardly saw him for weeks. Mummy was a lovely creature who popped into the nursery to say good night, dressed in chiffon and smelling of vanilla perfume. They were loving strangers to her in some ways.

Everyone had to make sacrifices now but she yearned to have a child of her own to cherish, one who would not be farmed out to servants all day. Without Gerald close by it was an impossible dream. War was causing such disruption even in this sleepy market town.

All the schoolmasters were called up for service and older staff brought out of retirement, married women were also back in the classroom. Farmhands, postmen and shopkeepers had all but disappeared. It reminded Plum of after the Great War when she was young and so many of her friends had daddies killed in the war. On market days it seemed as if the whole town was full of women, young boys and farmers, who had a reserved occupation. There were a few soldiers billeted around the streets but no army camps nearby.

She hoped that Arthur and Dolly would arrive back in time for Christmas. They were due to dock in Liverpool at the end of next week, if all went well. No wonder Maddy was excited and Pleasance was going around with a look on her face like her corns were pinching her.

'What have you got against Dolly?' Plum asked one night, after her return from London.

Maddy was in bed and the oldies were snoozing by the fire with their cocoa. Pleasance had looked down her specs at Plum.

'It's a matter of standards. Those sorts of girls . . . well, we all know what showgirls are like . . . actresses. I never expected a son of mine to get mixed up with one of them,' she sighed.

'But Dolly was singing to wounded troops when they met,' Plum replied.

'On the make, dear, just looking out for someone to be her meal ticket . . . It was all about the S word,' she whispered back.

'The what?' Plum could hardly believe what she was hearing.

'You know perfectly well what I'm getting at. Sex,' Pleasance mouthed in disgust. 'It was just sex with those two!'

'And so it should be at that age, Mother. Dolly's a lovely-looking woman. I've seen posters of her.'

'So why did they produce such an ugly duckling? I'm not even sure if Madeleine is Arthur's . . . I did warn him he was making a mistake.'

'Oh, enough! That's not very Christian. How can you say such a wicked thing when they've been out giving their services to the troops? Arthur sounds like the nicest of the brothers.' How dare Mother insinuate such a cruel thing about Dolly!

'I'm surprised at you. Gerald is the handsomest of all my boys,' Pleasance preened, looking up from her book.

Plum plonked herself down on the sofa, picked up her knitting. It was time for some home truths. 'I think this family must have a fascination for the stage. I know Gerald has. He's kept a mistress in London for years. In fact, he was seeing her before we were married. He says he's finished with her but I'm not so sure. If you want to criticise anyone, tear your own pretty boy off a strip, not Arthur. He's the only one with a happy marriage.' That would pop her balloon.

'Prunella, what's got into you? Don't be so mean. Gerry can't defend himself. Men are like that sometimes. It doesn't mean anything. You have to make allowances for their urges. They don't marry girls like that – not in my day, they didn't.'

'Didn't you have any urges then?' Plum paused, unimpressed by her argument.

'No I did not. I did my duty and gave him three sons. In return he gave me respect and didn't trouble me much after that. What Harry did in his spare time, I never asked, but Arthur wouldn't leave well alone; he had to go and marry the girl against our wishes. I blame him for Harry's death – letting the family down, going on the stage, refusing to go into the business with not even a grandson to inherit. Gerald was too young to take over. He's just a man being a man. It's a pity there's no child. You wouldn't talk so freely then.'

'It's not for want of trying.' Plum blushed with embarrassment. 'You missed out, not enjoying the physical side of marriage. It can be fun.'

'So much fun that my son seeks comforts elsewhere? Our sort of women are not bred for such . . . messiness. Next thing you'll be saying we should demand to be pleasured and equals like those damned Suffragettes making fools of themselves. There are women paid to give those sorts of services . . .'

Pleasance could be so cruel. 'And what wretched lives some of them lead,' Plum snapped back. 'I'm glad I've got the vote and have some say in things. Anyway, what has all this got to do with Dolly and Arthur? I just want them to be made welcome for Maddy's sake.'

'You're getting too fond of that child, spoiling her. She's not our responsibility now. We've done our duty.'

There was no budging Pleasance. No use carping at her.

'All I'm asking you is not to hold up Gerald and me as paragons of virtue. This last affair almost came to a divorce, but we've talked it through and it's sorted so you can sleep easy; end of subject. And who wouldn't be fond of Maddy? She's your only grandchild. Once that eye is realigned I bet our duckling will turn into a swan.'

'Oh, don't talk poppycock. I've never seen a plainer child. Now, if it was Gloria . . . she's got spark and those green eyes, she'll go far,' said Pleasance. 'Pass me my sherry.'

'Do you think so? There's something about her that worries me. I can't pin it down. Madge Batty says she's forever prancing in front of the mirror. Now there's someone who ought to be on the stage . . . Don't forget the school Nativity play on Monday. We'll have to support our evacuees.'

'Must we? The pews are so hard in the church.'

'Come on, Sowerthwaite expects its most prominent citizen to do her duty.' Plum smiled sweetly as she handed Pleasance the glass.

'I've done my duty sending my sons to war, opening my home to refugees and evacuees and putting up with disruption at my time of life. But listening to Juniors caterwauling on the stage is not my idea of a night out,' Pleasance snapped back.

'Bah humbug!' laughed Plum, her tension released. 'Who needs Dickens when Scrooge is alive and well in Brooklyn Hall?'

'Don't be facetious, it doesn't become you . . . making fun of a poor widow in her sorrows. Christmas is nothing without your family around you,' Pleasance sighed, sipping her sherry as she gazed into the log fire. 'Ugh! Is this the best we've got? Algie's been at the decanter again.'

'Hark at you. You've got a house full of relatives, a son and daughter on their way home, a hostel full of abandoned children and a granddaughter . . . Just thank God in His Mercy you have the means to give them all a wonderful time . . . The joy is in the giving.'

'Just leave the sermons to the vicar, Prunella,' came the sharp reply.

It was nearly Christmas and still no news of Mummy and Daddy. Maddy was so excited, waiting to hear their voices. Grandma didn't believe in having a phone at the hall but the Old Vic now had one for emergencies and Aunt Plum promised to let her know as soon as the trunk call came through.

'Can I go to the station to meet them with Mr Batty?' Maddy pleaded.

'Of course, but we must expect delays with the snow,' Aunt Plum smiled. She was putting the finishing touches to the playroom decorations, with Mitch and Bryan standing on the table fixing up paper bells.

They were going carol singing round Sowerthwaite with the church choir and it was snowing hard. The village looked just like a Christmas card, full of prewar glitter.

Peggy was sulking because her mother wasn't

coming until Boxing Day. There was a special train for evacuee families to come out from Hull and Leeds. Enid had begged to go to the soldiers' dance but Matron said she was too young, so she swore at her and was up in the attic bedroom having a screaming match, calling down the stairs the worst swear words she could muster.

Maddy was trying not to worry about Uncle Algie's latest news bulletin from the wireless. 'Convoys under attack. That means no bananas for tea,' he joked.

Maddy had not seen a banana or an orange for years, not since she was at St Hilda's. She thought of those poor sailors rowing open lifeboats in stormy seas. Thank goodness Mummy and Daddy weren't crossing the Atlantic.

She'd helped Aunt Plum prepare their room, air the bed with a stone hot-water bottle, put on crisp sheets and a beautiful silk counterpane. They filled a vase full of pink viburnum from the garden that smelled so sweet. The fire was ready to be lit in the grate. The bedroom smelled of polish and soot. She just couldn't wait.

Then she thought of their last Christmas together with Uncle George and Granny Mills behind the bar at The Feathers, Mummy singing 'There'll Always Be an England' to the airmen, and everyone cheering. It had been such fun being all together . . .

Suddenly she felt sick and sad and shaky. Nothing would be the same ever again. Last year she'd been safe – now she'd come to live with strangers. Her eye had been straightened when she was seven but now it had gone all wonky again. The patching wasn't working and sometimes she got two shapes, not one, before her eyes. Would they be disappointed like Grandma when they saw her, plain Jane that she was?

Tears rolled down her face; from deep inside great sobs poured out of her. Grandma came to see what the noise was and stared down at her.

'What's up now, child? What's brought this on?' She patted her on the shoulder like a pet dog.

'They won't come . . . they won't come . . . I know it,' Maddy spluttered.

'Now how did you come up with such an idea? Of course they'll come. They're on their way,' Grandma argued, but Maddy was too upset to guard her tongue.

'But you don't like my mummy and they'll go away again and never come back,' she blurted.

'Here, blow your nose,' came the reply. 'Now who's been telling you silly tales? How can I dislike her? I've never met her. You're too young to understand grown-up affairs. We'll have a perfectly pleasant celebration, so stop all this silliness, dry your eyes and go to the kitchen for a biscuit.'

'I don't want a biscuit, I want Panda,' Maddy sniffed. 'I just want my mummy and daddy to come home.' She felt foolish and awkward now. She'd poured out all her fears and Grandma didn't understand. How could she? She'd not even been to her parents' wedding.

'You're a big girl for cuddling toys, Madeleine.'

'I want Panda and Aunt Plum,' she argued, pushing past her grandma.

'Oh, please yourself, but stop snivelling and pull yourself together. Crying gets you nowhere. I was only trying to help,' said Grandma, turning towards her, looking hurt, but Maddy was off down the stairs in search of her beloved black and white companion.

Panda heard all her troubles and never answered back.

It snowed hard again overnight, drifting across the lanes into banks of snow, covering the railways lines with ice. Everyone's pre-Christmas travel plans would be disrupted with this snowfall, Plum sighed. Sowerthwaite had tucked itself in for the duration, used to bad winters and being cut off for days. The school was closed for the holidays, the food bought in and the children in the hostel were trying to be good, itching to be out on tin trays and sleds down the sledge runs.

Matron was huffing and puffing about the extra work, frustrated that her leave to be with her sister near Coventry might be cancelled. The news from the city was bad and she was worried by no word from Dora that she was safe.

'I'll have to go and see for myself, Mrs Belfield,' she insisted, and headed off into the snow to catch the first available train south.

Gerald sent a cryptic note from somewhere hot and dusty, but there had still been no word from Arthur and Dolly. That was only to be expected due to the weather conditions and delays. Everything was in place for their arrival and for the children to have a party at the Hall on Boxing Day. The excitement was mounting and once chores were done they were out on the hills having a great time.

Tonight was the Christmas Nativity play and they were all taking part except Greg, who was helping stack chairs at the back of the church. His voice was well and truly broken and he growled like a bear so that got him out of the fancy-dress parade.

Mrs Batty had warned them that Billy Mellor's donkey was brought out of its shed to do its annual turn parading down the aisle on its way to Bethlehem, no doubt leaving its annual deposit, which the verger would sweep up for his roses before it gassed the congregation. Hitler might do his worst but the donkey would do its duty on cue. Enid, Peggy, Nancy and Gloria were all kitted out as angelic hosts with wire halos on bands round their heads.

'I look daft in this costume,' Enid moaned. 'I'm too old for dressing up. Look, there's Alf and his mates.' She pointed out the line of soldiers in the back pew, sticking out her tiny breast buds in a silly pose.

'You're too young to be bothering about them,' Maddy said, but Enid ignored her, turning to Peggy with a loud voice. 'No one would look at her twice. She's only jealous.'

'No she's not.' Gloria stepped in to defend her friend. 'You're common.'

'Hark at the kettle calling the pot black, Conley! Takes one to know one!' Peggy added her pennyworth.

'Shurrup, fat face!' Gloria replied. The three angels jostled and nudged each other, knocking Nancy into the stone pillar until Maddy stepped in.

'Shush! You're in church. The play will be starting soon. It's too important an evening for quarrelling. Thanks for sticking up for me, Gloria,' Maddy whispered. 'But we don't need to bother with anything they say, do we?'

'Ooh, listen to Miss Hoity-Toity,' Enid giggled, and turned her attention back to the audience.

Maddy took her place in the choir, hidden behind the chancel screen. Everything shimmered in the candlelight. The church windows were boarded up in case any light shone through. How comforting that blitz and bombers had not stopped the Christmas festivities. How confusing that in Germany they would have their own carols and candles, all of them, allies and enemies, praying to the same God. It didn't make any sense.

When they all returned to the Vic and the children were in bed on pain of being given a sack of coal by Father Christmas for being naughty, there were still stockings to fill and parcels to wrap for tomorrow night. At least being busy there was no time to worry about Gerald. The Nativity had gone well and for once the donkey did his dump in the churchyard, not the aisle. The children had behaved impeccably and everyone was saying what a credit the Brooklyn children were to the Old Vic. She had to admit they played their parts on cue. Gloria sang out like a bell and Mitchell read his lesson like a trooper. There was hot fruit cordial in the church hall and spiced buns flavoured with home-made mincemeat that were wolfed down in seconds. The vicar gave a vote of thanks. Pleasance had made an effort, wearing her thick fur coat, Algie and Julia alongside, so the Hall was well represented. Poor Miss Blunt was stuck somewhere between here and Coventry and unlikely to return. It was turning out to be a good Christmas after all.

Plum'd enjoyed all the children's preparations, making sure they made presents for each other, all the secrets and surprises, letters and cards home, and the parcels arriving for some of the children who lived far away.

Without children the Brooklyn Christmas was a stodgy affair of much wine and little cheer, sherry gatherings and small talk and gossip, church and long walks. This was going to be a real Dingley Dell festival at the Brooklyn: the excitement of parcels unwrapped, extra food rations and treats, decorations in every room and fires lit, a great tree cut down and decorated, and above all the chatter of little voices singing carols. All they were waiting for was Dolly and Arthur's arrival by train to complete the picture.

Pleasance was fooling no one by pretending it was all a waste of time and expense, for even she had given a hand wrapping up parcels and sending cards this year. No one could say Sowerthwaite didn't look beautiful in the snow, icicles spiking down the rooftops.

Lost in these thoughts, Plum didn't hear the bell ring.

'Mrs Belfield! Phone!'

Plum raced over to the hall shelf. 'Sow'thwaite 157,' she smiled. At last! What perfect timing! 'It'll be

Maddy's parents,' she yelled to Mrs Batty, who was preparing the morning's vegetables in the kitchen. She smiled at her ruffled reflection in the mirror.

Then her expression went from grin to grimace in two seconds, her mouth tightening. She slumped on to the hall chair in a daze. 'When . . . ? How . . . ? I see . . . Yes, Yes . . . I see . . . Thank you for letting us know . . . Is there any hope? . . . I see . . . Yes . . . It is dreadful . . .' She slammed the phone down and sat winded. Some disembodied voice had just shattered hopes of a cheerful Christmas. Mrs Batty was hovering, curious.

'What is it, Mrs Belfield? Not bad news? Not Master Gerald? You've gone white,' she said.

'No, it's not him. I'm afraid it's Maddy's parents. Their ship was overdue, reports are coming in that it went down *en route* home in the Atlantic, somewhere off the coast of Ireland . . . enemy fire. They're not among the survivors . . . Oh dear God, what am I going to tell the poor child? It's almost Christmas Eve!'

6

'Mrs Plum, was I good in the show? Do you think Father Christmas'll know where me and Sid live?' whispered Gloria as she and Maddy skidded along the ice on the lane home from church, with little Sid and Mrs Batty, past the tall trees, their branches arching with snow. 'He won't know we left Elijah Street and if there's no one there, somebody's sure to nick the presents if he leaves 'em on the doorstep . . . Mrs Plum?'

Plum wasn't listening at all.

'Don't be a chump,' laughed Maddy. 'He's magic, he knows everything, doesn't he? We put our letters up the chimney at the hostel. He'll take them there or to your cottage, won't he, Aunt Plum?' Maddy turned round but their escort was not listening, walking behind them, lost in another world.

She'd been very quiet all day and Maddy had seen her dabbing her eyes when they were singing carols. She must be missing Uncle Gerald, who had come to visit them for a few days last month. He didn't look like Daddy at all. He'd ignored the children in favour of chatting to Ilse and Maria in the kitchen, but then popped half a crown in her hand when he left, so he wasn't that bad.

Aunt Plum was behaving very oddly, not looking a bit Christmassy at all in her black coat and hat. Every time she'd asked when Mummy and Daddy were coming she just shrugged her shoulders and turned away. 'It's this wretched weather spoiling everyone's plans and we can't change the weather, Madeleine. It's in the Lord's hands.' What a funny thing to say? Was Plum cross with her? No one called her Madeleine except Grandma.

They'd sung their hearts out in church although she loved the quiet ones best, like 'Away in a Manger'. The donkey pooed in the yard and made a stink, and Gloria sang her solo without forgetting her words.

The gang from the Old Vic had a great snowball fight outside church on the way home and Gloria got hit and had a hissy fit when her costume got soaked.

'*Gloria in Excelsis*!' they teased her.

'Shurrup! I'm not Gloria Chelsey,' she screamed back.

Maddy thought she looked silly in the long white gown made out of a tablecloth, and the halo, but now the two Conleys were so excited and Sid was racing ahead.

'Jungle bells!' he shouted. 'I'm listening for the Jungle bells.'

'It's bed and no nonsense, the both of you,' Aunt Plum said, shoving them through the gate of Huntsman's Cottage. 'The quicker you go to sleep, the earlier the day will come, won't it, Mrs Batty? There's church in the morning and dinner at the hostel. Tomorrow I want everyone to have a lovely day. Now shoo! Remember, we're last on Father Christmas's round so no disturbing Mrs Batty at all hours of the morning or you'll be disappointed.'

'Yes, miss.' Gloria waved, much too full of herself to listen to a word she was saying.

'Is there really a Father Christmas in the sky?' asked Maddy. 'Greg says it's all fairy tales. He's never had a proper Christmas and all his presents came wrapped up in the same paper from the Council. "It was the matron what done it," he said.' Maddy took hold of Aunt Plum's hand for the last lap home.

'Well, if Gregory doesn't believe, he'll just have to go without presents, won't he? He's jolly lucky to be staying here,' she snapped, and Maddy was surprised by her outburst.

'But he has no mummy and daddy, not ever,' she defended her friend.

'Lots of children have no mummies and daddies because of this damn war,' Aunt Plum answered in a cold voice, looking ahead. 'Come on, up the wooden hill to Bedfordshire, it's been a long day. We don't want to spoil the surprises, do we?'

'I just wish the telephone would ring for me,' Maddy sighed. 'Good night and God bless. See you in the morning.'

'Not too early,' came a tired reply. 'Don't worry, we'll have a lovely day, I promise.'

*

How can I say such a thing? How can Christmas Day ever be lovely again for the child? How can I spoil Christmas with such terrible news? Plum paced her bedroom floor, hugging herself to keep from shivering.

She should have taken Maddy for a walk in the snow and told her the truth when she had the chance but she'd flunked it. Why? What did it change? Why cast a gloom over the whole day, put the house into mourning for people they'd never even met?

The news would dampen all the joy of the surprises in store for the children, just for the sake of another twenty-four hours or more. Why not just let her open her presents and have their big party on Boxing Day as promised? Time enough then to break the terrible news.

She'd sworn Madge Batty to secrecy and not told her mother-in-law yet, but held the secret to herself. It hung heavily in the pit of her stomach like a cannon-ball, making her feel sick. She sat in the candlelight wishing she could take the pain away from the child herself. It was making her shake just thinking of ways to break the news gently – but there was no easy way to tell this news. Perhaps the vicar could do it? Perhaps Pleasance would see it as her duty, or they could do it together?

No, she was going to break it to Maddy and try to explain why she had not come straight out with it.

Oh, how she wanted to put off the moment when the child's face crumpled in disbelief, the moment Maddy realised she too was an orphan of war, that her future was now in the hands of others and that she must face life alone.

No, that wasn't strictly true. Maddy wasn't alone. They must take her on here. She was a Belfield child and no one would turn her away from Brooklyn Hall.

Plum shivered in the darkness as she shoved the little trinkets into the girl's red knitted stocking with trembling hands: ribbons, nuts, a mouth organ, a book, a little sweet shop, a cut-out theatre, a comic and some home-made toffee. The dress and the second-hand bike were waiting under the tree in the hall as her special presents.

Am I doing the right thing to hold back? What would Arthur and Dolly want me to do but love and comfort her like the daughter I never had? I must give her one happy day after all she's been through. Surely it's not wrong, Lord, to let the day pass uncluttered with gloom, but how do I tell her?

It was the one special day in the year when all the evacuees could forget this wretched war, stuff themselves with treats and have a big party. She had to think of the other children: Gloria, Sid, Greg and the rest. She must pin a smile on her cheeks and make sure the celebrations went ahead as planned. She thought of all the sad children in London, Coventry and Birmingham, children with no homes or toys, living as best they could. Her children were the lucky ones. It was so safe here. It was if there was no war going on at all.

As for Pleasance and Uncle Algie and the oldies, they would doze by the fireside waiting for their blow-out dinner, loosen their belts, dress up in their jewellery, drink sherry and pass pleasantries.

She would wait for a suitable moment after Boxing Day. It was not as if there were bodies to claim, nothing but the hush-hush phone call, perhaps further discreet communications to follow. It would not be announced on the wireless for days, if ever. No one wanted to hear such news around Christmas.

'The first victim of war was always truth,' she'd once read. Nothing was done to disturb public morale. Who wanted to know that a troopship was caught by submarines only a hundred miles off the Irish coast?

All over the country there would be other sad hearts receiving this call or telegrams around Christmas Eve. 'I regret to inform you that . . .' Her first thought had been that it was Gerald and then she was flooded with relief that it wasn't him. But now she was sickened by guilt at what she was withholding from the child.

Plum stroked her red setter Blaze for comfort. He nuzzled in for more. *What have I done? I just want to give Maddy a few more hours before I destroy her world. Every Christmas for the rest of her life will be spoiled by this news. It'll be a time of dread and sorrow. I just want her hope to last a while longer. What harm can that possibly do?*

Gloria could hear Mr and Mrs Batty whispering in the kitchen, after lunch on Boxing Day. It was something to do with terrible news at the Hall but when she popped her head round the door they drew back and changed the subject.

She was good at earwigging, hovering behind doors at Elijah Street, listening to stuff she shouldn't. That's how she'd learned from her aunties about the birds and bees and how babies got made, how rubber johnnies stopped them and how Old Ma Phipps could get rid of them if you was caught. Manchester seemed a long way away, and she wondered if Mam was thinking about them. Would she send them a present?

She'd never had a Christmas like this one. Elijah Street was just pop and sweets, singing and fighting and waiting outside the public in the dark. There was always a toy but it was broken by teatime. There was nothing about Baby Jesus in the manger and candles in the church, singing carols in the snow and making presents for each other. Everyone went to church in Sowerthwaite; only Freda and her mam went to the Kingdom Hall and they didn't believe in Christmas Day.

At Elijah Street they were sent to Sunday school to get out of the house of an afternoon but it was just a tin shack hall with no candles and decorations. She'd never seen such a big Christmas tree as the one in Brooklyn Hall. It smelled of disinfectant and melting wax. They spent ages decorating the one in the hostel with tinsel and paper chains. It was lovely.

Did Mam ever think about the two of them? How could she just shove them on a train with no word that they were safe? Sid had already forgotten their old home. He looked blank at her when she asked him about Mam. Gloria got hot and cold just thinking where she might be. One minute she was sad, the next spitting flames. What Mam had done wasn't right but coming here was great. She didn't want to worry about someone who didn't care about them, not now.

They were getting ready for the Boxing Day party at the Hall, and she was dressed in her new pinafore dress and shirt. It was navy-blue corduroy with rick-rack braid where the hem had been let down – not very partified at all but it was better than her other skirt and jumper.

Sid had on his new Fair Isle jumper that itched him, and his ginger curls were plastered down with Mr Batty's Brylcreem. Father Christmas had got the right address and Sid was thrilled with his toy farm and tractor, and she was pleased with her crinoline doll in its own box until she saw Maddy wobbling on her new bike on Christmas Day. Why hadn't he brought her one too?

Greg was helping her ride it on the path where the snow and ice were cleared away. Maddy was wearing a new velvet dress, all shiny and soft, the colour of peacock's feathers, under her school mac. It wasn't fair. She'd had two Christmasses – one at the Hall and the other at the hostel.

Greg was wearing long trousers and a new blazer, strutting around like the cock of the midden. Everyone was dressed up and on best behaviour. Maddy wanted her to see all the presents. There was a little toy sweetie shop with jars and scales and boxes of Dolly Mixtures given to her, and a book and presents from the staff. It wasn't fair.

Gloria begged for a shot on the bike but Greg said

her legs were too short to ride it and that got her mad, so she and Sid hid behind the sofa and scoffed all the jelly beans in the toy sweet shop. Aunt Plum was cross. She didn't smile once but, Gloria realised now, that would be because of the terrible news.

Now as they stood in the porch to go off to their proper party, Mrs Batty patted her head and told her to play nicely with Maddy. 'Be a good girl and no fighting . . .' They skated down the path and Gloria had forgotten her mittens. The snow was too cold to make balls without gloves so she darted back in through the open door to the basket where their hoods and scarves were put.

The Battys were still gabbing about the terrible news and she moved closer. What she heard had her running out into the chill. Wait till she told Maddy that she'd heard it first!

Maddy loved her new bike but it was too icy to ride on it properly. Father Christmas'd given her lots of nice surprises but not the one she really wanted, which was for Mummy and Daddy to arrive on time and sing carols at the piano and tell her all about their travels.

She'd begged to spend Christmas Day with the vaccies. It was fun at the hostel, with turkey and Christmas pudding with threepenny bits for everyone. They'd played silly games and charades and there was a singsong. Aunt Plum was very quiet, though, and looked a bit tired. Miss Blunt was away and the vicar and his wife came to help.

Now, on Boxing Day, Grandma was inspecting the buffet table for the bun fight this afternoon.

'I don't know why we have to do this?' she snapped. 'Children, let loose around the house like wild animals, are not my idea of fun. It'll all end in tears. Oh, do shift that vase out of reach, Maddy. It's priceless.' Maddy duly obliged.

'I'm not sure that sort of bright blue suits the child,' Grandma added, eyeing her dress again. 'You need red hair to carry off that colour. She'd be better off in a kilt and jumper, much more sensible.'

'Oh, Mother . . . let it rest,' Aunt Plum snapped as she dragged on her cigarette. 'Let her enjoy the party dress. There won't be many more in the shops if this blasted war goes on and on,' she sighed. 'If you can't dress up on Boxing Day, it's a poor show.'

'Who rattled your cage this morning? You've been a crosspatch for days . . . This was all your idea. What time are the hordes descending?' asked Grandma, lighting her own cigarette.

'Soon. I just think it's good for the youngsters to mix with all ages. It'll do the old codgers good to have a bit of life about the place. All they do is snore and eat. Uncle Algie's promised to do some conjuring tricks if I can peel him away from the wireless. Aunt Julia has promised to give a recitation . . .'

'Oh God, must we?'

'No, she said it was suitable for children.'

'How would she know? She's never had one of her own,' snapped Grandma.

The bickering went on but Maddy was too excited

to get upset. Those two were always sniping at each other, like Uncle George and Ivy, up and down the bar of The Feathers. It didn't mean anything. Then she thought of last Christmas and how so much had changed and how sad it was not to be back where she truly belonged.

Then Gloria and Sid arrived early and she thought she ought to let them have a try out of her bike.

Holding the saddle, she let Gloria sit up but her legs wouldn't reach the pedals and they kept slipping sideways. Two falls and she'd had enough.

'We mustn't get dirty,' Maddy whispered. 'I mustn't spoil this hem.'

'I'll have it when it's too short . . . It looks silly on you,' said Gloria, rubbing her fingers on the velvet pile.

'No it doesn't,' Maddy snapped back, pulling the skirt away from her. Why was she being so mean? Then she spied a crocodile of vaccies from the hostel coming up the drive, carrying their best shoes in baskets. She led them through the back entrance and the cloakroom to change their shoes and take off their coats.

The parcel from America had been full of shirts and trousers, and everyone was dressed up. Enid and Peggy were sporting earrings and painted lips – now they really looked silly – but Greg and the boys were looking smart and grown up. Maddy wondered if he still didn't believe in Father Christmas now.

Everyone collected chairs for the game in the hall, marching round the tiled floor to the music from a wind-up gramophone and rushing for the seats when the music stopped. The dining-room table was extended with a huge white cloth on which were plates of sandwiches, mock sausage rolls, mince pies and wodges of Ilse's crumb cake. They had to stand for grace, and then it was every hand for itself as the boys leaped to get platefuls of grub.

After tea and pop – Sid spilled his on the rug – Sukie and Blaze rushed round trying to mop up all the crumbs and then it was time for the children to sing for their supper to the assembly in the drawing room. Gloria did her usual show-off routine, singing 'Bless This House', which the vicar's wife had taught her on the quiet.

Then Great-uncle Algie appeared in a black evening cloak and top hat and tried to do a few card tricks, making them laugh. He conjured up eggs out of nowhere.

He asked for a volunteer and Bryan stood up as his assistant. The eggs came and went, and for his last trick he placed a magic egg on Bryan's head, said some magic words and cracked it with his conjuring stick. It broke all over his hair and dribbled down his face and onto his jumper. Everyone roared, but Aunt Plum was furious.

'That's his new jumper . . . How could you waste an egg like that!'

Poor Uncle Algie looked quite shocked at his telling-off but Grandma came to his defence.

'What's got into you? He's done his best to keep the natives calm. Thank you, Algie. We'll take the children back into the hall for pass the parcel. Really, Prunella, there was no call for that!'

Everyone pushed and shoved back out of the room, leaving Aunt Plum almost in tears. 'I'm sorry, Algie, I've a lot on my mind,' she sighed.

Gloria pinched Maddy's arm. 'I know what it's all about. She's had bad news,' she whispered.

'She never said,' Maddy replied curious now. 'Is it Uncle Gerald?'

''Spec so. I heard Uncle and Auntie in the kitchen talking about his ship going down, but don't say nowt. I was earwigging behind the door. She's a widow woman now, that's why she's been wearing black.'

'But why hasn't she told Grandma? She's got a red suit on. Uncle Gerry's her son. How strange? Come on, we'll be especially nice to her.'

Maddy kept looking at her aunt sideways. Plum must have kept her sadness all to herself to give them a good Christmas. How kind she was. Poor Uncle Gerry, never to see him again. How brave she was to bear such bad news.

The party seemed to drag after that and Maddy was glad when the last ones had gone home and she could put her hand in Aunt Plum's and squeeze it gently.

'I know,' she whispered. 'It must be awful for you.'

'Know what, Maddy?'

'About your bad news. Gloria heard the Battys talking. She didn't mean to but they were talking loud about Uncle Gerald's ship going down . . .'

Aunt Plum was staring at her hard. 'Is that what Gloria told you?'

Maddy nodded. 'Is that why you've been wearing black clothes?' Poor Aunt Plum was looking very strange and grasping her chest. Then she took her arm and guided Maddy towards the little morning room with French doors that opened out onto the side garden where the bird table was.

'Let's just shut the door for a minute. You're right, I've got some bad news but it wasn't Uncle Gerald's ship. You see, a ship did go down . . . We don't know all the details yet. There was a phone call the night before Christmas Eve. I thought it was best to let you all have a proper Christmas. Mrs Batty was there when the call came through. I don't know how to say this, Maddy, but it wasn't Uncle Gerald.' She paused.

In that split second Maddy saw the look on her face and knew what she was going to say and put her hands to her ears. 'No, no . . . Please, no, not my mummy and daddy!'

Everything went all fuzzy round the edges and her throat sort of froze so she couldn't swallow. There was a ringing in her head. Plum's words were faint, something about enemy action and a troop ship off the coast of Ireland, lifeboats and survivors, but it was all very quick. 'No, no, it's not true . . . ?'

Aunt Plum nodded. 'I'm so sorry, darling. I didn't know how to tell you.'

'But there are lifeboats and they can last for days? They found the children from the *City of Benares* when all was lost, days and days after!' Maddy was pleading for hope.

'It's been nearly two weeks. There were only a few survivors. It must have been very quick.' There was no comfort in her words.

The mantelpiece clock ticked and the fire crackled and blew out smoke. The blackbird was hopping around for crumbs and the icicles were dripping from the stone bird table. Time seemed to stand still.

'Then they're never coming home, are they?' she said, looking Plum straight in the eye.

'I'm afraid not.'

'So I'll have to go to an orphanage like Anne of Green Gables?'

'Of course not! Your home is here in Brooklyn.'

'But Grandma doesn't like me. She wore a red suit . . .'

'She doesn't know yet . . . about Arthur. I had to tell you first. I didn't see the point in spoiling your Christmas,' Aunt Plum sniffed.

'There's no Father Christmas, is there?' Maddy said, feeling ice cold inside. 'All I asked him for was to see Mummy and Daddy again and he sent them to the bottom of the sea. It's all lies! All of it . . .' she screamed.

'Maddy, I'm sorry, but Brooklyn is your home,' Aunt Plum stuttered, looking older and unsure. 'Forgive me if I've got it all wrong. I've never had to do this before. I just wanted you to have a nice time. Your home is with us now.'

'No it's not! I'll not stay where I'm not wanted. I'll go to the Vic and stay there. I'm not a Belfield any more!' she spat out, and jumped off the sofa, making for the door. She wanted to get away from this house. Grabbing her gabardine mac and galoshes, and the dog lead, which got Blaze bounding after her down the steps, Maddy stepped out into the dusky whiteness of the front drive.

There were no tears in her eyes. She couldn't cry. It couldn't happen twice, could it? First Uncle George and Granny Mills and now Mummy and Daddy? That wasn't fair. It didn't make any sense.

Maddy wandered down the lane in a daze, picking out the frozen footsteps of the hostel gang before her. She looked up at the tall poplar trees standing like Roman candles, the snow on the bark making pretty patterns. It was all so crisp and white and silent, so beautiful and so sad.

Would Mummy and Daddy know how sad she was? Did they care? Were they out there somewhere looking down on her, watching over her, with Granny too? She hoped so.

How strange that her own life was going on right now whilst their lives had been over days ago and she didn't know. All the time she was having fun at Christmas and the school concert, they were already gone. Her life was going on and they'd just disappeared. Now she'd grow and change and do things and they wouldn't know – or would they? Oh, how she hoped so. It was the only comfort she could cling on to.

Maddy looked down the avenue of poplars and thought of all those other boys who never came home, who were just names at the bottom of the trees. Now Daddy would be a tree on the lane with Uncle Julian. How strange all her family were in a far-off place and she couldn't reach them.

Now the dark chill wrapped itself round her but she

wasn't a bit afraid. She didn't feel cold. She didn't feel anything but a numb sort of tiredness as she made her way to the Victory Tree. She felt safe there tucked away, hiding in the crevice.

It was like sitting in the tree in The Feathers all over again, but without any hope of letters coming from Egypt. All she wanted to do was curl up and sleep until the war was over and things would go back to how they were before.

How could I have been so stupid? Trust Gloria to get it all wrong and spoil the moment; that silly nosy little tyke! Plum jumped up to follow the child. *How could I take it on myself to play God and get it so wrong?*

Pleasance would have to be told but not yet. First she must find the girl. It was too cold to be wandering about in the dark. Her footprints would be easy to follow and chances were she'd head for the Old Vic and to her friends.

Plum wished there was a phone in the house to warn Vera Murray, the vicar's wife, of the situation. It was not surprising Maddy preferred the shabbiness of the old pub to the genteel grandeur of her grandparents' house. Hurt puppies always headed for safety, where they could watch the world from under some table and lick their wounds.

Maddy wasn't running away, she was running to where she knew there'd be a welcome. To Plum that thought was no comfort at all.

*

When Mrs Plum arrived at the hostel everyone was still clearing up the mess before bed. The little ones had been sent up first and Greg was summoned into the kitchen to hear the bad news.

'Maddy's disappeared,' said Mrs Plum. 'Gone to ground. Have you the foggiest where she'd go, Gregory?'

It made him feel grown up that she always consulted him in a crisis, as if he was important.

'I think I know where she'll be, miss – up the garden by the big tree, in our Victory HQ. You'll find her there,' he offered, feeling so sorry for young Maddy. 'I'll fetch her back if you like,' he offered. 'She won't have gone far, not in the dark.'

'I'll come with you.' Mrs Belfield jumped up from the kitchen table.

'Give me five minutes so she don't run off,' he said, knowing that if it were him he wouldn't want grown-ups fussing. Maddy was a funny kid, even for a girl.

Greg crunched up the allotment path whistling 'Colonel Bogey' so she'd know it was him. 'I know you're up there, Maddy Belfield. I've brought some cocoa and syrup with condensed milk . . . Poor Mrs Plum is doing her nut wondering where you are,' he yelled, watching the steam come out of his mouth into the chill air.

'Go away! I'm not talking to anyone,' she shouted back.

'Don't be daft. It's freezing out here. Come down while it's still hot.'

'I don't care!'

'Yes you do. You don't want the dog to catch a chill,

do you? It's sitting on the icy ground.' There was silence and he saw her peering out into the darkness. He shoved the mug into the hand dangling from the tree.

'The vicar's wife says we can cook chips in the frying pan tonight if we clear up afterwards.' That was their favourite treat when The Rug wasn't around.

'I'm not hungry.' Maddy sniffed at the cocoa as if it was poison. 'What's it like being an orphan?' she added. Her glasses were all steamed up from the hot drink.

'It's just a label you get stuck on you. It don't mean anything. I've got no mam and dad, never had, and what you never had you don't miss,' Greg said, which wasn't exactly true but he wasn't sharing that with anyone. 'I've had loads of aunts and uncles, some good and some rotten . . . I just heard your bad news. I'm really sorry. You're not really an orphan, though, you know.'

'I was just trying it on for size,' Maddy answered, hugging the the hot mug for warmth. 'My parents aren't ever coming back. I don't know what to do.'

'But you've got yer gran and yer auntie. You've got family. Orphans have no one.'

'I don't want to go back to Brooklyn Hall, not now.'

'It's a bit stuffy there but it were a good do this afternoon for the little ones, and you belong with that lot, up there. Mrs Plum is your real Auntie.' Greg didn't want to admit he'd had a right good nosy around and grabbed as much grub as he could.

He felt sorry for Maddy and that was why he had taught her to ride her bike and get her balance, even if she looked a bit odd with her patch and glasses, her eye flickering all over the show. She was no Shirley Temple, not like Gloria, but he quite liked her funny stare.

'If you ever run away again, promise to take me with you,' she begged. 'I'm not stopping where I'm not wanted. Mummy and Daddy are drowned so I'm like you now.'

'No you're not and never will be. They'll look after you up at the Brooklyn. Mrs Plum cares about you. She's a good 'un.'

'But I'm useless at everything and Grandma ignores me,' Maddy sighed.

'Come off it! You're top of your class, not a dunce like me. I've missed so much schooling . . .'

'You make things with your hands. Enid can dance. Gloria can sing. Everyone likes her . . .'

'Gloria's a right little show-off.'

'You don't like her?'

'She's only a kid, OK as girls go,' he said quickly. It didn't pay to take sides between girls. He'd learned that one early after being bashed up in the first hostel near Leeds when he'd tried to stop a fight between two girls. 'Look, here's Mrs Plum coming to find you. She's been worried.'

'I don't want to see her,' Maddy snapped, darting behind the tree branches, spilling her drink and leaving a trail of milky cocoa for the dog to lick up.

'Oh, don't be daft, it's not her fault . . . She's doing her best to help. It is Christmas,' Greg replied, not knowing what to say now.

He looked up at the tall outline of the trunk, how it branched from the base into a V shape, outlined against the whiteness. 'Old Winnie would like this tree,' he said, making his fingers into a Churchill V sign. 'A proper V for Victory Tree is this. Come and see,' he smiled, pushing his fingers in her face. 'See!'

Maddy came down, stood back and looked up. 'You're right. It is a V shape. How clever of you to give it a name. It's our Victory Tree now. I like that but it doesn't change anything. I'll never ever have another Christmas again . . . It's all lies, isn't it?'

'Oh I don't know, I did rather well from Father Christmas. It pays to keep an open mind,' he smiled, thinking of his smart new blazer, long trousers and proper brogue shoes, his racing car annual and some shaving tackle.

'But you said there wasn't any Father Christmas. So if it's true, why pretend?'

'Because it makes grown-ups pretend and give us presents and treats, they play games and sing songs just for a few days in the year. It's make-believe but we get a holiday and people get boozed up. This's been the best one I ever had,' he argued.

'But it's all lies, all of it,' Maddy insisted.

'I think some bits are worth keeping, with this war being on and all . . .'

'I don't understand you. One minute you say one thing and the next you change your mind,' she snapped.

'Well, that's one thing I did learn in the orphanage . . . not to believe everything other people tell you. You've got to think your own thoughts and look after yourself.

When it's bad I do a bunk, when it's OK I don't,' he replied. He'd been let down so many times by being shoved here and there, smacked for nothing, made promises that were never kept.

'Was it really bad?'

'Sometimes, and other times . . .'

'There you go again, not giving me straight answers.'

'I wish I could,' Greg smiled. 'Here comes your auntie, plodding through the snow. It's time you went home before we all freeze to death.'

Poor kid, he thought, as the two figures walked slowly in front of him in silence. What a horrible Christmas present. He'd long ago stopped wondering why he was put in a home. He liked to think his parents were killed together and only he survived in a car crash. The thought that someone had just dumped him there and gone off and forgotten him . . . When he got wed and had kids he'd make sure his children were close by his side.

Grandma was sitting in the drawing room, knitting socks on three needles. She didn't look up when Plum and Maddy entered the room. They sat down on the sofa together opposite her.

She paused with a big sigh. 'Well? What is it now?'

'Maddy's got something to tell you,' said Aunt Plum, squeezing Maddy's hand to give her courage to say the hard words and not cry.

'Mummy and Daddy aren't coming here,' she said, waiting for Grandma to put down that blasted grey sock and ask why.

‘What’s it this time? Theatricals are always so unreliable,’ Grandma said, and carried on with her knitting

Maddy swallowed hard, trying not to be cross with her. She didn’t know the news and it was Maddy’s job to break it. Aunt Plum said she would tell herself but Maddy had insisted. It made her feel very grown up.

‘They can’t come home because they got sunk in a ship. My parents are drowned.’ Maddy felt the tears welling up but she stayed very calm as the knitting dropped from Gran’s hand.

‘Is this true, Prunella? Arthur’s dead . . . another of my sons is dead?’

‘And my mummy too. I know you didn’t like them but they were my mummy and daddy and I’ll never see them again.’ That’s when her tears just burst out and she couldn’t stop them.

‘Oh dear God! The ship went down? Where?’

‘The week before Christmas, Mother. We received a call at the hostel. I said nothing until after Christmas to spare you both, but Gloria Conley blurted out something to Maddy. I had to deal with it but I did mean to tell you first.’ Aunt Plum had gone very pink.

Grandma sat very upright, staring into the embers of the log fire, shaking her head.

‘Arthur . . . he always was musical. Heaven knows where he got it from . . . not me. He was always Harry’s favourite . . . mentioned in dispatches in the Great War. Now Arthur’s gone. I don’t understand.’ She talked as if she was very far away from them. ‘We never got to say our piece,' she whispered to herself. She suddenly looked very old.

'It's all right. Daddy wouldn't mind,' Maddy interrupted her reverie, hoping to give her grandmother some comfort, but it only made things worse.

'But I mind! Things were said that can't be put right now. I was hoping to sort out my papers with him.' She paused and stared at Maddy as if looking at her for the first time. 'I'm so sorry, Madeleine, sorry for your loss and your disappointment. You must be feeling very shocked. Come and sit by me.'

Maddy nodded and swallowed her sniffles as she crossed the great divide to sit by the old woman on the squashy sofa.

'We must pray that they are at peace. It's all we can do. Nothing I can do to put things right now, or say that will take the pain away, child.'

Grandma's hand patted her own but it was like all the feathers had fallen out of a bolster. She sagged in the middle, a new grandma cut in half, all crumpled up.

'I'll make some tea,' offered Aunt Plum.

'Damn the teapot, fetch me a whisky, a stiff one and no water.'

Maddy had never sat so close to Gran before. She smelled of cigarette smoke and almonds. They sat in silence as the grandfather clock ticked in the corner.

'I wasn't always this old prune,' Grandma sighed, pointing to the portrait on the wall. 'I was quite the belle of the ball in my day, but the Lord gives and takes from every woman in turn. Beauty doesn't last. I was hoping you would take after me or your mama. I hear she was quite something . . . we must do something about that eye for you.'

'Will I have to go away now?' Maddy asked.

'Whatever for? You're a Belfield, for better or worse, child. One day all this will be yours if Prunella and Gerald don't get their act together . . .'

Maddy looked into the fire, not really believing this change of heart.

'I can't make my peace with your father, and I doubt if he'd have accepted it anyway. He was just as stubborn as me. We were too alike, too sure of our own rightness, but you'll have to do. We'll make a silk purse out of you yet, Madeleine. Things will be different. We have to make the best of such sadness.'

'Will you plant a tree for Daddy?' she asked.

'Of course, and we'll have a proper memorial service for your parents. It would be expected of us to honour their sacrifice.'

'They'd like that,' Maddy smiled, taking hold of the old lady's hand. Her skin was like crumpled-up tissue paper. Her diamond rings sparkled on thin fingers flashing in the firelight. In that silence and sadness she'd have given the Crown Jewels to have her own mummy and daddy just sitting close beside her. It hurt so much inside she could hardly breathe. Tears dripped down her nose and Grandma produced a lace-edged hanky.

'Blow your nose, child. We'll just have to be brave soldiers marching on. Arthur sent you to us for a reason and now I know why.'

Maddy didn't understand. She was beyond tiredness on this, the worst day of her life, but she sensed a strange shift in the air. Life at Brooklyn Hall would be different from now on. The sofa was still full of doggy hairs, the knitting basket was on the floor, the clock ticked and the fire smoked. Nothing had changed but everything was changed. From now on this would be her home, whether she liked it or not.

7

Nothing was the same after the news broke in Sowerthwaite that Maddy's parents were lost at sea on a troop ship. Snowstorms were raging across the dale and playing out was too cold to be fun any more. Sid and Gloria were trapped in the cottage for days on end with nothing to do but fight and root in cupboard drawers for postcards to line up on the rug, imagining far-off places and examining the old stamps. The school was closed and Mrs Batty kept looking at her lodger as if she was a bad smell. It was freezing cold in the bedroom and the windows were iced over with Jack Frost. Gloria was in disgrace.

'If I'd thowt you was listening at keyholes, milady, I'd have tanned yer backside,' shouted Mrs Batty for the umpteenth time. 'You've shown me up good and proper with the Hall folk. We were talking confidential, Bert and me. Careless talk costs lives, and your careless talk's cost me my reputation. Thank goodness young Mrs Belfield is a lady and guessed what you'd been up to, blurting out such untruths to the poor little mite and her having to tell 'er the truth on t' matter. We don't want blabbermouths in this house. I hope you've learned your lesson?'

There was nothing to do but bow her head and get on with doing extra chores to make up for getting that news all wrong. They'd all attended the memorial service for the Belfields at St Peter's. The church where Gloria had been a candlelit star was now bare and bleak, packed with strangers in black.

Maddy wore a black armband on her sleeve. She had on a new coat made from a cut-down one of the old lady's. It was heathery tweed with a real black fur collar and cuffs and a matching hat. She looked like one of the Royal princesses, except for the glasses and patch. They sort of made her equal to everyone else.

Mrs Batty said Maddy'd be taken out of the village school and sent to a private one far away now that she was a proper Belfield. Gloria wondered if she'd ever speak to her again but no one was going anywhere in this blow-in.

She'd never seen so much snow on rooftops, piled up on the side of the lane in huge drifts like ice-cream cones. One morning it cleared enough for the gang to go out foraging and play up the Victory Tree as usual. She was glad that Maddy had come to join them. They climbed up together in silence and looked out over the snow.

'Do you think trees are real? Does it know when we play in it?' said Maddy with a sigh.

'It's not got a heart, it's just a tree,' Gloria quipped, and then wished she hadn't. She still had to make proper friends again but Maddy ignored her remark.

'But it's our special tree. We all talk to it and tell it things. Well, I do . . .' she sighed again.

Gloria was flummoxed. Maddy was talking rot again but she must be polite. 'A tree can't hear so I suppose it can't tell tales like Enid, and it don't talk back,' she replied.

'They groan and stretch and rustle. I think it listens to us,' said Maddy, pushing her specs up her nose to hide her squint.

'I think you're daft,' Gloria said. She'd done it again. Why couldn't she just keep her gob shut?

'No I'm not! A tree is a living thing, just like we are. Just think of all the things it must have seen long before we were born.'

'Like what?'

'All the birds nesting in it, for a start. People hiding up here, like Robin Hood . . .'

'He were never here, were he?' Gloria knew about him from her history book.

'I know, but there must've been soldiers keeping watch, sweethearts kissing. It must know hundreds of secrets.'

'You're mad, you are . . . it's just a tree.' Gloria was getting bored with this.

'It's our tree, our Victory Tree. We can always come here and whisper and no one else can see us,' Maddy went on.

'What do you want to tell it then?'

'Don't know, but I wish my daddy knew I was up here. I wonder if he ever played up here too.'

'And I wish my mam knew where I was so she could come to stay,' Gloria added.

‘Let’s make a wish then,’ Maddy smiled, and Gloria felt better and then went and spoiled it by saying, ‘But it’s daft talking to a tree.’

‘Then we could write our wishes down and post them into one of the cracks. Then the tree trunk will hold all our wishes for ever.’ Maddy was not going to give up.

‘That won’t do any good, it’s silly.’

‘No, it’s not. This is a magic tree. It’ll make our dreams come true, you’ll see, but we have to keep it a secret or it won’t work.’

‘Are we still friends, me and you? I’m sorry I got your news wrong, I’ve been in such hot water,’ Gloria blurted as they dangled their legs over the branch. ‘Just you, me and the old tree then?’

Maddy looked at her and nodded. ‘Just you, me and the tree: forever friends.’

Oh, what a relief still to be best friends. It had mattered to Gloria to be shoved out into the cold and not be welcome at the Hall. How then was she to ride on Maddy’s bike, or dress up in the big bedroom with the gold mirror, or be given sweeties from Aunt Julia and do errands for pennies? When she was there it was easy to pretend that she too was a royal princess with servants, not a nobody evacuee from the back streets of Manchester. Forever friends . . . that was the best news of all.

‘Have you heard the news about Enid?’ Peggy Bickerstaffe ran up to them as they climbed out of their hidy-hole. ‘She’s in big, big trouble.’

They were all ears. ‘This soldier turns up and says

he's Enid's cousin and could he take her out for the day on New Year, out for tea. The Rug's just back from her trip and brought him in for inspection while Enid comes down dressed to the nines with lipstick and stockings, her hair all done grown up, and they went off promising to return before dark . . . She's not been seen since, silly cow. Now she's for it! They sent for the constable and Mrs Plum, and it turns out, when they read her file, she doesn't have a brother or cousin and it was all a big lie so she could go out dancing in Scarperton. Do you think she's done it with him?' Peggy giggled.

'Done what?' said Maddy as they stopped by a drift of snow on the lane.

'Made babies . . . You do know what I mean?'

Gloria laughed but Maddy was blushing. 'Of course I do. People mate like animals. Everyone knows that.'

'No it's not. They have to kiss first, and dogs don't do that,' Peggy informed them.

'You don't make babies by kissing,' Gloria butted in. It was her turn to show them she was no dunce. 'You have to lie down and jump on the bed.'

'Do you?' Maddy looked at her with amazement as if she'd said something brilliant.

'She's such a fibber,' said Peggy. 'You have to kiss first or it doesn't work . . . like on the pictures, Rhett Butler and Scarlett.' They'd all swooned at the film *Gone With the Wind*.

'But he carries her up to bed . . . up the stairs,' Gloria insisted.

'If anyone carried Enid up the stairs it'd be like

humping a sack of coal,' Maddy replied and broke out into a grin. It was the first smile Gloria had seen on her face for weeks. 'We can ask her when she comes back.'

'She'll not be back here. I heard Miss Blunt saying she'll be put in a Home for Wayward Girls after this palaver.'

'But she hasn't done anything wrong . . . just gone for a bit of an adventure.' Maddy stood throwing wet sticks into the pram for kindling. 'It's better than this boring job.'

'This is war work,' Peggy argued. 'Enid's told lies and ran away, stayed out all night and let him have his way. She's a tart! No better than a prozzy. They do it for money and go to prison.'

Gloria suddenly felt giddy. She saw Elijah Street and the dressed-up women walking up and down in the dark, and men who jumped up and down on Mam's bed, and the big stone flour jar where she hid her takings. It all made sense like bits of a jigsaw puzzle coming together round a corner piece. If anyone found out her shame here . . . 'Perhaps he's done her in and hid her body,' she suggested. That's what baddies did in the gangster films. They both looked down at her in amazement.

'You do talk such bunkum,' sniffed Peggy.

'No! Enid could be in danger going off with a stranger like that,' said Maddy, coming to her defence.

'He weren't no stranger. It was one of them soldiers from the battery field. She's been chatting him up for weeks. He bought her some proper perfume for

Christmas, Bourge . . . joyce or something from Paris. She's nearly fifteen, old enough to know what she's doing, I reckon.' Peggy was put out that they were ganging up against her.

Maddy looked at Gloria and shook her head. 'I think she's really silly to run off with someone she hardly knows. What if he's cruel and leads her up the garden path? You know, like that *Waterloo Road* film with John Mills, where his wife goes off with a spiv. Mrs Batty saw it and she told Ilse when she brought in the washing. What a scandal! It's not fair on Aunt Plum.'

'You would say that. You don't have to live in this boring dump, miles from anywhere decent. There's nothing to do but play with soppy kids and go to school. Enid was going to run away with Greg anyway . . .'

That news shook Gloria but she wasn't going to show it. 'Don't be mean to the Belfields. They've got enough to worry about, what with Mr Plum being away and poor Maddy's terrible news.'

'It's all right, Gloria, I can speak for myself,' Maddy snapped, looking put out. 'Enid wasn't thinking about any of that, she's just being stupid and selfish, worrying everyone like this.'

'Who are you calling stupid, speccy four eyes?' Peg shouted. 'You stuck-up prig!'

'Shut yer gob, fatso!' Gloria threw her own brickbats. She was playground queen of calling names. The trick was to get in first.

'I'll have you an' all, carrot top!' Peggy struck out in her direction but Gloria was too quick and darted away, leaving the girl floundering and stumbling face down in the snow.

'Just stop it, both of you! She's not worth it, Gloria . . . She's just jealous that Enid went without her.'

'Oh, go and boil your heads, the two of you. See if I care.' Peg waltzed off, leaving them to push and pull the battered pram back down the garden track without losing any sticks. It was like old times chatting together. Gloria was glad they were alone.

'They say you're going to a new school?' she asked, wanting to be sure of her facts this time.

'When the weather gets better after Easter, I'm going to Palgrave House for a term. It's the prep school for Scarperton Ladies' College, but I'm not boarding, thank goodness, except in the winter. Aunt Plum says I can go on the train each day but we have to go on some Saturdays, which is a bore.'

'I wish I went to boarding school like the stories in my comic,' Gloria sighed. One minute she was a dunce at her reading and then it sort of clicked. She'd come on so fast that she could now read schoolgirl mags and follow some of the stories in a proper book, but Maddy going away would change everything. 'You'll be too busy with schooling to play out with us.'

'Spec so . . . lots of prep to do in the evenings.'

'We are still friends, though?' Gloria moved in closer.

'Of course, why not?'

'Can I tell you a secret? You may not want to be my friend when I tell you,' Gloria replied. Sharing this with

Maddy was the scariest thing she could think of to prove their true friendship.

Maddy nodded her head and turned towards her.

'My mam did it for money . . . you know, like what Peggy was saying. I think that's why she put us on the train out of the way, so she could earn more.' There, her fear was spoken, the awful truth laid bare for her friend to see.

'I'm sure that isn't true. Your mother looked very upset to me. She must have wanted to stop you having to . . . I don't know. It was a brave thing to do. I won't tell anyone, I promise but I think you've got it a bit wrong.'

Gloria could see that Maddy didn't believe her. What did she know of Elijah Street and all its dirty back alleys? How could she ever imagine such a world? Still, she hadn't run away from her in disgust.

'Thanks,' she replied. 'And Greg's got it all wrong saying you'll become a right snob when you leave Sowerthwaite.'

Maddy froze on the spot, looking at her in surprise. 'How dare he? What does he know? Gregory Byrne is talking out of his bottom.'

'Can I tell him you said that?' Gloria smiled.

'Tell him what you like,' Maddy sniffed. 'No, just tell him he likes the smell of his own farts!'

'Maddy! That's so rude,' Gloria giggled with relief as they both laughed all the way back down the lane in time for tea and pikelets at the Vic.

How dare Greg Byrne say she'd be a snob! Gloria's words rankled all the way home. In the end Maddy skipped tea and pikelets by the fire and refused to speak to him when he came in from the garage. The Old Vic wasn't her home and neither was Brooklyn Hall. Sometimes she felt like a barrage balloon let loose from its moorings, blown this way and that by this blasted war, not belonging anywhere. Nor could she understand why there was no news of the sinking in the newspapers; not in Uncle Algie's *Telegraph* or Miss Blunt's *Yorkshire Post.*

Bad news was hidden away as if it had never happened. Miss Blunt's sister had lost her house in Coventry and was living in lodgings. She said the whole city was just rubble and no one was allowed near, but there was nothing in the paper about it. There were terrible pictures about the Great Fire of London and how St Paul's was saved. Uncle Algie kept waving his paper about furiously but she couldn't look. She could still smell the flames and hear the screams when she shut her eyes. Nothing about the sunken ship either. It made her feel that Mummy and Daddy weren't important enough to be mentioned.

If she took the short cut across the fields, she could stop off and climb the icy branches of the Victory Tree again. It was cold and slippy up the rope but the snow had melted from the branches and she could just see the new buds swollen, ready for spring.

Would it really be warm again? Would flowers bloom and baby lambs fill the fields? Would the pain in her tummy ever go away? Up in the branches on the platform Maddy hugged her knees and stared out at the bleak grey fields, high up away from the smoke and soot of the chimneys. This was her home, high up out of sight. Everything was all muddled up in her head like Aunt Julia's tangled wool.

Gloria so desperately wanted to be her friend but Maddy wasn't sure she meant what she'd said to her about being 'forever friends'. Aunt Plum was trying to be kind but was so busy all the time, and now with Enid running away and Uncle Gerald being in danger . . . Grandma was trying her best to be interested in her school work as she helped her with her knitting stitches and asked her to fetch and carry spectacles and hot-water bottles for her bad back. Sometimes she just wanted to be alone up here but then she felt so lonely. She was nobody's child now.

There was an album of portraits of Daddy as a little boy in lacy dresses and knickerbockers, in school uniform with Uncle Julian, looking very important, and in soldier's uniform. Grandma sniffed on her hanky as she turned the pages.

'You don't expect to outlive your children,' she sighed.

Why couldn't she have done all this before Daddy left? Did you have to be dead before anyone said anything nice about you, Maddy thought. Suddenly Daddy was Grandma's long-lost beloved son and a hero, and Maddy didn't recognise him at all.

When she pictured Daddy in her head she saw him pounding the piano with gusto, smiling up as Mummy sang, sucking on his brown pipe as he read her a story before they left for the theatre, digging up the bowling green, cussing and swearing under his breath in his old corduroys and the jumper with the elbows frayed into a big hole, waving goodbye through the train window, hat in hand until the train was well out of her sight. She could never imagine him living here.

Nothing was fun any more, not listening to *It's That Man Again* on the wireless nor going to school in the snow. She just wanted to hide away under the bed covers and read. She'd devoured *Jane Eyre* again and *Little Women* and *Anne of Green Gables* for comfort. There was a lending library at the chemist – the books were too old for her but she read them just the same.

Books gave her comfort, knowing other girls had suffered death and sadness.

She no longer liked going to school and had tummy aches in the night and fevers and nightmares that allowed her a lie-in in the morning.

It wasn't as if she was afraid of going out, but she felt safer in the kitchen, helping Ilse, making milky drinks for the oldies who were scattered about, trying their best to get dressed and downstairs before noon.

It was like a hotel, comings and goings up and down stairs. Aunt Julia had her routine, Grandma had hers, Aunt Plum was always out with the dogs or seeing to the two horses for the trap or helping down at the Vic.

Sometimes Maddy could go a whole day without thinking about not seeing Mummy and Daddy ever again, but other days it just flooded over her like a wave of terror to be so alone in the world. Panda did his best but he was only a stuffed toy. She was getting too old for toys but he'd seen her through the toughest of years.

If she kept quiet no one noticed she'd not been to school until they assembled for afternoon tea on the dot of four thirty. She helped Ilse bake scones and oaty biscuits.

By the time Aunt Plum came rushing through the door and noticed her with a perfunctory, 'Are you feeling better, darling?' she'd nod weakly. No further questions were asked until it started all over again, wetting the bed, headaches and tummy pains.

She had managed to stay off school for a whole week but now the school was closed anyway. Grandma sent for Dr David to examine her. He prodded and poked, pulled out her tongue, inspected behind her ears and eyed her up and down.

'Just a wee bit run down, not surprising for the poor soul, but it's time we did something about that eye before it weakens her sight.'

He was always more interested in her squint than her tummy. Out came the tonic bottle from his bag and the name of a surgeon in Leeds.

'Let's get the girl on her feet before we start poking into her eyes. It appears the last man didn't make much of a job of it,' said Grandma. 'She's just skin and bone. You'd think we were starving her, not an inch of flesh on her,' she said, prodding Maddy in the arm as if she was feeling a chicken for the pot.

'Away with you, Mrs Belfield, she's tough and made to carry flesh like a thoroughbred, not a cart horse. But I'd send her to a ballet class to straighten out those humped shoulders before she gets a stoop. She's going to be tall.'

And that was why Maddy was going to be packed off to Madame Drysdale's Dance Academy in Scarperton to take a ballet class.

'Do I have to go?' she moaned to Aunt Plum. 'I'll be hopeless and it's a long way on my own. Why can't Gloria come too?'

'The Battys don't have the money to pay for classes, darling, and bus fares,' she replied.

'But we could pay for her . . . Please. I just can't face going on my own.' Maddy whined just enough times for Grandma to consent.

'Just for a term, mind, to see if it suits, but if you miss classes they will stop for both of you.'

She'd gone with Aunt Plum to visit the Battys and were shown into the front room that smelled of damp and soot and must. Gloria was out and they'd sipped tea politely, and Aunt Plum explained the scheme to Mrs Batty who nodded and smiled and said, 'How kind to think of her . . . especially after the unfortunate episode.'

Aunt Plum soon put her at ease with a wave of her hand and left it up to Maddy to tell Gloria this very afternoon, but she'd forgotten to tell her. Why?

As she sat up in the chilly tree loft she felt strangely distant from everything going on around her. Nothing was real any more. She just couldn't be bothered to tell her and watch the look of delight beam over Gloria's face.

Gloria would shine in the class and she would be dull. She was as pretty as Maddy was plain. An owl hooted from across the fields and she knew it was time to head down. She was being mean to Gloria and now she realised why. It was because of her spoiling Christmas with the wrong news, misleading her and lulling her into safety.

Maddy wanted to punish her friend a little while longer and then she recalled what Gloria had told her in confidence about her own mother being a harlot, as it said in the Bible. She must look it up in the dictionary in the study. Gloria's mother had given her up and run away; her own parents had no choice. It wasn't their fault or Gloria's fault. It just was. It was war.

Don't be mean, she thought as she made her way back to the warmth of the Old Vic, so she could walk back with Gloria and tell her the news then. It was the least she could do. But she was not going to speak to Greg Byrne ever again.

Plum rushed down to the Vic as soon as she heard the news that Enid had turned up safe, having been picked up trying to thumb a lift with her 'boyfriend', who was now on a charge of abducting a minor. She arrived to a scene of total chaos. From high up the wall, there were a pair of legs dangling from the upper casement window.

'Get down at once, Enid Cartwright! Stop making an exhibition of yourself,' shouted Avis Blunt. 'I don't know why they bothered to bring you back, you brazen huzzy!'

'What's going on, Gregory?' Plum turned to the young man staring up at the drama.

'The silly cow says she's going to jump out of the window if they don't let her see Alf. She won't be sent away to no home either.'

'Cook's left me to see to the pastry in the oven,' said Miss Blunt. 'You must deal with this now . . . Let her jump, for all we care. There'll be more for us if she does. I'm sick of her tantrums.' Avis turned back to the girl, wagging her finger. 'It'll be bread and no jam for you until you see sense, my girl. I never had this trouble with my prep school boys. My nerves can't stand any more of the likes of you. Don't scratch the paintwork!'

Plum was tired and in no mood for this drama. What with Maddy being difficult and moody, Mother-in-law off her food and being a martyred Minnie, Ilse giving her notice as she wanted to help in the local hospital, and the parcel of supplies to deliver, her head was throbbing.

Plum looked up at the gangling girl with her plump legs and ankle socks, her hair pinned up in a straggly Victory Roll, trying to look older than she really was. How did you reason with a defiant girl of that age? Call her bluff, she thought.

'If you're going to jump, Enid, do get on with it. Matron and I haven't time to stand here gawping at your dramatics. It's starting to rain.' Deliberately she turned her back and began to walk away, trembling at her own words. What if the silly girl did jump and she was accused of incitement to suicide?

'I'm not going to no home . . . I was coming back any roads . . . It's not fair, I ain't done nothing wrong,' Enid shouted, but the voice was wobbly and tearful.

Plum turned to see her half in and out of the window. 'Oh, Greg, can you talk some sense into her?' she sighed.

'Who said anything about another home?' he shouted up at her.

The would-be delinquent paused at this different tack. 'Shut yer mouth, Byrne. It's none of yer bloody business what I do!'

'Why should you be treated any different from the rest of us? What've you done to help out but moan and whine and skive off?' he replied.

'I went to school, don't I? I never asked to come to this dump. I done me chores but I'm not a kid, am I? I just want to do what the other girls in the village get up to . . . yer only young once, Alf says. There's nothing else to do in these hills. It's all don'ts in this place: don't show a light; don't leave a gate open; don't make a din; mind your manners and sit at the table. They think we're rubbish kids,' she called out to her audience.

'From where I'm standing, that's just what you deserve,' Greg yelled. 'You can't just run off and expect everyone to welcome you back with open arms. You let Mrs Plum down.'

'Hark at 'im. You'd be off down that road like a flash if there weren't a fancy car for you to fiddle with. You've gone soft, teacher's pet. I know your game. I'm not a kid, I'll be working soon and then no one can stop me and Alf being together.'

It was too much to stand by and let the boy try to bring her down. Plum was blazing mad as the rain poured down on them but now was not the time to show it. How had she ever got talked into this job?

'From where I'm standing, Enid, all I can see is next week's washing and a big baby making an exhibition of herself. I hope Alf isn't peering down his binoculars, seeing you in your glory; not very glamorous or grown up to get everyone worried and searching for you, and now your boyfriend's in the glasshouse because of you.'

'I don't care,' Enid said.

'Well, we do, young lady. Some boyfriend! And you don't even care what happens to him? Still,' she paused trying a different tack, 'if you fall we'll have to pick up the pieces and send for the undertaker to measure you up. So if you're going to jump, do it quickly before all these lovely American magazines in my bag get soaked. We've had another parcel from over the water full of tinned fruit and goodies. We'll share out yours with the others, if that's all right. You'll not be around to worry and Alf will find another girlfriend in your place,' she said, hoping this might tempt the disobedient young pup into behaving.

'What magazines?' Enid's sturdy legs were edging back over the window sill.

'Oh, just *Moviegoer*s, that sort of stuff, but I can send them for salvage . . . or I can send for the constable again and then you really will be in trouble. It's your shout,' Plum coaxed, sensing a shift in the wind.

'Keep yer hair on! I'm coming down. It's just not fair.'

Enid wriggled back through the window, to everyone's relief.

'That was good, miss,' laughed Greg.

'Sometimes the carrot works better than the stick . . . And what's this about you running away too? I thought you were starting work at Brigg's Garage?'

'No fear, miss. I know when I'm well off, and so does she, up there shouting the odds,' Greg smiled, seeing Plum's anxious look. 'Take no notice. It was hard at first for all of us to settle, what with the village lads calling us names, but once we'd bloodied their noses on the way home from school a time or two, we're sort of all one gang now, miss.'

Plum smiled, knowing a few of the matrons of Sowerthwaite had turned their noses up at some of the latest arrivals, especially young mothers in curlers, smoking fags on the doorsteps of their billets, hanging about looking bored. The town was full of newcomers unused to country ways. There'd been gossip about some of the young mothers complaining about there being no chip vans, dance halls or public houses, and giving lip to their betters. Perhaps if the locals knew just what some of these families had been through, they'd not be so quick to condemn.

Even Enid had chosen to run back here and take her punishment, sensing they'd be fair with her, the crafty little minx. It was a good sign when runaways returned to the fold like naughty puppies. Enid knew when she was well off too, however much she protested.

If only Maddy was that easy to settle. It was hard to get through the tough little shell she had grown in the past months. Her fears and worries were hidden deep behind a 'don't bother me' mask. Perhaps if they made sure her eyesight was secure, and straightened out the squint, it would give her confidence for when she started her new school.

If Plum had learned anything from working with these young girls it was that appearance mattered. How easy to forget how she'd agonised over spots on her own face and whether her nose was too straight. Poor Maddy had to wear those awful specs and the patch. She pretended not to care but she must be the butt of teasing and worse. How could they have left it so long? The girl was never going to be pretty so they must make the best of what she'd got.

8

Greg was in big trouble. It was not as if he meant to steal the soldier's motor bike. It was just there and he couldn't resist. He'd ridden it enough times across the battery field as a reward for doing errands and stuff. He liked going up there and watching them scanning the skies for enemy aircraft, oiling their machinery and playing football. It was one of those days when The Rug was on the warpath, nag, nagging, bending their ears with her petty rules and regulations: 'Wash your hands'; inspections behind the ears. He'd had years of this sort of rubbish and thought that a quick lick and a promise would pass muster, but not with Miss Blunt.

'Byrne, you are old enough to set an example but I can grow potatoes behind your ears so go and wash them again!'

Would he hell! Greg scarpered out of the back door and up the hill. There were times lately when he just needed to be on his own. All that fussing just pissed him off. When was he going to grow up proper? He was stuck in between a kid and a lad. There was a war going on and he wasn't in it. Real danger was coming, and all that old trout fussed on about was a few crusts behind his lugs. That was when he saw Barry's bike, mud splattered but begging to be started up. He knew which wires to cross to ignite the engine if the key wasn't there – he'd learned that at the previous hostel – but he was in luck as the key had been left for anyone to steal.

Barry was hiding behind some rocks canoodling with his latest girl from the town. He was a smooth operator. Greg had seen him chatting the girls up, necking with them in the fields. They were going at each other hammer and tongs so Barry wouldn't miss his bike for a few minutes. Greg could blow out on the tracks, scare a few sheep, rattle his bones. It would be brilliant!

Heading into the wind he drove like the devil, up the track winding across the main road. No one was around and he didn't care. Once he got up some speed it was as if it sparked an engine in his own head . . . Go, go, go!

How was he to know there was a milk lorry coming round the bend that swerved to avoid him? It crashed into him, knocking milk cans everywhere, milk spilling onto the road. Greg went flying and landed on his bum, dazed but unharmed. The lorry driver went berserk and cuffed him round the ears good and proper. The bike was a mess and he had to push it down the road. His new corduroy trousers were all torn and bloodied. Barry was nowhere to be seen but all hell broke loose at the Old Vic on his return.

He was up before the coppers for a caution, and the

biggest humiliation of all was when he was put back in short trousers, floppy grey ones, cut-offs that barely reached his knees like a kid, but he'd only himself to blame.

'If you behave like a tearaway you'll be treated like one,' screamed Miss Blunt.

Mrs Plum went with him to the police station, where the sergeant gave him a right dressing-down, saying something about wasting precious petrol that men had died in ships to bring to this country. He was wasting precious milk that the children of England will be deprived of and taking a bike without permission so a soldier at his duty was put at risk.

You'd think he'd started a fifth column of collaborators, waiting to sabotage the Yorkshire Dales, the way the sergeant went on and on. He saw poor Mrs Plum blushing with embarrassment as he was told off and was put under orders to behave himself or else.

He didn't care about the rest but he felt mean to have caused her bother. She didn't need to tell him he'd let her down. Her face said it all. It was The Rug who seemed to take pleasure in his disgrace, picking on him. Bad enough to be grounded, confined to the barracks for the foreseeable future. The gang thought he was a hero. But he just wished it would all go away.

Maddy brought him books to read and there was an especially good one that caught his interest. It was all about how boys hid in the wild woods and lived rough. Now that was something he fancied doing.

He felt stupid in his short pants, his legs were

growing like twigs, all bones and hinges. If only Miss Blunt would keep off his back – but she kept on sticking a needle in until he was ready to explode.

If she were a man he'd have clobbered her, but only a coward would slap a woman down. She was like all the past billet tyrants rolled into one, with her piggy eyes and roly-poly shape, the way her wig shifted when she got worked up.

He couldn't take his eyes off that wig. It made him laugh, taking his mind off her sarcasm. He knew it was only time before he'd take his revenge.

Maddy felt sorry for Greg. He just couldn't do anything right, and she overheard the meeting in the drawing room when Miss Blunt complained about his sullen insolence.

'In my book boys like that need breaking down. Byrne has too much spirit for a boy of the lower orders. He needs a taste of the birch, not a caution.'

'Gregory just got carried away,' said Plum in his defence. 'He's at that awkward stage, neither fish nor fowl. The in-between years can be trying but no real harm was done.'

'I must say, Mrs Belfield, you take all this very lightly. I'm not used to such indulgence by my clients,' said Miss Blunt.

'In my experience, I just feel the more we punish, the less response we get,' Plum replied. 'My puppies, for instance—'

She was interrupted. 'With respect, madam, this is a lad, not a pup.'

'I don't know . . . at this age there's not much difference, but breaking the spirit is never a good idea,' Plum defended her charge again.

'He'll have to be moved on. I'll not stand for much more. The others see him as a hero with his Victory Tree HQ. He sets a very bad example.' Miss Blunt was not letting go.

'Do you want me to have a word?' said Plum.

'You Belfields must do as you see fit,' came the guarded reply.

Maddy knew she must warn Greg to ease up on his campaign. Time to score some gold stars for himself, instead of black marks. Without him in the hostel it would be a very boring place and he was one of her special friends there. He'd taught her to ride her bike and she just liked him.

Rushing over to the Old Vic as soon as she could, Maddy spied them all having a troop review under the Victory Tree HQ, a line of troops for kit inspection. It was a war game they all played, a bit like being in the Boy Scouts, parading with pitchforks and spades as if they were guns, taking turns to spot planes in the trees. Greg was up the tree with the binoculars, but no sooner had she arrived than Miss Blunt came huffing and puffing up the steps behind her.

'Just stop these silly games . . . I want you all back inside at once. When you've done all your chores, you can play out but not before. And where is Byrne? If that toerag's skived off again . . . No one must take notice of a ruffian like that. He's the scum of the earth and he'll be ending up in gaol before long.'

The warden was facing them with her back to the tree, and Gloria, Sid and the troop were standing back. Everyone's eyes were trying not to look up as a fishing rod with a hook on the end slowly dangled down over Miss Blunt's head. Maddy gasped. The line was heading down silently towards Miss Blunt, down towards the thatch of rust-coloured hair. Slowly, slowly it descended as Greg, hiding in the branches, aimed for the crown as she droned on. She made to move, but the thatch lifted itself off neatly and swung in the air.

Once dislodged, it wriggled in the breeze like a wounded animal, dangling, exposing the fluff of her bare skull for all to see.

For a second, no one spoke, being too shocked, but Miss Blunt felt the jerk and then the draught, turning round to watch the wig disappearing from her grasp up the tree. She was speechless, her mouth opening and closing like a fish gasping for air.

'Byrne!' she screamed, shaking her fist into the tree. Maddy didn't know whether to laugh or cry, sensing Greg's triumph was going to be his undoing.

'This time you've gone too far,' said Mrs Plum, tearing a strip off the culprit standing before her. 'You might think it funny and clever, but what you did was wrong. Miss Blunt wears a wig for a good reason, to cover a disability, just as Maddy must wear a patch to cover hers, but to defy her in such a way – I'm ashamed of you! I trusted you and you let me down again. I stood surety for your last stupid prank. This time I have to inform the billeting officer to find you another hostel.

I have no choice. Oh, Gregory! What do you say for yourself?' she sighed.

'Sorry, Mrs Plum.' He looked suddenly smaller and lost in a short pants.

'Sorry isn't enough. You owe Miss Blunt an apology. Thoughtlessness is one thing. Cruelty is another. I won't have behaviour like this at the Vic. I just can't believe you'd be so stupid. And don't stand there looking as if you don't care because I can see through your act.'

Greg was standing with his head up, piercing her with those blue eyes. Had she met her match with the one pup she couldn't train or control? There had to be a reason for all this defiance. All her instincts sensed he was a good lad at heart. 'Why? Gregory, give me one good reason why I should keep you here?'

'Dunno, miss. I couldn't take no more. She's on at me night and day like a pain in the bum. She don't care for no one, just rules, and I'm sick of rules. Do kids who have mums and dads have to live by rules? Do they have to line up like skittles? Do they get slapped down? We're always strangers on someone else's stairs, shoved from place to place, and always rules! If I had a mum and dad, it would be different, yes? Why didn't I get one of my own? When I come here it was the best billet yet, but then she come up with stupid rules like all the rest and I can't stand no more of it.'

This was a side of Greg Plum had never seen before. It was as if for a second he'd lifted up that hard shell, showing the soft underbelly of the wounded boy. She wanted to take him in her arms, this motherless lad, confused and lost, who lashed out against the world that had never given him much of a chance. Here was somebody worth saving.

'If you will write a proper apology and try to make yourself useful, I'm going to try to reconsider, but I need your word of honour.'

'But I am not sorry, miss. She's just as hard as me.' Those ice-blue eyes stared ahead.

'But Miss Blunt is in authority over you. You can never win that battle. Sometimes we all have to do things we don't want to, make a truce with the enemy, find common ground, compromise. I know it's hard, believe me, but do you think you are man enough to do that?'

'Not in these ruddy pants, I'm not. She makes me wear them out of spite.'

'Long trousers don't make a man, Greg. It's in here.' Plum stabbed at her head and heart. 'This is where it counts, rising above petty rules and irritations. You behave like a proper man and I'll make sure you get your trousers back. That is my promise.'

'Thanks, miss . . . I won't let you down again.'

'I know you won't,' Plum replied, more in hope than certainty.

Two weeks later, Avis Blunt resigned, taking up a post in a private school.

'I'll not stay where my authority is undermined. I'll not ask for references from people who have no idea how to curb bad behaviour. That boy will prove to be everything I predict and more. You'll rue the day when you took his word over mine. He's a wild one, not easily tamed, and the sooner he's in the army, the better all round. We can afford to sacrifice riffraff like that! I wash my hands of this place. The trouble with the lower classes is they have no sense of their place in society. I blame the Great War for shaking up standards. Now we're educating children above their station. It'll be the death of this country, and you should be careful who Madeleine mixes with in future. Pack her off to boarding school before it's too late, is my advice.'

'Thank you, Miss Blunt, for your opinion,' said Plum, rising to her full height. 'But if the staff of any female boarding establishment resemble you in any way, that would be the last place on earth I'd ever put a child. Good day!'

9

It was the talk of Sowerthwaite that a plane had gone down somewhere up on the tops, high up on the moors on a grim night in mid-March when there was still deep snow and mist. Everyone heard the roar of an engine in trouble, but how far it had limped before crashing into rocks, no one knew. The moors were raked over by the army and RAF, closing off all the lanes and tracks to the fells to all but essential workers.

Greg held an emergency meeting at Victory Tree HQ. This was their chance to do their bit and Gloria was all ears.

'There'll be loads of metal souvenirs, shrapnel scattered for miles, so we've got to get it afore the other gangs in Sowerthwaite do.'

'But we're not allowed up there,' said Mitch Brown.

'So? They'll have cleared up the mess by now,' Greg boasted. 'I'll ask up at the battery field and then we can go off on our own search.'

'But it'll be dangerous,' said Peggy.

'So? You don't have to come. It'll be lads only then.'

'No!' yelled Gloria. 'I'm coming too.' She wanted to

have an adventure to tell Maddy, who was now at the other school.

'We'll go Saturday afternoon while it's light. Then we can say we're all going collecting sticks. It'll be fun, and Mrs Plum won't mind if we're doing something useful,' came the order.

Things had taken a turn for the better now that Mrs Plum was in charge and Mrs Grace Battersby, the new cook, kept an eye on things. She'd sort of made their rules fun. They got points and stars for good behaviour and were split into teams for chores. They had singsongs round the piano and concert nights. Mrs Battersby got them baking buns. They needed kindling for the stove, and sticking was something even the little ones could do.

There'd been no more snow so Greg's gang set out in the brightness of the blue sky on that Saturday afternoon, trudging uphill in a line, big boys racing ahead, scarves and balaclavas wrapping them from the cold.

Gloria's short legs couldn't keep up with the line and then they left the track and took a short cut over the fields, dodging the snow fence. Snow got down her gumboots and the cold chapped her bare knees but she wasn't going to complain.

As they scaled the fell, the sky got greyer and darker but no one was bothered at first, too intent on finding the crash site up out on the moorside. There were a few smoking embers in the distance to urge them on. They looked near but were in fact much further away. They were three miles up and it was an overcoat colder up there.

When they reached the ridge Mitch complained, 'There's nothing to see here.'

'Alf, at the battery, told me it was near the trig point, that triangle of stones sticking out on top of the rock. It's not far, but it may be still guarded,' said Greg.

'Will we see bodies?' Gloria asked, not sure if she wanted to see anything mangled.

'Nah! Poor sods roasted inside. Alf said they took them away first.'

Gloria shivered. 'It'll get dark soon – do you really know the way or are you just showing off?'

'Course I do,' said Greg. 'I've been up these rocks with the birdwatcher. There's a steep cliff with a cave up there. It'll be there.'

It wasn't, and now the mist was swirling round in wet murky ribbons, whipping Gloria's cheeks and chilling her legs even more.

'When're we going to see owt?' Everyone was complaining now.

Then suddenly there it was: bits of strewn metal, dead sheep's legs and the smell of burning rubber. There was no guard. It was eerie, only the wind moaning over the ghostly sight before them. Everyone fell silent as the mist wrapped itself round huge chunks of broken plane.

'I don't like this place,' Gloria whined.

'Shurrup!' The others ignored her, too busy collecting bits of cold metal to stuff in their pockets. There was a piece that looked like a huge silver bird's wing, all smashed up. What was left of the fuselage had been taken away in bits but on the floor she found a big leather glove, but she didn't dare look inside, in case there was a finger in it. She shoved it in her pocket and said nothing to the others. This was a sad place and Gloria didn't like it. She wanted to get back to the Old Vic, back to the kitchen Saturday night treats: crumpets and rhubarb jam, toasting bread on a fork in front of the fire.

'Come on, it'll be dark soon,' Gloria shouted, trying to round them up. Boys' adventures were boring, but she got no response.

The slippery limestone scree was rough with blocks sticking out from the melting snow like little flat pavements, and she started to jump from one to another. 'Come on, it's late. I want to go back!' she yelled, and then slipped and caught her ankle in the crack between the two blocks of stone. Boy, did she yell, but the sound was muffled at first by the mist. She screamed until Greg came running with the boys. He saw how her foot was all twisted in the boot and she kept screaming like a fox stuck in a gin trap.

'Lift yer foot!' he shouted.

'I can't, it hurts. It's stuck and I'm going to be stuck here and it's getting dark. I'm going to die!' she screamed.

'No, you're not going to die. You'll do as I say and it'll be all right. It went in, so it'll come out.' But even Greg could see that the boot was well and truly stuck down the crack. 'We'll just have to get your foot out of the boot. We could do with a shoehorn or something.'

By now Gloria was shivering with fear and pain and still screaming blue murder so Greg slapped her.

'You hit me!' she sobbed, gazing up at him with horror.

'Yelling doesn't help me think. They do that to women on the pictures when they have funny turns . . . sorry,' he replied.

'That's all right,' she whispered, calmer now. 'So what are you going to do?'

'Well, someone's got to go off and get help, for a start. You can't walk on that foot.'

'But we can't see,' said Mitch, and everyone was standing round. 'It were a stupid idea. And we'll all be for it when we gets home.'

'They'll send the army out for us when we're missed. Just think how we can make a torch or something. There's fuel oil spilled, we could make a pole and burn a signal.' Greg was getting carried away with ideas from the book Maddy gave him when he was grounded.

'First we can shove some down her boot and see if it'll shift it,' said Mitch. 'Happen she could walk then.'

'Good show,' Greg smiled. 'See, all's not lost. We're not far from the old caves; we can shelter in there and leave a marker here in the snow . . . a big arrow.'

'Just get my leg out of here or I shall never be able to dance again,' Gloria shouted. 'I want Mrs Plum.'

'Shut up, we're doing what we can.' They found some oil slicks and a cloth, and poked the oil down her boot. 'It's coming!'

'No, it's not,' Gloria wailed, unconvinced.

'It is, look . . . the other way,' he ordered, and she obeyed as he tugged at her boot, releasing the whole foot.

'You've torn my leg off!' she shrieked

'Don't be such a madam. I've got your foot free,' Greg snapped.

'What do we do now? We can't see a thing.' Gloria whined. 'It's all your fault.'

'Stop moaning, Gloria. You're making my ears ache. I'm not standing any nonsense in the ranks. We have to make our way back,' Greg ordered. 'It's too cold to be standing still. We can find a way.'

'How?' they all shouted.

'I'll think of something.'

Greg knew they were in deep trouble and it was all his fault. It was a stupid idea, setting off in the afternoon, and now he'd got to get them back to safety. In Maddy's book, the one about the boys camping out, living rough, there were some ideas, but that was in the middle of summer. It was hardly beyond winter, and they were about three miles out, and Gloria couldn't walk. She'd have to have a piggyback and he was the biggest. Being leader was easy in Victory Tree headquarters. Now he wasn't sure. There was real danger for everyone. It was cold, dark and misty, but he did roughly know where they were. If they made to the nearest stone wall and went down rather than up it might lead them to the main track, or it could lead them round and round in circles.

He thought about poor Scott of the Antarctic. Better to stay and take the safer option and find shelter. They'd already passed the old cave entrance, and that wasn't far from the drover's track. If they found their way back there he could work out a route home in the morning, but it was going to be a long cold night. Shelter and warmth was what they must have. And then he heard the sheep bleating . . . a few sheep for company, tied up would be like woolly rugs, just the job.

'I'm starving,' moaned Gloria.

'Shut up and get on my back, Gloria Conley. One way or another I'll find us a billet.'

When Maddy got back from a hockey match there was a flap on. Plum was on the phone to summon help from friends for the six missing children. It was Peggy who'd told them that the gang had gone to the wreckage on the tops in search of souvenirs. The lads from the battery field offered to take their bikes to locate them but it was too dark to see much, and too misty and dangerous. Everyone sat glumly in the Old Vic, trying to comfort each other.

'Poor little Gloria'll be so scared,' said Grace.

'At least Greg knows the area – he'll find them shelter,' said Plum. 'But those devils should have never been up there in the first place.'

'Boys will be boys, Mrs Belfield. My lot are like magnets to trouble,' Grace smiled with a sigh. She lived close to the church in a tiny cottage and had five sons and three daughters.

Maddy felt a strange envy of them being free to roam the hills and get into trouble. Gloria was in the midst of it with Greg, while she was still in her weekday uniform and not one of the gang any more. Going to a girl's private school was just like St Hilda's all over again, set apart just because she was a Belfield orphan, not a hostel one.

Poor Greg would be frightened. He'd be taking charge but this wasn't games at Victory Tree HQ; this was the real thing. How would he cope on his own? He'd been on his best behaviour for months. Soon he was going to Brigg's Garage on leaving school. What if they all perished on the moor before anyone reached them? There'd been some terrible accidents up there with people getting lost.

'Can't we do anything, Aunt Plum?' she whispered.

'We can all pray,' said Grace Battersby, bowing her head.

The treasure seekers huddled together in the entrance of the damp cave. They caught only two silly sheep and tied them with belts and ties and baler twine. The animals smelled, kicking out at them at first but soon they settled down and the gang took it in turns to warm themselves on their fleeces. Gloria's foot had swollen into a purple balloon and they bathed it in cold water as best they could. They all stank of oil and damp wool and they were hungry, but there was plenty of running water from a spring rushing off the rocks. They pooled what tuck they had left of their Saturday pennies spent in the sweet shop, and found some furry mint balls and a liquorice root to chew on.

Greg wrapped a snotty hanky around Gloria's bruised ankle and sat with her all night to cheer her up. She fell asleep on his lap and woke with a stiff neck. It was the longest night of her life, but one of the best so far. It was not every day you found your hero, she thought.

'I'm going to marry you,' she sighed when morning came and the sky was as blue as it had been grey. 'And you are going to marry me, one day.'

'Over my dead body!' Greg jumped up. 'None of that sloppy stuff here, gerroff me! Time to do look-out!'

They were halfway down the track when the army lads came up in a lorry and collected the bedraggled gang, stuffing them with chocolate and sandwiches. What a relief.

Gloria was bandaged up and fussed over, showing off her bandage in the kitchen. 'Greg saved our lives, took us to a cave and told us stories, so don't be cross with him, Mrs Plum. He saved my life.'

No one was cross.

'You showed great initiative,' said Plum. 'But I'd just wish you'd thought of another escapade.'

'We wanted to be first with souvenirs,' said Mitch, as out of their pockets came their treasure.

Plum looked at their booty. Was this what war did to children, risking life and limb for lumps of deadly metal?

'It were a terrible crash, miss,' Greg confessed later.

'That's me for the army when I join up, not the RAF after this. Better on land. They never stood a chance, poor blighters.'

Plum thought of her own brother, Tim, fighting the

Japs in the air, across the world. She'd not heard news of him for weeks now. The Far East was in turmoil.

'You're only just fourteen. The army is years away,' she replied. This boy was too young for war.

'I can go at sixteen . . . no one will stop me then.'

'Don't be in such a hurry to wish your life away, young man,' Plum smiled. She'd miss him when he left: this strange boy, half angel one minute, half devil the next. Thank goodness she'd given him another chance. A boy like Greg needed steering in the right direction – but heaven only knew what he'd get up to next!

10

March 1944

It was one of those mornings when Plum didn't know what job to tackle first: the annual spring cleaning in the Old Vic – beating rugs, scouring the lino in the bathroom, taking the blackout linings off the curtains to be steeped in the outhouse washing sink; or tackle the weekly accounts for the Town Hall inspection of her purchase and housekeeping ledgers. Then she must check that the butcher would deliver their coupons worth of meat for Grace Battersby's weekend stew and dumplings. She liked to check they got their fair dues with so many hungry mouths to feed. Then there was the heating playing up again, even though Grace's husband, Wilf, was a whiz with their temperamental coke boiler – coaxing it back into action with goal kicks worthy of Wembley Stadium.

Months had turned into years since those first evacuees arrived and Plum's greenhorn attempts to keep order in the ranks. Many childen had come and gone, and she'd learned a few tricks herself how to keep boisterous kids occupied on wet afternoons. Now there was a contingent of small toddlers living in with their mothers, who were easier to manage. With a bit of luck she'd find them all spring cleaning jobs to tackle and save her aching back from some of the tougher jobs.

The women formed their own little cliques, gossiping as they knitted and mended, leaving her to do the organising of supplies and deal with officials. She felt like an agony aunt, listening to their tales of woe, trying to console them if there was bad news, and stepping in if there were arguments with locals.

It wasn't the same as those first hairy days. These weren't her special charges and she began to look back on those first arrivals with nostalgia until she recalled how Bryan was almost gored by a bull, how Enid's lapses caused a scandal, how Peggy was caught sending raw bacon and eggs from their rations through the post to her family in Hull, and then there was Gregory's escapades . . .

New evacuees were delivered with depressing regularity, only to shoot back home at the first opportunity, danger or not, but the core of her originals remained. Gregory was now taken on by Brigg's Garage as their 'oily rag', but he was waiting for papers to join up. He was turning out to be a steady away young man, those bunking off adventures now a distant memory. There wasn't a mean bone in his body, not like Enid Cartwright, who now worked in the cotton mill and was courting one of the local evacuees in another billet. She could still get on everyone's nerves.

Life at Brooklyn Hall still ran round the routines of the elderly inmates and Pleasance's daily orders. Staff came and went, refugees mostly, whose ideas of English cooking were always spiced up with strange flavours that played havoc with bowels and their antique plumbing system.

Being in charge here got Plum out of the house, stopped her worrying about Gerald's dangerous posting and poor Maddy, who drooped under the pressure of homework, travelling by train each day to her day school in Scarperton.

They'd still not done anything about her eye. Somehow it never seemed the right time. She was like a bud wilting on a stalk, dreamy, slouching her shoulders to hide her height. If only Plum knew how to help her. Her own in-between years were filled with ponies and girl chums and parties. It was a tight-knit circle of girls from boarding school who met in the hols and played tennis, took shopping trips to York and London. Most of them were married off young – put out in the show arena as young fillies and snapped up by Gerald's dashing types. It felt like a hundred years ago . . . at the end of the war to end all wars. Poor Maddy was too young for the services and too old to fit in with the other evacuees, except Greg and Gloria.

The Conley transplants had rooted well in Huntsman's Cottage with the Battys. Gloria was shooting up into a pretty redhead and Sid was already helping out on a farm with his friend Alan from school. They'd blossomed in the fresh air like sturdy foals turning into handsome ponies.

Gloria helped out with the little ones when she was in the mood. She was company for Maddy at the weekends but their two worlds were different in so many ways. Maddy was clever and academic. Gloria was worldly-wise and rough round the edges, but she liked to run around the Brooklyn as if she owned it, and Maddy was too polite to tell her when she was disturbing her studying. Uncle Algie's old wireless was played loud with Light Entertainment music that got on Pleasance's nerves.

'When the war's over, can I stay on?' Gloria had asked Plum only the other day.

'I'm not sure. The hostel will be closed . . . You'll be eligible for a job soon,' she'd replied, not sure what to say as Gloria was almost fourteen. Once she started work, it would be time to find her permanent lodgings.

'I could get a job in Sowerthwaite . . . The Battys won't mind.'

The little minx had thought it all through. No flies on Gloria. She would make a good mother's help when her mind was on the job but she mooned over film stars and crooned over love songs not at all suitable for a girl of her age. She eyed up the boys in uniform who were home on leave, but give credit where due, she could be reliable and hardworking in the Old Vic.

Plum still watched over her with concern. It was inevitable that the first contingent of evacuees would be scattering now. How vividly she could recall seeing them on the station platform, her terror at being put in charge of such a raucous pack of puppies, and how fond of them all she'd grown, even poor Enid and lumpen Peggy, big Bryan and little Mitch. Cards came at Christmas from a few and the odd thank you letter from their parents, but nothing ever came for Gloria and Sid.

The Conleys were a mystery and no mistake, thrown onto a train, abandoned, sneaking into their carriage and clinging like limpets to Maddy. It disturbed Plum even to think of that strange collection of children. It was like being forced to rescue an abandoned litter of puppies, knowing nothing of their background or pedigree. No wonder she made so many mistakes.

You could tell a lot about a pup from the nature of the mother bitch. Pleasance had had to take back everything about Dolly Belfield's girl. Maddy was kind-hearted, clever, good with animals and a credit to her parents. Gloria was not so easy to predict, Plum sighed. Why judge Gloria on the behaviour of her mother when none of it was her fault?

Maddy had been forced to take responsibility for them when she had enough troubles of her own. Now Gloria was the only one left near her own age. Why shouldn't they be chums? Girls needed bosom pals and she thought of her school friend and fellow débutante Totty Featherstone, who'd married into some big estate near York. They'd promised to keep writing but somehow they'd lost touch. Sometimes she felt isolated. Vera Murray, the vicar's wife, was her closest confidante but Plum was always careful what she revealed about family matters.

Pleasance ruled over Brooklyn affairs, keeping a tight rein on their finances so they could keep up appearances on a very constrained budget. Maddy's school fees came out of Plum's own purse. She wished she could help Gloria more but it wouldn't be fair to pick her out from all the others.

It was something about the glint in Gloria's eager green eyes, the way she soaked up information in a desperate attempt to fit in, showing off in company, that worried her. The two girls went hiking together through the Dales, joined the local Guide troop and the church choir, all very healthy stuff – but one day soon, Plum sensed, they'd grow apart.

Plum shook herself from her daydreaming and looked at her wristwatch. Where had the last hour gone? Then she remembered the Warship Fundraising Committee in the afternoon and the minutes needed to be sorted out, and here was a line of blackout curtain linings to be pegged out.

They had strung a rope from the Victory Tree HQ at the top of the garden to the shed to get the most of the morning breeze when she heard the clang of the old doorbell on the High Street. Who was it now? Hadn't she enough to be doing?

'Go and see to it, Grace, and tell them I'm busy,' she shouted down the garden. Her hands were chapped in the cold air. It was March but it felt like November.

'It's Mr Ferris, the billeting officer, and a visitor, ma'am,' Grace waddled up the steps. 'I've put them in your parlour but I haven't had time to clear the dining room, this morning,' she puffed.

'Offer them some Camp Coffee. We've plenty of milk. I can't spare the tea ration, though. It's got to last the week. There'll be enough sugar to go round.'

This was not the day for an inspection, surely? It was going to be one of those mornings when all her plans would go out the window yet again.

Mr Ferris ducked under the low beams and held out his hand in greeting. By his side was a woman of about thirty-five with an extraordinary hat perched on the side of her head. It sprouted feathers in all directions like an Indian headdress, her hair was crimped into tight waves and her face was powdered and rouged with a slash of vermilion lipstick round her mouth like a wound. The woman smiled, narrowing her eyes. The perfume from her lapels was overpoweringly sickly.

'This is Mrs Delgado from Leeds. She would like a word in private about some relatives.'

'I am rather busy . . . I'm not sure I can help.' Plum nodded, puzzled as to why the woman was hovering like a hawk in flight.

'It's the Conleys . . . she thinks she might know them,' Mr Ferris offered, ushering the woman forward. 'I'll have to leave you, I'm afraid; another little problem up at Skally Hall.'

This was the other hostel across the river, where a bunch of toerags from Liverpool were running riot in their digs.

'I'll leave you in Mrs Belfield's capable hands. Duty calls!' With that he left promptly, and Grace brought in a pot of coffee.

'Please sit down,' Plum said, eyeing the woman carefully.

The stranger sipped the hot drink with a grimace and put it down, opened a packet of Camels and tapped them on the packet, lighting up without a by-your-leave or offering one to Plum. 'I only drink the real stuff. My hubby is American. We get rations, real coffee, chocolate, candy . . . He's in supplies.' She looked up with a grin, her eyes flashing.

There was something familiar about those eyes and that northern accent.

'How nice for you. We've not tasted ground beans for years. Now how can I help?'

'It's them two, Gloria and little Sid, we've been searching for them for years. My sister's been that demented. The little blighters got on that train by mistake. She's had the police searching. Our Marge didn't know where to turn. I'm Maggie, her twin sister. What with losing her man at sea and being in Dicky's meadow with her rent, she weren't thinking straight, wanting to join up and do her bit.'

'She's in the Forces then?' Plum asked.

'I'm not sure. She did a runner with some bloke but not before she told me what she'd gone and done with her babbies. They took a bit of finding. I got on to the police missing file. We thought they'd gone north, evacuated with a local school, but drew a blank until we traced their ration books and billeting officers. Hundreds, I've tried.'

'That was good of you.' Plum listened to this tale,

trying not to smile. 'They've been here nearly four years. What took you all so long?'

The woman didn't look up but dragged on her cigarette. She had the grace to blush.

'You know how it is – there's a war on, things get in the way. Now I'm settled, off to the States when the war ends. I've got a little lad of my own, Mikey Junior. It's only right Gloria and Sidney should be back with their own kin.'

'I take it you want to give them a home.' Plum replied, not believing what she was hearing.

'Oh, yes, Marge would want us to do that. She feels terrible what she done.'

'I should think she does after nearly four years, to abandon kids on a train with strangers. It's a matter for the Welfare Department if children should be returned to such a mother. They've settled down here in school.'

'Gloria will be fourteen soon.'

'Indeed she is,' smiled Plum. Now they were getting to the point of this visit. 'This is all a bit of a shock. I gather you'll have proof of identity.'

'Of course.' The woman ferreted in her handbag with shaking hands and brought out two birth certificates; well thumbed originals, genuine enough.

Plum examined them deliberately, not fooled by this rescuing angel act; not fooled at all. Gloria had never mentioned aunties or uncles, and certainly no twin aunt. Not that she talked about her life near Manchester at all. Sid was barely five when he arrived. Would he recognise any relatives?

'I think you'd better come back later, certainly after school. I'll have to prepare them for this news. It's all a bit unexpected,' Plum offered, but the woman shook her head.

'I'm not budging till I've seen them. I'm living in Leeds. It costs to come out here,' she whined, a flash of anger sparking in those jade eyes.

'And I'm not handing over two children to a complete stranger until I am satisfied you are who you say you are. They may not even recognise you,' Plum stood up and made for the door.

'Of course, they'll know their own.' Mrs Delgado stopped in her tracks. Her feathers twitched as she shook her head. 'Who do you think I am, a child snatcher? I've come here out of the goodness of my heart to rescue those babbies. I'm doing you all a good turn. It looks pretty crowded in here to me.' She stubbed out her cig in the hearth, showing off a neat ankle in nylon stockings and two-toned wedge-heeled shoes.

'Is that how you see yourself – as an angel of mercy? They're happy here, settled, safe from the bombing.' Plum felt her anger rise. How long was she going to keep up this charade?

'I have my rights!'

'And what might those be then? A mother throws her children on a train for whatever motive without saying goodbye or finding if they are safe—'

'I did say—'

'Yes, you did say, *Margery* Conley, and we still have the letter to prove it so we can stop this pretence right now. Auntie Maggie, my aunt Fanny! You conned your way in here with lies and half-truths. Do you expect us to just hand them over without suitable checks and safeguards? I wasn't born yesterday. I guessed just who you were the moment I saw your green eyes. Gloria has them too . . . I can't trust a woman who lies through her teeth.' It was harsh but it needed to be said.

Marge Conley burst into wails. 'I know, I know! I done wrong but I had to make it right. What I did was on the spur of the moment. I was out of my head with worry. It were wrong and I've not slept easy since, but it's all different now. I've got little Mikey and my Sergeant Delgado. He knows the score and it's fine by him. He knows I can't sail without them and it's taken ages to find them. I was scared I'd get locked up and then what good would that do? You wouldn't tell, would you?' she pleaded. She was still young, and pretty, albeit overdressed and shaking. It was hard not to feel some sympathy for her.

'They are Wards of the Court. Abandoned children can't just be released without papers, you know. It's only fair. The Courts have funded their care without any contribution from you or your family.' Plum could see she was dealing with a simple woman who acted on impulse like a cornered animal.

'I understand, but I'll make it up to them, I promise, if I can just see them and explain.'

'In due course, Mrs Delgado, when they have a chance to be prepared. They're both still young.'

'So when will that be then?' the visitor replied, gathering her bag and gloves and silver cigarette case.

'I suppose I'll have to go then. Little Mikey will need his tea. Will you tell them they've got a little brother? My neighbour's minding him.'

'Give me your address. There's no reason why you can't come back on Sunday for tea and a walk, get to know them and explain everything. This will give me a couple of days to sort out stuff. The Welfare will need your particulars.'

'I don't want no nosy parkers round my yard. We're respectable now, but if that's what must be . . .' she sighed. 'We'd better do it proper but thank you for trying to show me what's what. This is a nice little village, what I've seen of it. They'll have been comfortable here.' She was eyeing the place over, the shabby paintwork and scuffed skirting boards, the clutter of battered game boxes, the smell of vegetables stewing and a layer of ash on the old furniture.

'No, they don't live here. The two of them are lodged out with a couple.'

'I ought to be thanking them then. Where'll I find them?'

'On the Brooklyn Estate . . . The Battys will be sorry to see them go. Still, it's early days.'

'I shall have to write to them . . . What's their number?'

'We'll sort that out later, Mrs Delgado. I'm glad you understand how it must be, for the sake of the children.'

'Of course, Mrs Belfield. Silly me to think I could just turn up and take them home. You're right. Better be on my way to the station. And tell our Gloria things is looking up and I'll catch up with them soon.' The woman made for the door. 'Toodle-pip and thanks for all you've done for them.'

Plum ushered her through the doorway and pointed the way back to the station with a smile. 'See you on Sunday then? Sorry I'm rushing you but I've got dinner to prepare. They'll be tearing home for soup and sandwiches as soon as the bell rings.'

'Ta-tah for now.' Gloria's mother waved. 'I'll bring you some proper coffee next time. Them vaccies must keep you busy. Righty-oh! This is my telephone number. You can contact me at the Mason's Arms. They'll pass on a message. We rent from them in Peel Street.'

Plum watched her waddling down the Main Street, wobbling in her platforms on the cobbles, the tail feathers disappearing amongst the lunchtime shoppers. The morning had gone but thankfully Grace had quietly got on with the chores. All was not lost.

What a turn-up! You had to admire the cheek of her, trying to pass herself off as her own twin sister: crafty young blighter, in her tweed suit and fancy hat. It was the best wheeze yet. Nothing surprised Plum why some of their kids were such tearaways with parents who turned up when it suited them. The cunning lengths they went to avoid supporting their children, but Marge Conley was something else with those foxy eyes.

She'd taken a risk exposing herself here. No doubt her guilt was genuine but only when she'd come up in the world did she bother to find her kids. Plum was uncertain what to do next but it would be good for the Conleys to know they'd not been abandoned for ever.

If Marge'd turned up on her beam ends they could have offered her work here so Plum could keep an eye on her, but Plum knew that country life would never suit Marge, with her expensive tastes in nylons and coffee.

Don't be a bitch! Plum smiled to herself as she set the table for their meal. This news could wait. She still hadn't prepared the minutes and it was getting late.

Gloria was last out of the classroom, making for the girls' exit. She'd had to re-do her hemstitching 'cos miss said it was uneven. She'd had a rap on the knuckles for making marks on the material and she was fed up with school. It was dinnertime and her tummy was rumbling.

There was a woman waiting by the gate, the feathers on her fancy hat arching like cock's feathers. She was wearing a boxy swing coat and film-star shoes. There was just something about the way she was staring at her that made Gloria stop. It was as if a camera in her head snapped and a long-forgotten image surfaced, indistinct, but familiar just the same.

'Gloria!' The woman moved forward with grin. 'My . . . how you've shot up! Don't you recognise your old mam?'

The girl stepped back. 'Mam? What you doing here?' She was too shocked to think of anything else to say. Was she dreaming?

'I've come to collect you both. Don't worry, I've seen Mrs Belfield. She says it's OK . . . Where's our Sid?'

'Over there with his mate. He walked past you out of the boys' yard . . . in the cut-off trousers and balaclava. He won't know you.' The words came out as if this was everyday and normal, not this strange dream like a scene out of a film.

This wasn't right that Mam should just turn up at dinnertime after they'd not seen her for years and years. 'What're you doing here now?'

'I told you, I've come to take you home. Go and fetch the lad, there's a duck. I didn't recognise him. He's all legs.'

'I don't understand.' Gloria hesitated, unsure. Was this really happening to her? Was she, Mam, here after all these years, older, smarter, with crimson lips and painted eyes?

'I'll explain on the way to the station. Go and get your brother. We've got to rush if we're to get the half-past twelve to Leeds.'

'But we've got to get our things.' Gloria was panicking now.

'They're going to send them on by train. Hurry up, love.'

Gloria ran ahead and stopped Sid in his tracks. 'You're to come with me. You'll never guess who's turned up . . .'

Sid looked up and then at the woman waving. 'Who's she?'

'It's our mam and she's come to collect us.' Sid took one look and ran after Alan, unimpressed. Gloria had to drag him back. 'It's rude to run off. You've got to speak to her. She's come a long way to see us.'

'Why?' He looked the woman up and down as if she was a stranger.

'Don't you know your own mam? My, how you've grown too,' Mam whispered.

'You'd better shout. He's a bit deaf in that ear. He has to keep it covered,' Gloria said. So much had happened to them since Mam put them on that train. Sid was deaf and she had periods. They were country kids now.

Sid held back from the woman's hugging, rigid like cardboard. 'I told you he doesn't know you.'

'Course he does. He's the spitten of . . . I can't believe how big he's got.'

'What's she wanting?' Sid said.

'That's no way to talk to your mother,' Marge snapped.

She was not getting the rapturous welcome she'd expected, Gloria noticed. Served her bloody well right.

'Most mothers don't dump their kids on a train to fend for themselves . . . with not even a postcard to say where you were.' There it was said.

'I didn't know where you was and I have been searching. I thought I was doing the best for you both. It broke my heart to do it.'

'Well, you know where we are now. Why've you really come? If you think we're ever going back to Elijah Street . . . I know what went on there.' Gloria blushed at the thought of that time. She'd been such an innocent. Well, now she knew different. Enid had seen to that with all that name calling.

'No you don't, lady. Things is different now, I promise. I'm doing well for myself. Just follow me and I'll explain everything. Aren't you pleased I've come for you? A little late, perhaps but better than never,' Mam smiled. She smelled of roses and spice.

Gloria had to admit her mother was dressed in style and looked pretty. 'What took you so long?'

'We got blitzed in a raid and I joined up and then, well, I've got a little surprise. He's called Mikey and he's nearly two. Me and his dad are going to get wed as soon as he gets permission, but I call myself Mrs Delgado. He's a Yank so when the war's over we're all going to America, you two an' all. Won't that be exciting?'

Gloria had to admit that that was a turn-up but she tried not to show it. 'Does the Yank know about us?'

'Sort of . . . but it'll be fine. There'll be plenty of room where we're going. Arizona's near Hollywood. Just think of it – living among film stars. Sometimes I think I've died and gone to heaven. Mike's so handsome . . . look, here's his picture!'

She shoved a cracked snap of a man in uniform with bushy dark hair and a moustache, black eyes and fierce eyebrows. He looked like one of the baddies in a Western but his smile showed straight teeth.

'He looks old,' Gloria sniffed. 'What does he do?'

'He's in charge of a supply depot in Derbyshire. He drives a big truck and he can get us anything: sweets, fresh meat, tinned butter. I met him at a dance straight off the troopship. Come along or we'll miss that train.'

What were they to do? No one was there to see them off. It was not like Mrs Belfield not to wave them away – or was she just glad to see the back of them? In her heart, Gloria had always worried that the Belfields thought she was too common a friend for Maddy.

Sid wouldn't budge though. 'I'm hungry,' he said. 'Ma Batty'll have the soup on . . .'

'Then your real mam'll get you summat at the train station. Don't fuss.' Their mother was looking around them, not wanting to make a scene.

'We have to say goodbye to the Battys and Maddy.' Gloria was torn now. It was a surprise to see her real mother. How she'd longed for this moment, but it was all being rushed. On the one hand she was glad to see the back of school, but on the other all her treasures and Christmas gifts were in the cupboard at Huntsman's Cottage. What if they forgot to send them on?

Mrs Plum had taught them to say please and thank you and it was rude just to go away without saying goodbye. On the other hand, to be going to America on a ship, to play real cowboys and Indians in Hollywood was exciting. The other vaccies would be green with envy. She could send them long letters and show off her new life. She had a little brother she'd never seen and Mam was happy, anyone could see that. If it was all sorted with Mrs Plum then it must be all right.

'Come on, Sid, you'd better come with us. I'm not

going without you. Would you like to ride a horse and be a cowboy?'

'I want to be a farmer,' Sid sniffled. He'd got another of his colds coming.

'There'll be plenty of farms where we're going, young man. Home on the range for you. Hold my hand, quick, and let's skedaddle or we'll miss that train.'

Gloria took one last look across Sowerthwaite, the lush green up to the high hills. It was a fresh morning, blue sky and green fields dotted with white sheep. One thing was quite clear: they were doing the right thing. No one was bothered if they stayed or went. Better to leave now than to be chucked out later. They'd all be sorry when she was sunning it in the sunshine, but she would write to Maddy and explain.

Maddy was in school far away. She would be sad for her going. There wasn't even time to leave a note in the Victory Tree HQ, in their secret cubby-hole. Maddy would miss her and that made her feel better.

Maddy was busy with her French homework, huddled by the firelight in the drawing room among the snoring relatives, when there was a kerfuffle at the side entrance. Mr and Mrs Batty were standing in the doorway looking worried.

'Is young Mrs Belfield at home?' said Mr Batty, turning his cap round in circles.

'I'll go and get her,' Maddy replied, jumping up, glad to close her books. She raced up the stairs, two at a time, but Aunt Plum had heard the bell and her dogs bounded down alongside her, knocking past everyone in their path.

'What is it, Hilda?' she said. 'Down, Blaze!'

'Are Sid and Gloria still at the hostel?' Mr Batty asked.

'No, they should be with you . . . it's late.'

'They didn't come home for their dinner. I'd made shepherd's pie, special. I thought they'd been kept in but by four o'clock, not a sign of them . . . so I reheated it for tea. I thought the blighters had gone to Alan's farm again but Gloria should've been home for her chores.'

'Maddy, do you know anything about this?' All eyes turned on her and she was conscious of her patched eye. She shook her head. 'They must be at the hostel with Grace. Gloria sometimes helps out there.'

'I'll run down and check,' said Plum, grabbing her jacket.

'I'm coming,' Maddy said, not waiting for a reply. They piled into the old Morris, rushed down the dark drive and out onto the lane into Sowerthwaite.

At the hostel Grace Battersby was busy with the mending basket, turning collars on shirts and sewing on buttons. She looked up in surprise at the deputation on her doorstep.

'Are the Conleys here?' asked Plum.

'Gracious me, no . . . Not seen sight nor sound of them all day. Everyone's getting ready for bed and cocoa. Why?'

'Oh hell's bells! We're going to have to call the police. They really are missing. Were they in school?'

Grace shouted down John and Perry, the twins who were in Sid's class. They appeared in their pyjamas, red-cheeked, with grins.

'Was Sid in school today?' asked Plum.

'He were in this morning but not this affey . . . I saw him with the lady in the funny hat. Gloria was with him. They went for a walk, I think down town.'

'Oh goodness, that woman's gone and got them when I distinctly told her not to.' Plum went pale and sat down. 'How could I have been so stupid?'

'What woman? Not yon flighty piece that came this morning, who turned her nose up at my coffee?' said Grace. 'Was she not Welfare?'

'No, I'm afraid not. I've been such a fool. She was their mother, Margery Conley. She spun me some tale about being married to an American soldier, but did give me a name and number. I told her to come back to visit on Sunday but she went straight to school and picked them up . . . after four years silence. How could she? Poor Sid won't know her from Adam! Oh, I should have warned them at school. I never thought . . . What a mess! How could I have been so stupid? She said she was off to America and wanted to give the children a new life out there. I bet that was a pack of lies too. Stupid! Stupid me!'

Maddy had never seen Plum so upset. 'But they never said goodbye!' she cried. 'They've no clothes or anything, have they?'

'Everything is where it was this morning,' Plum replied. 'I can't believe they'd run off just like that without a word.'

'But I suppose it's just history repeating itself, dumping them without any clothes or provisions. I did see their birth certificates. There was no mistaking she was Gloria's mother, all right. I'll just have to call the police. She can't just snatch them.'

'Gloria wouldn't go if she didn't want to,' said Maddy, trying to make things better, but Aunt Plum looked frightful.

'That's true. She can be a stubborn little madam but she's easily led, and Sid wouldn't go without her. I suppose they must have hoped Margery would come for them one day but not like this, not without a single goodbye to her friends,' Plum sighed.

'She'll let me know where she is. I know she will, Aunt Plum. Their mummy wouldn't harm them, would she?'

'Of course not, darling, but I don't trust her. All this talk about going to Hollywood – Gloria's silly enough to believe it all.'

'There's nothing to be done until morning. That billeting officer will know what to do. It was him that brought her to our door. It's over to them now, I reckon,' said Mrs Battersby.

'How can I have been so trusting, so gullible? Any good sob story and I'm a sucker . . . after all these years in this job. When something seems too good to be true, it usually is. Come on, Maddy, home. We'd better drop off at the Battys and give them the bad news too.'

Maddy sat in the car in silence. After all this time, the woman who'd thrust the Conleys into her care had turned up and whisked her friend away to America.

The lucky devil! She still had a secret dream that one day her own parents would turn up at the end of the war as if they'd never been away: a great comfort to imagine on nights when the gales howled and she couldn't sleep.

It wasn't fair. Why couldn't it have been her turn too?

It was time to go, time to sign up and get out of Sowerthwaite, thought Greg as he marched up and down the square with the Home Guard, on parade for the last time, his long legs marching in time to the Silver Band. He felt daft playing at soldiers when the real war was hotting up. He'd never stayed anywhere as long as he had in the hostel but he wanted a change of sky.

It wasn't as if he didn't like his job with Brigg's Garage but there was no future there for him, not with all those sons to carry on the business. The hostel wasn't the same now that the old crowd had gone, and Maddy was busy with schoolbooks and a new horse called Monty. Any road, he was too big to be playing with schoolgirls. Greg was restless for adventure. It was time to get himself down to the barracks to sign on. He wanted to see other places than Yorkshire.

'We shall miss you, Gregory. Mr Batty will miss you, always keeping the car ready when it was needed for an ambulance.' Mrs Plum had shaken his hand when he'd gone to tell her he was leaving. There were tears in her eyes. 'I always knew you'd make good. You'll do well in the army, but promise to write to us. I'm sure Maddy will want to keep in touch too. If you're ever passing through you know there'll be a welcome at Brooklyn. Here . . .' She'd shoved some notes into his hand. 'Just a little thank you. Send us your address and we can make up parcels.'

'You shouldn't, miss,' he'd croaked, wanting to hug her but sensing he mustn't. Ladies like her didn't do such things.

Funny how this was the only place he'd ever been treated fair. Looking around him for the last time, he saw the old stone house with windows glinting in the spring sunshine, the tall avenue of trees on the long driveway and the daffs waving him off in the breeze. The days were pulling out, the sky was bright and the sheep were full of lambs. It was the nearest thing he'd ever had to a home. Not a bad place for a billet but it was time to move on.

Where he was going there'd be brick huts and concrete, barbed wire and guard houses. God only knew after that. What if he never came back?

Don't look back, he thought, trying to stride out with confidence and wink at the girls on the pavements ogling the lads. There'd be plenty of them when he got his uniform and his stripes.

He'd always hold Sowerthwaite dear in his heart. It was what they were fighting for, country towns and villages like this that were safe and wouldn't change, but who would he be when he returned? One thing was certain: when he came back to Brooklyn again it would be with his tail up. No one would ever look down on this vaccy ever again.

*

It had been a rotten day at Palgrave House School, three wet playtimes, lots of prep to do and Kay Brocklehurst on her back again. Why was there always one girl and her gang who took pleasure in sly digs at Maddy's squint, her lack of bosoms and her being top in French and Latin again?

Sometimes she hated her form so much that it made her sick to sit at her desk. They were all so cliquey and she looked different, so no one bothered with her except Elsie Fletcher, who was very plump. It was just the same at playtime and home time, jostling and shoving down the steps to the gate and the long trek to the train.

She'd no special friend since Gloria had left and she felt the loss. There were the occasional letters but not much news from Leeds. Now all the girls were giggling and ogling the grammar school boys, slouching in their cocked caps and gaberdine macs, everyone trying to look grown up and sophisticated in school uniforms. What a laugh! How could anyone look grown up wearing black stockings and a gymslip with a wide-brimmed hat in bottle-green felt? She felt like a sack of potatoes. Maddy tried to ignore the pushing but in her rush to get away through the gate she accidentally nudged Pamela Brownlaw, Kay's best friend.

'Here, you! Mind your manners, Maddy Isaiah,' shouted Kay. 'You cross-eyed stick insect, get out of our way!'

'I have as much right to the pavement as you,' she snapped back. 'And I'm not Maddy Isaiah.'

'Oh yes you are . . . one eye's higher than the other. Get it?'

Maddy tried not to let them see her distress. She was sick of these jokes at her expense so she put her nose in the air and ignored them.

'Who'd ever want to look at her twice? You're a freak,' Kay shouted as they spilled out onto the pavement.

A smart young soldier was standing on the pavement eyeing the girls coming out of school. Kay stopped and looked him up and down. 'What you staring at, Private? Looking for a girlfriend?' She nudged her friends. 'He's a bit of all right, don't you think?'

The young man stared down at her with a sneer. 'I'm not into cradle snatching, especially a foul-mouthed bitch like you . . . Hi, Maddy.'

Maddy stopped and turned, seeing Greg resplendent in his new khaki uniform.

'Oh, you've got leave at last! It's been ages . . .' He looked so grown up, tall and sophisticated.

'Just got a twenty-four-hour pass, so I thought I'd call and see everyone before I'm on my way back to York. I took a chance you'd still be here. Are this lot bothering you?' he asked.

'No more than usual but you get used to it, it doesn't matter,' she lied.

'Well, let's give them something to think about then,' he grinned. 'I've borrowed a car – no, honest, the owner knows I've got it – so hop in and I'll drive you back home.' The cluster of girls stared with amazement as he grabbed her arm and shot across the street to a little open-top roadster.

'Where did you get this? How on earth did you get petrol?' It was dark green with a belt round its engine bonnet, a real Morgan.

'A mate in the garage . . . I did a favour and sorted out his engine. Come on, I'll take you for a spin and let's give them an eyeful. Pretend you're my girl,' he laughed, kissing her on the cheek.

'I'll get a million detentions for this, if Miss Buswell sees me,' Maddy blushed, but enjoyed it just the same. Greg revved the engine up and they did a two-point turn in the road, leaving Kay Brocklehurst and her gang staring in disbelief.

That should shut her up for a week or two if I can be mysterious, Maddy smiled to herself. She waved back at them, holding on to her hat for dear life. 'Thanks,' she shouted into the wind. He'd made her feel grown up and not just a frumpy little schoolgirl. He was her friend for life now after such an act of kindness in this cold world. 'You can drop me off at the station, if you like.'

'No, back to Sowerthwaite for me too for a couple of hours. I'd like to see the old HQ for one last time. Don't know when I'll be back again.'

Everyone made such a fuss of him at the Brooklyn, plying him with buns and tea as if he was still one of the evacuees, asking about his square bashing and his new life.

Greg was like a stranger. He'd grown inches, his voice was gruff and his hair Brylcreemed. He'd grown up and away from them in the last few months. It was if a barrier had come down, separating them from each other. Maddy felt awkward and silly in her uniform. Greg was about to start a whole new adventure without her. Like Gloria he was disappearing from her life and she might never see him again. For the first time she wished she was pretty and grown up. She flushed at the thought of the peck on her cheek, given just to shock her silly school friends. That's all you got when you were fourteen, a peck on the cheek and a pat on the bottom from Old Uncle Algie. Kay was right. Who'd look twice at a cross-eyed freak?

Part Two

11

Leeds, 1945

Maddy sat up in bed and felt around the bandages, wondering when they'd come off and she could see the result of Mr Felstein's effort to straighten her left eye. It was strange sitting in darkness without the usual country noises off in the distance: lambs bleating, dogs barking and the rustle of leaves in the trees. All she could hear was Leeds traffic, mill hooters, the rattle of vehicles in the street below and that hospital smell.

They'd put off this operation for so long. Not that she thought it would do any good, and whatever the result she might still have to wear glasses, but the worst was over now.

What a strange summer it had been since D-day and the excitement that the war might be over by Christmas – but it wasn't to be.

One more year at school and then she'd be let loose on the world as a grown up. Grandma was already talking about some cookery course in the Cotswolds. Aunt Plum suggested a secretarial course, but Maddy wasn't in any hurry to decide. Everything was topsy-turvy now. She was waiting for the war to end and for life to start again.

There were only a few evacuees left in the hostel and she was too old to climb trees and do mischief with them, and since Gloria had disappeared and Greg joined up it wasn't the same. She spent her weekends hacking over the tops with Monty, helping out in the garden and trying to cheer up Grandma when she was in one of her 'slumps'.

Now she was the only one again in that rambling house. Uncle Algie had passed away suddenly. Aunt Julia was in a proper nursing home and her entourage dispersed other relatives. Uncle Gerald was still abroad and Grandma was busy ruling the roost so that all the old guests were leaving.

Their war had been an easy one compared to most – no bombs or devastation – but she still couldn't believe she'd never see Mummy and Daddy again, or Gran Mills and Uncle George. Sometimes it felt as if The Feathers and her life in Chadley had never existed, that it was all some dream. Only the smell of fish and chips brought it back and made her feel sick.

Aunt Plum was kindness itself, but inside Maddy was feeling strange stirrings of confusion now that she had messy periods. She didn't want to wear suspenders and stockings or put on a brassiere like the other girls. There was still nothing to fill it with, as the girls at school constantly reminded her. She'd grown so tall and gawky. Ballet had given her some grace to stand up straight but she was inches above the other girls at the barre.

Then there were the spots that kept popping up on her cheeks and her chin. Her dark hair was growing lank and greasy and she felt silly in plaits, but even sillier when Plum showed her how to pad it out into a Victory Roll.

Gloria was the one who had breasts and curls and a waspie waist. According to her letters she could jitterbug better than anyone else in her new job. It was such a relief when letters appeared at the Brooklyn from her friend. Gloria said things were fine and dandy and they were going to go to Hollywood once Mick Delgado was out of the army, but she was vague about her new job, her mother and poor Sid, who wasn't settling down back in the town and kept running away. She felt so sorry for them all.

There'd been one funny letter from Greg telling her about square bashing and being stuck in a hut, being put on a charge for being late and how they'd put him in the cookhouse even though he was a first-class mechanic. Poor Greg sounded fed up. Now he was somewhere in France, moving eastwards.

There was a flurry of nurses coming down the corridor, the squeak of brogues that announced the arrival of the eye surgeon on his morning rounds. Today was the day!

They fussed around her bed.

'Can you see him coming?' she asked.

'Don't be impatient. Mr Felstein will come to you in due course,' snapped Sister.

But Maddy was impatient. She'd been waiting so long to see if someone would straighten out her eye for good. She did so want to be like everyone else in school, not an object of pitying looks. She was sick of being called 'sken eyed' or 'speccy four eyes' by Kay Brocklehurst, but they'd laid off her a bit since Greg's stunt with the sports car and the public kiss. It had been an agony to be pointed at and there wasn't a name she hadn't called herself when she dared to look in the mirror.

It seemed like hours before the surgeon breezed in.

'Well, young lady, let me see my beautiful handiwork,' he laughed. 'Let's get those dressings off . . .'

'And then can I go home?' she pleaded, but the surgeon laughed again.

'Not so fast. I want to make sure there's no movement. You'll have to stay still a little longer to let things settle.' Fingers were loosening and lifting, easing off the dressing.

Maddy opened her eyes to a blur of light, feeling the pressure off her brow as she stared at the little man in the white coat.

'Will I do?' she whispered, hardly daring to breathe.

'Let me see . . . look this way . . . to my light . . . the other way to the wall. Hmm! That's better, Madeleine . . . much better. Everything's realigned nicely.'

She sank back into the pillow, hardly daring to move in case it all went wrong again.

'We must exercise the muscle but I want you still a little while longer. Be patient,' the doctor smiled, seeing her lips pout with frustration.

She was bored with sitting still but one more day

or two was better than doing it all again if it would make her normal. Aunt Plum would come on the train to visit her and Gloria knew where she was.

'There may be a slight shift, a little glide, but nothing like the last time, I promise.' With that he flounced out of the room to the next patient.

She was dying to find a mirror to look at his handiwork and see if the miracle was true – that there would be no more turn in her eye.

When her visitors arrived, for them it would be like looking at a whole person – they'd see the real Maddy Belfield at long last. She couldn't wait to see their faces. She stared at her wristwatch with despair, noting that it was hours before visiting time.

Gloria was determined to catch a bus into town to see her friend in the Eye Hospital when she finished her shift. Putting on her best skirt and blouse, borrowing her mother's duster coat with the swing back panel and a pair of real nylon stockings that she had to roll over at the top because her legs were still short, she primped in the mirror fixing her hair into a bang over her forehead.

There was no way she wanted Maddy to see her looking like a mill girl, with fluff in her hair and overalls. Nor did she want her to know they were living back to back in Hunslet up a steep hill that was a buggar to push her baby brother up in his go-chair.

She tried not to think of Brooklyn days, the green hills and gentle life they'd lived before Mam tricked them back with her lies.

The nearest they'd got to Hollywood so far was seeing Danny Kaye at the Rialto.

Every waking hour she hated living here, and Sid had run off twice as far as Skipton to be with his friend Alan. It wasn't fair, and now she would see Maddy and her old life would come flooding back.

It was all right lying in letters. She missed Maddy. They'd had such good times and no chance to say a proper goodbye. She didn't want anyone feeling sorry for her. One minute she'd been racing round Brooklyn on Maddy's bicycle, the next back on a train, with her mother promising them the earth and being as nice as pie. But it was all lies. She'd felt such a fool to have trusted her mother but with no money, no proper clothes, there was nothing she could do to get back.

How could she have believed all that guff about America? This was like living in Elijah Street, only worse somehow, because now she knew there was another world outside these mean streets.

Little Mikey was real enough, but the Yank had done a disappearing trick once he found out Marge had two more kids in tow. His letters just dried up with his money cheque, and Marge had stopped pretending she'd be a GI bride.

Mother was working in a garment factory piecing up clothes while Mikey was in a day nursery. Sid was put in school and Gloria'd been given a job slopping out in a woollen mill canteen. Sometimes she felt so angry inside she thought she would burst.

Mam just wanted her wage packet and a free baby-sitter for Mikey, and half the street seemed to think she'd sit for their kids too. If only she could tell her friend Maddy the truth – but she'd told too many lies in her letters about her wonderful life in Leeds. Better to lie than to be pitied.

She walked into town to save the bus fare and in her pocket was a pair of real nylons as a present for her friend, nicked from her mother's dressing-table drawer. They were payment for all the hours she'd sat amusing her brothers.

As she walked over the bridge, making for the Headrow, the wind beating her face, she smiled, thinking about the tree house HQ in the Victory Tree. Those hikes into the Dales with Greg and the gang carrying her on piggyback, trying to jog on Monty's back, the parties at Brooklyn Hall and the good times with Mrs Plum. It was all in another world. Coming to Hunslet was hate at first sight.

Sowerthwaite was another life all together, a softer way of living, where people were polite and spoke in gentle tones and wore smart, freshly ironed clothes, sipping their drinks, not ramming them down their throats. They ate with forks and knives, not picking chips with greasy fingers and slurping tea. Even their swear words were easy on the ear.

If only she'd not been so gullible last year as to believe her mam's promises, but they'd been too young to say no to a grown-up. It was obvious that everyone was glad to see the back of another vaccy family, off the books and out of their hair. She knew now that Conleys were common and looked down upon for being townies. When she'd tried to be ladylike at the table, remembering the manners she'd learned from the Belfields, Mam just laughed at her and told her not to be so lah-di-dah.

The Hollywood ruse was just the Yank's excuse to get Mam's pants on the floor. They'd all heard the joke about 'Utility knickers: one Yank and they were off!' Now there was yet another child to feed and Gloria felt trapped. Going to the pictures twice a week was no substitute for country life, and the food shortages meant queuing for everything they once took for granted in the country.

There was a queue waiting for visiting hours at the hospital. She'd left a note on the table telling Sid to go next door till Mam came home. There'd be a row when she got back and there was no tea on the table, but this time she was doing something for herself and it felt good. Mam could look after her own kids for once.

The bell rang and she walked down the corridor, wondering if Maddy would recognise her all grown up. She opened the door of the private room slowly and there was a roar of pleasure that made up for everything.

'Gloria! Gloria! You came . . . you look so glam!' Maddy's arms reached out to her. 'Sit down, sit down . . . I'm so glad you came.'

'Try and stop me . . . Wow, you look so different. Your eye is straight!' she peered at Maddy's grey eyes, which were blinking with excitement. She'd never noticed how thick those lashes were and how long, as they were usually hidden behind thick glasses. Maddy was sitting in striped pyjamas, with bunches either side of her head like a schoolgirl. 'How are things back home?' Gloria asked.

'Just the same. Plum and Grandma are at each other's throats. Uncle Gerald's in Germany now. Isn't it exciting – the war will soon be over!'

'Have you heard from Greg Byrne?'

'Auntie P got a letter. He's somewhere in Europe, fixing lorries, I expect. You know what he's like if there's any wheels to fix. I can't imagine him in uniform taking orders.'

'I can. He'd look good, don't you think? Have *you* got a boyfriend?'

Maddy blushed. 'I'm still stuck in a girls' school – where on earth would I meet a boy worth talking to?'

'I've had three since I came back, but they're not up to much. But I've had my first kiss and fumble,' Gloria lied, wanting to seem sophisticated and experienced.

'Gloria Conley!' Maddy whispered. 'You're far too young for boys.'

'You're never too young to get experience but I don't want to end up like my mam. I want to choose a good one who'll take care of me good and proper.'

'How's your job?' Maddy changed the subject.

'Which one, serving in the canteen or baby-sitting all hours down the street? I should open a nursery,' Gloria smiled, trying to make a joke of it all. But when she saw Maddy looking so young and carefree, she just crumpled with the unfairness of it all.

'You always were good with kiddies, not like me,' said Maddy, trying to be kind.

'When do you leave school then?' Gloria said, composing herself.

'Next year, all being well,' came the reply. No dirty canteens for Miss Belfield, she thought. Maddy didn't have a clue about real life.

'And then what?'

'Secretarial college, I hope. I'm not going to finishing school.'

'In London?'

'No, in Leeds. I don't want to go far away from home.'

But I'd love to be a million miles away from mine, thought Gloria, though she said nothing. 'Goody, we can be pals again here if I can stick it out long enough . . . It's horrible!' To her embarrassment Gloria found herself weeping real tears onto the bed clothes.

'What on earth's upset you? Is it something I said?' said Maddy holding her hand.

'I hate it here. After the Brooklyn . . . why did it have to all change? It was the best thing living there. I miss it so much. I'll never forget what you did.'

'Oh, don't get upset. You could always come back, you know,' Maddy suggested.

'And stay with you?'

'Well, no, but I'm sure Aunt Plum could find you a job. There are loads of ladies who might need a mother's help or something,' she offered.

'Do you think so? I'd never thought of that.' Gloria felt a surge of hope.

'Stay where you are, get a good reference and I'll ask Aunt Plum if she can help.'

‘You’re an angel. Then we could go out together like old times!’

‘Hang on, I’ve got exams to do and then I’ll be studying in Leeds, but it’s worth a try. You know the area. I’m sure someone will want you. Here, blow your nose.’

Maddy looked embarrassed, offering her a pretty lace hanky, and Gloria remembered the nylons.

‘I brought you these,’ she smiled, holding them out.

‘Gosh! Real ones. I’m still in ankle socks. Grandma says I’m too young for stockings and Plum says I’m not.’

‘Rubbish. I’m a bit younger than you and I wear them. It’s about time you glammed up a bit, new eyes and a new hairstyle, I say,’ Gloria added, sizing up the girl in the bed with a critical eye.

‘Do you really think so?’

‘We’ll be the sirens of Sowerthwaite, you and me,’ Gloria laughed, feeling suddenly like there was hope of a return to Brooklyn in sight.

‘But I’ll still have to wear glasses for things,’ Maddy sighed.

‘Not all the time, and you won’t look like Long John Silver any more, will you? I think you should get rid of those bunches, for a start. Have you got any scissors?’

‘In the drawer, but Granny will have a blue fit. It’s taken years to grow them, my hair is so curly.’

Gloria rooted in the bedside drawer and pulled out a pretty pink leather case with nail files, buffers and silver scissors. She combed out the tangled bunches and Maddy squealed at the lugs and tugs. 'I see what you mean about the length, but let's give you a bang at the front across your forehead like me.'

Before she could protest, Gloria snipped a fringe from the front hair and released the rest on either side. 'There, that's better!'

Maddy looked in the cabinet mirror. 'Oh, what've you done?'

'Made you look your age, that's what, Madeleine Belfield. The rest is up to you . . . forever friends, remember? You will ask Mrs Plum, won't you? I'll do anything.'

'Leave it to me, and do come again. If I've gone home you know where to find me. I've got your address. I promise we'll find you something, and let's write to Greg and tell him all about it. We can send him a parcel and some photographs of my new eye.'

'You're on, Maddy, and thanks.'

Gloria skipped down the dark streets with a broad smile across her face. One day soon she'd be on that train to Sowerthwaite and nothing would induce her back again. She was going home!

Greg sometimes wondered about the wisdom of the British Army in placing a perfectly able mechanic into a canteen. If an army marched on its stomach then heaven help anyone who trusted their strength to his feeble efforts at serving decent grub. No one took a blind bit of notice of his skills, only where the vacancies were.

Everything about this institution was about churning

men out in sausage machine regularity, ignoring their civilian aptitudes in favour of square pegs into round holes. He was better trained than most in institutional living and quite enjoyed his square bashing weeks: the marching parades, drums banging, kit inspections, the lads acting daft in the huts but before he knew what had hit him, he was ricocheting over the Channel onto Sword Beach in an old Bedford Truck.

'Keep yer head down when you get up there,' yelled the sergeant, pointing out a hill ahead. At least he was driving the canteen, and mounted up the ramp in a swift manoeuvre at the first attempt, and kept the show on the road, driving past lines of soldiers, military police and sullen natives. There were guns and artillery ahead. The convoy snaked round the high hedges, unsure of what lay waiting to ambush them.

When his truck died, everyone started hurling abuse at him as if he'd sabotaged it on purpose. 'Get that bleedin' thing off the road!' He bumped it over tussocky grass, terrified that there were mines in the grass sewn as thick as thistles. This was the moment that Greg's war began in earnest.

Someone brought out the petrol stove and tea was brewed – business as usual. It was a fractured petrol pipe that had done the damage but no one had a spare. The truck was going nowhere and neither were they, canteen or not, so all they could do was dig a slit trench and get stuck in for the night.

Enemy aircraft were flying low and Greg decided to try out his firing skill, aiming his gun high, pretending he was out with Mr Batty doing a bit of poaching.

When someone was out to get you there was an edge to the firing off like no other, he thought.

The rest of the night passed without incident and the truck was patched up when he went on a recce to filch a pipe from another abandoned truck. Only it wasn't as empty as he'd thought when he fell over the leg and the boot lying on the ground. He felt sick at the sight of what remained of the poor driver.

Once back on the road they trundled through the Bocage of Normandy, a slow tortuous route, when a sudden burst of sniper fire came from nowhere. Greg grabbed the nearest soldier and threw him into the ditch for safety so that they landed in a heap. The bullets rattled where they'd just been having a quiet fag, ripping through the truck side. Another bloody repair job to do!

The stink in the ditch was awful. They'd landed in a trench that had been used as a latrine and their uniforms were covered in shit!

'I owe you one,' said the broad-shouldered bloke with a stripe on his arm in a broad Yorkshire voice. 'But couldn't you have found a better hole, Byrne?'

That's how he and Corporal Charlie Afton became 'shit' brothers. It was good to have a guy on your side, who led from the front, fearless under fire and with a tyke's common sense not to court danger.

In the long trek over Europe somehow they kept in touch. From Jerusalem Corner, through Caen, Greg was filched for repair jobs and made a corporal. From Belgium into Holland, all those terrible campaigns that Greg would never forget – Gennep, Nijmegen, Grave, clearing the country between Maas and the Rhine – he and Charlie looked out for each other in billets and lofts, hay barns, fishing on lakes and birdwatching by rivers. Charlie was a good mate and no one survived long without a good mate.

Greg's canteen days were long gone when they realised what a whiz he was with broken axels, pumps and gearboxes. He had a knack of sniffing out spare parts in the most unlikely places. When he became a sergeant he began training up lads of his own to grovel under lorries and trucks, foraging for spares.

The only thing that separated the band of brothers was girls. They'd been initiated into the joys of *Maisons de tolérance* in Normandy. Standing in line down some backstreet, waiting for a turn to relieve their manhoods, was a farce.

Greg had faltered behind the door for a second on that first visit. This was not how he'd imagined it would be. It was all so rushed and perfunctory. 'Next,' shouted someone, shoving him forward. Whoever called this joyless plunge into a lifeless body a relief?

A sour-smelling woman stood before him looking bored. She was old enough to be his mother, with a sullen painted face, her empty eyes searing into him with contempt, and he felt a flush of shame and anxiety. After two more evenings of this he didn't bother again but sought out younger girls, grateful for a meal and a share of home rations. With his good looks and charm he found himself popular, and he and Charlie made a good double act, but Greg was cautious with his favours.

It was a matter of pride to get that first shot at sex over with just in case your number was up. Charlie, on the other hand, couldn't get enough of it – until he found couldn't pee, and ended up having treatment that made him more wary. Greg tried not to be smug.

'You're such a prude, Byrnie,' Charlie laughed. 'What a waste. If only I had your looks. I don't understand you. Even the local girls fall at your feet.'

Sometimes, though, he just couldn't look those starving girls in the eye. Hadn't they got brothers and mothers who were shamed by their desperate acts? He thought of Mrs Plum and Maddy and Gloria. How would he feel if they had had to do this to survive? He felt ashamed of taking advantage of them, but war was war and who knew when his end might come? He gave them what he could spare from his rations.

Later, when they were billeted near Hanover with a family, there was Marthe, a pretty blonde daughter of the house who threw herself at both of them in exchange for cigarettes, sweets, anything to sell on.

Charlie surrendered to Marthe's slender, starved body and long blonde plaits, but Greg was hesitant when she pressed her friends to accompany him. He made excuses to avoid her after that. He couldn't help his distaste. He kept thinking of Maddy and Gloria. If things had been different . . . He found himself distant, ignoring their charms and preferring to go fishing with a borrowed rod in the Steinhuder Meer. He once caught a two-pound perch, much to the family's delight.

Now and again there would be a bunch of letters waiting for him, a parcel from Mrs Plum with news of the girls. He'd been a chit of boy when he enlisted and now he felt like an old man. That part of his life he sealed away in a cigarette tin, close to his breast pocket, a world where there were proper roads and trees still standing, no mud, and girls with pigtails smiling from photo booths in school uniform, letters written in round childish handwriting. Good clean girls to come home to, virgins, not prostitutes.

He'd seen the worst and best in human kind. Sometime he woke with the faces of dead comrades before him, their eyes staring blank and despairing. He'd see stick-thin children with sunken eyes, and peasants lying bloated in ditches, covered in flies. War was a terrible thing and it haunted his dreams.

When the time came to be demobbed into civvy street where would he go? Perhaps he might stay in the army and retrain, but it was Charlie who was full of plans.

'When they let out us out of this madhouse you're coming home with me. You're too good a mechanic to let loose on our competitors.' Charlie's family owned a string of garages around Yorkshire. 'Besides, my mother will love you. I've told her you saved my life and don't drink much or smoke, and don't go with German girls; a paragon of virtue. She'll have you preaching in the chapel pulpit in no time! Don't forget . . . I owe you.'

The thought of going home scared him but perhaps Charlie would show him how to enjoy life again. The war seemed to bounce off him like water off slate. They'd paid their dues and now Greg wanted to be successful and make a life for himself as he'd always promised. He'd been spared for a purpose, given a second crack at life, and he wanted to be more than a garage mechanic.

Being an orphan and evacuee had taught him that you were nobody without money, connections and a half-decent family. He was not going to be put down ever again. He was going to live by his own rules. Move over world, he smiled, Gregory Byrne is going to make his mark, make a fortune and find his princess!

12

'Who's that dreamboat in the flannels? You could cut your bread on those creases,' whispered Gloria to Maddy. It was a Saturday afternoon in the summer of 1947, a scorcher of a day after the coldest harshest winter on record, and the Sowerthwaite Youth Club was playing rounders on the Fellings recreation ground.

'Crikey! It's him, the Jerry, the vicar's guest, the one there's been so much fuss about,' she added, pleased to be back on home ground with her old school friends from St Peter's. Mrs Plum, true to her word, had found her a job as a mother's help and it was her afternoon off.

'What fuss?' Maddy was the last to hear the gossip as usual.

'My dad says it's not right having one of them staying here,' said Beryl from the post office.

'But the war's over ages ago . . . we can fraternise now.' Maddy turned round to answer.

'Not for my dad it ain't. You saw what them Japs did to our Frank,' argued Beryl, folding her arms in protest.

'But the boy looks too young for a soldier.' Maddy eyed the young man with caution, taking in his brown hair, his height. He looked quite ordinary. She recalled how Aunt Plum had fought the vicar's corner when he offered to guest a German refugee, an exchange as an experiment with a view to there being further contact later on. She'd been too busy studying to take much notice but there were some facts at her fingertips.

'His name is Dieter Schulte. He's a theology student so he isn't a soldier. His parents died in the bombing of Dresden. He—'

'Trust her ladyship to know so much about him,' snapped Beryl, unimpressed.

'I don't. It's just there's been a lot of discussion about his visit in the local paper,' Maddy replied.

'I don't think he's much to look at, is he, Gloria?' Beryl ignored her.

Gloria shrugged. 'What do you think?'

'I don't think anything,' Maddy blushed, not wanting to make matters worse for the poor lad, who could sense they were all staring at him. 'But the war's over so we've got to make friends sometime or another.'

'Pity about the glasses with no rims on them; perhaps he couldn't afford any,' said Gloria. 'I've not seen any like that before. He's tall but his jacket's too small in the arms. I bet they put him in second-hand clothes. The Master Race doesn't look so masterful now.'

'There was a right ruckus in the church council about him coming,' said Beryl. 'My dad says charity begins at home and there's many a town kiddy who needs a good holiday in the country, never mind giving Jerries any favours.'

'I don't think it's like that. He's being sponsored by the Church in a gesture of reconciliation,' Maddy added, but that only made matters worse.

'Where do you think up such big words, Maddy?' Gloria laughed and then gasped. 'Hell's bells, she's got run out. Your turn, Beryl.' The line-up shuffled forward.

Since Gloria's return there was no living with her. She'd joined the new youth club and was eyeing up all the local boys as potential boyfriends. She even wrote to Gregory and his friends and asked for photos. Gloria was brazen.

Maddy had been restless in her last term at school. There was a whole new world outside the school gate and she'd wanted to get away from desks and school uniforms.

Grandma had sniffed and snorted, 'What a waste a university education would be on a girl of your class. Once you're out, you'll be getting married.'

'I don't want a season!'

'And why not?'

'I want to be useful, find a job, earn my keep and see the world.'

'You're very sure of yourself all of a sudden. Is this all your doing, Plum?' Grandma turned to see Plum shrugging her shoulders.

'Nothing to do with me. I'd have liked to see her at Oxford, but Maddy's mind's made up.'

'Since when did girls have any say in their futures?

I don't know what this world is coming to. Are there no standards left?'

'There's more to life than parties and frocks, Granny. I promise I'll work hard and make you proud, and I won't go far away. I just don't want to stay on after my exams . . . Please . . .'

Gran had huffed and puffed but given in to her pleas. From then there would be no more excruciating sports days and end-of-term concerts, just long weeks of summer hols.

Uncle Gerry was due home for good and everything was returning to normal at long last; soldiers returning in their striped demob suits and silly hats. The field batteries were dismantled, air-raid shelters now turned into pig arks and chicken coops.

With her eye straighter than ever before, Maddy felt normal, if not still too tall, towering in her pleated shorts and pumps as they watched their team getting thrashed by the lot from Beamerly St George.

Yet out of the corner of her eye she watched the stranger trying to make sense of play, trying to meld into the background, aware all eyes were on him. How would she feel if it was the other way round? Embarrassed, awkward in the glare of curiosity – she knew what it was like to be different and called names.

'Why don't we ask him to play on our side?' she whispered to Gloria. 'It's mixed match.'

'Don't be daft. Who wants a Jerry on their team?' came the reply.

'He can have my place. I'm hopeless,' Maddy offered,

knowing she'd be out first ball. Hand and eye coordination was never her strong point.

'He's wearing glasses, for goodness' sake. What use will he be?'

'I wear glasses only for distance now.'

'Exactly,' Gloria sniffed. Only a friend spoke the truth like that and no offence was taken. Gloria had taken to speaking as she found since her return. There was a hard edge to her scorn sometimes. 'I bet he's useless.'

'Bet he's not. Germans are supposed to be good at games,' Maddy snapped back. 'What've we got to lose, anyway?

'Bet ya?'

'How much?'

'That lipstick you had on last night.' Aunt Plum had given Maddy 'Cherry Glow' to wear, but she thought she just looked silly.

'Done!' They slapped hands like farmers over a market deal.

Gloria turned back to the match. 'You'll have to ask him. I'm not going near him.'

Maddy edged out of the line, sidled over to the boundary where Dieter was standing with the vicar's wife, Mrs Murray.

'Ah, Madeleine, come and meet Dieter, our student.'

'Hello,' she replied, looking him straight in the face. 'We wondered if you'd like to play. You can have my bat,' she smiled, staring into the bluest eyes she'd ever seen.

His cheeks were pink and his neck red as he bowed,

and for a second she thought he was going to click heels like the Nazis did in the films.

'*Danke* . . . thank you, I am delighted,' he smiled. He was really good-looking behind those stern glasses. Taking off his tweed jacket, he rolled up his sleeves. His arms were tanned to a nut brown and the fair hairs stood up against the dark skin. He looked very muscled for a theology student. He walked with her to the back of the queue while she explained what he must do to stay in the game when his turn came round.

He towered over the other members of the team but not over her. Everyone turned to look him over with interest.

'That was a kind gesture, dear,' said Vera Murray when she returned. 'Poor Dieter must be getting a little tired of our ancient company. He's been working on farms. His English is good. It puts our feeble German to shame and he is so polite.'

Maddy prayed he'd not be shown up when the Beamerley team sussed out his background. They would show him no mercy. She felt mean now betting Plum's present away.

Gloria did her usual harum-scarum dash and got run out. Beryl was caught. Derek Brigg from the garage got a rounder but they were three behind and in for a thrashing. Then it was Dieter's turn. He carefully took off his spectacles and put them in his pocket, stood four square and, after the first miss, he whacked everything they threw at him.

Gloria whistled in amazement.

'Run, you daft bugger!' the lads screamed from the

sidelines. He tore round at breakneck speed and scored another rounder. Then he missed and was nearly out. The next ball he whacked into the trees.

'Bloody hell! Where did he learn to hit like that?' Another rounder, and another. The last one he pitched too high and was caught out – but they had drawn the match.

'Not bad for a Kraut!' was the verdict, and Maddy nudged Gloria with relief. Her new lipstick was safe.

'Here, you,' yelled Gloria. 'How come you can play rounders so well?'

'I play baseball with Americans. It's the same, *ja*?' Gloria was looking up at him, flashing her green eyes. He was the enemy no more.

'Thank you, Miss Madeleine. It is good to stretch legs. I enjoy very much,' he turned to give her a warm smile and her heart took a funny leap, a fluttery jump when she looked up. A boy who towered over her was a novelty, especially a boy with periwinkle-blue eyes and streaked brown hair. He handed her the bat and bowed again; this boy had nice manners too. There weren't many of them in Sowerthwaite.

When they went into the church hall for tea and biscuits, she sensed his eyes burning into her back. He was watching her and she felt hot iron tongues snaking up her cardigan. For the first time in her young life she knew she was being stared at not for being an oddity but with admiration, interest and gratitude.

Suddenly the room went fuzzy round the edges and she wished she could walk right up to him and find out more about his life. An inner voice told her not to be so public, not in front of Gloria and the girls. They wouldn't understand. They would tease her and take it the wrong way, make fun of them both and she couldn't bear that to happen.

Somehow she had rescued him, made him a hero and saved the match. That was enough for now, but her gesture had not gone unnoticed and Vera Murray was quick to seize the moment, bringing the boy round to the Brooklyn to meet the Belfields.

That was when Maddy found out he was going to be a student at Thubingen University on a special scholarship. His father was a Lutheran minister, a friend of the martyred pastor Dietrich Bonhoeffer, who had been hanged in Flossenbürg Concentration Camp for preaching against Hitler's regime.

The Russians were in Dresden now, and it was not easy for Dieter to return to the East to see what remained of his family. Vera was fishing for him to be included in some of the summer activities. 'We want him to meet lots of young folk while he is here.'

There was already talk of exchange visits between English churches and German youth groups.

Pleasance looked him up and down, knowing there were rules about non-fraternisation, but said nothing. Dieter endured this scrutiny, sitting, observing the drawing room, the furniture, the pictures, putting a brave face on his circumstances.

Somehow they were equals now, thought Maddy, having suffered the same injustices, woundings and sadnesses, both survivors and victims. When she heard his story she felt no animosity or anger, just sadness that his family, like hers, had been devastated by war.

She met him again in St Peter's the following Sunday, where he endured yet more sideways glances. Dieter was not film-star handsome but there was something about him that took her eye. She sensed he was serious about his studies and a gentle giant. They were used to prisoners of war in their ugly uniforms, digging roads, hay timing in the fields, marching or lounging on the backs of lorries. They were defeated men but cheerful. Some were crude and common, like any rough soldiers, but Dieter was different, his body taut from farm work, his long limbs tanned in borrowed shorts. She'd never really studied a man's body before and it made her go all hot.

When he entered a room her heart did a secret dance.

She took extra care to pin up her hair into soft curls, stopped putting it in bunches with ribbons. She scrubbed herself down, splashed on eau-de-Cologne and tried on her new lipstick. Going to church was now an appearance, not a chore. There was the annual harvest homecoming soon and Maddy prayed Dieter would still be around to enjoy the fun.

Gloria was too wrapped up in her new job as mother's help to Dr Gunn and his raucous family to notice this change of mood. They'd sent a letter to Greg but Maddy made no mention of the new visitor. Greg might think them silly to be entertaining the enemy in the Brooklyn. She couldn't share the feelings that bubbled inside her like fizzy pop with anyone.

Sometimes she sat in the window box of the study

with a copy of John Donne's poems. He was her favourite of the moment and so romantic.

I wonder by my troth, what thou, and I
Did, till we lov'd? were we not wean'd till then,

Shakespeare, in the Sonnets, and Emily Brontë knew what she was feeling. All that boring school stuff was coming alive.

Any excuse and she found herself calling in at The Vicarage to catch a glimpse of him, and once on the way back from riding Monty they met by chance – or was it?

They both halted, smiling, blushing and trying to act normal; as if nothing stupendous was happening to both of them.

Maddy dismounted and they sat on the stone wall looking over the fields.

'It is so beautiful here, very peaceful, no smoke, no bomb-bings. You had no war here, I think?' he sighed.

Maddy shook her head. It was important he didn't think it was all easy. 'My family was bombed,' she attempted to explain in her schoolgirl German. 'Grandmother and uncle killed. My mother and father drowned in a ship. I have no family. The war brought me here to safety.'

Dieter turned to her. 'It is terrible. Why did it happen for us?'

She shook her head. What was there to say? 'It happened, but it mustn't happen again, Mr Schulte.'

'You are very kind to me, Madeleine. Please, call me

Dieter.' She loved the way he pronounced her name. It sounded so exotic.

'Call me Maddy. You would have done the same for me.'

'I'm not sure. Things are bad when you lose a war – no hope, no food, no money. People are angry and do not understand why it comes this way for us again.'

'You got too big for your boots,' she replied, and he looked at her puzzled for a second and then laughed.

'Ah, yes, I understand. We wanted everyone else's boots but they wouldn't let us have them so we tried to grab them and now they push us away and take our boots and now there are no boots for anyone.'

That wasn't quite what she'd meant. 'Let's not think about that. It's over. It will get better.'

'Memories are long, Maddy. It will take many years for our people to be friends again, many years,' he said, taking off his glasses and polishing the lenses with care. 'Are you going to the dance tonight? I have nothing to wear for a ball.'

'Oh, it's not that sort of dancing,' she smiled. 'It's a barn dance – country dances in circles and groups. You have to walk around and follow the caller,' she explained.

'The caller?' Dieter pushed up his glasses. 'How do I call?'

'No, he calls out what to do and you do it to music. I'll show you how. Take your partners and bow.' She mimicked doing a gentleman's bow. 'Take my hand . . .' She marched him up and down the grass but he had two left feet.

'Ah, follow my leader! I don't think I am good at that,' he said.

'Wait and see. It's fun, and you can dance with all the girls, one by one.'

'There is only one girl I am dancing with,' he whispered.

'Who's that?' She crinkled her face, knowing full well who he meant. Her heart was pounding as they drew closer and then drew back. 'You must see how the natives play. All the girls will want to dance with you.'

'Not your friend. She does not like when I talk to you,' he said.

'Who? Gloria? Take no notice of her. She can be very pig-headed.'

'Why pig's head?'

'Stupid, no brains . . . like a pig.'

'But pigs are very intelligent animals. I like pigs,' he argued.

'Dieter, you are too serious. It's a joke, just a saying . . . Gloria and I are always calling each other funny names. I'll see you tomorrow then?'

'If you think I will be welcome, yes, tomorrow. I shall be looking forward to dancing with you.' He helped her onto the horse and stood watching her, waving as she trotted down the lane.

Maddy rode upright, flushed with his words and hoping she looked good from the back on a horse. Tomorrow she had a date with Dieter and she didn't care who was watching.

*

It was the usual Sowerthwaite harvest hop: bare wooden floors, tables stacked with paste sandwiches, scones and fancy buns. The fiddler, pianist and drummer were at one end of the hall, and the caller, Fred Potts – in his checked shirtsleeves with fag in his mouth – was gathering sets together for the first dance. They had put straw bales for benches and strung paper lanterns across the beams, flowers on the windowsills softening the smoky fug in the church hall.

There were the usual suspects standing outside smoking, eyeing the girls as they went inside: lads in flannels and open shirts. The girls were in ankle socks and best dirndl skirts with faded lines in the creases where the hems had been let down.

The vicar and his wife put in an appearance for form's sake, and Aunt Plum. Gloria was swanking in a pretty cotton gingham dress made from curtain material, lent to her by Mrs Gunn.

Maddy had agonised what to wear. She'd got so used to wearing slacks, but there was a pleated skirt and fresh blouse that would have to do since she had no coupons for anything frivolous. She put a petticoat under her skirt so that her modesty was intact when they swirled about on the dancefloor. She wanted to look her best.

She'd arrived too early and helped Plum set out the room, watching the door in case Dieter came, but as the dancing began to hot up there was no sign of him and she felt first dismay and then anger at being let down. She sat with Gloria and the girls, feeling fed up, knowing the evening was going to be a flop.

She was trying not to feel bothered. He was only a German student, a stranger. What future was there in that? He had made the decision for them and copped out of this appearance. Perhaps it was for the best. Better to stick to her own kind, the sort of public schoolboys who were sons of Plum's friends, who came and went each holiday – but none of them had ever made her tremble like Dieter did when he smiled at her.

There was something in his sadness and quiet presence that touched her. He was strong yet gentle. He had picked her out. Why had he said she was the only one he'd dance with if he'd not intended to come? Why had he stayed away? She felt sick with disappointment. Was she too tall? Was her eye turning again?

Gloria was rattling on by her side but she didn't listen, her eyes glued to the door just in case . . .

At suppertime, Maddy could stand it no longer and sidled up to Vera Murray as calmly as she could.

'I thought your student would want to see us English at our playtime,' she offered.

Vera turned from the tea urn with concern. 'Oh, I should have said earlier, our student has had bad news in a letter from home. His sister, Mechtilde, is sick and now he wants to go home but his aunt says he must stay in the West. He didn't feel like dancing or mixing tonight.'

'I'm sorry. Would it help if I go and visit him?' Maddy offered, ashamed that relief was her first thought, relief that it was nothing to do with her.

'Would you? We had to come over tonight but Archie

will keep him company later. His sister has never been strong. She lives near Dresden. Things are not easy there. I think he feels guilty that he was singled out for this visit.'

'I'll go at once, Mrs Murray.' Maddy plonked her supper down and made for the door.

It was Gloria who came after her. 'Where are you off to now? You've not had a dance all night.'

'Won't be long, gone to see a man about a dog,' she blurted, and darted out of the door on her errand of mercy.

She felt nervous but grown up as she walked up to The Vicarage drive on this mission of mercy. It was an old farmhouse with a stone porch and the drive was lined with purple asters and Michaelmas daisies bobbing in the breeze. They had escaped the first frosts of autumn. There was a nip to the night air – which the locals called 'backendish' – but it was still light enough to go for a walk It had been a rotten summer for weather and the lambing had gone badly but the thought that this summer was coming to an end startled her. Dieter would soon be gone and they hardly knew each other yet.

He was sitting at the piano, fingering notes and looked up with a half-smile when she tapped on the window.

'Mrs Murray told me you'd had a letter . . . Would you like some company? We could go for a walk and you can tell me if you like,' she said. He nodded, grabbed his pullover and made for the door.

Dieter was very quiet at first. She walked him up the Avenue of Fallen Soldiers, explaining about Uncle

Julian and her father and the men of the town lost in battle. They crossed the footpath across the field and took the track to the old beech tree. Dieter seemed lost in his own world.

'Come and meet my tree . . . our Victory Tree, but not over you. Over Napoleon, I'm told. Look, the ladder's still there. This is where I come to think, to chew the cud,' she said, pointing to the platform on the branches of the tree.

Dieter turned round at this expression, puzzled, so she mooed and pretended to be a cow munching its grass. His eyebrow raised and he laughed.

'Let's climb up out of sight.' She knew it would be dark and the lights of the hostel were off as everyone was at the hop.

Dieter sat with his knees bent. 'I am so worried now. Tilde is my youngest sister, her chest is bad and now there are few hospitals and medicine. My uncle is not a wealthy man. They took us in after my father was taken. I should be looking after her but I am stuck here.'

'When does college start?' she asked, not knowing what else to say.

'October . . . I must go home. I must do work for medicine. I should not have come but I was curious. It was selfish but I wanted to see real British people. We saw soldiers, of course – some good and bad, some angry and some merciful. War makes animals of us all, I am thinking. There are no real heroes but here I find only kindness and friendship.'

'She'll get better, you'll see. In the next letter you

will have good news,' Maddy offered, more in hope than certainty. Through the gap over the wall she saw the lights of town twinkling. 'You know, it's strange to see lights on. We got so used to pitch-darkness and just the stars. I used to sit here dangling my legs, waiting for Mummy and Daddy to return but it never happened. Tilde will get better. I just know it.'

'I have met no girl like you, so kind and pretty. Why do you not have a boyfriend?'

'I have lots of boyfriends. Gloria and me, we write to Greg, who's in the army, and his friend Charlie sometimes.'

'No special one, no sweetheart,' he whispered.

Maddy laughed. 'When you have a bad squint and stand six inches over a boy, no one wants you to be their sweetheart. Now my eye is straight I don't care for any of them,' she replied.

'But you are beautiful and you are growing a kind heart,' he replied. 'My father used to say that a loving spirit is the greatest beauty of all.'

Maddy could hardly breathe. 'He must have been a good man.'

'Yes, he was. But now I must ask your permission to kiss you, but perhaps I go too far?'

'I don't mind,' she whispered.

'You don't? I've never kissed a girl before.'

'And I've never kissed a boy except when they were babies.'

They kissed with lips shut, chaste, firmly but dry. He tasted warm and salty, with a hint of tobacco and fresh soap. She sat in his arms, looking up at the stars.

My first kiss, she sighed, and from a German boy. Who'd've thowt it, as Beryl would say.

Then caution hit her, splashing over her like cold water. What would the Murrays think of her, taking advantage of him? Plum would be furious. No one would understand this magnetic pull towards him.

'We have to keep this secret,' she said, sitting up straight. 'I don't think anyone will understand how it is for us.'

'Like Romeo and Juliet?' he smiled.

'Oh, don't say that!' She pulled away. 'That's a sad play. We're not sworn enemies, are we? I shall tell no one yet. We can write to each other when you go home and perhaps I come and visit you one day.' Her mind was racing ahead already. Her first proper boyfriend, her first kiss all in one evening. How wonderful to be loved and needed.

'When can we walk again?' Dieter grasped her hand tightly.

'Tomorrow, down the bridle way. I'll walk the dogs and I know a quiet path down to the foss, the waterfall. I'm free until I go to college. Tomorrow I'm going shopping with Aunt Plum. She's promised to buy me something new with her own coupons.'

'You are lucky. My sister wears only rags, I fear, but I must write to Tilde and go on a ride with Mr Murray. We are looking at places for students to visit when they come to Yorkshire. We have been to Bolton Abbey and tomorrow it is Ingleton Falls and some special caves, I think. But I think it will be a long time before they come. Not everyone likes us here.'

'How can anyone not like you? I like you very much, and you can take some of my clothes to Tilde if you like.' She couldn't bear to think of anyone having so little when she had so much.

This time they kissed longer and deeper and stronger, until Maddy's legs went weak and her tummy melted with a fluttery sensation. 'We'd better get down before we fall out of the tree,' she laughed, breaking the tension between them. Time to walk back to The Vicarage and for her to make the last few dances of the evening. Her feet were floating two feet off the air so that might be difficult.

'Where on earth have you been? The dance is over,' Gloria snapped, her lips pouting with disapproval. No one seemed impressed with her new dress and the local boys weren't worth staring at.

'It's not my sort of dance,' Maddy replied.

'Too common for Lady Muck, are we?' Gloria laughed.

'No, of course not, silly. I just popped back to the Brooklyn. Uncle Gerry's due back soon and I wondered if there was any news.' Maddy's cheeks were pink as if she'd been running and her grey eyes flashed like polished steel.

A likely story, thought Gloria. Something was different about Maddy. It was hard to detect if you didn't know her but it was something to do with that German lad at The Vicarage. He'd put a smile on her face, for some unearthly reason. He was tall and OK-looking, not her type at all in those spooky specs and funny clothes. She'd noticed the way he eyed up Maddy at the rounders match. She couldn't possibly be falling for a Jerry, could she? How stupid was that? He'd be gone in a couple of weeks and he was too stiff even to come to a friendly hop.

He was one of those bookish parson types. She couldn't imagine anyone marrying a vicar. A doctor or a farmer maybe, but a po-faced parson like old man Murray, never!

She must write to Greg and tell him all about it.

Why had Maddy found a fella so easily? She hardly wore any make-up, didn't bother to keep her hair up to fashion. She never wore a bra and looked like a lad in shorts, but she had made an effort this evening. Maddy was such a beanpole – no high heels for her, only pumps if she wanted a partner.

The two girls were like peg and prop together, and it suited Gloria to be the glamour puss. Her new employer, Mrs Gunn, was pretty and lively, and if she played her cards right there'd be more cast-offs to make her own. She'd already been through her wardrobe while the couple were out one evening, playing dressing-up with six-year-old Sarah: fur coats, suits, a ball gown, they'd tried on everything and they fitted her perfectly as Denise was short like herself, and her dressmaker shortened all her clothes beautifully. It was an Aladdin's cave of gorgeous clothes in Mrs Gunn's dressing room.

She liked it at the Gunns', minding Sarah and Jeremy, and there was a new one on the way. They lived in a fine old house just outside Sowerthwaite that she biked to each day.

The doctor owned a big car for emergencies and his wife had a roadster for her shopping. Sometimes they all squashed into it and took the high road to Harrogate when they had petrol coupons to spare, or outings into the Dales for picnics. How different from life with Mam and Mikey. Mam was furious when she upped and left without so much as a by-your-leave. It was tit for tat. Served her right for what she'd done to them all those years ago.

With not a word from Mike Delgado for years, Mam marched up to the depot in the camp and demanded support for her baby. They took photos of little Mikey and she filled in her complaint. They accepted her claim but closed ranks, making it impossible for her to get any information about the soldier. Trust Mam to find herself in Dickey's meadow again. Sid was pining to come back to Sowerthwaite when he left school and Gloria was going to help him find a job on a farm.

Now she was back living in the hostel but it was dull after Leeds. There were no theatres, no big shops, but it was better than Peel Street and watching Mam back to her old tricks, entertaining strange men in the night. Some of them eyed her up with interest and it scared her, but she'd not told that to Maddy.

What Gloria wanted was never going to be found in this countryside back of beyond. She wanted what Denise Gunn had acquired: a husband who made money, enough to live in a big house, have a daily and a gardener and someone to mind her kids as and when they came along. Gloria had already planned to have just the two, a boy and a girl.

She wanted pretty dresses and shoes, time to have her nails painted and long visits to the hairdressers, to be taken to expensive restaurants in a fur coat, like film stars wore in *Picturegoer*.

She could just see herself in a white fox fur wrap, fluffy, warm and soft to the touch, a long sable with matching hat or a short mink for visiting friends in town. Gloria laughed at herself; dream on, lady, but her heart was set on this goal. If you didn't make big plans how could dreams ever come true?

She'd keep herself straight, pick up tips and good manners, and one day find a fella as would make it all come true. But until such times she'd have to up her game and learn to be a lady herself. After all, she was as good as Maddy any day.

They were still friends even though she thought Maddy daft to go mooning over a Jerry. Nothing would come of it. Old Mrs Belfield would make sure of that.

The few late summer days seemed to go on for ever, the green grass tinged with gold. The sky was bright and everything shimmered in the heat. Hay time had been poor and the lambs were still puny. It had been one of those dismal summers so the sunshine was welcome. They'd chosen a good day for the youth club charabanc outing to the Lakes and the seaside. They'd all strolled down the prom at Morecambe and sang on the coach back. Maddy had sat with Gloria, and Dieter with the vicar's wife, both trying not to draw attention to themselves. It was as if the summer hovered to enjoy one last fling before the morning dews drenched the grass and the long trek into winter began.

When the school bell rang out on the first day of term, Maddy was glad her own schooldays were over. How could she ever have continued her studies when she was in a torment of confusion over her stolen kisses with Dieter?

His sister had recovered but there were barely two weeks until he returned to Germany. They had walked the heels off her brogues, talking and reading poems together, sharing their beliefs. He gave her a list of the books that had convinced him that Christianity embraced the whole of life, not just Sunday worship; how it should be at the centre of daily life and work. Most of his philosophy just went over her head because she just wanted to be close to him.

They held hands and kissed, lying side by side, sharing thoughts. She'd never met anyone who thought so deeply about everything. He knew so much more than she did about real life.

Sometimes he told her a little of how they had survived the war, living on scraps and hiding from marauding soldiers, who wanted to grab young girls for their pleasure. His mother had died for want of medicine when her wounds became infected. They had sold everything just to live, and his faith had been tested to its limits, but just when things could get no worse, someone would help the family, take them in and shelter them. His father died in an internment camp but for months they'd hoped for good news. There were so many people to thank for kitting him out to come to England and he was determined to go back East and thank them before he went to college.

'You will write to me?' Maddy pleaded one evening.

'Of course, but our words are censored. It will not be easy to write. A thank you letter perhaps.'

'Oh, don't say that.' She sat up, suddenly afraid. The thought of never seeing him again became real. 'You are so wise. I wish I knew all you know.'

'*Liebchen*, I am full of envy. You have everything here for a happy life: food, beauty. No wonder your soldiers fight so hard to keep it safe.'

'Stay then, don't go back . . . you can do your studies here. We need ministers too.'

'It is not possible. I must see my family, what is left of it. This is just a holiday for me. I owe many people for this wonderful time.'

'Am I just a holiday romance?' she snapped.

'Of course not. We are alike, you and me, with serious loving hearts. I will write to you and we will find some way to be together.'

'And I will come and see you all,' she smiled.

'It will not be possible . . . not yet. In a few years—'

'A few years! We'll be so old then,' she cried, snuggling into his side.

'You are a funny girl, so . . . what is the word? . . . never wanting to wait. All good things have to wait. It is God's will.'

'But there's only two weeks left, Dieter!'

'Then let us make the most of what we have been given.' He rolled over to kiss her and they wrapped each other in a parcel of arms and legs and hugs. How they got to undressing, she'd no idea but it was so natural to peel off the layers and lie on the prickly ground almost naked but for underwear. Dieter fingered her white skin, gazing down with a frown on his brow.

'This is not right. Mr Murray will be angry with me to treat you so. I am their guest.'

Dieter was uncertain but Maddy was unrepentant. 'We love each other, no one is to know. "Come live with me, and be my love, And we will some new pleasures prove",' she whispered Donne's daring poem into his ear whilst fingering down into his shorts, feeling the hardness underneath.

'No, Maddy . . . This is for marriage. We must contain ourselves.'

'Yes, but we're doing what our bodies want us to do. What is so wrong with that?'

How could she be so brazen? But if John Donne could make love to his mistress when he was a minister, then so could she to her love.

'I've never taken a woman, it isn't right,' he protested, but she kissed him and stopped his words.

'And I've never done this before but we have so little time and who knows when we can meet again?' she whispered, pressing his hand on her thigh. 'What is wrong in giving each other pleasure?'

'I don't know . . .' he groaned as she caressed him.

'Like this?'

He groaned again and she placed his hands deeper between her thighs and squirmed until he was touching the very centre of her excitement. They rolled together, feeling the tension mounting, writhing until they both burst with relief.

'That was good, and we didn't break the rules,' Dieter sighed.

'Oh, you are so strait-laced,' Maddy laughed, and he looked at her and grinned. Then he became serious. 'One of us has to be careful. We must not do that again.'

But they did. Every evening she rode out at dusk on Monty to the bank overlooking the foss where there was cover and shade and the rush of falling water.

They brought each other to climax and lay content as if there was all the time left in the world.

When Maddy looked back on those tumultuous days it was as if there was only sunlight and shadows, probing fingers and spilling fluid as he spilled over her and she lay, letting it soak into her. There was no risk, no blame, no breaking of the chastity rule against penetration. She was still virgo intacta in name but not in deed. How could such blissful innocence ever end? When he left she would write to him, and they would meet when visas and permits allowed.

On the last night they clung together, hardly daring to breathe, watching clouds scudding across the moon through the rustling trees, listening to the night sounds, the whinnying of the horse, the cascade of water over rocks.

They made love but not fully, and each time it got harder to resist that final joining of bodies, but Dieter pulled back and came with care.

'How can I ever leave you after this? It is the most wonderful summer of my life.'

'And mine too . . . I'll see you to the station.'

'Better not to come, Maddy. I might cry and everyone will know.'

'I don't care who knows that we are lovers,' Maddy protested.

'You will have to live here after I am gone. No one will thank you for choosing me.'

'Time will change it, you'll see.'

'I hope so, Maddy. I pray so, Madeleine. I love your name. Always be proud of that beautiful name. You will send me pictures?'

'And you will write to tell me your address. You have my new address in Leeds.'

'It is in my wallet next to my heart.'

'I can't believe this is happening: that we should find each other and grow up like this. In spring I was just a girl, now I'm a woman and you have given that to me.

'We are not as we were, *Liebchen*. I have wonderful memories to take to my grave, precious loving times. What we do I see now it is sacred and special.'

Maddy shivered. It was dark and damp and chill. Summer was over.

'Don't say that. We'll be together soon. I'll come to you, I promise. But we'd better go. It's getting late.'

They walked the horse back slowly and Maddy felt sick that it was time for their dreaming to end.

Plum was anxious. It was dark and Maddy was still out with Monty. What on earth was she doing till this hour, wandering over hills getting lost? The girl had seemed to be living in a dream for the past few weeks. She had that starry-eyed, half-listening head on her as if she was far away in another world of poetry and novels and private daydreams. Her cheeks had bloomed in the fresh air and sun, her skin tanned with the wind. Maddy had changed so much in the last year.

Why begrudge the child a bit of respite from exams and beginning real study? If the truth were told she was disappointed that Maddy wouldn't go on to study for university but the girl was adamant she wanted to do the secretarial course in Leeds.

'I want to come home every weekend.'

'But London would be more exciting, or Oxford. Leeds is so . . . well, ordinary,' Plum had argued.

Maddy had given one of her steel-eyed truly Belfield stares when roused. 'Yorkshire is my home now.' End of discussion.

At least she'd had a good summer and done Vera a favour in taking Dieter to the youth club. They taught him to play darts and she accompanied him at the piano in duets, laughing and giggling together.

'That girl's not getting silly over him?' sniffed Pleasance after one performance.

'Of course not. They're still children,' Plum had snapped back. She didn't want to think of Maddy as growing up and away, especially as the child was at an awkward age. Poor girl was more aware of the imperfections of her shape and height, her bunches were gone and she'd jumped at the lipstick when it was offered: nearly seventeen was a funny age, being neither one thing nor another.

When Plum was that age she was put out into the débutante circuit to hunt balls and cocktail soirées. She'd met Gerry, when she was barely more than a child bride herself. Thank goodness the war had changed all that nonsense. Girls were no longer just objects to be auctioned off like useless ornaments and had proved themselves in war work equal to men. Now they must make a future for themselves, homes or jobs, or both perhaps. Maddy was right to insist on practical training. When all the men came home, they'd have to compete in a different marketplace.

Plum leaned on the portico with her cigarette, relieved as horse and rider trotted up the avenue without a care in the world.

'Where've you been, darling? I was getting worried.'

'I went to say goodbye to Dieter. He leaves tomorrow.'

'I know. You've been a good friend to him.' Plum smiled, sensing there might be more in this but saying nothing.

'I'll just see to Monty.'

'Cocoa?'

'Super . . . Can we have a chat?'

'Of course. You know you can talk to me any time,' said Plum, suddenly feeling flushed. Was this going to be one of those birds and bees jobs? Oh Lord! What had she been up to?

Plum trusted the biology mistress had sorted the details out long ago on the section on rabbit's mating.

Maddy was a country girl; she'd seen foals born, tups with the rams. Oh hell!

How Plum wished she'd been more informed on her wedding night. Her mother only whispered one bit of advice: 'Don't move, let him get it over with. It won't hurt too much, you ride horses, you'll be fine.'

Gerry had always been a bit of a tally-ho galloper, riding rough on her until he was satisfied. Not much fun in that department. How could she sour Maddy's innocence with such details? The flushing spread over her body as it did lying in bed. Was this a sign of that time of life when her hopes for a baby would be over for good?

Gerry was coming home soon and she wasn't sure how she felt about that. They'd just have to make a go of it for the Brooklyn's sake – and Pleasance. Divorce was unthinkable.

If only there'd been a son. Maddy was the nearest to an heir. It was all so complicated. Then she smelled burned milk in the pan and a hiss as it all boiled over.

Hell's bells! I can't even make a cup of cocoa.

Her job at the hostel was finished, but she was still warden, clearing up the debris of years, wondering what they would do with the building. Mainly it was back to listening to the moans and groans of her mother-in-law. She would have to find something for herself or she'd go mad. There was only so much voluntary work she could do. What would happen when Maddy left?

Maddy and Plum sat in the kitchen, as they did most

evenings. It was easier to heat and less distance to carry things.

'Here you are. It's a bit skinny on top,' she apologised.

'That's OK,' Maddy smiled. 'Do you think I could visit Germany?'

'To see Dieter?' Plum smiled too. So it was this after all. 'You've taken a shine to each other. I did wonder.'

Maddy was blushing. 'We're going to write to each other, pen pals like Greg. Golly, I've not written to him for ages. Gloria has . . . But can I go and visit Dieter?'

'Has he asked you?' Plum was fishing now.

'Not really. It's difficult for them with permits. His family's very poor now.'

'I don't think you'd be allowed into Germany yet. Why all the hurry? Are you sweet on him?'

'We're a bit sweet on each other. He's my first proper boyfriend and he's so clever. Not like any of the other boys round here.' Maddy was blushing as she spoke.

'That's because he's a foreigner, a stranger from a far-off land . . . a Sheikh of Araby,' Plum laughed.

'But he makes the other boys look silly.' Maddy looked so serious in his defence, it was touching.

'I always thought Gregory was your special friend?' said Plum.

'Yes, but we've not seen him for years. He's never bothered to visit us and his letters are grown up, all about making his fortune in bricks and mortar or some such. He thinks we're still kids.'

'You're nearly seventeen, I suppose things are stirring . . .'

'That's old enough to die for your country and grown up enough to . . .' She paused trying to avoid the word.

Plum was on alert. 'Enough for what? You've not done anything you shouldn't, Maddy?'

'What do you mean?' Maddy was on the defensive again. 'It's nothing like that. We know what's right and wrong.'

'Oh, that's a relief. Only things happen when young love gets carried away.' Plum smiled, trying to sound relaxed, but her heart was thudding. *Take it easy now.*

'Like Billy Forsyth having to get married to Eunice Billington?'

'How did you know about that?

'It doesn't take a mathematician to work out little Sam was christened only six months after they came down the aisle, but there's nothing wrong with making love, is there?' She looked directly into Plum's eyes.

There was still a slight turn in Maddy's left eye but it was hardly noticeable now. Plum was trying so hard not to blush and fluster.

'Of course not, in the right time and place within marriage.'

'That's just what Dieter says,' Maddy replied.

Phew! What a relief, thought Plum. No danger there then. 'He sounds a thoroughly decent chap with a sensible head on his shoulders. You must correspond with him, perhaps take up German again to improve your letters. A secretary with good German might be able to get a position—'

'Abroad! Brilliant, Auntie Plum. I could go and work in Germany while he is studying. I can do a night school class.'

'That's not quite what I had in mind. It'll all take time and you'll know then if this is just a crush or the real thing,' Plum said, hoping Maddy would take the hint that first love never usually lasts, especially when separated by the Channel.

'Oh, it has to be the right thing. Love comes just once,' Maddy sighed.

'You've been reading too many romantic novels.'

'Just *Romeo and Juliet* and sonnets . . .'

'And look how that ended. First love is special, intense, and you think it'll never end but it's a sort of practice loving to set you up for the real thing later,' Plum said, thinking of how she'd fallen head over heels for the gardener's son. They'd barely had time to blush at each other before Daddy whisked him away to farm work. 'It's like a firework, a burst of flame and then nothing.'

'But it feels so wonderful. Dieter is kind and clever.'

I hope he's been a gentleman too, thought Plum, seeing the ecstasy on Maddy's face, luminous with rapture. What on earth did they get up to? Still, it all sounded innocent enough – stolen kisses in the park. How sweet!

She couldn't ever recall feeling that about Gerald. It was all such a whirlwind of dances and parties, dress fittings and invitations. There never was a proper courtship. If there had been she'd have soon realised that behind those tight-fitting trews and Green Howard jacket was a cool and calculating bounder, who played away whenever he got bored.

Sitting across the table, watching her niece bright-eyed and enraptured, Plum felt the green knife of jealousy twisting her guts. She's young and has all her life ahead, she thought. I wish I'd my time all over again. I wouldn't be sitting here, that's for certain.

13

In the weeks that followed Dieter's departure, Maddy was too busy gathering her stuff for college to think how they might meet again. There were eye checks and dental appointments, clothes to make and the trunk to send ahead to West Park, to her new lodgings. There were farewells and thank you teas for all the kind gifts people kept handing her for her new life: a lovely writing case from Plum and Grandma, hand-embroidered hankies from Grace Battersby, and a tapestry pencil case from Vera Murray, who told her they'd had a brief thank you note from Dieter with an address near Dresden. There was a powder compact and puff from Gloria and the new girls in the hostel. It was being let out now as lodgings.

She had everyone round for tea to show off her new tweed suit, made by a bespoke tailor in Scarperton in a lavender and heathery tone. Grandma produced a string of pearls to finish off her lilac knitted jumper.

'Guard them with your life!' she ordered. 'They're heirlooms for your daughter.'

'No, they're not,' whispered Plum. 'They're a wedding

gift from a client. She just likes to make out the Belfields are old money. You'll have all of mine when I pop my clogs and they go back for generations.'

They were always scoring points off each other these days. It was something to do with Uncle Gerald not coming home for some reason.

Maddy didn't want any pearls. All she wanted was not to be going to a strange house in a strange city. Although Leeds was only fifty miles away it felt like going to another planet.

Every week she'd written to Dieter but so far he'd not replied. She wondered if something was wrong with Mechtilde and he'd not gone to college after all. It was as if those wonderful starry nights by the foss – the wind whistling over them, the stinging nettles prickling their bare bodies and the darkness like a blanket – were just some faraway dream, to savour perhaps on dark nights when there was homework from college to complete.

Her digs were on the top floor of an enormous Edwardian villa just off West Park Road. There were two other students staying there, both at the university, and Miss Ffrost was keen to have only respectable 'gals' from good homes nesting in her attics.

Plum had packed her favourite quilt and ornaments, along with photos of the summer outing in a frame, to make her feel more at home. There was a special photo of Dolly and Arthur, a studio portrait of the Bellaires in evening dress in its square silver frame. It was all she had left of her parents.

There was a watercolour of the Brooklyn done by Aunt Julia, and a sketch Greg once made of the Victory Tree HQ that she'd kept for sentimental reasons. He'd done it from memory when he was stationed in Germany and sent it to Gloria. Gloria had given it to her as a present and written on the back 'Forever Friends'.

It made her think of all the fun they'd had, and how Greg had comforted her when her parents had died and, later, rescued her from catty Kay at the school gate.

Now her memories were of comforting Dieter in the very same tree the night they sat in the branches and he poured out all his turmoil, the night they became soul mates.

Gloria was coming as far as Leeds with her, as she was visiting her mother on her day off. The two Conleys were back in one of their friendly phases and Gloria liked to keep an eye on Sid, but she was very put out about Maddy leaving Sowerthwaite.

'You'll forget us all when you get college mates,' she accused.

'No, I won't. Forever friends,' Maddy reminded her. 'I'll be back at weekends when I can. Then we can go out together, go hiking, and we can meet up when you come back to Leeds, go to a milk bar and spot the talent.'

'Promise?'

'I promise. I'm not going to Timbuktu, only Leeds! Have you heard from Greg?'

'Nah, I think he's forgotten us. I expect he's got a

girlfriend by now. Charlie mentioned someone called Martha in Germany.'

Maddy had never thought about Greg being smitten like she had been by Dieter. He was always solid and somewhere in the distance, in his khaki uniform and his hair sticking up. She'd not seen him since he went abroad. She wondered where he was.

'Don't suppose we'll ever see him again then,' Maddy said.

Their letters had sort of dried up. They lived in two different worlds, she supposed. When was the last time she'd bothered to write to him? Two could play at that game, but they ought to send him a card and parcel before Christmas.

Without Greg and the gang those first years at Brooklyn Hall would have been awful, but they were children then. Now she was beginning a new life in silk stockings and court shoes, with lisle stockings and brogues for daytime, and one of Plum's cast-off pony-skin jackets that she was too polite to refuse. The thought of the skin of a poor pony like Monty slung across her back filled her with horror but it was too good to give away. She might sell it on and buy something more modest. It was a little too short and neat, and not her style at all.

They sat in the carriage, staring out alongside the muddy waters of the River Aire. Green turned to grey, and factories, stone mills and sooty chimneys filled the view. Maddy smiled, thinking about that first journey with Gloria when they were small, that first adventure into the unknown.

'We've come along way since 1940, kiddo,' she whispered, thinking of the skinny redhead with the little boy in a balaclava with the runny nose, wailing for his mam.

'You saved our lives on that train. Who knows where we'd have fetched up?

Now we're two young ladies on the town. Are you nervous?'

'Not half! I just want to get the first day over with. You will write to me, even if I forget to reply?'

'I might,' Gloria winked. 'Don't look like that. Forever friends, you and me. If you find a nice rich young man for me to dazzle, I expect you to let me have first go, seeing as you're spoken for.'

'Is it that obvious?' Maddy nudged her.

Gloria winked again. 'Love's young dream, all those secret rides in the dark. Everyone knew you two were at it like rabbits.'

'No, we were not,' she protested.

'Pull the other one. I've seen your face. You've gone and done it, I can tell.'

'No, I've not. We never . . .'

'Well, something put a smile on your face and it wasn't reading bleeding Wordsworth.'

They parted at the station, hugging as if Maddy was going to cross the Arctic solo. She went straight into a taxi without a thought while Gloria must hike over to the bus station and get to the other end of town. That about summed it all up.

Maddy was up to something with that Jerry boy.

She was different, more confident, prettier and striding out as if she owned the place. She didn't have to hold on to her cherry, cross her legs when lads came fumbling up skirts with wandering palms. She had prospects and a whole new world to explore. It wasn't fair. It never had been.

Now she must trudge up to Peel Street and hope Mam was in one of her good moods and not being silly over some new toerag who promised the earth and never delivered anything but bills.

Gloria was worried about Sid scarpering off from school again. He'd never settled back in the town and it was all her fault for going back with Mam so eagerly all those years ago. What a fool she'd been, but at least she was back in a decent job and she'd not brought any silver for anyone to filch from her pocket. She'd stopped that game when she found her coat pockets empty on a previous visit. There were just some precious eggs in her basket from Mrs Plum. Now there was a real lady.

How could two girls from the same place and time have such different lives? Here's Gloria at one end of the city, tripping over rusting pram wheels, the smell of boiled fish up her nose, and Maddy sitting in her taxi, all prim and proper. Everyone knew she'd been with that Gerry; all over him like a rash, Beryl whispered. Why was there one rule for the rich and another for the rest?

It was a good job they were best mates or she could hate her guts.

*

The Yorkshire Ladies' Commercial College was a bus ride down from West Park, close to the university on Woodhouse Moor, that green leafy stray that separated the town from the suburbs. The college was housed in a large terraced house on four floors that once must have been a family home. It was now a much-battered series of mock offices and classrooms where everything was stripped to essentials: desks with typewriters, a working library with boardroom desk, more study rooms with a mock interview room.

On her first morning Maddy arrived too early and paced around the street trying to get her bearings. As she looked up at the tall white towers and grand steps of the Parkinson Building, she felt very nervous.

The sooty acrid air smelled so different from damp Dales wood smoke, but despite the smoke, and the fumes of buses grinding up and down, there was an excitement at starting something new – no more uniforms, no more prep and new people to meet. She only hoped that she'd be up to the tasks ahead.

Soon there was a queue of girls chattering in the chill September morning. Everyone stood around until a tiny woman darted off a bus and rushed with her keys to the door.

'Where is that stupid caretaker? He should've opened up hours ago. I'd keep your coats on, girls. It'll be freezing in there.' This was Maddy's first introduction to the Principal, Hilda Meyer, who ran the establishment with her sister, Hermione; the one who had interviewed her, months ago.

Never were twins so disparate. Miss Hermione had iron-grey hair drawn back into a severe bun and wore black. Hilda sported a marcel wave clipped with pins into a style that could only be described as curious, each bumpy ridge held in place like little boats on a sea of raven black.

Miss Frobisher, who took dictation and shorthand, hovered nervously with a man in a tired tweed jacket, with one sleeve tucked into his pocket. This was Mr Beckett, who took account keeping and business studies. They completed the staff.

Being a two-year course, there were students who knew the ropes bounding up the stairs like giddy sixth formers to bag the best seats. Had Maddy exchanged one set of rules for another? Miss Hilda soon had this new year's intake gathered together in the largest drawing room to give them a pep talk.

'Now, ladies, to break the ice before we commence, I want you to line up and each of you to introduce the person next to you.'

Maddy wanted to rush out of the room right there but the girl smiled. 'I'm Caroline,' she whispered.

'I want you to get to know your fellow students and listen carefully. Then I'll ask you to introduce them to the rest in turn.'

Maddy turned to her neighbour on the other side who was called Nan Pinkerton. She was a farmer's daughter from a place near Harewood. She was one of three sisters and wanted to do farm accounts. She was engaged to a young farmer called Malcolm and they were getting married next summer to run their own farm. Maddy tried to store all this information into her head.

A tall elegant girl sauntered up to Maddy and eyed her up and down. 'God! I didn't expect this. Mummy said those two were loonies but, hey ho! I'm Arabella Foxup. Who are you then?'

Maddy tried to explain she'd just left school and wanted to do something useful.

'Did you see Madeleine Carroll in *The Thirty-Nine Steps*? She was killed in a plane crash – or was that Carole Lombard? Welcome to the madhouse. No point in being useful, darling. All we're fit for is breeding – like brood mares, my pa says. Haven't a clue what I'm doing here. Alexander, my intended, is in the army and we're getting hitched soon. Can't see any of this being of any use, can you?' With that, Arabella breezed off to chat around the room.

The moment of truth came when they had to introduce each other to the group. There were Ruth and Thelma, who were both members of Hebron Hall Evangelical Mission, and were keen hikers and knew the Dales well. They wanted to work as secretaries to missionary societies. They'd sort of cheated on the task as they knew each other beforehand and never said.

'Some of the "Thou Shalt Not" brigade,' whispered the haughty Arabella, waving her huge sapphire and diamond engagement ring up everyone's noses. When it was her turn to introduce Maddy, she couldn't remember a thing Maddy had told her, only that she had a film stars's name.

Maddy felt flat and a bit stupid. Miss Hilda had missed nothing.

'Madeleine, is there anything you'd like to add, seeing that the Honourable Miss Foxup's concentration was obviously elsewhere?'

'Bitch!' whispered Arabella, looking daggers at the Principal.

Maddy smiled, shook her head and said, 'That's fine, Miss Meyer.'

'This may only be a stopgap between school and husband for some of you, but we take this commercial college seriously. These aren't games we're playing but an exercise to flush out how good you are at mixing and sharing and relating to other people other than yourselves. A dozen girls in a confined space takes tact and co-operation – you've a lot to take in in a short time. Some of you are seriously committed to your task, whilst others may not be so sure of their futures. It is my aim to give you time to learn, process and contribute. There is a waiting list for places here so anyone not prepared to knuckle down might as well toddle off right now, for you'll get no quarter from my staff. It's a waste of good fees to turn up and idle your time away. Three absences without reasonable explanation and we cancel your place and keep the fees. That is the contract. *Comprenez-vous?*'

Miss Meyer was staring hard at the Honourable Arabella, who fingered her manicured nails.

She shrugged and turned away, blushing, muttering under her breath. 'Keep your hair on. OK!'

'Miss Foxup, you wish to comment?'

'Fine by me,' she said with an air of nonchalance that fooled no one. A truculent puppy had been brought to heel. Aunt Plum would've been proud of such direct action.

'Good,' replied Miss Meyer. 'So let's sort out the timetable, rooms and housekeeping. We have an affiliation to the University. There are some courses open to the public. You can have tickets for the library and I have connections with the theatres so you can view some dress rehearsals and matinées for free.'

And so that first term passed in a flurry of typing practice, shorthand and hard slog. It was a wet dreary autumn, and Maddy found herself walking home in pea-souper fogs on November nights alongside lines of folk with hankies over their mouths fumbling towards their streets in the acrid air.

There was a basic German night class that she tried to attend, but homework and the trek back to her digs made the effort to turn round again easy to miss. No wonder she was always exhausted.

On Saturday mornings she walked down to City Station to catch the train north, back to Sowerthwaite, to Monty, Grandma and Plum, back to fresh air and fields and quiet, and Gloria's third degree of questions.

On the train home there was time to split her world into two, town and country. She loved both in their own way but it was all so exhausting. She'd never felt so unfit, with no more lacrosse, tennis or long hacks. She'd filled out and grown breasts, much to her delight, and treated herself to a smart satin bra from Marshfields store on the Headrow.

The students at college separated naturally into little cliques. Maddy stuck mainly to Pinky and Caro. Arabella ignored them at first, but lately tagged on to them to talk horses. Under all that bravado she was quite studious and came top in bookkeeping and accounts. Bella's father owned acres of farmland and her mother was the daughter of an earl. Her fiancé was training at Catterick Camp and they were preparing for a huge summer wedding next year.

Sometimes she persuaded Maddy to trawl the bridal stores, not that there was much on display. Everyone wanted satin with sweetheart necks, but Arabella wanted something dramatic, like the lacy patterns in the American bride magazines.

They'd been to Marshfields and Marshall and Snelgrove so many times that the assistants smiled when they arrived. Pinky came only once and sniffed at the prices and the coupons, shaking her head in disgust.

'Why waste money on just one day in your life? I'm going to have my mother's gown remodelled. Wedding dresses only end up in a trunk.'

'Don't be such a boring farmer's wife,' Bella hooted in her pukka aristocratic voice that filled the salon so everyone could hear. 'Think of your picture in *Tatler* or *Yorkshire Post* or the *Field*. Mummy says, when in doubt, spend. Daddy's footing the bill so I'm spending.'

Maddy yawned with boredom. She knew every dress on the rack.

'Poor you, marrying that Hun chappie . . . God love us! What next . . . ? I have to admit some of them look appealing in their jackboots and peaked caps!' Bella roared seeing their disapproval and milking it.

'How could you!' Pinky replied. 'You know she's not heard anything for weeks. Don't joke about Nazis.'

'You're all so bourgeois!' Bella stomped off.

Maddy wondered if she was ever going to see Dieter again. She had talked to her new college friends as if they were engaged, but without a single letter or contact it was becoming clear that this was just a childish dream. Plum was right. First love was all fireworks, a flash in the pan. Perhaps he'd write at Christmas.

Mrs Murray was planning to send a big food parcel to his address with socks, clothing and treats for his family. It was going to be another hard winter, especially in Europe, but not as bad as the last few, Maddy prayed.

All the changes in the last months had upset her system, tired her out, so sometimes she went to bed with a Horlicks as soon as she got to her digs, even before supper. Miss Ffrost's suppers were on the mean side: dried-up cutlets, tired vegetables, watery soup and blancmange that turned her stomach. In fact, the tiredness was so awful she wondered if she was short of blood. Everyone said she looked peaky.

Going home at weekends enabled her to catch up on decent vegetables, bacon and egg pies. Pastry was her favourite thing and she took to buying Eccles cakes in her lunch hour to keep hunger at bay. She was always hungry. Her sweet ration was used up in great binges of eating chocolate, which then made her feel sick.

Her heart would lift as they chugged out of Keighley

station and the moors began to stretch out before her to Skipton, Scarperton . . . and then Sowerthwaite.

There were always familiar faces to chat to on the bus with news of all the local gossip. Gloria kept her on the dot about who was courting whom and who had left the youth club.

Plum heard from Greg that he was soon going to be demobbed. Good for him, Maddy sighed. If only things were brighter at the Brooklyn. Uncle Gerry was home for good now and the atmosphere was frosty between them all. Sometimes Maddy felt it was better to keep to her room out of the way, or nip down to the hostel to spend the day with Gloria, Beryl and their new friend, Cynthia. All they talked about were boys she didn't know and other girls she didn't care about, and who was on at the Picture House. That was when she longed to be back in Leeds with her college friends.

'No word from loverboy, then?' Gloria asked.

'I do wish you'd stop asking. If I'd anything to tell—'

'Hold your hat on! I was only asking.'

'Sorry, but it's been three months and not a letter.'

'That's lads for you: love you and leave you. Thank goodness you didn't end up like Enid Cartwright. You know, the one who went off with that soldier when we were kids? She's ended up in a home . . . for girls in trouble somewhere in Manchester. Poor cow,' Gloria whispered, enjoying the scandal.

'Can't she stay at home?' Maddy asked, knowing Eunice Billingham had married her boyfriend in the town. They were a nine-day wonder, but nobody bothered about them now.

'Where've you been lately? Her mother threw her out on the street so she came back here to see Mrs Plum and Mrs Battersby. I heard Mrs Gunn saying the doctor fixed her up out of the way so no one will know her disgrace.'

'That's what comes of giving your all,' sniffed Beryl, with a smug grin on her pudgy face. 'You won't catch me delivering the goods until I have a ring on my finger and the church booked.'

That'll be a long time off, thought Maddy, feeling mean at them all. They knew nothing about being in love. 'When you're in love, girls get carried away,' Maddy offered. 'Like in *Romeo and Juliet*.'

'Hark at her, the dimwit. There's ways and means, French letters, rubber caps . . .' Gloria winked. 'You don't have to get in trouble, not if you're careful. Mrs Gunn gave me a lecture. I shall plan my family – a boy for him and a girl for me,' she announced as if it was already in the bag.

'Like your mother, then?' Maddy snapped back, tired of all this sex talk.

'You leave my mam out of it. She knows what men are like – one thing only on their minds, and up and away. Dieter's just like the rest, as I said.'

'No, he's not, he's . . . oh, I don't know. I know he would write if he could and he will write soon. I feel it here,' Maddy sighed, pressing her hand to her heart in a dramatic gesture.

'Then you've nothing to worry about, have you?

Don't look so po-faced. Let's go and listen to the wireless. It's *Variety Bandbox*. There's that singer on. "Bless You for Being an Angel",' Gloria crooned.

Maddy smiled and waved them on. 'I'll just sit a bit longer and get some air in my lungs.'

'Up the Victory Tree? How's that going to help you?'

'Don't know, but I like it up there. Remember when we used to post notes down the nooks, in our secret pillar box?'

'When are you going to grow up? We're too old for climbing trees and passing on notes,' Gloria laughed, her eyes crinkling. 'You're such a card!'

'I know, but I still want to do it,' Maddy insisted. Gloria and Beryl went off arm in arm, sniggering. Maddy climbed up to her perch and hugged her knees. Nothing was turning out as she had hoped and there was something else on her mind, something she'd not even considered until now.

In the branches of the old tree, she could be a child again or roll back the clock to the night when Dieter had made those tender promises. Why hadn't he written? Was it all over between them?

Yet another Christmas with rations and restrictions. Will these shortages ever end? thought Plum as she looked at her lists one more time. She'd met Maddy for lunch in town at Marshfields, having procured a beautiful calfskin leather briefcase for all her niece's notepads and files. A shopping bag was not quite the image for the Yorkshire Ladies'.

It was good to see her niece blossoming at the

college, her cheeks filled out, flushed with excitement. They were holding some posh frock evening at a hotel just outside Leeds and she was going to invest in a proper gown for the occasion.

If only Maddy wasn't so tall. The short ballerina-cut length just looked silly on her. They were on the last lap of the shopping trawl, hoping there'd be something affordable in the evening department. It was too late to have anything made up for her.

Maddy knew the shop and its prices and the coupon count from her boring excursions on Bella's bridal hunt. 'We can get something cheaper than these,' she whispered.

'Darling, you're only young once. You've worked hard and done well, and the Miss Meyers are pleased with your progress. Come on, let me treat you to something glamorous.'

'I'd rather have new jodhpurs and a hacking jacket,' Maddy said. She'd grown out of the waistband of her old pair.

'No, you wouldn't. Don't spoil it for me. This gives me as much pleasure as you. I know Christmas isn't an easy time for you. Still no word from your German pen pal?' Plum said, with concern in her eyes.

They fingered through the hangers in silence. It was good to distract herself from the coming weeks. Gerald was going to tell his mother that they were separating for good. They couldn't go on living a lie any more. He'd got a good post in London and was living with Daisy again. He'd never really left her. She'd heard him whispering to her over the phone, pretending it was a business call. He'd had the decency to blush. They'd kept up this pretence for months but Pleasance would be horrified: a divorce in the family was such a disgrace! She'd take to her bed in despair after dinner, which would be eaten in silence, punctuated by sniffs of disapproval at both of them. Although anyone could see their marriage had been in trouble for years.

'War Hero Returns to Safety', said the *Gazette*, with a colour picture of Gerald in uniform on the front page. He'd been back a month in theory, but he was exploring some post in London.

It was such a pity that they had nothing to say to each other any more. The war had strained the ties between them to breaking point. The gap between their separate town and country worlds was unbridgeable. He was still handsome, bronzed, but cold as ice when the bedroom door was closed, reading with his back to her, going through the motions of being pleased to see her in public but ignoring her the rest of the time.

How had she not noticed that his lips were mean, tight drawn and thin, his grey eyes like cold fish eyes on a slab when he looked at her? How different from that Hunt Ball in 1925 when he'd gathered her up into his arms and whisked her around the floor as if she was the love of his life.

Gerald wanted city life while Plum wanted to retreat back into the safe world she knew, a world of dogs and hills. She'd hiked for miles in the past few weeks agonising whether or not they were doing the right thing. She'd even talked it over with Mr Murray and

Vera, wept over them in distress. They had been kindness itself.

'Not every marriage is made in heaven,' Archie said to comfort her. 'The war has a lot to answer for. It's disrupted so many lives and changed couples from friends to strangers with nothing in common any more.'

It was a comfort to know she was not the only one but it felt as if she was alone in the world, ashamed and such a failure. Plum was not going to pretend any more.

Now was not the time to tell Maddy, though. She hardly knew her uncle. It would not mean much to her if they parted, nothing like losing her parents and family. Now that Dieter Schulte had let her down, the poor girl had her own sorrows – so why not blow all her coupons on a flashy cocktail ensemble with a pinched waist and fishtail skirt at the back, à la Paris mode?

The Dior fashions were making waves in magazines and Leeds women were eager to follow the fashions. The Jewish matrons made sure of that, with their boutiques and expert eye for fabric and design.

'Maddy, look at this one,' Plum said, pointing to a rich turquoise brocade with a neat bolero jacket. 'Try this one on, it's such a pretty colour against your dark hair.'

'Wait,' interrupted the vendeuse. 'Let us model some for the young lady. Veronique!' she called, and a tall blonde girl simpered into view. 'She will show you our latest range.'

It was going to be a long afternoon as the girl dutifully posed in six outfits at varying lengths and prices, but it was still the turquoise one that they liked. 'Would madam's daughter care to come into the *cabine*?' said the saleswoman.

For a second Plum looked at Maddy and wondering if she should put her right but Maddy smiled and carried on. How lovely they assumed she was her daughter. It had been worth the expense for just that moment of recognition. Maddy was like a true daughter. Whatever happened over the next year with Gerry, no one could say she and Maddy were not real Belfields, with ties stronger than blood.

How awfully boring her life would've been without Maddy and the Old Vic Hostel and the gang of misfits who'd brought it to life.

When Maddy appeared Plum gasped. She looked so grown up, so filled out, her bust pushing out of the gown and that glamorous, dark hair against the shimmering fabric. When had that skinny crossed-eyed orphan, who'd stood on that station so forlorn, turned into a beautiful young woman?

'It's pulling a little on the waist but we can let out an inch, perhaps,' the vendeuse fussed. 'If miss will wear a proper corselette . . .'

'What has Miss Ffrost been feeding you on?' laughed Plum.

'It's all the snacks at lunchtime. I've got such a craving for custard vanilla slices,' Maddy laughed, blushing. 'I shall have to starve after Christmas.'

She tried on two more, a gold lamé and a red satin

that looked tarty on her. This had to be the one and it was worth every penny.

Plum recalled buying that turquoise velvet dress in Harrods during the war, for that first terrible Christmas. Now she was going to spoil Christmas again with bad news, or wait until the New Year perhaps. Gerald would have to broach the subject with his mother before he left for good. Pleasance would take it badly and she'd be left to pick up the pieces. There were dark clouds ahead.

'Your daughter is perfect mannequin size, so tall and straight in the back, with a little adjustments, perfect. She is at home, yes?

'I'm a student in Leeds. Yorkshire Ladies' College.'

'Ah, yes, I know, the finishing school for Young Yorkshire.'

'No . . . the sweat shop they call the secretarial college,' Maddy said. 'My nails are broken with all that hammering on keys, but it's fun and I'm so glad I came.'

'We hope to see you again, young lady. Your height shows off clothes well.'

'Not at these prices,' Maddy whispered in Plum's ears as she darted into the cubicle.

'Your figure is a little full, but she is perfect for a mannequin. We are always looking for lovely gels of her sort,' said the vendeuse.

'I'm afraid Madeleine's hard at work, she's more *Horse and Hound* than *Vogue*,' offered Plum, surprised at the woman's interest. She'd never thought of Maddy as full-figured, but her shape had changed, rounded and thickened, and it suited her.

'Ah, Madeleine, even a model's name too, very French and very romantic.'

Perhaps the saleswoman was just buttering them up, pleased with her expensive sale on a wet afternoon, perhaps not? Maddy a mannequin, now there was a laugh!

Gloria was wrapping Maddy's present up in brown paper dotted with potato prints of Christmas trees and stars. She had amused the Gunn kids for hours on the kitchen table, making reams of new wrapping paper out of old wrapping newspaper just like they'd done at the Old Vic. There were a few days' leave due to her, but it was not going to be a happy homecoming in Peel Street.

Sid was staying up at Alan's farm. Now Mrs Gunn had high blood pressure and was on bed rest. The Gunns had wanted Gloria to stay but she did fancy a change, a trip to the panto with young Mikey, a chance to trawl the shops for a bargain. It was pandemonium in the doc's house – Sarah and Jeremy were so excited – but she was good with kiddies, always had been. She sort of let them run off the leash but sensed just when to haul them back to heel.

Maddy was going around with a face like a wet weekend in Brid, moping up the Victory Tree like a soppy cow. Sometimes Gloria wondered if she was quite right in the head. Every day of the holiday she cantered over the fields on Monty, and when Gloria called for her she was never there.

Something was up at the Brooklyn or college. How

could anyone be miserable when they possessed the most gorgeous frock? It must have cost at least two months of Gloria's pittance. It made her going-out stuff look so homespun and tatty, with its cheap trimmings and wrinkled fabric. Maddy's new dress was too posh for Sowerthwaite, though.

No doubt it was dear Dieter who'd put the mockers on her Christmas. She'd seen the letter he'd sent to the house; just a few lines and not so much as a hanky for a present. Anyone could see that romance was going nowhere so perhaps now she'd wake up and get herself about town with her posh mates, Caro, Pinky and Bella, and pick up one of their brothers. I ask you, what sort of handles were those, she smiled. That lot lived in another world. They didn't worry about coupons for corsets or stockings, or worry about what Mam got up to of a night when she left the garment factory with her dizzy cronies, picking up lads young enough to be her sons.

Marge would never learn but Gloria paused with a sigh. She did have a mam and that was more than poor Maddy had. Oh hell! That was it – Christmas and the telegram, and me getting the wrong end of the stick and her being an orphan, she thought. Poor sod, no wonder she looked washed out and miserable.

The present sparkled in her hand. It came from Leeds market. It was a metal photograph frame, second-hand, with lots of hammered tulips and flowers. It was for Maddy to put in her digs in West Park, but Gloria hoped she wouldn't waste it on a picture of Dieter Schulte.

*

Maddy could hear the row going on from the top of the stairs. Uncle Gerald was standing in the hall, wagging his finger at his wife, his voice cutting in its cold reproof.

'Just stop right there. A divorce in the family is not an option. Why on earth did you say all that to Mother just now?'

'But it's the only way . . . all this secrecy for years. I'm just not pretending any more Gerry. It won't wash. I've had enough. You tell her it's over, *finito* . . . I can't carry on. What's the point in this charade?' Aunt Plum was fiddling with the large Christmas decoration, shifting the foliage this way and that, then throwing the shrivelled ivy across the floor in frustration.

'The point is, while Mummy is still with us I'll do nothing to disgrace the family name. I will not divorce you. The shame in the newspapers would kill her. You know how she likes to keep up her standing with the county set. We'll carry on as we always have. You're free to stay here.'

'Oh, thank you, very kind of you. I'll not be put away quietly, then? Though why I should want to stay in this empty barn beats me!'

'Oh, Prunella, be reasonable! Nothing needs to change. Why go and spoil everything? You knew it would only spoil Christmas all round. Now you've gone and upset things.'

'If you're so worried, you tell her the full story – how we've lived this lie for years. Surely Daisy has some say in things?'

'Daisy understands that this is how it has to be.'

'Then she's a bigger fool than I thought. The stupid woman must be a dimwit!'

Maddy saw Gerald move forward as if to strike his wife.

'Shut up, shut up, both of you! They can hear you all over the house. Please stop it,' she cried, running down the stairs.

They both looked up, shocked.

'Maddy, we're just arguing. This is a private matter,' Plum explained.

'Then say it in private, not in the hall. I don't want to hear it!' Maddy cried, storming out, feeling such a rage of fury. How could they spoil Christmas like that, bickering at the table and now shouting at each other?

Christmas was a holy time, a family time, and now they were splitting up. Didn't they know that the Belfields were all the family she had left and soon there'd be nothing? It wasn't fair. She didn't want atmospheres, sullen silences and bickering, not after her own disappointment. It was bad enough recalling that first terrible Christmas here when she lost her family. Now she had lost Dieter for ever, and if Plum went away too . . . ? It was too much.

Maddy stormed across the fields in the frosty air. Shivering in her pullover and slacks, she climbed up the Victory Tree to the hidy-hole to sulk and swear. Burning a hole in her pocket was the one letter in all the world she'd been longing for, one sheet of crumpled thin paper with whole sentences blacked out.

Someone had read it and blocked out precious words and there were so few words left.

My dear friend Madeleine,
I am writing to thank you all for your parcel. My aunt and sister are grateful for the gift and kind thoughts. It is most welcome at this winter time.
We are well enough. It is hard to say what changes in our lives are. We think of you often wit joy and sorrow. We will not be meeting ever again, of that I am certain.

The next two lines were blocked out There was no mention of university, no special words to her, just this polite thank you except for one line.

Summer harvest is ever in our minds. Forgive me.
Your friend in Christ, Dieter Schulte,
Mechthilde and Gisele Schulte

There was not even a return address. The message was clear. Dieter wanted no further correspondence with her. That was what hurt most of all. What on earth was happening over there? Had Dieter forgotten how they had kissed and made promises? Was he in danger for writing to her? Her feelings were so mixed up: anger and pain, disappointment and frustration, and longing to see him again.

Gloria had gone home to Leeds. What was left of

Christmas was ruined so what was there to stay for but rows and recriminations? Better to be alone in West Park than be surrounded by warring Belfields.

Maddy walked home calmer now, pausing to look up at the skeletal branches of the avenue of trees. Spiky and cruel, they raked the sky like claws. It was indeed an avenue of tears on that bleak winter morning, she sighed.

She packed her bags, said her goodbyes briskly and caught the first train back to town without a backward glance.

Miss Ffrost was away and the house was chilly. She turned her key in the door, hoping that one of the students might be there for company but the house was empty. Then it snowed and the small barred electric fire gave no heat. She piled on her clothes over her pyjamas and was glad she'd not abandoned the pony-skin jacket. The tiredness didn't go away and with it came the shivers and aches, so much so that she could stand it no longer and made an appointment to see the doctor at his surgery off St Chad's Road.

Plum sent a long letter of apology, saying that Gerald had gone to London. Grandma was resigned to their separation but angry, but there were no plans to change things at the Brooklyn immediately. She was sorry that Maddy had witnessed the bust-up but in a way she'd made Gerry face up to the truth of what this was doing to Plum.

Maddy felt mean to have run out on them as she read the rest of the letter. The weather was bad and the drive was blocked. Pleasance had taken to sulking in her room but Plum said she was glad it was all out in the open. 'Secrets are so draining,' she confessed.

The snow piled up in the drive of Arncliffe Road too, and Miss Ffrost came back a few days later needing a hand with the shovel. Maddy found herself exhausted and couldn't shift snow like the others. What was wrong with her?

College restarted early in January but Pinky was snowed in and late to arrive, Caro was digging with her married sister in Bramhope and Bella arrived straight from a party in London full of New Year's resolutions. It was good to have her friends back. They'd all gone to the panto and she'd treated herself to a symphony concert. The music soothed her anxious spirit at first and then came Beethoven's Fifth making her think of Dieter, stirring all those feelings up again.

Thelma and Ruth were on a recruitment drive for their Saturday Night Fellowship meetings: 'You'll meet some good people there. It's fun and gets you out of yourself.'

When she heard how Maddy's Christmas had been so sad, Ruth offered advice, 'Trust in the Lord and he will provide.'

Ruth was right, Maddy thought, as she sat in the doctor's waiting room, feeling sick with apprehension, but what if she was sickening for something serious? It was one of her own New Year's resolutions to get herself fighting fit again. If she was anaemic there were pills to perk her up. She couldn't ever recall a time when she'd felt so low, perhaps only after the eye operation. Sometimes when she looked in the mirror she thought her eye was turning again. It turned when she was tired and she was tired all the time now.

'Miss Belfield?' A voice summoned her into the little sitting room at the back of a large family house. A man with a white beard sat behind a desk and pointed her to the leather upright chair facing him. 'How can I help?' He leaned forward, his glasses falling over his nose.

Maddy told him how tired she was and how she felt faint for no reason and was hungry all the time.

'And when was your last monthly course?' he asked.

'You know, I can't remember. Before Christmas, I think . . . I'm never very regular . . . I never have been . . .' she replied. What had the curse got to do with anything?

'I see,' he answered, and came across to look under her eyelids and in her throat, her ears, took her pulse and blood pressure. 'Have you lost weight?'

'No, in fact I've filled out. I was always skinny,' she answered, puzzled by the direction of his questions.

'You've had no periods, you've put on weight, do you feel sick?'

'No, not really just tired.'

'Since when?'

'Since I came to Leeds in September,' she said, struggling to recall when all this began.

'I'm going to have to examine you.' The doctor pointed to the screen. 'Please remove your stockings and suspenders and pants.'

She obliged quickly, really worried now that something was terribly wrong. She lay on the couch while he felt her stomach.

'Does this hurt?' he pressed.

'No.'

'I see . . . Have you had an examination before . . . inside the passage.'

'No.'

'Well, I must do it. I can call my wife if you would prefer,' he said, sounding suddenly very curt.

'No . . . I'm fine.' She opened her legs and felt a burn as he probed inside her with his fingers.

'You are still a virgin, I see . . . That is strange.' He stared down at her with concern. He pressed her stomach and her insides together? 'How unfortunate,' he sighed, taking off his glasses.

Now Maddy was really worried. 'Have I a growth?' she mumbled, thinking the worst while she stared at the green curtain of the screen, a sad theatre gown shade.

'You have a growth but not what you think. How it got there . . . Have you had sexual relations with someone recently?' he asked, not looking at her directly but through the corner of his eye as if he was trying to sum her up.

'No!' she protested. 'I did have a boyfriend, but not now.'

'When was that, then?'

'In the summer holidays. Actually, for a few weeks, and then he left to go abroad to Germany.'

'In the Forces?'

'No, he was an exchange student . . . What's this got to do with me feeling tired?'

'I'm sorry to have to tell you, Miss Belfield, but you are going to have a child.'

Maddy sat up, rigid. 'But I can't be. We never did . . .' She paused, feeling so shocked.

'So I see. No penetration occurred but enough seepage to, well, swim its way . . . you young people will go in for heavy petting, I think is the term.'

Maddy blushed. 'We were close, yes, but we . . . we thought it was safe. He was so careful . . .' Her words faded away.

'Not careful enough. I'm afraid you've been most unlucky but these things happen.' Maddy was shivering. 'But we were careful. We knew it was wrong to go inside before marriage.' She pulled down her skirt, desperate to hold on to some dignity.

'You were very foolish. A little sperm goes a long way and even a virgin has a few gaps. You ride horses perhaps, or do ballet?' the doctor asked, washing his hands in the sink.

'Both,' she replied. 'But it can't be true?'

'You say you can't recall your last monthly course. I would guess it was last July so that makes you about five months into your term. I can feel this by the size of the womb. Haven't you noticed any changes in your body, young lady?'

'Only that I had filled out – I was so pleased not to be straight up and down . . . but I can't be pregnant! What'll I do?'

'Is there any chance the young man will marry you?'

Maddy shook her head. 'He lives near Dresden. Since he went home I have had only one censored letter. I think he is trapped there.'

'That's a pity for both of you. Then it gives me no option but to book you into a home for unfortunate girls like yourself where you will be confined until such times and then we can arrange for adoption. Have you a family to support you?'

'My parents died in the war. I have an aunt and grandmother in the country but I do not want to worry them.'

'You should've thought of that before you engaged in such sexual behaviour. You have been very silly and unlucky. Very few are caught this way. I will give you iron tablets to build up your strength. You are run down. This baby is draining strength from you. You are entitled to milk tokens and welfare juice but I have to charge you for examinations. Unfortunately this new National Health Service hasn't started yet so treatments must be paid for.'

Maddy stood up and then felt faint and sat down again.

'You're in shock, young lady. This is not what you expected.' The doctor's voice was full of concern now.

Maddy shook her head trying not to weep. 'I thought I was just run down. Things are not easy, My uncle and aunt have separated. My grandma is furious. I can't burden them with this too.'

'You have work here?'

'I'm a student.' She preferred not to say anything more. 'I do have a little income of my own. But I've let the family down. What am I going to do now?'

'Go back to your digs and try to rest. There's always a way forward. The growth in your stomach is new life, not something sinister. Unexpected and unwelcome it might be but it is another human being to bring into this world. To bring a child up alone will take money, support and understanding people around you. A child needs loving parents to nurture it. Are you sure you are the right person to do this? Are you strong enough to face the disgrace to come for your family and your standing in society?'

Maddy didn't want to hear another word. 'How much do I owe you?'

'The lady at the desk will see to that. Go home and rest and pray to your God to guide you through to the right decision. We will make arrangements for your confinement at our next appointment.'

Maddy stumbled out of the surgery into the grey afternoon. The wind was ripping through her tweed suit and up her legs. The pain was still smarting from his examination. Her eyes blinked back the tears in the dusty street. She stood at the bus stop in a daze, letting buses pass by and turned north to walk uphill to the roundabout at West Park, her heart thumping in her ribcage.

Pregnant, with child . . . It was all thundering around her head like a tolling bell. All this time she'd not noticed . . . or had she? She'd seen the blue paper package of the sanitary towels sitting unopened in the back of her drawer for months, and she'd refused to see the message they were giving her.

This was the loneliest walk of her life, worse even

than the night of the blitz. She had done this to herself. Up the hill, she trudged, round the bend where the white stuccoed house in Arncliffe Road was waiting, up the brown varnished hallway and stairs with the brass rods across the mottled green carpet – not forgetting to take her shoes off as was Miss Ffrost's rule – up two flights to the attic. She walked over to the drawer to see if those towels were still there and yanked them out, throwing them across the floor in disgust. How could she have been so blind?

Staring at herself in the mirror, she turned this way and that. She was still slim even though her waist was thicker. In a long cardigan and jumper no one could tell, but she knew she was changed for ever by this startling fact.

Inside her was new life and one day it would grow so big that she'd have to let it go and the whole world would know what she'd done. Dismissal from college would then be on the cards, she'd be the talking point of Sowerthwaite, and Grandma would have an apoplectic fit. She was no better than poor Eunice Billingham or Enid Cartwright. They'd had to face the furore and now it was her turn.

Maddy curled up on the bed, piling all the blankets over her head. She could hang on a little longer, not show her secret shame for a few more weeks. She was going to pretend none of it was happening yet, go about her studies, keep herself to herself, and just hope when the time came she'd have the courage to face it all.

Curled in a ball she could hide from this cruel world. She didn't want to think about any of it. She'd gone for some pills and this was the bitter pill she'd have to swallow alone. Then she recalled something in her autograph book that Grace Battersby had written all those years ago when she was sad. Painted over some dark clouds was a rainbow and the words: 'All things pass, so will this.'

But it didn't feel like that now. Once a child was born it was there for ever. This event would never pass. It was just the beginning of for ever.

Maddy sobbed and hugged herself, waiting for sleep to overcome her.

14

Plum stared into the firelight – yet another freezing winter in Sowerthwaite to endure. Brooklyn Hall was an ice box to live in. Pleasance Belfield hugged the fire too, but there was little warmth to glean from it. She refused to sit by the Rayburn stove in the kitchen. That would be lowering her standards too much. It was bad enough in her eyes, having only a daily now and no live-in help. Grace Battersby came in with her cheery smile from her cottage on the High Street as she had done with the evacuees all those years ago.

Maddy hadn't been home for weeks, since the weather in Leeds was awful and she was preparing for a typing speed test and exams. Gloria said she'd met her by the town hall steps and they'd gone for lunch, but no one had news of anything in these grim months.

Gerry kept away but wrote to his mother. He'd found a new position in a city bank, but no mention of his mistress was made to upset Pleasance. He said he might be back to shoot in the autumn and do a little hunting – just to keep things looking normal, Plum thought –

but he was content to let things stew on the matter of their divorce.

In truth she'd put off seeing her solicitor too. There were a litter of pups on the way and horses to exercise. They were all acting as if the events of Christmas hadn't happened but the chill between the Plum and Pleasance inside Brooklyn was not as easy to address as the freezing temperature outside.

This place was too big, too empty, too cold and sad. It should be sold, except no one would want to live in a barn like this unless it were a hotel or a convalescent home for old miners with bad lungs. It could make a good prep school with playing fields, noisy children bringing the house back to life. It needed children, not old folks now.

Plum had seen Pleasance stumbling up the stairs, clinging to the banister rail for dear life. How she'd aged in the last few months. Disappointment had sucked in her cheeks and tightened her mouth. Naturally she wanted to blame Plum for not being a good enough wife.

'You should've gone to London . . . never taken on that blessed hostel. You could have sorted things out. Gerry needs a firm hand. It's beyond me! Whatever will people think when they find out?' she whined like a child deprived of its sweetie.

'Oh, Mother, what does it matter? We're not the only ones going through this, I'm sure. Gerald is his own master. I was always just the little country wife to him, expendable. We've grown apart. We married too quickly and never got a chance to know each other . . .'

'You should've kept some mystery, some allure. Look at you, dressed in old slacks like a farm labourer. You scrub up perfectly when you bother to take the trouble. A man likes to see his wife at her prettiest, eager, ready to greet him when he returns. He always had to root round the kennels to find you.'

'At least dogs don't let you down,' Plum snapped, tired of this constant criticism. 'I'm sorry I couldn't keep your errant son from straying off the porch. I'm sorry I'm not the kind of glamour puss he obviously prefers and I'm sorry I didn't give you an heir to train up. No, I mean, I'm glad there's no poor boy to be spoiled and trained in his father's footsteps!'

'Prunella! That's not like you! I didn't mean to bring up that subject.' Pleasance put down her knitting and sighed.

'Oh, but it's there, underneath the surface, day in and out, and I'm so sick of hearing how I have failed in my duty. It's me that keeps this blessed place going. I do my duty in Sowerthwaite. I kept the home fires burning so I think it's time for a life of my own. I shall leave at the end of the month. It's time I found my own place and started afresh.'

'But what about Brooklyn? I can't manage on my own.'

'I know that, but you have choices. Get Gerry to pay for a housekeeper . . . that's all I've been for the past six years. Look around you, Mother. This mausoleum needs a new life or pulling down. It's too grand and ridiculous. We'll become two old biddies rattling round waiting for someone to visit us. It's pathetic,' said Plum, surprised at the venom of her words. Years of frustration were spilling out of her mouth.

'You ungrateful girl! How dare you talk to me like this? I've sacrificed two sons for my country. You've had it easy all these years. You never were my first choice for Gerald.'

'Oh, and don't I know it! I've had that fact seeping into my pores for years but I had my uses, or had you forgotten? How much of my own income has kept this tanker afloat? Gerry's wartime pay never made a dent into the upkeep of this mausoleum. Now it's about time the place kept itself. You're living in the past, Pleasance.' Plum sat down, suddenly weary of their quarrelling.

'The past is all I have these days . . . no future to look forward to but creaking bones and killing time,' came the reply. 'When there's no heir to pass on all you've created, no Belfields to come—'

'There's Maddy.'

'She's a girl.'

'So is Princess Elizabeth. Maddy's a Belfield and one day she'll make us proud. You can pass it on to her and let her make something of this albatross round our necks.'

'Oh, that's enough, Prunella. I'll not be ordered about in my own home.'

'I've not said nearly enough,' Plum snorted. 'But someone has to see to dinner.'

'I'm not hungry.'

'You will be when it's ready. Meals don't just rise up

through the table unaided. Grace can only do so much.' Plum rose from the sofa, wanting to get out of the room and the atmosphere.

'You are being very cruel to an old lady.'

'You're not old, but you will be if you keep up this moaning Minnie act. We have to pull together, not tear each other apart.'

'What's the point? You're leaving . . . you just said.'

'Oh, not yet. How can I? Not till everything is in place to your satisfaction, though why I bother, I don't know.'

'You've become hard. Go now, if you're so discontent.'

'I might just do that,' Plum shouted as she fled through the door. How she needed a cigarette!

In the noise of the kennels she calmed down. Sweeping out the muck and exercising the bitch in the field, staring across to the limestone crags was soothing. She felt oddly serene now all that venom was out of her system.

I love this place, she smiled as she drew smoke into her lungs. I love the old house, the space around it, the gardens, the trees. It's my home too – so why should I leave?

In the cool fresh air their quarrelling seemed so silly and childish and so bitchy.

Perhaps it was all this wretched sweating and hot flushes giving an edginess to her mood.

Poor old Pleasance was slowing down and she couldn't defend herself against Plum in full flow of righteous indignation. Brooklyn and all it stood for was her pride and joy, a sign of her status in the district.

She was losing everything now. Everything Mother'd wanted to achieve was in these old stones: the grandeur of the sweep of stairs, the fine marble on the hall floor, the silver. This was all she had. Selling it would be disastrous since house prices were so low. No one wanted to take on such a big place.

Plum pulled off her gloves and saw her reflection in the window. She'd let her hair go uncut and frizzed at the edges, her collar was grubby and she did look a mess. Pleasance was only trying to give her some home truths. Now she felt mean and sorry that they'd argued so much. Time to go inside and make a soothing cup of china tea with Grace's special ginger biscuits on a Spode plate as a peace offering.

When she strode through the hall there was a strange noise, a funny groaning coming from the drawing room, and Plum rushed in to see Pleasance slumped across the sofa, her face lopsided, her lips drooling with distress.

Plum cried out, made her comfortable and rang for the doctor.

Sergeant Gregory Byrne read Plum's letter on the ship home. They'd docked briefly in the Med in Gibraltar. He'd climbed the rock to see the monkeys and the view. He fingered his post with interest – Plum was his only link with civvy street now.

Since the war ended his regiment had been all over Europe on mercy missions, opening kitchens in displacement camps. He'd seen such sad stuff: camps with people in rags; children with swollen bellies, too feeble to beg; families living under tarpaulins, filthy; beautiful cities razed to the ground – enough horrors to last a lifetime – and now they were on their way home.

Old Ma Belfield had had a stroke. She was in bed and couldn't move much. It sounded as if Mrs Plum was rushing all over the show just keeping things ticking over. No change there then.

Her husband, the posh bloke who no one ever saw, had returned to see his ma but she was hanging on for dear life. That sounded just like the tough old bird who'd shouted at them for mucking up her carpets all those years ago.

Maddy had come home briefly from Leeds to see her gran. She was a student but she couldn't stay at home long either. She'd met up with Gloria Conley again and they were still pally. No change there then either.

Greg wondered what those two birds looked like, skinny mallink and the ginger knob, no doubt. Plum said Maddy was quite bonny these days, and loved cream slices and pies. In other words, Greg smiled, she'd grown fat.

> Poor Gloria's not enjoying her post at Dr Gunn's any more. Their new baby is called Heather and rather sickly. She says she stinks of milk, and Sarah and Jeremy, the other children, are playing her up. She's considering making another move into Leeds since there are plenty of opportunities for her to be a mother's

help. Sid now works on a farm and I don't think he'll ever budge from the Dale again.

I think she finds Sowerthwaite a little dull after the town. She told me if you've seen one sheep you've seen the lot! I think she's grown tired of being a country bumpkin.

When will you be demobbed? What are you going to do next?

The poor hostel is nearly empty and they're thinking of shutting it down. Gloria says it's very creepy at night time when the girls have gone home for the weekend.

How is your friend Charlie Afton? Is he still courting a German girl? You will find England very dull and grey when you come home. We have so many shortages and rations, but nothing to what you must have seen abroad.

It doesn't feel like we won the war but our local farmers are doing well enough. They've all got vans and machinery now, so I'm sure Brigg's would be glad of a good mechanic.

I'm afraid you will find us all very scruffy and gloomy. Do look us up when you return and tell us all your news.

Good Luck.

Plum Belfield.

How far away was that cosy world now. Gloria and Maddy would be strangers, grown up but still kids. He'd had one letter from Gloria, along with a photograph of her posing, trying to make herself look older.

Was she still all red hair and freckles? And as for Maddy, doing shorthand and typing, getting fat and eating cakes . . . that wasn't the Maddy he remembered. Perhaps her eye had turned again . . . Poor kid, stuck with the oldies in that big house.

They were just names on paper to him now in a faraway one-horse town in Yorkshire. He'd seen the ruined cities of Europe in all their glory, lived so long in barracks he'd forgotten what a real house was like.

The war had taken the shine off him, hardened his features and muscles to granite, and turned him into a first-class mechanic, stripper, fitter, ducking and diving. When he got out he was going to do something about making money from all he'd learned. There was a whole new opportunity waiting in Blighty and he was going to make himself some dosh one way or another.

One day he'd have a Brooklyn of his own, with a paddock and pony for his kiddies, and a wife who thought he was Mr Universe. But it would have to be in Yorkshire, in the hills, quiet and grand.

Funny that he'd seen mountain ranges, volcanoes, Alpine peaks, but he couldn't wait to see that green grass of the Dales again – but not until he could possess some of it for himself. It might take one year or five, but he knew what he wanted. He'd not gone through the bloody battlefields of Europe to end up in some dead-end garage pit looking up the arse of some Austin Seven Ruby . . . no way.

If he worked on anything it would be a Daimler or Roller or a Fangio racing car, something with class, speed and fury. Perhaps he could get into a racing team, making tea, carrying spanners at first, but he wanted to see his heroes at close quarters and his women would be top-notch birds too, classy and clean. He'd seen enough scrubbers and sad acts to know what he was looking for, but perfection didn't come cheap.

The army had given him skills. There was no engine he couldn't fettle up. He fancied his chances in the building trade, doing up ruins for a quick profit; with all the bombs dropped there was bound to be scope for rebuilds and slum clearance. Even if he had to start as a builder's mate, it was worth a try.

Maddy came when summoned, hugging her smart new briefcase and some overnight clothes. Miss Meyer had asked her to redo some accounts while she was away.

'You're all over the place, Madeleine. You sit with us, but I think your concentration has gone to Timbuktu.'

'Sorry,' she said. 'My grandmother is sick and I'm worried. I need to go home, she's very ill.'

'Of course, you must see to that, but I must have your work in on your return, dear. Life has to go on even when the ones we love are passing over,' said Miss Hermione, patting her hand.

I don't love Grandma, I never have, thought Maddy with guilt, but she would go back to Brooklyn. The last phone call to Miss Ffrost's house had been a reprimand from Aunt Plum: 'She won't last long. I need you here, Maddy. Please come home.'

Maddy had taken to wearing a tight corset to hide

her six-month bulge. Her pot belly was showing so she'd found a sort of gymslip without the belt, and a long jumper, and tried to look hip like the girls in the jazz club that Bella had taken them to after college. In the dark smoky basement, she could forget all her troubles in the smooth rhythms of the music.

How she longed to trust them with her condition, but she couldn't bear to see pity flood into their eyes. Ruth and Thelma would want to pray for her, and Pinky was too wrapped up in going to see Malcolm and lambing to even notice that Maddy was not her usual self. If only she could trust one of them, but they were only college mates not confidantes. The only friend she had was Gloria, and lately she'd shoved her away too. There was always the fear that she might blab her shame all over Sowerthwaite in a careless moment of chatter.

Aunt Plum was distraught about Grandma and nursed her with devotion. She kept saying it was all her fault. Grace Battersby was running the household in her cheery way, and Mrs Hill in the cottage nearby came to do the laundry and shopping.

Now Maddy must go home one last time.

She'd not gone back to Dr Klein or the Welfare Offices. Better to carry on and get her exams passed, get her speed certificates, but she was all fingers and thumbs, making silly mistakes, and her grades had plummeted. She had calculated her birth date. If she could make an excuse for an absence on holiday, perhaps she might conceal the truth and come back with a baby?

No! She just couldn't think so far ahead. It was all so unreal. The doctor said one thing and she wanted to do the opposite, in her usual disobedient fashion. Perhaps she could pay Gloria to be her mother's help, but with what? She needed every penny to buy clothes for her baby, a pram and other expenses. She must find a room, but all the ads in the paper for places she could afford said 'No children'.

Where would she deliver without going into a home?

Now she must screw her face together, pull in her stomach and trust no one noticed her condition when she got home.

Everyone was tiptoeing around at the Brooklyn.

The vicar came and went, smiling at her. 'How are you, young lady? We're so glad you've come. Mrs Belfield will be pleased to see you.'

Oh, no, she won't, thought Maddy. My shameful news would kill her off at once.

Plum rushed round the corner, carrying a tray. 'Oh, darling, do take this up to the nurse. She needs a break. Just sit with Granny for a while. She'll know you're there . . . I'm rushed off my feet. Uncle Gerald's out on Monty. He's up from London to make his peace . . . It's not looking too good.'

Maddy carried the tray into the big bedroom with the four-poster bed facing the window overlooking the moor. The room smelled of Lysol and smoke: the scent of the flowers on the dressing table made her feel sick for a second. The dark brocade curtains were draped back so the old lady could be propped up to stare out on to the fell, an uninterrupted view. She looked about a hundred, her face pinched and crooked, her eyes glassy and a dribble coming out of the side of her mouth.

This wasn't Grandma; Pleasance Matilda Belfield, the famous old battle-axe. In her place was this little pixie of a crone from a fairy-tale illustration straight out of Grimms', a shadow of the woman she once was.

Maddy recoiled at the sight of her. The day nurse, in her starched cap and apron, smiled, took the tray and retired to the dressing room next door to smoke while Maddy touched Granny's hand. It was like a bony claw.

The hawk eyes turned in her direction.

'Just me, Madeleine . . .' she smiled.

The old lady tried to speak but it was a garbled mess of noises. How terrible to be trapped in such a feeble body, unable to move or speak, just a wizened little half-smile and a sigh. So Maddy rattled on about Miss Meyer and the girls at college, about Miss Ffrost's awful dinners, how cold it was and sooty and smoky in Leeds city centre. She patted Grandma's hand, trying not to cry, for it was a shock to see such a sad end to such a proud life. Everything was fading away like the corners of the curtains bleached grey by the afternoon sun.

The nurse came back into the room and Maddy was relieved of her post. She sped to her own bedroom, suddenly achy and weary. The journey had been long and her back ached. Exhaustion overcame her again. She lay staring up at the familiar plasterwork on the ceiling, willing her bump to lie quiet within and give her some rest, but the fluttering inside made her want to scream, I don't want to feel you. I don't want to know you're there. Go away!

The atmosphere at dinner was strained. Plum and Gerry were being extra polite. The night nurse was ready to go on duty.

This extravagance was Uncle Gerry's idea and Plum didn't protest about the expense. She looked so tired and washed out with worry. Her hair was scraped back into a bun and she wore a grey twinset and grey flannels and pearl earrings, but suddenly Maddy saw that her aunt looked jaded, middle-aged and so unhappy.

Any fleeting hope of confiding in her was quashed. Plum looked at the end of her tether, strained with keeping up appearances and caring for her sick mother-in-law. Maddy wondered how long the old woman upstairs would last. This nursing had been going on for weeks and it was clear there would be no recovery. Her heart would decide when it had had enough or another stroke might see her out of this world.

The nurses were chatty, uninvolved and told her exactly what to expect: 'We'll call you if there is any change. Poor dear won't be long before she slips away.'

Grandma would hate to be referred to like that, but Maddy was too tired to protest. All she wanted to do was go to sleep and soothe her aching back.

In the morning Maddy was halfway to the stables when she changed her mind about riding Monty. She felt so tired and achy, as if she was coming down with flu. Then she recalled it might be Gloria's day off so there might be a chance of a bit of young company. Carrying her briefcase full of homework just in case no one was there and she could read through her notes under the Victory Tree, she sniffed the springtime air along the lane with relief.

It was one of those special Dales mornings, the rough breeze chilly from the snowy tops of the fells, birds chattering, darting among bare twigs along the grassy bank topped by the dry-stone wall that led from the house to the hostel. There were primroses in the shady banks and clumps of purple violets, coltsfoot and lush green foliage. Everything was springing alive again, bringing summer ever closer, when she must give birth too.

To her relief she saw Gloria hanging out her smalls, her flame hair twisted under a headscarf like a gypsy. She looked up and smiled.

'Maddy, you're back at last . . . What's the latest news? I heard things weren't so good,' Gloria said.

Maddy shook her head wearily. 'Cup of tea on the go?'

'I can do better than that. Hot Vimto, Bovril, dandelion and burdock – name your poison,' Gloria laughed, picking up the wicker laundry basket and heading for the steps. 'It's a grand day for a line of washing.'

'Am I glad to see you . . . It's awful up there. Everyone's waiting for Grandma to die. I thought she'd go on for years. Aunt Plum is like a shadow, flittering around at everyone's beck and call.'

'I hear as it was her as found her. They'd had a row, poor Mrs Plum. I hear his lordship's living in London for good. They say the Brooklyn will be up for sale soon as old Mrs Belfield's gone . . .'

Maddy wasn't listening as she felt a strange warm wetness running down her legs. She felt down to see where she'd wet herself. 'Oh, no!' she cried out.

'What's up?' Gloria said, and then saw the pool on the stone slab. 'Crikey, what's that?'

'Nothing, I'd better go. I've just wet myself, would you believe it – at my age!' She made to go back up the steps but a stabbing pain tore through her belly and she doubled up. Gloria rushed to her side. 'You'd better come inside and quick. Is it diarrhoea?'

'No . . . I don't think so . . . I think I'm in labour,' Maddy croaked, unable to look Gloria in the eye. She had been reading up on childbirth in the reference library on the sly.

'You are having me on! Pull the other one, Lady Jane,' Gloria roared, stepping back to take a closer look at her friend. She saw the panic on Maddy's face and knew it was no joke. 'What've you been up to in Leeds?'

'Not there, here, last summer, Dieter and me, we got caught. It shouldn't have happened but it did. I'm having a baby but not yet, surely not now!'

'Does anyone know up there?' Gloria nodded in the direction of the hall.

'Of course not. No one knows but you. You have to help me. It's coming early and I don't know what to do.'

'How early?' Gloria asked, her freckled nose and sharp eyes glinting with concern.

'I don't know but it's not due for ages.'

'If we lie you down and rest, happen it'll stop. Come on, lean on me and I'll get you upstairs. There's only Alice Nuttall staying, and she's on early shift, then she's having her hair permed at Susan's. There's no one at home but me.'

Gloria helped her up the stairs to the top bedroom. It was a jumble of unironed clothes, magazines piled on a single bed, make-up tumbling over the dresser and a little cracked mirror in a frame. 'You lie down and I'll boil the kettle like they do in the films.'

'What for?'

'I don't know, but that's what they always say, and towels, loads of towels to mop up the . . . Oh, and newspaper for my bed. I don't want any mess on it. It'll have to be *Picturegoer*s – that's all I've got. There might be a *Gazette* in the common room. Crikey, Maddy, it were a good job it were my day off.'

'How's things?' Maddy tried to act normally but the pain gripped her again. It started in her back and then gathered like a tight lasso around her stomach.

This wasn't right. Dr Klein had suggested she wasn't due until June, and this was only early April. In her head she knew she should send for Dr Gunn. Better just to lie here and see if it settled down. She couldn't think straight for the pain. Her slacks were soaking wet, sticking to her legs. Her corset needed unhooking. She felt she was bursting inside.

They struggled to get her clothes off and Maddy into one of Gloria's old nighties. Gloria rushed down for a basin and a pile of dishcloths, then down again for magazines and the one newspaper. Up and down, her curls bobbing and her cheeks pink.

Between them, they stripped the bed and put towels and papers over between each pain.

'We ought to call Dr Gunn. If it's early he'll know what to do. I've never done this before . . . you'll have to tell me what to do.'

'But I don't know either,' Maddy confessed.

'Didn't you read up?'

'Only a little bit. I didn't want to think about it until I had to. I'm sorry . . .'

'Then we'll just get on with it as best we can, keep everything clean and the baby warm. How funny her up in Brooklyn passing over and another life coming in her place. They'll get one hell of a shock when you show your face with a bundle in your arms.'

'But it's too soon. It won't be right.'

'Oh, I don't know. Next door's babby in Peel Street was a seven-month job – and they hadn't a stitch for it so her gran went and bought a lace burial gown off the second-hand barrow, so as not to waste her money but he's three year old now, bright as a button, not a mark on him. They just kept him warm by the bread oven until he was up to fighting weight. Babies survive, you'll see.'

Maddy said nothing, knowing this one would be just over six months old not seven. It seemed like for ever, lying on the bed. Alice came and went to the shop for fags and then on to her hair appointment, unaware that Maddy was hiding upstairs with a flannel in her mouth to stop her groans.

'Are there only the two of you here now?' Maddy whispered. If she screamed now she might give the game away.

'The Old Vic's like a morgue these days. I'm thinking of packing it in with the Gunns. Babies are hard work and Heather is a right little mitherer, whines all day. Shall I go and fetch someone?'

'No!' Maddy gasped as the pain hit her again. 'Not yet . . . please don't leave me, I'm so scared.'

Gloria couldn't think what to do next. Maddy was in agony and had been sick in the basin, tossing and turning and crying out. Giving birth must really hurt.

Mrs Gunn had gone into a nursing home for two weeks and came back clean, slim and smiling with her bundle of joy as if it were a trip to the seaside.

Gloria knew how babies were born but what to do when they came out was another matter. This labour was going on for hours and she was scared. The kettle was boiled dry for hot-water bottles, on the little electric ring.

It made sense to wrap the babby in hot towels to keep it warm and clean, but they had nothing but clean dishtowels, the ones kept in the second drawer on the left for best, utility towels with red stripes at the end. They would do for a start, and she might be able to snaffle a few bits from the Gunns' nursery to tide them along. It would give Maddy time to think.

In her heart Gloria knew she ought to go for help, no matter what Maddy insisted – but then she might be in trouble for delivering a baby without help. There wasn't really time. Her pains were coming so fast now. Maddy's face was covered in sweat and she kept asking for sips of water. It was hard to know how to comfort her in this state.

'I need to push now,' Maddy groaned. 'Help me!'

'Like a number two?'

'Yee . . . s.'

'Oh Lord. You'd better squat down like the natives do, then. They can deliver theirs behind a bush and then go back to work, so the missionary said,' she offered.

'Well, that's a lie! This is bloody hard work . . . oh . . . Gloria I'm scared.'

'So am I,' she whispered, peering between Maddy's open legs, fearful of what might be there.

Maddy screamed and pushed and something slithered out in a gush – a purple bundle onto the towel and the *Gazette*. It had a cord dangling.

'We have to cut the cord. Bitches bite on them and clean up their pups,' Gloria suggested. They'd both seen enough lambs and pups born to know the score.

'Wow! It's come, Maddy!' she smiled, while Maddy was pushing something else out that looked like a large piece of liver from the butcher's. There was such a mess of everything all at once.

'What do we do now?' she cried, knowing the baby needed air to breathe. It was so small and not like a baby at all, more a tiny doll. 'It's a baby boy,' she offered gazing down at the little mite, not much bigger than the size of her hand. It lay all curled up and silent.

'We have to make it breathe.' Maddy looked down. 'He's so tiny and beautiful, I'll blow in his face.' She scooped up the limp baby and blew and blew. 'Why isn't he breathing?'

'I told you we should have got help. Dr Gunn would know what to do. Let me have a go,' Gloria snapped, feeling fear trickling up her spine.

The baby's skin was still purple, his eyes shut and peaceful, all curled up in his own little world like a little skinless bird thrown out of the nest too soon. Gloria was sweating now with fear. The tiny thing in her hands had veins through its glassy skin and still no breath. This was all going wrong. It should be breathing by now. Then she recalled a film where the doctor dunked the baby in water to shock it into breathing. All she had was cold water left and she raced downstairs to run the tap.

Maddy screamed from the bed, 'Hurry up!'

Up the stairs she struggled, grabbing the baby and dunking it in the water but nothing happened. Seconds turned into minutes and only then was it obvious that there was no life in this child.

'You should've let me go for help, Maddy. Now what are we going to do?'

'I don't know, I'll think of something,' Maddy sighed, and lay back, overcome by exhaustion, closing her eyes and drifting off to sleep, the baby cradled in the towel by her side.

It was the longest day of Gloria's life, sitting there, the enormity of what had happened hitting her like a hammer. They had to do something before Alice Nuttall returned. How could Maddy just turn over and sleep like that?

She stared down at the bundle, knowing it was up to her to do something about it now. Poor Maddy needed her sleep after all that pain and effort. She'd have to go back to the Brooklyn as if nothing had happened. No one would be any the wiser but the mess would have to be cleared away – and fast.

The fire was lit downstairs and she could burn the papers and stuff, but how to give this little thing a burial? Perhaps they should call the vicar, but it was too late now for anything proper. Gloria was on her own with this one. It wasn't fair to be dumped with such a terrible thing but her friend had needed her and they must stick together.

Perhaps one day when she needed a favour Maddy would oblige. That's what friends did: helped each other out.

There was no time to shillyshally, she must do the necessary, and quick. Better that Maddy knew nothing more about this. In films midwives took stillborns away quietly and put them somewhere. It wasn't as if the little mite was ready to be born. He'd never breathed – it was just too soon. In a funny way he'd done Maddy a favour in slipping away so quietly. There'd be all hell to pay if anyone found out.

Gloria took one last look at him, lying like a skinned rabbit, perfect in every way but lifeless. She wanted to cry. This wasn't right and he'd never stood a chance. It was left to her now to sort out his final resting place.

*

Maddy's dreams were full of tunnels with water rushing through and she was trapped on a ledge, but the torrent pushed her out into a swimming pool and there was little Dieter swimming towards her, pink and smiling. As she swam to him he began to sink and she couldn't reach him or find him at the bottom of the pool. Diving under the water, she was blinded by green murk, feeling around searching, searching to catch his limb, like catching soap in the bath. He slipped from her and she woke in a panic, sweating, but it was only a dream.

Her room had changed into the attic at the Old Vic and then she sensed the soreness in her belly and the towels between her legs. Suddenly wide awake she knew something awful had happened.

She sat up and her head swam. Where was the baby? Where was Gloria? What had happened last night was a fuzz of images. Was the baby still inside her? She felt the flatness of her stomach, someone had battered her insides and she struggled for the gerry pot. Everything burned and there was blood beneath her.

Then Alice popped her head around the door, sporting her new frizzy perm. 'You've had a bad monthly,' she sighed. 'They're such a mucky nuisance. Do you want some more STs? I've got some towels in my room. You do look like death warmed up. Shall I make a cuppa?'

Maddy nodded meekly. She must try and get up and behave as normal, but her slacks were nowhere to be found and Gloria had vanished. There was nothing to give away their secret. The room was tidy, the sheets were clean and she had no recollection of getting out of bed, but the dream was spinning in her head; Little Dieter's sculptured face, lifeless in her arms. Where was he? Her arms ached to hold him again but it was as if he was never born on 3 April 1948.

Alice brought in some tea and a slice of soggy toast. Maddy was hungry and grateful.

'Gloria's gone to the Gunns,' she said, and sat on the end of the bed. 'She'll pop back at dinnertime. She's such a good mother's help. How's your gran doing? We heard she was failing fast.'

Everyone knew everything in Sowerthwaite and the Belfield doings were always a source of speculation. She mustn't add to the family woes. In one supreme effort of will Maddy got out of bed, trying not to let Alice see the state she was in.

'Gloria's dried your clothes . . . it's awful when you get caught short,' smiled Alice. 'I'll bring them up if you like.'

She'd never been so grateful in all her life for these simple acts of kindness, or the fact that trusting Alice believed their story. The cover had held. She accepted another pad, hoping it would hold until she got home. Her breasts were sore now. It was an effort to hook herself into her corset, but she must look normal – as if nothing had happened. As if her insides had not ripped open and delivered a life of sorts.

Mustn't think about that now, but get dressed, gather her stuff and leave a note for Gloria on the kitchen table, asking her to call round.

They must meet up and then she'd know where little

Dieter was and yet she didn't want to know. Last night was just a blur of pain and fear.

Her mind was racing; confused one minute, relieved the next. What she didn't know and hadn't seen wasn't real. The birth never happened, that was it. Would it be wrong to conceal a birth? Was it a crime? It was all a nightmare and she couldn't remember. It was as if it had happened to someone else.

Would she get Gloria into trouble? She couldn't think. It'd never lived so there was no proper birth to disclose. Round and round the excuses, the lies, the images flashed in her fuzzy brain.

The walk back to Brooklyn took every ounce of her strength and all her concentration to put one foot in front of the other. All she could think of was climbing those stairs and creeping under her eiderdown to sleep for a hundred years.

She staggered up the avenue of tears. If it'd lived . . . What would they have made of this new Belfield, this German–English hybrid? If it had lived would she be making this walk now? Why did she call the thing, it? She didn't want to recall any of it ever again.

There were cars outside the portico on the gravel drive, black cars and a man in a frock coat came down the stairs and doffed his bowler hat.

'Ah, Miss Belfield, our deepest condolences on your sad loss,' he whispered. 'Sowerthwaite will be diminished by her passing.'

Maddy nodded, not taking in his words at first, but she knew it was Alfred Platt, the joiner, owner of the funeral parlour. Her heart was thudding when she saw

Plum scowling as she came down the stairs. Her lips pinched with disapproval.

'Where on earth have you been? Staying out all night. As if I hadn't enough to worry about. Couldn't you not have stayed at home one more day and seen it through with us?' she snapped.

'I was only at Gloria's. Someone could have rung there,' she replied. 'Has Grandma . . . ?' She couldn't finish the sentence.

'This morning, very early and peacefully. We were all at her side but you should've been there. It was the least you could do after all she'd done for you.' Maddy had never seen Plum so vexed and agitated. 'It's not like you to let us down. I am disappointed in you.'

'I'm sorry . . .'

'So you should be. I thought you might at least have rung to see how things were, but no, when you young ones get together, there's no thought for anyone else. I might know Gloria Conley would lead you on.'

'It wasn't like that. I had a bad period and she looked after me. I couldn't move. I get them like that and I fell asleep. I'm so sorry,' Maddy wept. Tears of sadness, frustration and exhaustion were rolling down her face.

'You do look a bit off. Never mind,' Plum sighed. 'Everything's under control now that Platts are here, but you'll need something black for the funeral. At least we can give her the send-off she deserves. Oh, Maddy, I wish you'd been here. It would've helped me.'

What was there to say to that? If she had blurted out that while Gran was dying she was giving birth to a dead baby, what good would that do?

'Would you mind if I had a bath? I'm still feeling a bit wonky,' Maddy said, gripping the banister rail for dear life. It was the only thing holding her up. 'Are there any aspirins in the cabinet?'

'Oh, go and sort yourself out. Then you can help me send out funeral invitations for the service. We're not going to hang about. Gerald is seeing to it with the vicar. At least we're both hitched to the same wagon on this one.'

Maddy crept up the stairs, checked the hot-water tank, ran a bath with some Dettol in it. She sank into it slowly, letting the heat warm her through and soothe the soreness.

What was she going to do with her blood-soaked clothes? Then she noticed liquid seeping out of her breasts, trickles of juice for a baby that would never suck, and she wept and wept for all that was lost.

She had never felt so alone, so unloved and unnoticed. It was as if something of her had died with the thing she'd birthed last night. Grandma was gone out of the world at the same time. Had she met her baby in the avenue of tears when she joined all her sons in that far-off country? Were they all looking down in disgust?

She could have bled to death but for Gloria's care. She ought to thank her but to see her would bring it all back again. For a second she wanted to dunk her head under the bathwater and never come up. Who would care what happened to her now? Dieter didn't care or know her terrible fate. Plum was angry, Uncle Gerald uninterested. No one had a kind word for her. She was on her own again. That was nothing new.

It was time to make herself decent, stuffing pads into her brassiere to soak up the flow. She felt so weak it was all she could do to get downstairs and try to look useful. The whole day went by and still she'd not seen Gloria. They must make their stories tally if Plum was on the warpath.

The next few days were taken up with receiving visitors, ringing guests, finding Maddy something to wear, arranging flowers for the church and trying to stay upright.

The funeral took place on the Friday with all the due ceremony befitting a Belfield; a horse-drawn carriage, men in top hats and frock coats walking before the hearse, curtains were closed and flags lowered, the church bell tolled a bell for every one of her years on earth, as was the custom. There were the usual clutch of aged aunts and companions, with sticks and ear trumpets.

The reception was to be at the house. Maddy helped Grace prepare canapés, but outside caterers would see to all the other arrangements. Plum was too busy to talk, Gerald looked distinguished, brisk and brusque with her, but jovial and chirpy with his hunting cronies. It all looked fine on the surface but Plum and Gerry were not speaking to each other.

Maddy was the bridge between the two, relaying messages of condolence. There was no time to visit Gloria and she was hurt that her friend had not bothered to come and check on her.

But maybe she had a point. Better to stay away. The longer they stayed away from each other the easier it was to pretend the birth had never happened. There was nothing to link the two of them. The fact that Maddy looked like death, pale, stumbling and stooping, would be put down naturally to grief.

In her head she thought that the sooner she got back to Leeds and college, the sooner she could put this nightmare behind her – but that gave her no comfort at all.

Somewhere there was a little body laid to rest, hidden away when it should have been here alongside its great grandmother, but that would never happen now.

The Belfield reputation had to be respected and this was no time to draw attention to her own shameful secret.

Gloria went with the Gunns to the funeral, as was expected. The church was full, the vicar droning on about Old Ma Belfield's virtues, but Gloria could only remember her being a cantankerous old cow, until she recalled that first visit when Mrs Belfield picked her out as one of them by mistake. Thinking she was Maddy.

They were stuck in a side aisle and she didn't get a chance to speak to Maddy until the handshake at the end.

'How are you?' she whispered.

'I'm fine,' Maddy blushed, not looking her in the eye. She wore a navy coat with a fur collar, a silly hat perched on her head like a pillbox, over which a black net veil hid her puffy eyes as if she were royalty.

'But we have to talk . . .'

'I know. Later,' Maddy said. 'Not now . . . not here.'

'Come over to the hostel and we can sort things out.'

'What's there to sort out? You did your best and I'm so grateful, but it's over with,' Maddy replied, turning away to greet the next in the line as if she was just some onlooker.

'But I thought you'd want to know what I did with—'

'Shush! Not here. People will hear . . . I have to go.' Maddy darted from the line-up.

Gloria was puzzled. It was if Maddy didn't care about any of it now, as if she was pretending it had never happened.

She'd taken a huge risk, thinking on her feet, burying the evidence as best she could, saying a prayer. She'd even baptised him Dieter, just to make sure, like they did in the pictures when a baby died. Now she was being spoken to as if she'd done nothing special.

She wanted to tell Maddy about the nightmares she was having when his little face kept peering up, eyes open, pleading with her to let him breathe. What if he wasn't dead? Why should she carry the burden when there Maddy was, Lady bloody Bountiful, all airs and graces, greeting the gentry, ignoring her friend as if she was a nobody.

That wasn't what friends did. They stuck together

through thick and thin. She'd chew off her ear when the funeral was over, tell her what was what.

Maddy owed her big time for concealing this birth. What they'd done couldn't be ignored. Gloria felt her eyes smarting with tears of frustration. It was like being turned away all those years ago, the childish fear of being rejected for getting the wrong end of a tale, fear of being thought common and silly and of no consequence.

How could they know how hard it was to pull yourself out of the gutter, she thought, distancing herself from Mam and her Peel Street cronies. She'd found a steady job, for starters, and she had ambitions. This wasn't fair after all she'd done for her. One day she'd put Maddy and all those snooty Belfields in their place. No one was going to put her down again – especially after what she'd just done and what she knew. Gloria was shocked how angry she felt at her friend's behaviour.

You owe me, Maddy Belfield and one day I'll make you pay your dues.

Three days later Maddy caught the early morning train back to Leeds in fear of Miss Meyer's wrath. She'd lost her new briefcase and notes somewhere in the hostel. Search as she could, she'd not found it. Alice had looked under the beds and in the cupboards but it was gone. It was not in Gloria's room either. It had all her homework in it. Now she'd have to add another lie to her collection of fibs about it being stolen on the train.

She felt hot and cold and shivery, her breasts still solid with stale milk, and she was in agony. In desperation she tied a tight bandage over them to squash them, and that relieved the pain enough so that she could think straight.

It was awful to have avoided Gloria when she called in at the Brooklyn to see her. Maddy'd hid in the stables like a coward until she'd gone. She didn't want to talk about any of it. It was too terrible to dwell on that fearful night. Now she was running away, sneaking off without saying goodbye, leaving a note for Plum.

This was mean and a poor show, but she felt so drained and miserable, bursting into tears at the slightest thing – hearing music on the gramophone, watching the sun set, the lambs bleating in the fields. No one must see the state she was in, not even Gloria. She was too ashamed and it was agony to be so close to where she and Dieter had made love by the foss, and yet he was so far away now. Memories of happier times flashed into view. She'd written three letters to Dieter confessing what had happened but then tore them up. The price of her freedom must be silence. Now she had to be strong and carry on as if nothing had happened.

Going back to Leeds was like starting afresh in a new place. She was a different person from the one who had left not long ago, growing up overnight into someone colder and more calculating. No one must know the truth. If Gloria said anything she'd deny it all and call her a liar. Gloria had let her down before.

She must get away from her friend in case she was tempted to spill the beans. Maddy's Brooklyn life was over.

Plum was staying put at the old house but Gerald had gone back to London in a huff. Grandma had made sure of that. Her will was making sure they didn't divorce or he would lose out on everything. If he remarried, the house and land would revert straight to Maddy and her heirs, and he was furious. Plum was not sure now what she was going to do. None of this made any sense to Maddy.

The cherry blossom was frothing in the avenues in West Park, pink and vibrant. The fresh spring green of the grass and the new leaves brightened the streets. Lambs were dotted around the fields, new life burgeoning, but it was still winter in her heart, grey, murky and oh so cold.

How glad she was of the silence of her attic room, the routine of college classes, the bustle of the busy city centre distracting her, pushing the terrible events of the past few weeks to the back of her mind.

How easy it was to shut this pain into a secret place, lock it away with a padlock, out of sight. Every time she passed that door in her mind she scuttled past and thought of something else. Only in dreams did her heart betray her. She found herself running down the hallway, listening to the cry of a baby, opening every shut door, searching for the source that never appeared. The pram was always empty and the crying continued until she woke up with tears streaming down her face and the shame began all over again.

From the safety of her billet she wrote a polite letter to Gloria, thanking her for all her kindness and concern, promising to meet her sometime in Leeds for lunch but giving no specific date. It was better that they kept apart for a while and got on with their own lives.

She could never forget what her friend had done, and she didn't ask for the specific details of the burial, but suggested they never mention the birth again. What was done was done. That was the condition of their continuing friendship, in her own mind: no harking back to what they couldn't undo.

Dismissing her old friend was cruel and it didn't sit easy within her. The new friends around her now knew nothing of her shameful past. They would fill the gap that Gloria had left. They weren't kids any more but girls about town. It was time to have some fun, forget all that April grief.

There was money coming from Grandma's estate, money enough to have brought up a baby alone had it lived. She brushed aside this thought. No going there, she sighed, the what-might-have-beens were pointless. All that was over.

Sometime later, when her monthlies returned, she wondered why her baby had been so early. Was there something wrong with her insides? Another fear she must shove in the cupboard, out of mind.

Yet healing was quick and her weight dropped off as her appetite was poor. No more vanilla slices or sweet stuff. Straight up and down she was now, back to that boyish figure without any effort. She wanted no reminders of that terrible winter.

The turquoise cocktail dress hung on her and needed taking in. She might even take it back to Marshfields for alterations if she needed it for one of Bella's smart parties or she might not.

Nothing really mattered but work, concerts, flitting round the shops like any other young Yorkshire woman. All her worst nightmares were over – so why did she feel so sad inside so that nothing gave her much pleasure at all?

Gloria cried when she read Maddy's letter. She didn't understand what she was getting at. How could a mother not want to know what she'd done with the baby? Why were her words so cold, as if she was writing a polite note to a stranger, not her best friend? Where had she gone wrong? In staying away, or speaking out of turn at the funeral?

She'd wanted to leave Sowerthwaite to see more of Maddy in Leeds, go dancing, go to the pictures and join her new friends. It was pretty obvious now she wasn't welcome, she wasn't part of that world, she wouldn't fit in. No point in going where she wasn't wanted so she might as well stay put, but not at the Gunns'. No more nappies for her to wash. Oh, no, she'd find something more to her liking, but where?

For Plum, the months after Pleasance's death were fraught with anxiety. What to do: go or stay? Part of her wanted just to sit it out in the Brooklyn; the other wanted to pack her bags. She wasn't old and there was still time to find another life, but here were her beloved dogs, the horses, the estate cottages, so many silken threads that bound her to this place.

She wore a path around the neglected gardens, trying to think out her future. There were no staff left now to keep things trim, except the Battys at Huntsman's Cottage, who were getting on in years.

She stared up at the house that had once been such a refuge. It looked so shabby and neglected – unloved and tired. Why should she stay where she wasn't wanted?

Maddy had raced back to Leeds like the ungrateful child she still was in not staying to help her with clearing away Pleasance's room. They'd spoiled her, and yet it was all her own fault. She was the one who'd encouraged the girl to reach out for something other than this small town and domesticity. As Plum paced over the old path to the hostel she smiled, thinking of the times when she'd been so happy here to rush across and lend a hand.

The beech tree was full out, resplendent in its fresh green coverlet. It was still a magnificent specimen and when she shut her eyes, she could still recall a line of dangling children's legs of those hiding in the tree house from Miss Blunt. The ladder was there, the rope knots still firm.

Oh, what fun they'd had, as well as tears and tantrums: Maddy climbing up and refusing to come down, Greg marching his troops, the raising of Miss Blunt's awful wig – such good times as well as sad.

Plum sat under the Victory Tree, hugging her knees. Those were her glory days of being in charge, housekeeping, catering, managing staff. Never had she been so busy or so fulfilled. Now the birds had all flown the nest – husband, niece, evacuees. How quickly memories fade, but not these.

Then there were all the oldies in the Brooklyn. She'd kept them in order, pandered to their diets and foibles, fed and watered them through the war, and put up with her mother-in-law's demands. Now they too were gone but the house remained. Was it possible to fill it again?

A germ of an idea like a seed was sprouting in her mind. What if she . . . ? What if it was opened as a holiday guesthouse or a hotel even? No, perhaps not a hotel – too many staff would be needed – but she could run a guesthouse herself.

The house would have to be distempered right through, smartened up. She'd need help with guests. Perhaps Maddy might take over one day . . .

Plum sniffed the new spring undergrowth and smiled for the first time in months. If she budgeted carefully and followed ration requirements, it might just work. Gerald would have to know but he didn't care as long as the rents came in and he didn't have to do anything.

She shot up from the damp grass, brushed down her corduroys from loose soil and dried beech mast. This was more like it, she thought, striding back at a pace, taking in the surroundings as if for the first time; the swelling ridge of hills, the beck running down to the foss. It was an idyllic place for a rest from city life: silence, scenery and good plain Yorkshire baking. That was not beyond Grace Battersby, and they grew so much stuff themselves.

She'd train up someone to keep the guest rooms changed and fresh, a girl from the village with a bit of nous about her. There must be a way forward to bring the Brooklyn back to life and give both the house and herself some purpose once more.

Part Three

15

Greg was sweating as he hagged the ends off the old oak beams, hacking off the burned timber to a smooth finish, his shoulders aching, his palms blistered. He thought he was fit in the army but now that he was working as a navvy on a bomb site, salvaging what was left of this burned-out mill, he'd found muscles he never knew he had. They were stripping down everything: stone flags, beams, metal – anything that could be sold or reused again.

Sometimes he cursed that he hadn't taken up Charlie Afton's offer to work in their garages but it wreaked too much of old-man Brigg's set-up. Whatever he did from now on, he wanted to do for himself and strike out solo, but he needed cash and this job was as good a way as any to start.

All day he was up and down planks, lifting timbers and stone setts onto lorries and away. Their boss was an Irishman who took no prisoners, and tolerated no shirkers. When he took his shirt off he looked as if he could kill a man with his shoulders alone. You didn't argue with Mr Malone.

Greg soon learned to keep his head down and his mouth shut. Reclamation was a dodgy business at times. Things disappeared overnight, and nothing was said. It was cash in hand and piecework, and left him time to do a bit of moonlighting on the side, fixing up cars and getting them back on the road after the war years; all those bricked-up chassis in garages needed fettling up now that petrol rationing was not so bad.

Greg lived life like a clenched fist. It was bad enough wasting his best years fighting battles, but now it was time to make something of himself. He couldn't wait to start something up. Perhaps doing up bombed houses, and selling them on was a sure start on the property ladder. There was a shortage of houses, and thousands of soldiers with new wives and babies who wanted a roof over their heads. Money was to be made in property and Greg wanted to be at the head of the queue. No time for billiard halls and pubs, night school classes and the like. He was lodging in a back-to-back terrace near Kirkstall Abbey. It was rough, but clean and cheap. Greg was on a mission and deep in his heart he knew he'd make it one day. There was still that vision of his own place in the Dales and that ambition had grown from a neat villa to a mansion with a paddock and a fleet of cars. He'd be a muck-and-shovel boy until he got enough cash to get a foothold on the first rung of that rickety ladder of success. Growing hard muscle, a thick skin and tunnel vision was the only way, and nothing was going to stop his progress.

He found his billycan and sat down for a smoke

and a mash of tea, bringing out Plum's letter. She'd kept her tabs on him even though he'd not written for ages. She'd sent a letter to Afton's Garage near Harrogate, hoping to find him there, and Charlie had passed it on. She didn't miss a trick, that one.

The old Brooklyn biddy had passed over and he'd dropped a line for old-times' sake, just a polite letter of condolence. But here Plum was writing to him again. Secretly Greg was pleased to know they still remembered and cared what he was up to now.

Dear Gregory,

Thank you for your letter on the death of Mrs Belfield. She has left many gaps in the district that I am trying to fill. You will be pleased to know my new venture will soon be up and running.

I am hoping to find someone to train up, with strong legs and lots of energy. You asked after the girls. Gloria works locally but Madeleine is elusive. I expect her new friends and course keep her busy.

The door is always open should you be passing this way. Please feel free to call without an appointment. We go back too far to stand on ceremony. Good luck with your new position.

Regards,

Plum Belfield

If only she could see him now, with string tied round his knees, in hob-nailed boots and a collarless shirt, covered in muck and sweat; not a pretty sight, but he didn't care.

He smiled, thinking about the antics at Victory Tree HQ with snotty little Gloria and pony-mad Maddy – not his sort at all but when he'd made his packet he'd find his own classy bird.

Women were the last thing on his mind. He could take his pick but he'd always been choosy. Girls cost money and there was nothing to spare. His cash was going into his property fund. He'd find an old house to do up, and a decent car.

Charlie would be as good as his word in finding him a decent saloon to do up, something that made him look prosperous when the time came. Charlie was into racing, time trial rallying, and needed a good navigator and mechanic.

Greg had no time for such fun, not yet, not when there was a fortune to be made in fixing up old buildings. That was where the future lay for him. The rest could wait.

One day he'd return to Sowerthwaite, but with his tail up, and show them all this vaccy was a man of substance, a man as good as any of them. He'd not be calling until then.

He stood up, folded the letter in his pocket; time to 'tote that load and shift that bale', as the song went . . .

What am I doing here? thought Maddy. She was sitting in a disused drill hall, singing choruses to a harmonium and trying to look as if she was enjoying herself. They sat on hard benches listening to Mr Sandy

Blister, who stood, Bible in hand, thumping on the pulpit that she must be born again, must rise from her seat and commit herself to Jesus or be damned to hellfire.

Maddy looked around at the gleaming earnest faces singing and swaying with ecstasy. What a strange way to be spending a Saturday night.

It was summer now. There was Roundhay Park, Temple Newsam to visit, concerts to hear. She could walk to college, to Adel and Eccup, through Lawnswood and out into the country for miles. She'd borrowed a bike from one of the medical students in her digs and cycled around Cookridge and as far as The Chevin ridge near Otley. Although it wasn't the Dales it would do.

But weekends were the worst, when her college friends, Pinky and Caro, went home, and Bella disappeared to her cronies near York to prepare for her wedding. That was when loneliness hit her, the hours stretched out and the cupboard door strained to spill out all her secrets. Ruth and Thelma, those would-be missionaries, sensed her weakness and filled that gap, inviting into her circle. She was too grateful to resist at first.

There were tea and sandwiches, lots of young student types from the university in tweed jackets and grey flannels, who carried Bibles and belonged to the Scripture Union.

She'd taken their pamphlets, read the passages with Thelma's sour breath puffing over her shoulder. She didn't use Lifebuoy soap and sweated a lot. They were kind to invite her but she just couldn't make sense of this strange new world. How could she be mean about these good people? For three weekends she'd sat rigid in her seat until she could feel their disappointment when she didn't respond to the preacher's call.

Tonight her mind was all over the place. The preacher'd said something about sin against the Holy Spirit, the one unforgivable sin. Sin . . . sin . . . sin. It was all about sin and she knew enough about that. It made her want to scream out, 'Oh, do shut up and think about all the lovely things in this world!' but she sat in sullen silence.

The room was full and the air felt stale, the walls seemed to be getting smaller. With Ruth on one side and Thelma on the other she was being squeezed until all the air in her lungs expired and she couldn't breathe. There must be a way to escape this noise.

Was there no hope for a girl like her, steeped in guilt and wickedness? Her legs began to shake and her heart thudded in her chest. She couldn't bear this a minute longer; the pressure, the heat, the smell and the droning seductive voice.

'I've got to go,' she whispered, pulling herself out of the chair. They smiled, thinking she was stepping up to the front, but she turned out the door, to freedom and fresh air, taking great gulps of air.

Thelma was at her heels. 'The Holy Spirit has got you at last,' she smiled.

'No he's not. I just felt faint. It's stuffy in there and I don't know why I'm sitting inside on such a glorious evening. I think I'll go for a long walk over the Ridge and take in God's scenery, chimneys and all. I'm sorry, but this is not for me.'

'Don't turn your back on the Lord,' Thelma pleaded. 'This is the Devil tempting you.'

'Don't be silly. I can't go back in there again. I don't believe it helps me.'

'Me, me, me, Maddy. It's not all about you. It's about our Lord's sacrifice. He's calling and you are rejecting him, crucifying him all over again.'

'Oh, stop it. I'm not crucifying anyone. I'm trying to be honest with you. If I want to go to church there's St Chad's up the road not this . . . this shed.'

'Maddy, the Lord doesn't dwell in temples of stone,' Thelma argued, her eyes bulging with concern. A soul was slipping past her grasp and she was determined not to give in without a fight.

'Nor in temples of wood, Thelma. Thanks for your concern but I'll find forgiveness in my own way and my own time.'

'Ruth and I will pray for you. I fear you're fast in Satan's grip.'

'No, I'm not . . . I'll find my own way to faith . . . I must go!'

All Maddy wanted to do was escape from Thelma's bewilderment and hurt.

Once out into the street she watched children with a skipping rope jumping up and laughing. When was the last time she had jumped for joy?

Ruth's crowd meant well enough but their religion was not for her. It was with relief she strode northwards from Woodhouse Moor, glad to be alone with her own thoughts.

The Ridge, overlooking the city, was a wooded escarpment full of bluebells in the spring and courting couples on summer nights. Tonight Maddy felt like skipping along the path out of sheer relief. She was free at last and strangely relieved.

Amidst all the sadness and emptiness of the past few months was another growing certainty of relief. She'd been spared the shame of an unwanted pregnancy. She didn't have to worry any more. That secret was safe, locked away, but it was all so confusing. Here she was on this lovely evening, safe and reprieved. Now she would grab life, work hard and try to make up for her mistakes as best she could. If only she didn't feel so burdened with guilt. It lay on her like a lead cloak.

The bell on the café door clanged. A new customer was arriving. No one was more surprised than Gloria to see Mrs Plum coming in to the Cosy Nook café for a cuppa and a smoke. For once she looked like a proper lady, not a dog woman in her old greatcoat and wellies. She was dressed in a smart fur coat and wore a head-scarf over her windswept hair.

Gloria had packed in the job with the Gunns. Children were all right in small doses, but Heather had never taken to her for some reason, and the novelty of being a mother's help had worn off. Her plan to go to Leeds was shelved so she'd taken a summer job with the Temperance Café, serving mock cream teas to cyclists and hikers who came out at the weekend, but come the autumn she'd have to think again about going to the town and maybe even Peel Street for a while. Not a cheery thought.

'I heard you were working in here, Gloria,' Plum said, sitting down and removing her gloves. She ordered a scone and butter. 'Fresh, are they?'

'This morning,' she replied, feeling proud she'd got the knack of knocking them up with the best of them. Tray bakes, jam slices and pastry were her best efforts.

For once Gloria took extra care with the service, cleaned up the tray, no smears, fresh pot of tea, tea strainer, brew well mashed, hot water jug, and found a spoon that wasn't chained to the sugar bowl.

She was wary around Mrs Plum these days, sensing she disapproved of her, blaming her for keeping Maddy away from the deathbed of the old woman.

If only she knew the half of it, but Gloria's lips were sealed. She'd made a bargain and she was sticking to it. What was done was done in good faith and friendship – in ignorance maybe, but nothing would've changed the outcome.

'Have you heard from Maddy?' Mrs Plum asked as she sipped her tea. The café was quiet so Gloria tried to look busy polishing tables with a damp cloth.

'No, she's gone very quiet. Exams, I expect.'

'Perhaps . . . I was hoping she'd be here for the holidays. There are some changes I'd hoped to discuss with her. If you hear from her, do tell her to give me a buzz.'

'Of course, but I doubt we'll meet up again soon.'

'Have you two fallen out? You were always such good friends.'

'Yes, forever friends,' Gloria said, blushing. 'No, no . . . nothing like that. Just gone our different ways, like you do. I expect she's got lots of college mates. Sowerthwaite's a bit of a dead end for a young lady about town.'

'What a pity. She's been acting strange lately. Perhaps her grandmother's death upset her, seeing as she didn't get there in time.'

'Perhaps,' said Gloria, knowing full well she'd been dumped, ditched, thrown over because she reminded Maddy of what they had done. 'She was sick that night, you know.' Time to put the record straight even though she felt hard done by and let down.

'Yes, I realise that, and it was good of you to help her but that's not what I'm here for, Gloria. I have a proposition to put to you. I know you've left Dr Gunn. Denise tells me you've been much missed there. Only I'm thinking of some changes to the Brooklyn, turning it into a guesthouse, taking in paying visitors. I'm looking for staff to train up . . . housekeeping, catering, that sort of domestic service, and I was wondering . . .'

She wants me for a skivvy, thought Gloria as she bustled around, hiding her dismay.

'Er, what does this entail? I was thinking of returning to Leeds. It gets so quiet in the winter here.'

'I'd be thinking of opening all year round, taking parties, ramblers and as wide a clientele as I could reach. There's a lot of preparation work, redoing rooms . . .'

This was tempting. She'd get a good training with Mrs Plum but it would be hard work.

Mrs Plum smiled, sensing she might be tempted

'I've always thought you hard-working and conscientious, good with people, honest, and with that extra bit of flair I'm looking for. Perhaps you'd like to think about it.'

'Where would I stay?' she asked. 'The hostel's closing now. It's hard to find rooms here.'

'You'd live in, of course, with your own room. It would be a full-time appointment after a trial period on both sides. I need someone to run things when I'm not around.'

Live in the Brooklyn! It was always her childhood dream to share all Maddy had taken for granted. Even if she was only a domestic there was scope here, scope to save up, to meet interesting people, a chance to observe a real lady at work, to learn how to do things properly.Who knew where that might lead one day? This was just the ticket.

'When do I start?'

Maddy returned one weekend to the Brooklyn unannounced, only to find Plum going through the rooms like a whirling dervish, sorting out clothes, furniture, buckets of distemper lying everywhere while old Mrs Batty was turning the place upside down.

The fact that Gloria was busy stripping off old wallpaper in dungarees and turban disturbed her even more. From the laughter and joking and shared cups of tea, it was easy to see those two were as thick as porridge, slopping paint like children. They were smartening up the décor for as little cost as possible. News of Plum's new venture came as a shock.

The kitchen garden was raked and weeded through. Brooklyn Hall was to be a registered guesthouse and Gloria had been given the biggest bedroom on the third floor with a sitting room off the side. She looked like the cat that got the cream.

Suddenly Maddy felt left out and superfluous. Was this Plum's way of saying she could manage the house, make a living and cock a snook at Uncle Gerry – and punish her for not being around?

Everyone was busy and enthusiastic. She hadn't the heart to be mean, but wasn't Brooklyn her home? Hadn't Grandma left it to her one day? Oughtn't she to be consulted? But who could blame them? She'd not been home for ages.

If only Plum had asked her opinion, she'd have offered to do the bookkeeping when they took in their first guests but it was much too much of a mess to be ready for the autumn deadline.

'Autumn in the Dales,' read the brochure. 'Enjoy the peace and tranquillity of quiet country lanes, warm log fires. Bring your ration cards and we will supply appetising breakfasts and evening meals for your pleasure.'

Grace was going to cook. Plum was the host and Gloria was in charge of domestic services and laundry. In other words, she was a glorified skivvy in overalls, but her friend was acting as if she owned the place, swanning around, showing her all their improvements.

'Of course we'd like sinks in every room but there

is a toilet and bathroom on each floor.' The cheek of her, as if she didn't know that already, Maddy sniffed.

The dogs were banished to the washing out house and that damp doggy smell was replaced with the scent of fresh paint and varnish. That in turn would be replaced by beeswax polish and fresh-cut flowers. It all looked very inviting, but not to her.

She felt like Billy No Mates stuck in a corner. Grandma would be hovering in fury as they'd stripped her bedroom of all its dark brocade and put back the shutters and voile curtains to let in the light. The parsley-coloured walls were newly papered with a border around the picture rail. Maddy was miffed at all the changes and desperately trying not to show it. This wasn't her home any more. It didn't even smell like the Brooklyn.

'Isn't it gorgeous?' said Gloria. 'We've worked so hard to smarten it up. Your aunt's done a great job.'

'It's OK,' Maddy replied, reluctant to give them any praise.

'Is that all you can say?' Gloria snapped back. 'We thought you'd be thrilled.'

'We' . . . 'we' – there were too many 'we's for her liking. 'It's just not how I imagined it would be.'

'The trouble with you is that you've stayed away so long. You've forgotten how drab and dirty it all was. Look at my hands – I'll never get them smooth again.'

'I've been busy.'

'So I gathered, too busy to drop me a line. What did I do wrong?'

‘Nothing . . . let’s talk about something else,’ Maddy said, feeling her cheeks flush. ‘Don’t go on about it!’

‘Hold on, I’ve said nowt. What’s the matter with you? You’ve sulked all afternoon.’

‘No I haven’t!’

‘Suit yerself . . . I’m not bothered. I’ve too much to do here. By the way, guess who’s living in Leeds?’

‘Go on, enlighten me.’

‘None other than Greg Byrne. He’s working on a building site so if some lad gives you a wolf whistle, you never know, it might be him. He wrote to your aunt. I’m going to write and see if we can all meet up again.’

‘Please yourself. I wouldn’t know him from Adam. He won’t want to see us.’

‘Who trod on your toes, missy? You had a lucky escape and no mistake; don’t be so mardy.’

Maddy stormed off and went to say her goodbyes. There was just time to get the afternoon train back to Leeds. It was evident that she wasn’t needed here. Sitting in the carriage, she felt ashamed of feeling so jealous, so out of sorts and so unkind to Gloria. She owed her friend her new life. What would have happened if Glory hadn’t stood by her side? What was the matter with her these days? She was jumpy and tetchy, sleep was broken and full of nasty dreams. She didn’t like herself much for running out on them, but going back was a mistake, churning up all those old feelings of panic.

Leaving the station in a stroppy mood, stomping out of City Square, she wasn’t quite sure what to do with herself now. It was raining as usual. There was time to trawl the shops to see if there was anything to spend her few coupons on. She needed cheering up and fast. Time to look to see if there were any new shoes in the stores or pretty fabrics, find something in a pretty colour to soothe her tired eyes.

She sauntered towards Marshfields, which was Bella's stamping ground; the bridal department with its rich silks and satins, ball gowns and evening wear bedecked with sequins, lace, braids and ribbons. She fingered them all lovingly, the materials soft and silky in her palms, smoothing her own ruffled feathers.

The assistant eyed her up. 'Modom is looking for something?'

'Not really. They're all so beautiful,' she sighed. 'But too expensive for a student.'

'You'd like to try them on, yes?'

'I can't afford them.' Trust her to land a pushy saleswoman.

'This would look lovely on you . . . try this on. I'd like to see for myself how it looks.' The blood-red gown was shoved in her hand, she was told to strip in the *cabine* and then the vendeuse buttoned it up, throwing a sequined bolero over her shoulders.

'Let's just brush your hair up off your neck, like this,' she insisted, and Maddy was beginning to feel trapped and uncertain. She'd only come in to have a look round.

'Perfect . . . Now walk this way. You live in Leeds?'

'Yes,' muttered Maddy. 'West Park. I'm at college.'

'Excellent. Wait one moment.' She closed the curtain

and when she opened it again, a man and a woman in black were eyeing her with interest.

'Don't you think?' whispered the vendeuse. 'What's your name, dear?'

'Madeleine Belfield.' Now she was really in trouble. They were eyeing her up like a piece of steak.

'Ah, La Madeleine. Beautiful, yes.'

Then to her surprise everyone clapped and she blushed as the other customers stared at her. They were making a big mistake if they thought she was going to buy this dress. 'Please, I can't buy this,' she said, trying to look firm.

'But we are all getting the pleasure of seeing how this gown should be worn on a lovely young woman with the perfect figure. See, our customers are gathering to admire you, looking and wondering if they too will look like this in it.'

Sure enough a clutch of women hovered and smiled. Then she caught sight of herself in the wall mirror. Who was this elegant stranger with sloping shoulders, slim-hipped and flushed in the cheek with such a long neck? How strange, she was stopping the traffic through the department.

'Now we will have you in the gold.'

Another quick change, this time into a slim figure-hugging jacket in gold and black with a bouffant skirt. A pair of court shoes was shoved onto her bare feet and she posed and nearly fell over as she towered over the proceedings.

'*Brava!*' The vendeuse clapped her hands, nodding to the man in the suit, and he nodded back.

Maddy tried on three more outfits and paraded round like a dressage horse, then changed back quickly into her tweed suit.

'Mr Percival will see you in his office,' said the lady in the black frock with the phoney French accent. What had she done now?

She knocked on his door, wondering what was going to happen next. The whole afternoon had been so bizarre.

'Come in, Miss Madeleine. You were very brave to go with Madame Delys's little whim. She has an eye for talent and you have it in spadefuls, young lady. Tell me about yourself.'

Maddy gave him a bare outline of her life to date.

'And your family?' She told him about her parents.

'Ah, the Bellaires. I remember them well on the wireless: such a pity for them to be lost and you so young. And you have their presence: tall, graceful, very arresting to the eye. We could use you . . .'

For what? she mused. Who on earth was he talking about? Surely not herself? Her puzzled look made him explain.

'We like to have floor walkers, mannequins to show off to special customers, models for parades and events, tall girls who carry clothes well and know how to walk. You will do perfectly.'

'But I'm at college,' she explained.

'Naturally, but not every day. We can use you on Saturdays, perhaps in the vacations to cover for other models at first.'

'But I have no experience,' she said, still not taking all this in.

'We will take care of all that – how to walk and sit and pose. That can be taught, but a clotheshorse has to be born, shoulders, ankles, neck, face and height. These can't be altered, only disguised. Our customers are just from the street, with flaws and lumps. When they see you gliding around in that "Scarlet Passion" number, they see themselves transformed. You carry the dream of what they might be.'

Maddy didn't know what to make of this offer. She'd never thought of modelling gowns for a living. It was the sort of thing Bella's friends did in their spare time for charity and magazines. She was going to be a secretary to an important businessman one day, not a tailor's walking dummy, but some of those dresses were rather beautiful.

'Let me give you some advice. Finish your course, by all means – you can be a secretary all your life, but a mannequin is for a short time only. Alas a few years, then other girls will come and take your place. Why not enjoy the chance of a career here? It will take you out of Yorkshire and beyond. Why not give it a try?'

The man in the pin-striped suit with razor-sharp creases and slicked-back hair smiled a warm smile. 'Think about this offer. It's genuine.'

Why not? Maddy breezed out of the department store with both feet off the ground. Why ever not? This bit of news would give them all at the Brooklyn something to splash on the walls, and the Misses Meyers too. Bella would be envious, Ruth and Thelma appalled, Caro and Pinky nonplussed. Their hearts were stuck in muck and sheep; they wouldn't care either way. But Madeleine Belfield, a mannequin?

Skinny mallink, boss-eyed Maddy? Who'd 'a thowt it! She laughed all the way back to her digs.

16

'Come on, Charlie, pedal to the metal!' yelled Greg as they tore across the forest track at breakneck speed.

'You just concentrate on the map and stop giving me orders. This bit is going to be tricky in the slush and mist,' said Charlie Afton, Greg's co-driver.

It was only the second time that Greg had navigated for his friend and he still hadn't got the hang of it. They were making good time, but Charlie was cautious round the bends. Only he who dares would win this time trial. It was fun, but Greg knew he ought to be back supervising the guys on the building site. He didn't trust them to keep at it without him beating the stick.

He navvying days were almost over, but if need be, he would take off his jacket and muck in with the best of them. He'd bought some land, just a derelict plot outside Headingley, jumped in quick and made an offer, and now he'd got four semis going up, with inside bathrooms, proper kitchen-cum-diners, in the American style.

All of them were sold just from the plans alone,

and he was on a deadline and shouldn't be out enjoying himself. But hell, it was good to be getting some fresh air.

'Where next?' Charlie said.

For a second Greg had lost concentration. 'Sorry. Just keep going ahead, I think.'

'Keep your flaming mind on the bloody job, Byrne!'

They were still arguing when the car skidded, crashed into the side of a tree and spun off the road into a ditch.

'That'll teach you to concentrate on the job. You can pay for the damage!' Charlie was furious but unhurt.

'You OK?' Greg sighed, knowing he should've stayed in Leeds and got on with his building. He jumped out of the car and went for help.

The motor rally was in full throttle, engines roaring through the forest in the distance when Maddy Belfield arrived late for the photo shoot in the park. It was one of those dark winter snowscapes, a grey light, monochrome, with the old house etched against a darkening sky as a backdrop.

They wanted her to model the latest fur wraps and jackets, and she was frozen stiff standing in the muddy slush, trying to keep her teeth from chattering. There was a rush to get her hair coiled into a chignon. She must give her best Lady Muck look, standing by her sleek Daimler hired for the shoot.

Nobody had warned her how unglamorous being a photographic model could be. Piers, the flamboyant photographer, was fussing like an old hen, clucking about getting the right light and shadow for the glossy shots needed by Marshfields store, who were promoting this winter advertisement in a Yorkshire magazine.

As one of their favourite mannequins, they had demanded Maddy made herself available.

Her toes were numb in the patent court shoes and her make-up had to be touched up to disguise a blue nose. The assistant had shoved a hot-water bottle up the hidden back of the coat just to warm her through.

They'd borrowed the big Georgian house outside York where Bella's family lived, so at least she had a bed for the night.

Since leaving Yorkshire Ladies', Maddy's feet had scarcely touched the ground, much to Miss Meyer's dismay.

'We didn't train you up for you to go off and be a window dresser's dummy,' sniffed Hilda as she handed over Maddy's certificates. 'You young gals . . . where will it end?'

It was Miss Hermione who wished her good luck and slipped a lovely compact into her hands. 'You enjoy yourself while you can,' she whispered. 'Don't listen to her. We never got much of a chance after the Great War – no young men left for us. Hilda is bitter. I shall look out for you in the papers.'

Now her weeks were filled with fittings, rehearsals, shows, parades. Sometimes she was sent into the big warehouses for their seasonal show for buyers. It was hard work, stripping off and on, keeping her hair smart, pouring into waspie waist cinchers and silhouette corsets and huge petticoats, trying not to snag her nylon stockings.

Sometimes she did feel like a painted doll, especially when she looked in the mirror. In her eyes she was still plain Maddy with the gawky frame and hunched back, but now she could switch on and become 'La Madeleine' the minute she walked down the catwalk.

If Plum was disappointed in her new career she said nothing. She was too busy with her own business. Her sidekick, Gloria, ignored all the fuss over this new career and never showed any interest when her picture appeared in a local magazine.

Maddy preferred to think she was in demand because she turned up on time, didn't complain when they stuck pins in her, was pleasant to buyers and tried to show off the clothes as best she could, even though some of the stuff was ridiculously froufrou and over the top with beading or lace. Tight waists were *de rigueur* now, full skirts à la Dior, which took yards of material, fussy hats and gloves that must be spotless, make-up that must not be smudged or look too theatrical. She suffered constant backache from standing in high heels, trying to look haughty and sophisticated, which gave her a fixed smile. This was the look for now.

For all the glamour on the outside, there was still a burning part of her inside that remained distant and uncertain, as if all this was happening to someone else who deserved this success, not her.

'Madeleine, hold that faraway look,' someone shouted. When she was tired her slow eye turned slightly, but no one seemed to mind and it didn't show on the full shot.

Now, on this freezing slushy afternoon all she could think of was a hot bath and a mug of cocoa, of being wrapped in a thick silky eiderdown, but the roar of the engines kept whirring, disturbing her reverie and she turned.

'Don't move!' yelled Piers. 'Just one more.'

How many times had she heard that line? 'It's only a motor rally in the forest. Take no notice. They'll be gone soon . . .'

But the engines seemed to be getting closer, and they heard a screech of brakes and the unmistakable crunch of metal against tree, and then silence.

'What was that?' Maddy shouted, turning as someone came running out of the woods in mud-splattered leathers and a helmet like a parachutist.

'Where's the nearest phone? There's been an accident . . .'

Then he stopped, staring at this strange set, backing off.

'Oh, I could use you for contrast . . . just move over closer to Mads,' said Piers. For a second the man stopped again, distracted by the scene, and then he ran on.

'Go up there,' Maddy yelled, 'to Foxup Hall . . . We ought to go and help too.'

'No need, love,' shouted the mystery man in his dark leathers. 'Just need a bit of a shove out of the way. Only a prang, no bones broken.'

'The driver?' Maddy asked, wondering just how bad it was.

'A bit shook up. We don't want to hold up the race, though. The marshals are seeing to it.'

The man raced off up the drive and soon Bella and her father were racing down with the gardener.

'Damn rally boys! I knew it was a mistake to let Alexander's lot loose. This is all your doing, Bella. That bloody husband of yours . . .'

'Oh, Daddy, it's only a bit of fun, a practice run, and no one's hurt – well, not too bad.' She turned to Maddy with a smile. 'Darling, you look absolutely frozen. Go back up and thaw out, the light's going. You will stay for the party tonight?'

Maddy shook her head. 'I'd better get on my way. I promised Aunt Plum I'd fetch her up for her birthday.'

'That's tomorrow. Saturday night is party night and you're going nowhere. Come on, chop chop.'

'Do you mind?' yelled Piers. 'We're not finished yet! Mads, keep your pose.'

'We'll send you the medical bill if she catches pneumonia,' Bella yelled back, unimpressed. 'Slave driver . . . See you later, darling!'

Maddy had stayed up at Foxup before. She hadn't gone to Bella's wedding, making a feeble excuse. She'd not been feeling sociable for months but she'd asked Plum to find some beautiful skin fleeces and they'd sent them as a gift. Bella had written back to ask her over for a weekend to meet Alexander and somehow they'd stayed in touch. The house was a huge pile of grey stones and inside was as cold as a Frigidaire, full of grand furniture, portraits and stag horns on shields. It was twice the size of Brooklyn Hall but the family always made her welcome.

Bella's brother, Morgan, was just out of the army and a bit of a handful. He and Alex spent every waking hour under the bonnet of some fast roadster. Bella and Alex tried to make them a foursome but Maddy found him a bit of a buffoon; anything on four legs or four wheels and he was off boring for England. Now they had made part of the forest a time-trial track for rally teams.

It was funny how out of all the girls at Yorkshire Ladies', the two friends who'd stuck were Bella and Pinky, the farmer's wife. Thelma and Ruth had never forgiven her for running out of the Hebron Hall meeting: 'You've sold your soul to a worldly occupation. How can you parade yourself in peacock's finery when half the world is starving?'

There was no easy answer to that but she was earning her own living, paying her way, and it kept her away from Sowerthwaite.

She needed no excuse to stay away from Brooklyn Hall as reminders of her secret shame hit her whenever she walked out of the station and smelled that fresh damp Dales air.

Gloria was still being cool and disinterested in her travels. Aunt Plum was full of how former evacuees had returned to see her. Big Bryan Partridge was now in the army and had roared up the avenue in a Jeep with his friends to show them where he'd spent the war.

Walking up the Avenue of Tears to Brooklyn brought back such painful memories. She hated going back, but tomorrow she must brace herself and make a special effort, snow or not.

Now she was too weary and chilled to protest when the housekeeper, Mrs Pilling, ran her a bath in the great roll-top tub and brought her a hot toddy of whisky, lemon and hot water on a silver tray.

'Her ladyship's orders,' she smiled. 'Get that down you. Dinner is at eight.'

Luckily Maddy had her best woollen two-piece in her overnight bag, which was otherwise full of accessories for the shoot. A mannequin needed to have gloves, scarves, bits to dress up the clothes if the dresser's stuff was boring or plain awful. At least she had her Shetland wool spencer, light as gossamer, to wear as an extra vest. She had a paisley cashmere shawl that had belonged to Grandma, which wrapped round like a blanket and kept the draughts from howling up her skirts. It was a night for Gran's pearls too.

Lady Foxup was wrapped in a white fox fur stole, Bella wore a fancy plaid jacket and Alex wore tweeds. The fire was lit but it usually made no impact on them sitting round the table. The best was to hope that one of the dogs took a fancy to her and warmed her feet under the table.

'Will you take the horses out tomorrow after church?' Bella's mother turned to the girls.

Maddy shook her head. 'I must get back. It's Aunt Plum's birthday tomorrow, we're having a special tea.'

'I was meaning to ask you about your aunt Plum. Was she, by any chance, a Templeton? Prunella Templeton of Underby Hall?'

'Yes,' Maddy smiled, her soup spoon pausing in the air.

'Good Lord! Prunes and Custard . . . We came out together. Tell her Totty Featherstone was asking after her. She married Sir Jasper, didn't she?'

'No . . . Gerald.'

'The same,' grinned Totty Foxup. 'We used to call him Sir Jasper. N.S.I.T. – not safe in taxis! How are they getting on?'

'Fine. Uncle Gerald works down in London most of the time.' Maddy hesitated, not wanting to give too much away.

'Do tell her to ring me and we'll have lunch. What a hoot, Prunes and Custard being your aunt.'

The soup, made of indeterminable vegetables, was followed by roast lamb, then stewed fruit cobbler and cream: rib-sticking fare that warmed her through.

'I've invited my rally cronies back for drinks, a bit of a party,' Morgan said, smiling across the table at Maddy. 'No bones broken this time but one of the chaps is a bit dazed. They're down in the kitchen warming up. Pilling's doing a grand job keeping them entertained and sorting out their boots. We'll put the gramophone in the billiard room and they can have a bit of a singsong. Car's a write-off, by the way,' Morgan added. 'An MG roadster, all souped up. Pity . . . some chaps from Leeds or Harrogate, new recruits. You girls must come and meet them all, chivvy them up.'

Maddy groaned, wanting to go to bed to be ready for an early start in the morning, but she was their guest so must oblige.

There was a bunch of guys hugging the fire in the billiard room, some faces she'd seen before, regular chums of Morgan's, standing in steaming socks and leathers, sipping from crystal glasses and looking awkward.

Morgan did his best to introduce them all. 'That's poor Charlie – father owns a string of garages, and his co-driver over there. This is their first time and they're a bit brassed off, losing their car like that. Silly mistake, eh, lads?' Morgan was off round the room, trying to make everyone at ease.

Maddy recognised the tall young man in black leathers who'd shot out of the wood to raise the alarm. Without his helmet and gear he was handsome in a rugged Yorkshire sort of way, she thought, rough round the edges and looked you straight in the eye.

He was staring round at the panelled walls, the trophies and swords. There was something about his stance, his eyes, something familiar. Was it a trick of the firelight on that shock of fair hair, those lean features? Something about him tapped into old memories but she just couldn't place him. It was a pity he'd not given his name but better not to embarrass him by singling him out in front of the others.

'Now I want you to meet my friend Madeleine,' Bella suddenly announced above the clatter. 'She's the poor soul trying to sell fur coats out of our driveway when you lot interrupted the proceedings, Mr Afton. Rallying can be a dangerous game but that's what it's all about, isn't it?'

Maddy caught the driver eyeing her up with interest. She walked over in his direction. 'Hello, I'm Madeleine,' she smiled. She smelled the whisky fumes on his breath.

He'd been knocking them back. 'I hope your friend is recovering.'

He laughed. 'I knew a Madeleine once, long time back.'

Charlie Afton rose to greet her. 'You never told me about that one, Greg. Watch him, miss.'

Maddy was searching his face with renewed interest. 'Greg? . . . Not Gregory Byrne?'

'Who's asking?' he replied, as light bulbs of recognition went on in both their eyes. 'Not . . . Maddy Belfield of Brooklyn Hall? You were the girl in the fur coat freezing down on the drive. Maddy? I don't believe it. How's everyone? Mrs Plum and Gloria and old Mr Batty . . . ? Surely not? This is Maddy, one of the evacuees I was telling you about, Charlie. Maddy, is it really you?'

'I'm afraid so. I knew you were in Leeds. Gloria told me.' They shook hands, laughing. Maddy drank him in with relish. 'It's incredible! After all these years . . .'

'You are now speaking to Byrne Bespoke Builders Inc,' Charlie interrupted. 'He'll give you his card given half a chance,' he laughed. 'And he wrote off my MG this afternoon.'

'Ah, that's definitely the Greg I remember. Tell Charlie about the motor bike on battery field. I can't believe it's really you, and here of all places.'

'It's a bit grand for the likes of us,' Greg said, Charlie nodded.

'And me too,' Maddy smiled. 'But Bella's my friend from college. We borrowed her grounds for the shots.

I work for Marshfields store. As you saw, I was nearly frozen to the spot.'

Greg stood before her, rough hewn, broader, but still the same straw hair parted neatly, and those electric-blue eyes flashed. Suddenly the rest of the room faded into a blur as the noise in the crowd silenced and she stood fixed to the spot. It was as if all the lights in the room were turned off and just the spotlight surrounded them. How strange on a freezing winter's night to feel such a warm glow, such a sense of peace. It was Greg, her old friend, but when she looked at him it was not friendship she was feeling but that strange excitement she once felt for Dieter.

Greg stared down at Maddy as she circled around the room, no longer a lanky schoolgirl with a turn in her eye but this slender, elegant vision in lavender. How strange that their paths had crossed once more. How strange to find her in here, in this barn of a mansion – but then why not? This was her world, after all – a private education, a finishing school, county friends, horses – a world away from his tough building sites. This was not where he'd expected to spend his Saturday night. To think, he'd nearly done a bunk to the nearest pub.

Charlie's rally cronies were a wealthy lot and thought nothing of racing all over the county over borrowed land, cadging hospitality where they could. Now they were waiting for the garage to bring out a towing truck to get the roadster back to dock. It looked a crumpled mess but there was just a chance the big end had not gone for a burton.

When he was nervous Greg drank too much, gulped too fast on an empty stomach. He'd met Arabella once before. She was OK but he couldn't stand the usual toffee-nosed 'gals' who'd never done a day's work in their lives, poring over the sports cars in the garage, feigning interest, draping their long legs in and out of the seats, knowing that they looked good. They were all the same and made him nervous. Coming to Foxup Hall was a first, and he felt out of his depth with all this old money and grandeur, but they'd made them all welcome.

Now he felt such a scruff in these old cords and jumper. He was so busy ploughing money back into his business that he never bothered to put it on his back like Charlie and the others. But Maddy seemed genuinely pleased to see him, so warm and so welcoming. His heart skipped a beat at the sight of her.

Could this really be his old mate? How could that skinny kid become the perfect princess of his dreams, handed to him on a plate by the fates, the sort of girl he'd always wanted to find? All his firm resolutions crumbled at the sight of her. Just one look was all it took to hear himself mutter under his breath, 'I'm going to marry that girl.'

Then icy reality gripped him. Why should she look twice at a scruff like him, a jumped-up labourer with nothing to offer but hopes and in uncertainties. He was not in a position to court a princess, especially one who'd known him since he was in short pants. It wasn't part of his plan. She'd come too soon into his life and yet . . . For once he was gobsmacked by the coincidence.

'What a beauty!' Charlie whispered. 'Blimey, I'd go for her myself but she seems to be eyeing you up with interest. So go for it!'

'I can't . . . not yet.' Greg hesitated. All sorts of obstacles flashed before him: lack of money, a decent car, his rough callused hands, not even a decent suit to his name. How could he even think of it?

'Don't be a fool. Take your chance or it might not come again. Morgan Foxup is hovering over her like a vulture and I never took you for a coward.'

Greg felt sick as he strode up behind Maddy. He straightened his collar, slicked his hands through his hair and swallowed hard, trying to look casual.

'Now that we've met up again there's so much to catch up on. Are you around tomorrow? We could go for a walk. It looks as if it will stay fine. I'll be staying here until we sort out the car.'

'Pity,' she smiled. 'I've got to go back to Brooklyn. It's Aunt Plum's birthday and I can't miss it again.' They both paused with a kind of sigh. 'There's not a chance you could come too?' she asked. 'It'll be a lovely surprise for her, and you'd see everybody then. I'm going by train but you could come on, later.'

Greg knew that he ought to go and check the brickwork on the building site, but it was a Sunday and they weren't allowed to work then. Charlie's car was a wreck, however, and it was going to be difficult to get transport.

'I'll try,' he said, 'but now I know you're in Leeds, perhaps we could meet up again.'

She looked at him and smiled. 'Of course, but I'm here, there and everywhere where the work is.' Maddy scribbled her address on the back of an envelope she'd pulled from her handbag. Then she turned away to circulate again among the other drivers, glancing at him from time to time, while he stared like a tailor's dummy, transfixed by this unexpected meeting. He just had to get to Brooklyn tomorrow. There was only one thing for it. Grabbing another drink, he shoved it in Charlie's hand.

'Can I ask you the most almighty favour?'

Charlie had already read his mind. 'Just get that wreck back to the garage first. Never let it be said I stood in the way of true love.'

Gloria hugged her secret to herself on the train back to Bradford on her day off.

Was it only three weeks ago since she'd followed her hunch, knowing the photographer's card was burning a hole in her handbag? She'd taken extra care with her appearance, rolled up her curls, bathed and powdered her white skin, dressed with care, polished her shoes for the interview.

Maddy was not the only one to be a photographer's model. Now she was one of his regulars and this was going to be Gloria's most daring session yet.

It all started when Ken Silverstone and his 'wife' arrived for a weekend at the Brooklyn six weeks ago. He'd booked the best suite and Plum thought they might be on honeymoon, but Gloria, sharp-eyed as ever, saw that the girl had no ring on when she'd first taken off her gloves. It had only appeared, when they turned up for a late breakfast.

Ken was very chatty to Gloria as she served on the table, but his girlfriend looked daggers at her when he kept going on about her red hair.

'I'd bet you'd look good in a bathing costume. I do a lot of catalogues. They're always on the look out for unusual colourings – you know, a touch of the tar brush or Rita Hayworth hair is always in demand.'

'Is that where you met your wife?' she snapped, waiting for the girl to blush.

'Who, Dulcie? She's not—' he began, and then a wince screwed up his face as she kicked him under the table.

'I'm a secretary,' sniffed the bottle-blonde Dulcie. 'Nothing to do with Ken's business. Come on, darling, time for our bracing walk,' she giggled.

Not in those high heels you're not, thought Gloria. She'd seen the state of their bedroom. It smelled of yeast and perfume, and something else that stirred her interest.

It was when they were packing their suitcase into the boot of the Jowett that he slipped her a business card along with a tip.

'If you ever fancy a change from changing beds, come and see me. I'll do some shots for free and see where that leads,' he winked, leaving her on the steps, trying not to laugh. The cheek of him!

Still, it was a change from the humdrum routine of

the Brooklyn. Much as she loved it, things got dull in the week. Some weekends they were rushed off their feet, others were yawning gaps of boredom, but this week was Plum's birthday. Maddy would be gracing them with her presence and this time Gloria was not going to be outdone by all her glamorous assignments. She'd had one of her own.

The studio was up a side street not far from Forster Square, next to a pub, up a flight of rickety stairs; a bit of a dump, if she was honest, but artists in the films always seemed to prefer studios with character.

Ken Silverstone's studio was smaller than she imagined, really just a bare room. On that first visit she'd opened the door gingerly, clutching her handbag. 'I thought I'd look you up,' she lied. 'I was doing some shopping in town.'

The walls had black sheets on them. Silver umbrellas and headlamps, a cloth screen like the ones round hospital beds were the only bits of furniture. He was busy in a dark room and came out at the clanging of the bell on the door, recognising her at once.

'Ah, little Miss Redhead, I thought you might be tempted.'

Gloria smiled. 'I am interested to see. I wouldn't mind a shot at some modelling. I have a friend in the business,' she added.

'It's not those sorts of mannequin shots, love, more the glamour end of the market.' He took her over to a table strewn with papers and photos, opening to a page full of brassiere and corset adverts, girls in lacy undies and see-through nighties.

'For this sort of work you have to have the right sort of figure, full and shapely so the lingerie looks good,' he winked again.

'I see.' Gloria gulped at the sight of so much flesh on display.

'Very tastefully done, of course. Good lighting and subtle poses make the best shots. We have to check there are no awkward blemishes or angles. I need to take a few tasteful shots first.'

'I see.' Gloria gulped again. 'Do you think I'd be any good?' Part of her was wishing she was a hundred miles away from this dark room once she'd seen those photos.

'With your figure, fantastic, a natural,' he replied. 'Shall we try out a few poses first so you get used to it?'

'I've come all this way so I might as well have a trial, but no stripping off. That's not what I want to do.' Better to be firm and state her case. There must be no misunderstandings. She was a good girl.

'Of course not, love, but we need to do artistic shots, discreet but classy. If I had a body like yours I'd want to show it off. You can go behind the screen, keep your slip on and your panties. Then I can judge how you'll match up . . . just head shots, at first.'

On that first visit it was chilly and she felt stupid. Thank goodness she'd put on her silk slip and French knickers, peach with coffee lace, which Maddy had bought for her last birthday. They were nicer than anything in his catalogues she'd seen so far.

He sat her on a chair and fussed with the lights and made her turn this way and that until her back ached. This was boring and she yawned.

'Fancy a little snifter?' he smiled, waving two glasses and a bottle of brandy in her direction. 'I always keep a bottle handy to warm us up. Just let the strap down off your shoulder – that's better – and your hair up is not right, it needs ruffling onto your shoulders. Shame to waste curls like that.'

Before she could protest he'd unpinned her hair and spread it like a cape over her shoulders, pulled down her bra so her breasts were almost hanging out.

'Much better, just relax . . . splendid, gorgeous. You've got great tits, shame to hide them.'

Gloria felt herself tensing up. This wasn't quite what she was expecting but she'd posed many a time in the mirror and her breasts were high and full. The spirit had gone to her legs and she smiled, slid off the bra and leaned forward so both breasts were out. 'Like this?' she said.

'Gorgeous. Now we can let the dog see the rabbit.'

On the second visit and another tumbler of the fiery spirit, she felt her reserve vanishing a little more. Then he posed her again, this time on a fur rug.

'Let's get those legs on display, perfect, turn round, oh yes. I can see we'll get a lot of work out of those, beautiful. What a bum! Just one more . . . Can we get rid of those frenchies and have a peep . . . ?'

No! It was as if cold water was thrown over her. What was she doing, half naked in front of a stranger? This didn't feel right. Maddy didn't do these sorts of poses.

'That's enough. I didn't come here to do a strip!'

'I know, love, but there's no modesty in this business. You have to be prepared to give the customers what they want,' Ken argued, giving her a tight hug. 'A girl like you should be proud of her assets. Why not show it off – tastefully, of course?'

'I thought I was going to do corsets and bras,' she replied, confused by his suggestion.

'Come on, Gloria, that's bread-and-butter stuff. You can do more than that and it will be good money. Glamour shots for a specialist magazine.'

'You mean, like *Titbits*?' she asked.

'Perhaps . . . but you have to relax and give them everything they ask.'

'I'm not sure. I need to think about that,' she hesitated. 'Do I get these shots to keep?'

'I'll pick out the best and let you know when you can view them.'

'Send them through the post,' she suggested. It was costing her to come by train, and she'd not earned anything yet.

'I'd rather you came back. We could have another session. Fancy a drink next door? You've been a good girl and I'd like to use you as my model.'

'Would you?' Gloria was relieved and flattered. She was a natural and perhaps she might just take her clothes off. He'd not suggested anything improper. Ken had his girlfriend. He was dark and short with a thin moustache, too old, and not her type at all.

'I'll think about it. When shall I come back?'

Now she was back a week later on her Saturday off. If she was going to make some money there was no time to lose. They had the usual drink that seemed to fill her limbs with jelly, and set to work as usual

The shots he'd taken were what he called 'exotic' poses. Some of them were a bit naughty and she was glad there was only her and Ken. The drink seemed to make her go dopey and silly, and then she didn't care where she put her arms and legs, or her clothes, which always ended up piled out of sight, leaving nothing now to the imagination. Ken said her shots were exciting and provocative, whatever that meant.

Gloria staggered back to the station with her head swimming. As the train rattled northwards, she began to shiver at what she'd just done. Had she gone too far? Was she making herself cheap? It wasn't very ladylike, but as Ken insisted, it was her duty to show off her lovely body. There was nothing wrong in nudity, was there? It was art, after all. She was a proper artist's model now, but it must be a secret, a delicious secret. Little Miss Redhead was going to give La Madeleine a run for her money

It was turning out to be a lovely birthday, even though Plum was now almost fifty. Archie and Vera Murray called in for drinks and afternoon tea. Gloria and Grace had baked a Victoria sponge with jam and cream filling. Maddy came up on the morning train from Leeds, carrying a gorgeous bunch of cut flowers, extravagant blooms to fill the vase in the hall.

Maddy looked so grown up in her lavender suit and Pleasance's pearls. She was turning into a beautiful young woman, with a sparkle back in her eyes.

Even Gerry had sent Plum a card. They'd still not divorced, but lived apart, and she hardly gave a thought to him or the fact that he lived with Daisy Abbott as his wife. It was all very civil, and yet unfinished business between them. How would she ever break free and start again?

The Brooklyn was her life now. Bookings were spasmodic but enough to keep Gloria on. Yet sometimes in the evenings, when there was only the wireless for company and the dogs wrapped round her feet, the house groaned and creaked and she missed the bustle and complaining of the oldies during the war. How had it all shrunk down to this?

Maddy sat tucking into their Sunday tea with gusto, full of the discovery that Bella's mother was her old school friend Totty Featherstone.

'Good heavens, so that's where she went, bagged Hugh Foxup . . . I'll give her a ring some time.'

'She called you "Prunes and Custard". What's that all about?' Maddy laughed, seeing her blush.

'She was the custard blonde and I, well, with a name like mine . . . Better than some of the laxative nicknames they dished out. It was all terribly competitive, this débutante thing, being presented at court, finding rooms for parties and balls. It nearly beggared my parents but it was the done thing then, you just did what you were told. Totty and I were up from Yorkshire and shared a few dos but she had a title and got first pickings. It was such a farce, like some glorified cattle market for fine-bred heifers, but it served its purpose, I suppose, in making sure we didn't step out with unsuitable boys from the wrong backgrounds. Well, well . . . Totty Foxup. I'd love to see her again.'

Just thinking about those far-off days made Plum sad. She and Gerry were thrown together, too young and silly to know they were unsuited. She would make sure Maddy made her own choices in that department when the time came.

It was lovely that Maddy was going to stay for the night to catch up – that was the best present of all. She hoped tomorrow she'd be up early, in her old togs, mucking out and gossiping with Gloria in the kitchen like old times. They were her family now.

She was always grateful for Archie and Vera's company, her friends on the WVS committee, but young voices filled the house with chatter and noise and such energy.

Gloria came to life when Maddy came back. Sooner or later her young helper would up and marry away. This was no life for a lively girl. She'd trained up well and was a spotless cleaner. She'd made the guesthouse business possible, with her eye for detail. You couldn't fake that sort of eagle eye, and Gloria had flair. She suggested changes to the way the furniture was laid out, little adjustments that made all the difference to their comfort. Plum herself had no time for fussing around the rooms. There were still estate matters to distract, horses to exercise, dogs to walk and the garden to keep in some sort of shape. Gloria was proving a reliable member of staff.

'This is delicious,' said Maddy with cream on her lips. 'Who made it? Grace?'

'No, me,' smiled Gloria, looking smug. 'I'm not just a pretty face.'

'So I see.' Maddy paused, hearing a scrunch of brakes on gravel. 'You've got another visitor, I think.'

Plum stood up to peer out of the window. She was not expecting anyone else. There was a dark green sports car parked up and a tall young man in a blazer and grey flannels was striding towards the steps.

'He must be one of your friends, Gloria,' she said, making for the door. 'We've no guests booked in, have we?'

'No, I kept it free . . . Let me see to it. But I don't know anyone with a car like that.'

Plum examined the smart vehicle, puzzled. Then suddenly there was a roar from the hall.

'Mrs Plum! Look who's here? You'll never guess in a month of Sundays. Come in . . . come in!' Gloria ushered in the young man, who stood in the doorway, hesitating.

'Mrs Belfield, it's Gregory . . . Gregory Byrne. I hope you don't mind, but I've been meaning to call for some time.'

'Greg! How wonderful.' Plum darted forward at once to greet him. 'My, how you've grown, so tall! You've filled out. What brings you to these parts? Last time I heard you were in Leeds. Come and meet my guests. Remember the Reverend and Mrs Murray?' She pointed in their direction. 'Greg was one of my first evacuees,' she reminded the vicar and his wife.

Everyone stood up to shake hands except Maddy, who for some reason looked away, flushed, and smiled.

'Maddy, look who it is!'

'Hello, Greg. We meet again,' she grinned, and they

stared at each other. He just couldn't take his eyes off of her.

'I made it. Charlie lent me a show car. I'm so sorry to be late.' His cheeks were flushed as he stood fiddling with a cufflink.

'We met at Bella's house last night,' Maddy grinned. 'Couldn't believe it was our Greg. Would you know it, he wrapped his rally car round a tree at Bella's and got out without a scratch?'

'You should've said he was coming,' Gloria sniffed. 'I would have made extra.'

'Sorry, I didn't know . . .'

'Come and sit down. Grace has already gone to fetch another cup and plate. How lovely to see you. You must stay the night so there's time for you to tell us all about yourself. We'd almost lost touch with you. Oh, what a super end to my birthday. The unexpected guest is always the most welcome . . . I can't believe it!'

How wonderful, out of the blue like that, like the long-lost hero from the wars returning, Gloria sighed. How dare Maddy not tell them Greg was coming?

When had he grown so tall and handsome and confident? Gloria couldn't take her eyes off him for one second. She was preening her feathers, flirting, offering him cake, knowing she was being ridiculous but she didn't care.

Soon he was settled by the fireside, telling them about the army and Germany, full of his new business, his plans for the future. He kept pausing to look at them both, smiling like the cat that got the cream.

Gloria couldn't tear her eyes away from Greg's face.

It was a film star face, with a blond Brylcreemed quiff, slicked back at the sides, those piercing blue eyes, and his car, the racing-green sports car with an open top, outside for all to see. It was a Morgan on loan on pain of death from his friend Charlie's garage. He'd just swanned in like the old times. He was always Mrs Plum's favourite evacuee.

Gloria was so glad she'd got on her new tan dress, bought from a proper dress shop with coupons Ken had given her for doing that extra bit of business yesterday in Bradford.

She felt hot thinking about how he made her pose, straddling the seat of a chair as if she was riding a horse with a whip and a top hat and high heels but nothing else.

'You're a natural, Gloria, and gorgeous!' he'd kissed her on the lips and she'd not resisted.

He'd still not told her where he sold her pictures and she'd not done one straight corset shot yet. When she'd asked to see them he just waved his hand.

'Your body is wasted covered in pink cotton and whalebone. It needs to be admired. You'll be proud of my glamour shots . . . just one more.' How she hoped he knew what he was doing. Some of the poses made her feel silly.

Yet the thought of Greg peering down at them made her squirm. What would he think of her? He might not understand their artistic value. Nudes were OK in museums and art galleries, but just in a plain photo . . . Why had she let Ken coax her into doing some of this stuff?

For all that he was short and dark and a bit greasy, he made her feel good and important and special, and she didn't mind when he kissed her. He was the first man to make her feel like a real woman. Here was the second.

'I can't believe it's you, after all these years,' she whispered.

'And here you are, just as cheeky and just as bonny,' he laughed. 'And Maddy here is a real mannequin at Marshfields. Charlie does old man Marshfield's cars . . . the Bentley coupé and the Daimler. How long have you been working there?' He turned back to Maddy, looking straight through Gloria as if she was glass.

'She was at a typing school and got spotted, didn't you? Now she's all over the place – Manchester, London, it'll be Paris next,' Gloria added, not wanting to be ignored. 'I've been doing a spot of photographic modelling myself, not like Maddy, but it pays well for knitting pattern books, catalogues,' she lied, but it sounded good when she said it out loud.

'Really?' Greg smiled, turning back to Maddy. 'How about going for a spin tomorrow before I go home . . . out into the hills and I'll put the Morgan through its paces?'

'Jolly good!' Gloria could hardly contain herself. She could see herself whisked through the country lanes with all heads turning to see who it was.

'And you too. I suppose I could squeeze three of us in at a push,' Greg added.

'I'd love to, but I ought to exercise Monty first,' Maddy replied. 'How's poor Charlie?'

'Just a bit sick,' he replied. 'He's in bed today. He'll be fine in the morning.'

'I'll be ready even if Maddy's not,' Gloria piped in, not wanting to be ignored.

Why was Maddy looking daggers at her? What had she said? It was no skin off her nose if Maddy didn't come. One less distraction, and Greg would be all hers for the morning if Mrs Plum gave her the time off.

'I think that's an excellent idea,' said Mrs Plum. 'But Maddy should have some fresh air too. Her face is much too pale.'

'I can take Monty out for a hack, the exercise will do me good and then I really must get back to Leeds.'

'I'll give you a lift back?' Greg offered without any prompting.

Gloria felt panic rising. Why was he making a fuss of Maddy and not her?

'That's kind, but enjoy your trip down memory lane with Gloria first. Aunt Plum will have lots of things to show you. We can catch up later,' she said, blushing pink.

Well, goody goody, gumdrops, Gloria thought. It left the coast clear for her own invasion plans. Gregory Byrne was the best thing to drive into town since the army left for good. She was going to make sure he returned.

Greg paced over familiar territory in the chill November wind, down the field track, over cow pat fields, to the Old Vic. Everything seemed smaller, shabbier, but just as green and beautiful. The smell of peat smoke, coal fires, horse dung and hay – still that real country aroma.

Sowerthwaite hadn't changed since he was here as a vaccy: the grey stone church tower where they went bat hunting, the squat wide market square with the three-storey houses lining the cobbles, the low Dales cottages, the hostel still as it was, but empty and sadder, somehow, for being so.

He'd been happier here than anywhere; up the Victory Tree, spotting planes and hiding from old Ma Blunt, swopping picture cards and marbles.

Now the tree stood bare, its branches stripped by the wind, a carpet of rusting leaves at his feet. He looked up, expecting to see a line of dangling legs, the rope ladder and tree house where they'd always been. It brought a lump to his throat.

He was so glad he'd come back and could prove he was somebody, not just a scruffy evacuee. He'd come with his tail up, even if it was in a borrowed car. He had to see Maddy again. He couldn't get her out of his head.

He was on the road to success, given time. There was cash in his pocket. He knew his trade and he had the gift of the gab to sell himself but one look from those flashing eyes and he was lost. When she looked at him, he was knocked sideways. There was something so imposing about her on horseback, or lounging in the drawing room, that stirred him; her eyes, her warmth and attractiveness roused him even as he thought of her. She stirred desire inside him, a longing even before he'd known who she was. It was as if he'd been struck stupid all over again, just like the night before.

She was his Maddy, his friend, the first good deed he'd done on that station all those years ago when Plum had entrusted him to find her.

Gloria was lovely, bubbly, cheeky and full of fun. She'd not changed, eager to be included, pretty and curvaceous, a head-turner in her own way, but she wasn't Maddy. He'd not be ashamed to have her on his arm if there wasn't a first choice. She was more of his own class than the young lady at Brooklyn Hall.

Why was he feeling so angry and anxious? He hadn't come north to face all this being stirring up, but it was mixed up with being here as a child: so many memories crowding into his head, his lonely childhood and longing for a family of his own.

The Aftons were kind to him but it was work that kept loneliness at bay, work that gave him satisfaction, work that gave him pride. Bella and Alex's crowd were not his type. They had too much money and life had been too easy for them.

Coming back here reminded him that he was poor, alone, an orphan, and how much he had lost in life. The Old Vic had brought a family of sorts, as had the army, and staying with the Aftons. He didn't belong at the Brooklyn, however welcoming Mrs Plum was to him.

He must put all this sentimental nonsense behind him. Now was the time to grab his chance, have some fun and forget all that stuff – but how could he do that if he didn't have Maddy Belfield by his side?

*

Maddy woke sweating from a dream. It was a nightmare of explosions and railway stations where she stood trying to catch a train that wouldn't let her on board. She was being carried far away, against her will and she couldn't reach the train home to Plum and Monty. The stables were burning, Monty was trapped, and she couldn't rescue him. She was tearing the bed sheets and woke gasping for breath, sitting bolt upright in the darkness. Where was she?

Then she recalled it was Sunday night, she was safe in her own room, and along the corridor was Greg Byrne in the blue guest room. Her feelings had turned upside down in twenty-four hours, all because of his arrival in her life.

Out of nowhere he'd turned up and shaken her to her boots. It was the shock of seeing him grown, handsome, so physical in his leather suit the first time she saw him in the snow. She could almost sense him in her nostrils like a horse senses fear or danger or attraction.

She felt wary, uncertain, curious and confused. She'd wanted to stay safe. The last time Maddy had let her emotions rule, look what had happened. That must never happen again. Yet there was something in his stride, his long limbs, the curve of his stance, his enthusiasm, she was finding hard to ignore, like a stallion let loose in a field of brood mares. It made her feel hot all over.

Aunt Plum had quizzed him all evening, and the Murrays were all ears about his travels in Europe. He'd asked about Pleasance and the oldies, the Battys, the other evacuees, as if he was really interested. They talked about his letters and the terrible trek through Northern France.

She'd seen the shutters closing over his eyes when he talked about the war. He was filtering what he said to them. Everyone sat listening, enthralled that this was their Greg, returned to them.

Gloria sat with her hands wrapped over her knees, gazing adoringly into his face in the firelight, willing him to look at her and admire this devoted attention.

Greg kept glancing at Maddy all evening and she stared back, holding his gaze as if sending a signal that she longed to be alone with him. She sensed how nervous he was, seeing through his bravado.

He'd had a tough time as a soldier and now he was trying to forge a new life for himself. She sensed it was a struggle. It was Charlie's money that brought them to the rally. Who was she to look down on his efforts? He'd had none of her advantages and that made him all the stronger in her eyes.

She was just a clothes horse, showing off expensive outfits to women with more money than sense. There was not great merit in her work and yet she was admired for the mere accident of her figure and face, neither of which were any of her doing. The configuration of her limbs and features were an accident of birth. Only her eye had been tampered with.

She fitted the clothes because of her thinness and height. She was there to emphasise the cut and design of the fabric, nothing more. She was no more than a doll for dressing. She'd not battled across the

Rhine against gunfire and shrapnel. She'd not watched her friends shot to pieces or starved in war-torn cities.

They'd lived out the war in comfort, even though she'd lost all her family. He'd never had any family to mourn. The war felt like some strange dream now, so unreal, shoved to the back of the cupboard of her mind along with all the other stuff.

Greg's arrival brought it all back, her memories of the war, and his kindness to her at the station. How he'd stuck up for her when she was bullied.

They were both orphans, children of war, evacuees and refugees. How could you – forget all that? They had so much in common.

Maddy lay back with a sigh. He really was quite a dish.

'How do you get enough petrol?' screamed Gloria, clinging on to the side of the car as they spun round a bend. She was terrified and feeling sick, a silk scarf wrapped round under her chin, but she was enjoying the run too much to spoil his showing off. Greg looked so dashing in his thick army coat and racing goggles.

They'd taken the high road to Malham and kept stopping to open gates. They scared sheep, which scattered in all directions. She'd posed by the gatepost to show off her shapely pins and ankles, pulled in her waist belt until it hurt and tried to look cool and sophisticated, windswept and mysterious, like the stars did in the pictures.

Greg was such a fast driver, with no sense of danger,

that her heart was in her mouth but she tried to imagine they were in Monte Carlo.

'This is fun!' she yelled, strands of hair whipping her eyelids, though the urge to retch was getting stronger by the minute. 'Stop and let's have a look at the view,' she suggested, knowing she was going to be sick.

Greg jerked to a halt and stared across the expanse of moorland.

'I'd forgotten how grand this scenery is. One day I'll build myself a house up here in the hills, just for the summer,' he announced with a wide sweep of his arm.

'You could always stay at the Brooklyn now Mrs Plum's made a go of it,' she suggested, but he was not listening to her, his eyes were roaming over the fells in a daydream.

'What happened to Gerald? Was he killed?' he asked, fumbling for his cigarette case in his pocket.

'Nah, he went off with his fancy woman. I'm not sure if they're divorced. She never says anything but she still wears her wedding ring.' He offered her a cigarette and lit it with his lighter just like a film star on screen.

'And your family. Where's Sid?'

'On a farm up the dale, happy as a pig in muck . . . You know Mam came back for us, after you left? She was going to marry a Yank but he was killed in France, or so she said. You never know with Mam. I couldn't stick the city and ended up back here when Mrs Plum got me a job as a mother's help. Now I'm a housekeeper but I do my modelling on the side with Ken Silverstone Associates.' Why had she lied to him, when it was Maddy who'd brought her back here?

'He's your boyfriend, this Ken?'

'Not really. He's my manager and finds work for me,' she lied.

'And Maddy – does she have someone too?' He turned away, staring out again as if he wasn't interested but she knew he was quizzing her for information.

'Dunno . . . never in one place long enough to go steady. I've never heard of one but you see how she is. Never still for a moment.' Gloria stopped smoking, feeling her belly in her throat and groaned. 'Oh shit!' She shot out of the car to throw up by the stone wall. This was not how it was supposed to be. You never saw that in the pictures, except in comedies.

'Sorry,' she croaked, getting back into the car, feeling foolish.

'Better out than in!' Greg laughed, until he saw her green face and drove sedately back to Sowerthwaite on the main road.

They turned into the drive just as Maddy was on the doorstep with her case. Plum was down the stairs in a flash.

'Gregory, dear, you will give Maddy a lift to the station?'

'I told you I can do better than that. Hop in and I'll give you a lift back to Leeds. It's the least I can do. I have to return this Cinderella carriage to the garage before it turns into a Morris Minor.'

Gloria fell out of the car on wobbly legs. She was still feeling sick and also miffed, knowing that she'd have to get on with her chores and leave them to it.

'Time we had another afternoon get-together one Saturday, Maddy. Meet you outside the Queens as usual?' she offered. It was worth a try to revive their friendship.

Maddy smiled. 'That'll be good. Tea and the pictures, it is?'

'You and your friend Charlie might like to join us?' said Gloria, not one to miss an opportunity. 'A foursome would be fun. I can always stay over with Maddy, if it's my weekend off.' She threw a look of desperation to Mrs Plum, hoping for the next weekend off.

'I'm sure we'll think of something, Gloria. I might come and do some shopping myself and make a day of it,' shouted Plum. 'Keep in touch, young man.'

No, no no! Gloria groaned, not you as well. How can I get to know Greg again if the whole of the Brooklyn is watching? A chaperone was the last thing she needed.

'We can't both be off at the same time,' Gloria said, hoping to nip this idea in the bud.

'Silly me, of course not. No, you're right. Another time, perhaps.'

'But I'd like to take you to tea, Mrs Plum – just a little thank you for your hospitality. Perhaps the others might like to join us. I shall write and confirm a date,' said Greg, roaring the engine back into life.

'Tea'll be lovely.'

No it won't, thought Gloria. If she goes, I'll have to

stay, and it'll be Maddy who gets the treat, not me. It's not fair. She waved them off half-heartedly.

'They make a lovely couple, don't they? Very distinguished,' whispered Plum as she watched the car roar down the avenue.

'Do you think so?' Gloria replied. 'I don't think Greg is Maddy's type at all. He's only a builder.' The east wind blew across her face and she shivered. Why didn't all of them recognise that he was just Gloria's type of bloke? What must she do to make him look at her twice?

They drove as far as Skipton in silence. Maddy shivered and Greg stopped to put the roof on the car when it started to sleet. They both spoke at once, breaking a strange silent tension that had grown on the journey, each aware of the other one sitting close, aware that this was the first time they had been truly alone together but not knowing what to say.

'Thanks for the lift. I'm glad you came,' said Maddy. 'Do you remember picking me up outside school that time? It did the trick.'

'I do, and those awful girls . . . If they could see you now . . . We didn't get much time to talk, did we?' said Greg.

'There'll be other times. We mustn't lose touch again.' She smiled, turning to him.

Greg grinned back and his eyes sparkled like dancing water. 'The Brooklyn hasn't changed, spruced up a bit but still the same old place, and Plum is just as kind.'

'I wish she'd sell the damn place and get herself a

real life. She must get so lonely,' Maddy replied, relaxing into the bucket seat.

'Gloria's a laugh, quite the little glamour girl. I'm surprised she's hung around so long, what with her new career and her Ken.'

'This Ken is very elusive,' Maddy said. 'According to Plum he's not given her quite the opportunities she was dreaming about. No one has ever seen any of her portfolio shots. She's very secretive but so desperately wants to do what I'm doing. She thinks my world is so glamorous and I keep telling her the truth of it. You saw us all hunched in the snow, standing frozen, waiting for the right light, take after take. Sometimes I get so fed up I want to scream, but it pays well, and I do get to some interesting places. I never know who I'm going to meet.' They both laughed.

'I bet there's not many jobbing builders on your sites.'

'There is now,' she smiled, turning to him.

'Oh, aye? And who's that then?' he joked. 'Do you get much free time?'

'Oh, it's either a famine or a feast – frantic fittings for shows, photo shoots and sittings for magazines, and then sitting around waiting for the phone to ring. Miss Ffrost, my landlady, is not amused if I'm late with the rent.'

'Could I take you out to dinner sometime soon, when you're free?' he asked, and his cheek was twitching with nerves.

'I'd like that; then we could catch up properly. You have to tell me all about rally driving if you can bear to. I must say it looks pretty dangerous . . .'

They smiled and nodded and sat this time in companionable silence. She kept pointing the way to the nearest bus stop but he'd have none of it and drove her straight home to Arncliffe Road.

'Now I know where you live I can pick you up, but it won't be in a Morgan, I'm afraid.'

'Four wheels will be fine or shanks's pony,' she laughed. She hadn't felt this happy for years.

'Just the two of us, on Thursday night then?'

'Thursday night it is,' Maddy said as she made to get out of the car. 'Thank you.'

'Remember when I rescued you last time, I got a reward,' said Greg, leaning over the seat to kiss her.

She didn't resist but kissed him back on the cheek, waving him off until the car had gone from sight. Suddenly her suitcase was lighter, her step springier. He was still the old Greg after all.

There was a message waiting on the hall table from Marshfields, asking her to report for some big buyer's bash in Manchester from Wednesday until Thursday. Poor Greg would have to wait for his date and that thought gave her no pleasure at all.

17

In the weeks following that first chance encounter with Maddy, Greg couldn't believe how his world had changed. They met every week when she was free but he was cautious. This was his first serious affair and he must pace himself.

Maddy wasn't one of his quick conquests. She was the sort of girl who would expect him to do things properly. It was 'Gently Bentley' with his lovemaking. There was all the time in the world now, but he couldn't wait. He wanted to make her his own and treat her like she deserved, no matter what it cost.

He sat on the rooftop looking out over the city, wanting to shout out to the world that he'd found his girl, the one who'd make him the proudest of men. He whistled on the job and the brickies wondered if he was drunk.

He was drunk with the scent of her, the anticipation of meeting her outside Marshfields, even if there was only time for a cup of tea in the station buffet before she disappeared off across the Pennines on another assignment.

Now there was something more in his life than making money, he thought as he whistled away, something more than creating yet more business. He was besotted with his princess.

Now he even noticed children in prams – perhaps one day they might have a family of their own – but most of all he felt that he wasn't alone any more. Every day and evening they spent together was magical. She took him to an orchestral concert in the Town Hall, quite highbrow stuff for a rough chap like him, but the music stirred him. Then they spent a morning going round the City Art Gallery. They ate a picnic in Roundhay Park, in the car, because it was still cold, and climbed the Cow and Calf on top of Ilkley Moor. They kissed each other until he ached with wanting her, but he sensed hesitation, a reluctance to go too far so he tried not to rush things. Maddy was respectable, his perfect princess, and he still couldn't believe she could look at him twice – but the miracle was that when she did, he was putty in her hands.

'What's got into you this evening?' snapped Ken Silverstone, trying to focus his lens in on Gloria's plump breast. 'Your skin's gone all blotchy. Go and powder them down.'

His subject got up from the rug and wrapped a dressing gown over her body. She wasn't in the mood for looking sexy and come hither, dressed in only a red velvet cloak with a cotton wool trim that smelled of other unwashed bodies.

Plum had had another letter from Maddy saying

she'd lunched with Greg Byrne in a big hotel by the Otley road. He'd spared no expense. They walked in a nearby park and had got tickets for the Grand Theatre for the weekend.

This was not how it was supposed to be. She was seeing too much of him. Greg was Gloria's challenge and target. Maddy had enough opportunities to meet with rich cronies; she didn't need to poach the one decent man to come into Gloria's life.

Ken had his moments, in a gruff Yorkshire sort of way, but he talked rough, and was a bit common. He'd made a real fuss of her and one night after a drink too many he'd shown her what's what in the love department, shown her how it all fitted together. It had been a bit disappointing, going all the way on a stained rug in the studio, a bit overrated, a push and shove and, Bob's your uncle, it was all over.

He'd suggested it was good for her career to have experience so she could have the look in her eye that men would recognise, the 'I'll give you a good time' look that suggested she'd be fun in bed. It might give them a thrill, but she'd felt nothing but pain and embarrassment.

At least he'd worn a rubber johnnie. There must be no accidents. Maddy's mess had taught that – and Mam's too. It was all a thunder of nothing, as far as she was concerned, but Ken seemed to get excited when he took shots, fiddling with himself and getting worked up so they ended up rolling on the floor. He then carried on taking his shots naked and she thought how silly he looked, and how stupid she looked in these costumes. 'Mother Christmas in Santa's Grotto!' This was not how she'd expected to end up. It was all so cheap and made her feel dirty. Why did she keep doing it then?

He'd even asked her to do some shots with Rita, who did more specialised angles, he called them, wanting them to lie together and do silly stuff but she told him straight to cut it out, she wasn't that sort of girl and she didn't want to be his model any more if this was how he saw her. She was fed up at never seeing any of her shots. When she asked to do respectable work he'd laughed at her.

'Listen, love, this is all you're fit for. Once a tart, always a tart!' That was when she slapped him hard and he hit her back, and things were getting nasty.

'I'm off! I'm not coming back,' she'd screamed. 'You can find another muggings!'

'There's plenty more fish in the sea, darling,' he'd sneered. 'You're not that special. Anyway, you like it really. You'll be back. There's a club I know that could give you a slot, stripping for gentlemen. Now that would get you on a circuit – free booze . . . instant stardom, Gloria. My Little Miss Redhead does it again!'

She should've walked out there and then, but she didn't, and now she was back doing silly Easter Bunny shots. Why was she still pretending there was any future in this but dirty postcards?

Yet something happened when she climbed those wooden stairs to the studio that made her feel important and special and sexy. Here she was Gloria, the model, a star in her own right, not just a poor relation or a domestic in someone else's house. When she posed under those lights it felt as if she had an audience of hundreds drooling over her body. Ken was very persuasive, with his presents and drinks. This was her secret world no one knew about but her, where her body had the power to stir men's lusts, or so Ken said. This was where she felt secure, in some strange way, noticed and wanted.

If only people in Sowerthwaite knew what she got up to on her evening off . . . but it was cold outside and her skin had come up into a pink mottled rash and she was brassed off at not getting a date with Greg on his own because Maddy had got there first.

They'd had one foursome with his mate Charlie Afton, a blokey sort of man, nothing about him at all but a line of garages. He'd sat in the cinema not saying a word, separating her from Maddy and Greg and doing nothing to show he was interested in her. If only she could get Greg on his own he'd soon see what he was missing. He had to know there was another offer on the table from a girl who knew what it was like to be poor and shunted around, but who'd make a lovely home for him.

Now there was talk of him coming over for the weekend. It was her turn to charm the pants off him, dazzle him and seduce him good and proper. Maddy had had her chances in Leeds.

Gloria needed Greg to give her a better chance in life. Maddy must have plenty of suitors. She wouldn't miss Greg. She didn't need him to help her career or support her. It wasn't right to steal from your friend,

Gloria thought, but sometimes you have to take your chance, grab the life raft and cling on in stormy waters.

She would cook up some delicious stews, buy a whole new outfit with the funny coupons Ken had got hold of, have her hair restyled. This was where the photo money came in handy. She might not be up to Maddy's dizzy heights although she could cut a dash in her own way – but she must clear a path to get Greg alone. There must be no competition.

Gloria powdered down her red skin with talc and hoped it would do the trick. She went back into the darkness, pinning a grin on her face. The show must go on for a while longer, even if it was beginning to pall.

Next morning she was walking across the footpath to the shops with the dogs. A Yorkshire spring was still a long time coming, the wind whistling through the bare branches as she opened the rusting iron gate into the Old Vic yard. The hostel was now let out into lodging rooms for mill workers but she still used the short cut.

The great beech tree towered above her, buds now visible; a promise of summer to come, but without Greg it was all so pointless. She paced around the trunk in a frenzy of frustration.

I must have him. I've never wanted anything so much in my life. He'll never be suited to Maddy. Why can't anyone see that? She's not for him.

Her frustration was like a ravenous hunger inside, this need to make Greg Byrne love only her. She stood entranced for minutes under the tree, its outline silhouetted against the leaden sky. It's V-shape like two fingers into the sky, defiant.

How it brought back memories of their wartime escapades, living up the tree, forever friends, those posting boxes in the bark of its trunk where they had played spies sending messages, of being in a gang of off-comers in that first freezing winter, of getting Maddy's news all wrong, of being second best.

Then she recalled that terrible night in the hostel when, blinded by fear, she'd helped Maddy deliver the baby and hidden the evidence. It was something they had both blotted out from their lives. Neither of them had spoken of it again, acting as if it never happened, whether through shame or guilt, she didn't know.

Now the remembrance of that night rose up, blinding her with sudden knowledge.

There was a way . . . oh, yes, there was a way: all was fair in love and war, they said.

She owed Maddy nothing but Maddy owed her a great deal. It was because of her that Maddy was free now to be a mannequin and lead such a glamorous life. No one would have looked at her twice with a baby on her hip. Why should Maddy have all the chances when her own life was going nowhere? Only Greg had brought excitement into it and even that was threatened by Maddy's charm.

Neither girl would be young for ever, but Maddy would always have Brooklyn and her inheritance, her connections and plenty of men of her own class to choose from.

Gloria needed Greg and his ambitions to give her a well-deserved lift in her rough life. Maddy would just have do without him.

Gloria recoiled at these angry devious thoughts. It was not going to be a very friendly thing to do but she must take her chance when it came. Maddy would thank her in the end. A plan was forming in her mind and she had the Victory Tree to thank for it.

Gloria strode into town, heading into the wild wind with a smile on her face. To the victor the spoils. Who'd have thought their school motto would come in so useful?

Maddy peered into the powder-room mirror with satisfaction for once, touching up her lipstick and perfume. The peacock satin ball gown shimmered under the lights, the satin elbow gloves decorated with motifs in blue, black and green sequins sparkled, and she felt her heart skipping with anticipation.

She'd asked Greg to be her partner at Marshfields' annual charity ball. They'd got a whole evening of dancing in front of them. It was all so romantic and she wanted this night to go on for ever. She'd been looking forward to it for weeks. Greg coming into her life was the best thing ever, better than having Monty to ride, making exits down the catwalk under the spotlight, better than Christmas. She wasn't alone any more: there was someone to share all her gossip and mess-ups, someone to wait for at the end of the day.

Plum and Gloria, kind as they were, faded into the background, being so far away, but Greg was close at hand and such fun. He took her to the fair and they spun on the waltzers and drove the Dodgems; he bought her candy floss and silly toys. He'd taken her to her first football match, screaming Leeds United to victory in the pouring rain. He'd showed her around his latest building site like a king striding over his castle. Greg was so enthusiastic and thoughtful. She'd never been so happy in all her life. What she had felt for Dieter was puppy love, just as Aunt Plum had said, a rehearsal for the big event. She'd been so young and impressionable then.

Greg was rough but he had been there in that terrible time in her life when Mummy and Daddy were lost. He was all mixed up with Brooklyn but he had gone on to find his own way unaided: a warrior who'd found a good friend in Charlie, a businessman who worked as hard as any navvy. He could mix with all types and not be overawed. He loved the countryside as much as she did. He was the only man who'd known her when she was inflicted with her squint. It didn't matter that he was not public school or a professional, that he was struggling to make his dreams come true. He was all she ever wanted in a man. Was this how Daddy must have felt when he met Dolly Mills over a piano stool? Class barriers hadn't bothered them. They knew they were soul mates, and Maddy sensed now she had found hers.

The Assembly Rooms were festooned with flowers and hothouse plants, the dinner was over and now it was time for dancing the night away. Work had taken her away from him lately – buyers' parades, the new season's range to model – but this night had been kept clear. Tonight was her turn to show him off to the world; this thoughtful man who left flowers on the doorstep after a long day, letters and cards in the post. He often waited for her late into the evening to bring her home, foot sore and weary. He cooked her the only thing he could make, hot vegetable broth and grilled chops, in his little flat off Mornington Road. There was always his cheery taxi service to rely on.

It wasn't hard to fall in love with this dashing young man in his borrowed tuxedo. She needed to repay his generosity with a gesture all of her own. All the other mannequins lusted after him. She knew Gloria found him attractive too, but Greg was her man, her future and she was so lucky to have found him again.

Tonight the orchestra were playing all their favourite tunes: 'I'd Like to Get You on a Slow Boat to China', 'I'll Be Seeing You', 'Anything You Can Do I Can Do Better', which they mimed and laughed, and then he took her into his arms for the slow croony tunes.

Maddy wanted this night to go on for ever as they sat together in comfortable silence, smoking and watching the other dancers drifting across the floor under the spotlight. There was a smell of perfume, leather seats, cigar smoke and lust in the air.

When you were so in love, words were not necessary; just eyes catching and holding, fingers caressing each other through satin gloves.

All too soon the band played the National Anthem and it was time to go.

*

Greg hoped his surprise would go down well. He felt nervous about asking her to the hotel he'd booked nearby. He wanted to show her how much he loved her. He sensed she was nervous about lovemaking, holding him at arm's length. Alone together for a night they could relax and take all the time in the world. It was his way of saying thank you for the expensive tickets. She hadn't let him pay and that unnerved him at first. Charlie had loaned him his dinner jacket but his patent leather shoes had pinched him all evening.

Tonight was made for being as close as a man and woman could be, he mused as he waited while she collected the little white fox fur cape that Plum had given her. She looked so sophisticated. She kissed him on the ear and smiled, 'Home, James.'

'I've got a surprise. I hope you'll like it,' he whispered, leading her by the hand out of the foyer into the chill night.

'Not another of Charlie's flash taxis? You've spent enough money.'

'No need,' he said. 'Look over there . . . The George. We can go in there now.'

Maddy smiled and looked across. 'For a drink? The bar's closed by now.'

'But the hotel's not. I've booked us a room,' he said, waiting for the hug that didn't come.

'Thanks, but I'd better not. It's late and I've got an early start,' she said, and he felt her stiffen as if he'd said something wrong.

'I've booked us a room,' he insisted. 'I thought you and I might like . . .'

'And that's why I can't come with you. It wouldn't be right,' she replied.

'Not right?'

'You know.' Her voice trembled. 'I can't spend the night with you . . . I'm not ready . . . It's not right.'

'But I thought—' he said.

'I'm sorry, Greg, but I'm not that sort of girl.'

There was a silence between them and with a sinking heart he knew he'd got it terribly wrong.

'Forgive me. I think too highly of you to compromise your morals . . . I love you too much,' he added, kissing her forehead.

'And I love you.' She didn't look at him.

'So what's wrong?' he asked, puzzled by this unexpected resistance. 'I respect you and I can wait. I know you're not the sort of girl to mess around with. When I was abroad, well, you know what soldiers are . . . I did the usual things, but you are so special to me.' There was an awkward silence. 'I just thought it was time . . . I got it all wrong, didn't I?'

'A bit . . . I made my mind up ages ago not do anything until I'm married. I want to make it special on my wedding night. I want things to be perfect.'

'You want a ring on your finger . . . I see. I'm not quite in a position for that yet. In a year or two . . .' He was too stunned to continue.

'Neither am I, Greg. Let's not jump the gun . . . just forget all this.'

Her words were like ice in her heart. He suddenly felt stupid. How could he have misread the signals?

'It's not that important,' she added.

'Oh, but it is,' he replied. 'You're right. I'm glad you've got standards. I saw too many poor girls flinging themselves down on their backs for the price of a loaf, selling their bodies so cheaply. I want my wife to be mine alone. I don't want a slice off a cut loaf so I'm willing to wait.'

Somehow the romance of the evening evaporated from that point onwards; the balloon popped and there was nothing he could do to rescue things.

Maddy pecked him on the cheek. 'I'd better be going then. I can get a taxi.'

'Don't even think about it. The car's parked round the back. I'll walk you to the door.'

They drove back to her flat in silence and she jumped out, feeling sick at this turn of events. She kicked off her slippers and raced up the stairs with her key, her lips trembling with disappointment, fear and confusion.

What is wrong with me? I've ruined everything. Why can't I just jump into bed with him? It's not as if I don't want his body and his love. I've humiliated him. He thinks I don't care, that I'm only interested in marriage. How can I explain how afraid it makes me to let myself go . . . without telling him the truth? I am a slice off a cut loaf. He couldn't have spoke truer words.

The last time I let myself be carried away . . . I can't risk the fear. I have to be safe, safe within marriage, no more mistakes. Damn and blast, the past is past and I *can't alter a thing. Would it matter to him if I wasn't a virgin?*

Somehow she sensed that it would. That was the scariest thing of all. Maddy threw off her gown and flung herself on the bed, sobbing into the pillow. How could she have got it so wrong? There was still so much to Greg Byrne she didn't understand.

Greg drove back to the hotel in a daze. How stupid could he get, trying to be sophisticated! What a total mess he'd made of it! Was he out of his mind? It wasn't that didn't want her. He'd made love to her in his mind for months, ever since the first night he'd clapped eyes on her – but perhaps she didn't feel the same. A girl of her class would want a honeymoon in Paris in the best hotel. Maddy deserved only the best, a lovely wedding day, a precious ring. He couldn't give her any of those things yet. Now he'd spoiled everything. She thought he was looking for a quick fumble.

She was his princess. Everything must be perfect and if it meant taking things slowly, he'd wait even though his groin ached with longing to touch her and make love to her.

Old habits died hard. She was a Belfield, after all, a posh bird, as Charlie called her. Perhaps he ought to write to Mrs Plum and ask permission to court her seriously like they did in the olden days. There was no one else in her family to ask.

What if Plum turned him down as unsuitable? Once an evacuee, always an evacuee . . . the outsider, one of the roughies bounced from one place to the other. He had good prospects. He was as good as any other man, he'd fought for his country but somehow it wouldn't be enough. He had no parents, no education, nothing but his hands to make his way. He would hold his own with any of the rally crowd, given time. His accent was rough but it could be tempered to suit polite company. He'd learned early to bend the truth to please and do the chameleon act when needed. He would not be put down by anybody.

He'd thought the two of them were soul mates, who together would make up for their own sad starts in life, no more wars and disaster. He could see it all in his mind's eye. He'd work his fingers raw to make sure no one looked down on his family.

They must have what he had never got: a loving family, a stable home and a decent education. He needed no handouts to provide for his own.

Perhaps Maddy hadn't understood how desperately he wanted things to be perfect and now they were all muddled up. To her everything must be done in the correct order. That was the big mistake.

As he parked up in the side street under the gaslamp, pulling out a cigarette, he felt like a seven-year-old stripped of his treat. He wanted to cry. How could he have got it so wrong? How could he make it right again?

Spring was late but Plum had sniffed romance in the air the last time she saw Maddy with Greg. There'd been a sparkle in Maddy's eyes she'd never seen before and this was the season for new blossom and hope.

Maddy was busy as usual, but they were all going to be together like old times. Food rationing and austerity could go hang this weekend. They'd have all the trimmings, fires in every room and flowers everywhere.

Springtime in the Dales was so lovely: the shimmering greens of the leaves, the crocuses and daffodils, and aconites in the drive, and if they were lucky the bleating of the new-born lambs in the lower slopes.

Gloria was bustling around, whistling to herself. She was a strange girl, with her up-and-down moods. Perhaps she'd bring over her Ken from Bradford – the one they'd never met. Dancing was her latest craze and she was off on the train with Alison, who worked in the local chemist, her new friend to find dance halls and better partners.

'I wonder if we'll be hearing wedding bells,' Plum voiced to Gloria as they were dipping hard-boiled eggs in onion skins for the Sunday School Easter Pace egg race, when painted eggs were rolled down a steep slope on Pie Crust Hill.

'Whose wedding bells?' shouted Gloria, dunking the shells in the dye.

'Why, Maddy and Greg's, of course!' Plum laughed. She heard an egg crack as it fell on the stone floor.

'What gives you that idea, Mrs Belfield?' Gloria bent over to pick up the bits of shell.

'It's pretty obvious what's going on between those two lovebirds, isn't it?'

'Maddy's said nothing to me,' Gloria snapped. 'I'd think I'd know summat. He's not her sort . . . you know.'

'Isn't he?' Plum was puzzled. She'd thought them well suited in looks and height.

'Nah! Maddy's all for her career. It'll fold if she gets wed. I don't think she's ready to settle down proper or spend time slopping out nappy buckets and dusting china, not after the life she's having now.'

'You do surprise me. I always thought she'd love to settle down with a family of her own. One day this house will be hers now Gerald's not in the picture. Oh well, perhaps I got it all wrong. I must be getting out of touch with you young folk. Pity though. They'd make a fine couple down the aisle.'

Gloria nearly squeezed the egg into her hand. Lovely couple indeed! It was not going to happen. Greg was meant for her. He might not know it yet but he'd soon get tired of Maddy's quiet homebody ways if they lived in the country.

He was full of energy, get up and go. A man like that was going to get rich and join all the best clubs in the district. He'd needed a woman to satisfy those energies and desires: someone as ambitious as himself.

He'd need someone who'd enjoy spending money, dressing up to show off her figure. He needed a girl like Gloria, someone who would not be afraid to flash his wealth around.

Maddy was boring. All she wanted to do was ride Monty, walk the dogs and read books by the fire when she came home. She'd sensed there'd been a cooling off between the couple of late.

It was her duty to stop this right now, at a stroke.

Greg was going to make an awful mistake if he hitched himself to her. Gloria must save him from himself. Could he not see that she was the right girl, waiting in the wings to pick up the pieces?

They had both hurled themselves up from nothing. They were two of a kind and made for each other. He couldn't see it yet because he was dazzled by Maddy's fancy looks and manners. That was all show. Underneath she was plain boring and ordinary and not glamorous at all, while she, Gloria, was a daredevil, a naughty girl who'd excite his passion and give him the best sex now she'd learned a few tricks from Ken.

She'd soothe his brow and then make him wild. Ken said she was a born sexpot but first she had to make Maddy disappear from the scene. Once she was gone then it would be Gloria's turn to console him. She had to be cruel to be kind to both of them. One day they'd thank her for it.

It was a relief to be back in the Brooklyn. Maddy was kneeling on the rug, wrapping up Greg's birthday present in her bedroom. She'd bought him a cashmere jumper that had cost all her clothing coupons.

They'd sort of made it up since the misunderstanding after the ball, but were still being careful with each other. She tried to feel flattered by his proposition but she still didn't feel comfortable explaining her reluctance. She hardly understood it herself. The fear of another pregnancy would always be at the back of her mind, no matter what precautions they took.

This weekend they were going to go walking together, talk things through, and she half wondered if he'd suggest putting things on a proper footing. It was a few days to enjoy the Dales and give Greg a well-deserved rest.

Then Gloria barged in without knocking. 'Sorry to disturb, but I need a word.'

'Fire away, Gloria. I'm just finishing off this. It's a jumper for Greg, and this,' she said, holding up a wrapped package.

Gloria laughed. 'What's that, carpet slippers and a pipe?'

'No, it's a holder for his maps, made from calfskin leather. I know they shove the maps in the back of the car but I just thought it might be useful, don't you think . . . on rallies?'

'I suppose so, but a bit boring. I've got him some aftershave lotion, cost a bomb. Strictly under the counter but, what the hell, he'll smell divine.' Gloria grinned.

'That's a bit personal . . . aftershave?' Maddy looked up, surprised.

'Not at all. Anyway, I've known him since Adam were a lad. It was me who started writing to him in the army. We're good mates. You don't own him.'

'Of course not, but it's just that this weekend is special. I think he's going to tell Plum we'd like to get engaged soon,' she whispered, blushing.

There was a deafening silence. Then Gloria plonked herself on the bed and sighed.

'Do you really think that's wise, Maddy? He's not

your type at all. I'd not rush into anything yet. You don't really know him. It's only been a few months since you met up.' There was something in the way Gloria was shaking her head that was unnerving.

'You know how it is,' Maddy replied, shocked by Gloria's words. 'Love comes and suddenly it feels so right. It happens and you just know,' she smiled, hoping to win her friend round.

'Do you? I'd think with your history you should be careful.' Gloria's eyes were full of concern.

Maddy sat up, puzzled. 'What do you mean?'

'Well, there's poor old Dieter, for a start, and his baby . . . That's not something you spring on a fella like Greg, now is it?'

'You wouldn't say anything about that?' Maddy said, sensing the atmosphere in the room tensing.

'Of course not – I'm your friend. I'm just trying to be honest here. Although you can't deceive him about something as important as that, can you? I'd walk away from him now before he gets hurt.'

'But I love him!' Maddy felt tears welling.

'I can see that, love. I'm just making the point why I think you and Greg are not suited. Underneath all that charm, he's ambitious, an old-fashioned guy at heart, like the rest of them. Believe me, he'll not take kindly to your confession. We don't always get the response that we want, do we? We both know that. You've got a wonderful job, the envy of thousands of girls.'

'But I'd give that up willingly. I don't care about prancing around in new clothes.' Maddy stood up, staring out of the window, feeling sick. Gloria's honesty was chilling her heart.

'Well, we do! We're all so proud of you. Don't be a chump. Don't spoil your career just as its going so well. There'll be other Gregs, but you can't deceive him or let him down.'

'But if I refuse him, I am letting him down.' Why was Gloria taking this stance?

'Look, do you want me to prepare the way? Then you could let him down gently. It's in his best interest.' Gloria continued fingering the presents with a sigh.

'But what about mine? He'll think I've rejected him and he'll be so hurt. He'll think it's a class thing . . . You know I don't care about any of that,' she pleaded, knowing they'd only just got over the last misunderstanding.

'So what if he thinks it is? We'll stand by him. Charlie, me and Plum will make sure he doesn't go too wild. Don't worry, leave it with me, but you must tell him the truth before you both commit to each other. It's only fair.'

'Are you sure?' Maddy's mind was racing to keep up with Gloria's argument.

'Trust me. I'm more experienced than you. He'll be fine . . . Men get over these things quicker than us.'

'But Greg will understand. He was a soldier, he did things – he told me himself,' Maddy argued.

'But it's different for guys. They like to think we girls're all pure as snow, virgin brides, not mucky slush.'

'Hang on, I'm not mucky slush! I made a mistake, but that's all in the past. It was an accident and then

I miscarried.' Maddy struggled to speak those words out loud.

'I know, I was there, or have you forgotten that too?' Gloria replied, spearing her with fierce green eyes. 'How do you think he'll feel, knowing you had someone else's kiddy and never told him? Doctors can tell, even if you don't say anything.'

'But it died,' Maddy whispered. 'It never happened. Why should I tell him?'

'Because you should. Because it's only fair and honorable, and you owe it to him or you're not the Maddy I know. If you can't, then perhaps in your heart you know you don't trust him to understand after all. I'm sorry but I'm trying to help you face facts. You've always been straight with me. Now it's my turn to speak out.'

'It's good to know I have a friend, Gloria. You've made me face up to how things are, but I must deal with this myself. It's nobody's business but mine. Thanks, for the offer. I'm sure Greg will understand once I explain.'

'I wouldn't be so sure if I were you. He's set you up as his princess, his bit of totty. I think he'll be gutted when he finds you're no different from any other. He'll go cold on you, mark my words,' Gloria sighed.

'Oh, no, not Greg! He's got a big heart. He knows I love him. It was such a long time ago. It can't affect us now.'

'It's only a few years ago . . . Face the facts, it'll never work out between you once he knows. The longer you leave it, the worse it'll get. Don't go breaking his heart at the last minute. Better come clean now and see what he says.'

'But how? I can't . . . you're right,' Maddy wept. 'No man would forgive such a slip-up. It's hopeless, isn't it?' she said, suddenly feeling limp. 'I don't know what to say. The truth is so brutal, even when a friend spells it out.'

'It's nothing. What are friends for but to help each other out? It just wouldn't work. I mean, I was with you when you did that awful thing.'

'What awful thing?'

Gloria hesitated. 'I don't like to bring it up. You know, with the baby. You must have been off your head . . .'

'What did I do?' Maddy went cold.

'You left it to die. You refused to get the doctor out to help us.'

'But it never breathed.'

'Well, it wouldn't as you neglected it,' came the reply.

'How could I have done that? I don't remember.' Maddy sat rigid on the chair, suddenly afraid of what she was going to hear.

'You passed out afterwards. I couldn't rouse you, but I saw what I saw. I went out of the room and when I came back, it was dead and you had gone to sleep . . . Don't worry, my lips are sealed.' Gloria sat facing her, her green eyes flickering with anger. 'You should have got the doctor in when I asked.'

'But you could've gone for Dr Gunn yourself,' Maddy replied.

'I did what you wanted and didn't go. It's worried me ever since.'

'Is that why we never talked about that night? I don't remember,' Maddy whispered. 'It was a terrible night. I was so scared but I didn't let my baby die. It never breathed. We tried . . .'

'So you remember bits . . . I saw it all and I'm telling you it's not the sort of night you ever forget, hiding everything away like that.'

'What did you do with him?' Maddy said those awful words for the first time. She was shaking.

'Not now – I can't . . . Let's forget about that but you see why you can't marry Greg. Men don't understand, and in my book living a lie is no basis for a marriage,' Gloria said, brushing down her tweed skirt, her head bowed.

'Everyone has secrets,' Maddy argued.

'Not those sorts of secrets, and you can't go down the aisle to the holy altar in white with that sort of stuff on your conscience.'

'I wasn't planning on a white wedding,' Maddy countered, feeling sick at the emotions being stirred up again.

'Then you would hurt Plum. She's been planning your bash for years: the country church, the beautiful gown. It will be a whole pack of lies to live down. Think about it, Maddy. Better to stop things right now.'

'Oh, Gloria, how will I live without him?' Maddy sobbed.

'Like you did before, get on with your life . . . travel, perhaps go to London? You've got your friends there.

You'll be doing the right thing. You wouldn't want to make him unhappy, out of his depth, ashamed of his lack of education and all that stuff that no one will ever talk about?'

'You've got Ken in your corner, who'll be in mine if I let him go?'

'You've got plenty of friends, you'll get over it. Look at my mam – two fellas killed in the war and a few more besides. She survived.'

'But she let you and Sid down.'

'Everyone lets someone down sometime. You should know that by now,' said Gloria, not looking at her.

'But I love him so much, and Greg's my friend. He'd understand if I told him.' Maddy was screaming inside.

'Can you take that risk? Greg's a survivor. He's got a fortune to make, and fast. He's a simple man who grabs life by the balls. Do you want to see the look of revulsion on his face when you confess your sins to him?'

'If I turn him down I wouldn't want him to think he wasn't good enough for me,' cried Maddy, weakening to the power of Gloria's outspokenness. 'Are you sure I'm doing the right thing?'

'Trust me.'

Maddy fell into her arms, weeping. 'What would I do without you, Gloria?'

The answer came swiftly. 'We'll allus be forever friends, you and me, come what may. We smile through our tears. Auntie Glory to the rescue once more.'

Maddy couldn't see those green eyes flash in triumph. Her heart was broken.

Later she sat in the window seat staring out on the Avenue of Tears and the bright flowers dancing in the breeze. This just couldn't be happening on such a lovely day, surely not, just when she was beginning to feel secure in Greg's love and their future?

But underneath all their passion were terrible truths lurking untold, stuff she'd hoped to take to her grave, nobody's business but her own. It wasn't fair to let Greg think she was pure and innocent. Gloria was right: he deserved better.

Easter lay in ruins. She would have to pretend that her world hadn't crashed over her head. There was no escape, no work to run to. She was going to have to put on the biggest act of her life and it was killing her to think about it. In letting go one of the loveliest things to have happened to her for years, part of her very self would be destroyed. How would she tell Greg to walk away?

Gloria had sown terrible seeds of doubt about that fateful night. Had she seen Maddy do something neglectful? Hard as she strained, she couldn't recall anything other than fear and pain, blood and tears. Could any of her observations be true? If they were, then she must not risk exposure. She didn't deserve any happiness, if that was the case, and losing Greg must be her punishment.

Gloria couldn't stop shaking at what she had just done to her friend. She saw the joy die in Maddy's grey eyes as her terrible arguments sunk in at last. She was surprised how easily Maddy caved in, quicker than she would have done if the roles were reversed. She'd watched her friend's confidence crumble at the suggestion she had allowed the baby to die of neglect in not calling the doctor.

That was a terrible thing to suggest, and the weight of her accusation hung on her neck like a yoke, like carrying buckets of coal around her heart. How could she have done this? The words just sprung out of her mouth fully formed, tipping the balance in her favour. Maddy had wilted under them and retreated.

As Gloria walked down the avenue to have a quiet smoke and calm herself, she felt the branches arching over in the wind, pointing fingers at her. The wind rattled up the drive making her shiver. What was said was said, no turning back now, but in her heart she felt the first stirrings of guilt and fear. Somewhere, sometime, she would have to pay for what she had just done.

For once the Yorkshire weather perked up into sunshine and showers. Greg drove over Blubberhouses Moor from Harrogate to Skipton with the hood down on his new roadster. He couldn't wait to show it off to Maddy and the gang. He drove up through Skipton High Street, admiring the church and the castle gate, stopping off to find some chocolate eggs with his coupons.

He was back home in the Dales, home among familiar streets and faces he recognised in shops, that familiar accent. He stopped off for a pint in The Crown, where the barman recognised him: 'Now, then, young Greg. How do?'

He wore a grin from ear to ear in anticipation of his birthday bash. In the glove compartment was a very special package he'd picked up from Fattorinis, the jewellers, only that morning; an antique engagement ring in its brown box with a cream satin lining. He was the happiest man in Yorkshire – two days off and the most beautiful girl in the world waiting for him. How could he have been so lucky? Everything was going right for once.

He'd just won a contract to build offices on a spanking new commercial estate. There was money in Harrogate. It would be a good place to set up home. Maddy could do some work in Leeds if she wished. He was just bursting with news. Each bend in the road brought him nearer to his dreams coming true.

It was Gloria who came running down the steps to give him a hug. She smelled of summer roses. 'Lovely to see you!'

'Where's Maddy?' She was always his first thought on seeing Brooklyn.

'She's out riding, been in a funny mood all day . . . women's stuff, I expect.' Gloria tapped her nose with her finger and winked. 'She can be a moody cow, sometimes.'

'Oh, I don't think so,' Greg replied, striding up the steps, ignoring her, making for the kitchen where Plum looked up. He threw his cap round the door.

'Greg, how lovely! Sit down, the kettle's on. You're on time.' She gave him a floury handshake. 'Good journey?'

'Bumper to bumper through Skipton as usual. So

many cars on the road, business must be booming at long last.'

'I hope so. We're full for Easter. I think folks just like to get some fresh air in their lungs over the season . . . Can't you just smell the spring?'

All he could smell was Gloria's overwhelming perfume. It made him want to sneeze but he sat down.

'Everything OK? Maddy busy? She didn't ring last night,' he said.

'Oh, she's fine, just a little tired. I told her to take Monty out for a canter. It clears the head. She won't be long.'

He was half watching the door for what seemed hours, for the sound of the hoofs in the courtyard. When she came in she was flushed and dishevelled.

'Hi, Greg! Must have a bath, won't be long.' But she was ages upstairs titivating herself, and when she came down, she was in a smart suit and hat.

'Going somewhere special?' He couldn't resist saying, she looked so haughty.

'Just some last-minute shopping.'

'I'll drive you down.'

'I can walk, thank you. Won't be long. Gloria will look after you,' she smiled, and left. They all sat in silence, not knowing what to say.

'Told you she could be moody, Greg,' whispered Gloria. 'Come on, let's get you unpacked and sorted. You can give me a lift if you like.'

And that was the pattern of the next day. Maddy went to church to do the Easter flowers, Greg helped old Mr Hill in the garden. They met up for evening dinner with the guests and still nothing was said about their engagement. He was puzzled.

On Easter Sunday morning, it was the tradition for everyone to go to church, but if Greg was looking forward to walking there with Maddy he was soon disappointed.

'Happy Birthday!' She pecked him on the cheek. 'Must dash . . . I'm helping the children make the Easter garden display. See you later.' With that she pedalled off on her pushbike out of sight.

He had to make do with Plum and Gloria for company as they joined the queue outside the porch, admiring the floral displays. This was all women's stuff, but he sat politely through the communion service, the Easter hymns, the procession of children with their Pace eggs and recalled how once he'd done the same thing all those years ago but he'd been hungry, and snaffled the hard-boiled egg, which was rock hard and tasted disgusting. He'd hated them ever since but in Germany they'd been glad to boil any egg they found when they were foraging for meals.

How things had changed. Everyone was sporting something new to wear – new hats and dresses, smart ties – rationing or not. There was always some trimming to make a hat look newer than it was. It was the tradition on Easter Day to celebrate with new outfits.

They were making a special birthday luncheon for Greg. Gloria had baked a cake and there were wrapped parcels waiting in the drawing room for him to enjoy. It was going to be a memorable day: the day when he and Maddy announced their engagement to the world, but first he had to speak to Mrs Plum. It was only polite to inform her first.

Maddy stared at the stained-glass window behind the altar, trying not to cry. This was going to be such a lovely weekend and she was ruining every hour of Greg's visit. How could she pray and take the sacraments when she was deliberately hurting the one she loved by avoiding being alone with him, not returning his loving glances, making excuses to get out of his reach. She could see the bewildered look on his face as she flitted around the house, never sitting still, pretending to be Miss Oh-so-busy and leaving him to make polite chatter to their holiday guests.

Even now she could feel his eyes boring into the back of her straw hat, the pretty one she'd bought especially for Easter. It was the hardest thing she'd ever had to do in her life. Lying awake, pacing the floor, going over all Gloria's arguments, she knew she must let him go but was this all a ploy for Gloria to have Greg for herself? Then she recoiled from such a mean thought. Gloria looked after number one, always had and always would. She was a survivor but she wasn't a thief or cruel.

She was right in telling her they'd risked danger in not sending for the doctor on that fateful night. Perhaps he could have done something? They'd never know now.

Greg deserved someone better than her. She'd hoped by keeping their lovemaking until they were married she would somehow write off the debt she owed to fortune in saving her from public disgrace. Gloria was right again. If they had a child together, a doctor would know it was not her first. How would she explain that away if there were complications? Lies and more lies wouldn't do then.

Oh God, forgive my weakness. Help me to do the right thing, give me the strength to do what is honorable in Thy sight. Temper the wind to the shorn lamb.

Maddy was sitting with the Sunday school lines, looking pretty in her straw hat with ribbon twisted round it. Greg kept thinking of the moment when he walked her down the aisle, the organ playing something stirring and the sun shining through the stained glass, catching sunbeams on her veil. She would look so beautiful. He could feel himself choking with emotion.

The vicar's sermon wasn't bad. It was about new life and renewal, and the joy of the Resurrection to the friends of Jesus who thought he was dead. Greg didn't know what to make of all that, but spring was such a relief after winter, and the thought of beginning a new life with Maddy after years of war was wonderful.

After the service everyone went up to Pie Crust Hill and rolled the coloured eggs down the slope in time-honoured fashion. The day had pulled out into a proper dazzler – blue skies, light fluffy clouds, and everywhere the green of hills and leaves that only spring could provide. Then it was home to luncheon at the Brooklyn and the smell of roasting lamb.

First there was sherry in the drawing room and he opened all his gifts with genuine surprise. Birthdays had never been much of an occasion before – a swift half in some public house with Charlie. He was twenty-two years old and sometimes he felt going on fifty. The war had done that to all his generation, he thought: made them old before their time, guilty for being alive when so many of his friends had not made it through to the end.

He fingered the leather map case and the jumper from Maddy, the bottle of strong aftershaving lotion from Gloria. Plum had found some suede leather driving gloves. It was wonderful to be so honoured.

'When shall we tell them?' he whispered to Maddy as they were going into the dining room.

'Tell them what?' she said, distracted by finding everyone a seat.

'You know, about us,' he whispered.

'Not now, Greg.' Maddy coughed to hide her words. 'We need to talk about it first.'

'What is there to talk about? Why are you avoiding me?'

'I'm not,' she snapped. 'Shush, Plum's going to give you a toast.'

'I can reply then,' he smiled. He wanted to tell the world about their news.

'You'll do no such thing, not before we've had a talk in private.'

'Chance'd be a fine thing. We've not had two minutes alone since I arrived.'

'I'll speak to you later,' she whispered.

'Is that a promise?' he laughed.

Maddy ignored him and reached for her glass.

'Happy Birthday, Greg!' she smiled with her lips but not with her eyes. Something was wrong.

Gloria kept trying to fill the gaps in the conversation at the dinner table they were sharing with two couples and pair of hiking lady guests. It was very stilted, the usual guff about the weather and the best footpaths and how nice the local lamb tasted. Greg couldn't wait to leave the table and get Maddy on his own but when they all cleared away the plates into the kitchen, suddenly Maddy had disappeared again. Her vanishing act was beginning to annoy him.

When he could stand it no longer, Greg burst into the stable where Maddy was giving Monty his rub down. It was time to say his piece.

'What have I done wrong? You've hardly said a word in my direction since I arrived.'

'Nothing, Greg. I'm tired. I just need to be alone for a bit.'

'Well, you've made that quite plain. What's biting you? You can tell your uncle Greg,' he smiled, trying to coax her out of this strange mood.

'No, I can't. I've just got a lot on my mind, that's all.'

'Then let me tell you all my good news. I've got a big contract in Harrogate. We can set the date now. I can support the two of us . . . Isn't that wonderful?' He waited for her to hug him but she turned her back on him.

'I'm very pleased for you,' she said, and carried on rubbing Monty down.

'Don't I get a kiss?'

'No, but I said I was pleased for you.'

'Have you got a date in mind, yet? Midsummer would be romantic,' he continued.

'I don't think that's a good idea.'

There was a silence as he took in her words.

'What's wrong, sweetheart?' he tried again.

'It's too soon, Greg. We don't really know each other. There are things we need—'

'What things?' he interrupted. 'I told you all about Germany and stuff. You know my views on things. The past is the past. We've got such a future. If it's your job, you can carry on as long as you like. Let's make it Christmas, then,' he offered.

'It's just . . .' she turned away so he couldn't see her face, '. . . I can't marry you . . . I never could. We're not suited.'

Greg felt a stab in his gut at her words. 'I don't believe you. We've had such fun these last few months.'

'Yes, we have, and fun is all it's been for me. I'm not ready to settle down. I've got a chance to work down in London and, who knows, maybe Paris. I'm not ready for a house and children yet. I want to make a success of my career before I'm too old. You do understand, I can't be held back.'

Greg stood rigid with shock. How could she say all this stuff and not look him in the eye? 'Yes of course, I understand now. You'd not want to be held back by a working man who came from an orphanage and whose accent is rough. I wouldn't fit in with your London pals.' The shock and disappointment spilled out of his mouth, bitter to the taste.

'You've got it wrong, Greg, completely wrong. It's

not that at all . . . Oh, I wish I could explain but it won't work out. I know it now. I tried but, believe me, I'm letting you off the hook. You'll thank me later . . . I'm not as straightforward as you'd like to think.'

'Then tell me,' he pleaded. 'What's so hard that I'd not understand – or am I being gently dumped for one of Bella's cronies?'

'Of course not. There's only ever been you,' she pleaded, and there were tears in her eyes. 'But I can't marry you, I'm sorry . . . Just leave it at that, please.'

'No, I won't. I thought you felt as I did. Is it that business of the hotel? I thought we'd got over my mistake? Look, I can wait. I promise I won't rush you into anything.'

'Stop it, please,' she snapped. 'Leave me alone. We're just not suited. Leave it there. Don't go on. I'll not change my mind. Please, go.'

Maddy's dark grey eyes blinked back tears. She looked down as if she was ashamed. He knew she was lying but there was no give in her stance.

His head was spinning with this unexpected rejection. All he wanted to do now was to jump into the MG and head for the nearest pub to drown his sorrows until he couldn't feel a thing. What a bloody Happy Birthday!

'Well, a gentleman knows when he's not wanted, I'll take my leave,' he said with a mocking bow. 'Give my apologies to Mrs Plum but I'm not stopping where I'm not wanted. You know where to find me if you need me, if you change your mind.'

He left her to her grooming and didn't hear her

agonised wails as he revved up his car. How could he stay now? He roared down the avenue, fumes smoking behind his retreat. The package was still unopened in the glove compartment. He didn't care if he never saw it again.

Maddy collapsed on the floor, hiding in the stall among the bedding straw until she heard his engine fade away and out of her life. How cold and cruel she'd become. How had she spoken such horrid things to him? But what had to be done was done.

It had to be done for everyone's sake, but the pain in her stomach made her double up. She felt her head bursting with horror. She'd sent him packing, done the deed, salvaged the family honour, for what it was worth – and for what?

Maddy sat back, exhausted. Her energy was drained by pain and frustration, but retreat was always a good tactic. The look of disbelief on his face, the hurt in his eyes – this rejection would be with her for ever. He'd looked like a little lost boy for a moment. What had she done to him? How much she must have hurt his pride, but she daren't risk the alternative.

'Oh, Monty, we had to do the right thing,' she whispered to her horse. Being cruel to be kind was no comfort at all.

Tears were falling, great gulps of anguish pouring out, shaking her body until she was too exhausted to move. She fell asleep in the stall and awoke hours later, red-eyed, puffy and itching all over.

It was almost time to face Plum and Gloria but

not yet. Time enough to explain Greg's sudden departure when she'd pulled herself together. Gloria would back her up. Thank God she still had a friend to lean on.

'I wish you'd tell me what's going on,' said Plum as they waved away the last of their guests from the drive. 'Why did Gregory rush off like that without a word? What was so important for him to return to during his holiday? Have you two quarrelled?'

Maddy carried on waving. 'Nothing like that. He's got a problem to see to. Papers to sign or something. We're fine . . . I must dash back to Leeds too.'

Something was going on. Plum could almost smell it in the air. Maddy was smiling, her cheeks pinned in a rictus of a grin, convincing no one by this act, and flitting from one room to another, never still for a second. Gloria tiptoed around trying to be extra helpful in the kitchen. When she walked in a room, Maddy and Gloria were deep in conversation, jumping apart when she came close, treating her as if she was invisible. By the end of the weekend she was glad to see the back of all of them.

Greg wrote to thank her for the weekend and for his present. He said his move to Harrogate would mean no time for weekends away until he had licked his team into shape.

Then Maddy telephoned to say she was off to London on an assignment that might lead to something permanent and not to worry if she couldn't make too many home visits this summer.

'Darling, that's fine, but what about Greg? Are you still seeing him?' Plum asked.

'Oh, no, it's over between us. We've agreed it's run its course, Plum. We're not really compatible and there's no point in flogging a dead horse, is there?' There was a wobble in her voice and it wasn't a crackle on the line. Maddy was getting in a dig about her uncle and aunt here, but this news was still a shock.

'Do you know anything about this?' she asked Gloria, who had the annoying habit of hovering in the doorway, listening in to conversations.

'I told you there was no future there. Maddy's got better fish to fry and now she's off to London. Actually, I'm thinking of a change myself, if you don't mind. Me and Ken aren't hitting it off either. I expect you're wondering why I never brought him here. He's a bit old for me and doesn't like the countryside much. He was pushing for us to tie the knot but I'm not ready so I'd like to make a clean break and move away too.

I hope you don't mind but with all the valuable experience you've given me, I've applied for a domestic post in a boys' school near Leeds – assistant domestic bursar, would you believe. I was hoping you'd give me a reference.' Gloria smiled sweetly, her cheeks flushed with freckles.

'But the season's only just starting. I shall need you for a little while yet,' Plum replied, shocked at this sudden desertion.

'Don't worry, I'll not let you down. If I get the post, I don't think they'll want me until after the big holidays,' she replied.

Gloria's new posting was closer to Harrogate than Leeds, judging by the address, but Plum wrote a glowing reference and suddenly all the young ones were flying the coup. Soon Brooklyn would be silent and empty again on weekdays with no guests. Plum tried not to feel let down when Gloria broke her promise and promptly left at half term and one of Grace Battersby's girls came to help out, but she wasn't a patch on Gloria.

What did she expect? Sowerthwaite was never going to hold youngsters for long, especially if they were bright sparks, full of ambition. Plum sighed and got on with the jobs herself.

One afternoon in high summer, a large saloon car drew up, and a plump youngish man in a striped de mob suit jumped out of his seat, demanding to speak to Gloria.

He didn't seem to know she'd moved away and then tried to wheedle her address from Plum. He said he had some catalogues to show her but he didn't look Plum straight in the eye when she asked who he was. So this was the famous Ken Silverstone. Plum sensed he was a shifty piece of work. She had the feeling that she'd seen him somewhere before. She never forgot a face. No wonder Gloria hadn't introduced him earlier. Then she recalled their first guests.

It was the man, who, way back, was one of her very first customers. But when she smiled and recognised him, he didn't seem too pleased, especially when she fumbled and refused to give him Gloria's new address, saying she'd mislaid it somewhere.

He was not who she imagined at all from Gloria's description of her boyfriend: a florid little man who looked like a private eye in a gangster film, all teeth and moustache.

She was glad Gloria had given him the elbow. There was something of Gerald in his arrogant manner that irritated her.

They must do something about the divorce papers and end their shillyshallying once and for all. Who was there now to embarrass if the Belfield name appeared in the decree nisi columns? There must be thousands of couples all over the country getting unhitched from hasty wartime marriages, judging by the lines of names in the *Yorkshire Post*.

Perhaps Maddy had been right to call things off with Greg before it all got complicated, but they had seemed so right for each other. Where had it gone wrong?

She hoped Maddy was not turning into a snob, thinking Gregory was beneath her?

She no longer understood young people these days – safer to stick to dogs and horses. They never let you down, she smiled, but it was all so unsettling.

Should she give up the catering business and rent the house to a proper family? It seemed such an indulgence to live in such a barn of a place on her own, but it wasn't hers to sell or rent. By rights it would be Madeleine's one day, after Plum died.

Perhaps it was time to let out rooms to lodgers, who could help to heat the place and give her some company. She could still run the guest rooms as a side line when it suited her.

Mr Hill was still struggling to contain the jungle in the kitchen garden.

At this rate, what with the WI and the church and guests, plus the garden, she'd be too tired for company in the evenings. The dogs needed her too, and the horses, she sighed, feeling sad and very alone.

How beautiful the garden looked in the setting sun, she smiled. Shadows across the lawn and the tall poplars lining the avenue on sentry duty, the swifts wheeling and swooping in the ink-blue sky and the bats darting around, the scent of the old Yorkshire rose dripping from the high wall in cascades of blooms, the old stones shimmering pink in the dusk.

How could she ever think of leaving here? Yet if Brooklyn didn't earn its keep it'd have to go, Maddy or not. There wasn't much left in the kitty for repairs. Sunshine and shadows together, pleasure and pain, black and white and all shades of grey in between: that was how her life felt now.

18

Maddy sat in her dressing gown, staring at her face in the mirror. She looked like a panda with huge made-up eyes – like a ballerina on stage. This look was all the rage in the *cabines* of the London mannequins. Other model girls in full make-up were sitting around waiting for something to happen, chewing gum, smoking with elegant holders, sizing each other up like race horses in stalls ready for the off. She'd been lucky enough to be taken on trial to see if she suited and now she was part of Mr Raoul Henry's stable of fillies.

It seemed months, not weeks, since her first nervous arrival from Leeds clutching her portfolio of photographs, bedding down with Bella's dizzy cousin Fay in a pad off Marylebone High Street.

She'd spent days traipsing from warehouse to warehouse, up rickety stairs and over bomb sites around Great Portland Street, in the heart of the fashion industry, hoping to find a job showing off the latest designs to buyers.

Now that clothing coupons were finally abolished there was a dash to feed the frenzy of women looking for a new wardrobe after years of making do with drab and dreary sludge. Rouge Dior was the big colour in Paris and London, and being dark, Maddy suited the striking deep scarlet and always wore a scarf in that shade around her neck to highlight her pale skin.

Maddy had scoured her *Vogue* magazines eagerly, looking for ways to groom herself to the highest standards. She wore gloves, hat, perfect stockings, knowing she must provide her own accessories, with shoes – pretty pumps and smart court shoes – all lugged around in her holdall. Coming south was a huge gamble, but she couldn't stay north after what had happened. It was too painful to stay in the town where she'd been so happy only a few months before.

Her hair was getting longer and she practised sweeping it into an elegant chignon anchoring it down with precious kirby-grips and combs. She mustn't look like someone up from the country when she went for interviews, lugging her heavy portmanteau containing all her *batterie de beauté*.

Along the busy streets she trundled, around the heart of the rag trade, Great Portland Street, Margaret Street, up and down, until her legs ached in her scuffed shoes and she despaired of ever getting work.

The ballet look was everywhere. The film *The Red Shoes* had seen to that, but she was no Moira Shearer even if she scraped her hair into a bun and pulled in her waistband, trying to look as if she'd just stepped out of the stage door.

'You're more a ballroom girl,' said one owner, looking her up and down. 'Débutantes and society weddings, that's your look. Why don't you try Hardy Amies in Savile Row? They do glamorous evening wear for the rich and famous.'

She found no joy there, but one of the *vendeuses* took pity on her and gave her another address. 'Try round the corner. Go and see Mr Henry's salon, but don't say I sent you. I know one of his models has just got married to a lord; she's now on her honeymoon in the South of France. Try there and good luck!'

With aching feet and heart, Maddy followed her instructions, climbed to the elegant steps to ring the bell. The brass plate by the side of the door said: 'The House of Raoul Henry'. Eventually the door opened to her.

'I've come to see if there's a vacancy for a house model,' she said smiling, hoping they wouldn't noticed the dust on her shoes, the grubbiness of her white gloves or her tired face. It had been a long day.

A woman in severe black ushered her in, 'Are you from the agency?' she snapped in a heavy French accent, ushering Maddy up the stairs quickly. 'This way. Mr Henry is going out shortly.'

They left the glamour of the marble hall behind and climbed up indeterminable steps towards the attic hubbub of the workrooms with a rainbow of cloth bolts lining the stairs, and the smell of fabric and sweat and perfume all mixed together.

'Your name?' said the woman.

'Madeleine Belfield. I've brought my portfolio,' she said, holding it up, but the woman didn't even give it a glance.

‘Wait here,’ she ordered, and Maddy waited for what seemed hours, wondering what fate lay in store, praying that the girl from the agency wouldn’t turn up and queer her pitch.

A small man in the doorway stared and eyed her up. ‘Let me see you . . . stand . . . walk this way. Your height?’

‘Five foot ten,’ she offered, adding half an inch for good measure, trying to look sophisticated and used to inspection. She smiled.

‘I don’t want smiles, I want haughty,’ he commanded. ‘You’d better strip behind the screen and let me see your shape.’

Maddy did as she was told and strode out in her underslip as she had been taught.

‘Good,’ said the man. ‘Long limbs and a straight back for once, but can you move? Hortense, put her in the gold brocade and call me back when she is respectable.’

He disappeared while the woman in black fussed over her and brought up a ballgown that barely fastened up the back.

‘You’ll have to get rid of some of this,’ she said pinching her hard in the back. ‘There’s too much muscle. Mr Henry likes straight-up-and-down gals. At least you have no bust; he likes to create that within his gown.’

Maddy stood as they fixed her straggling chignon into the nape of her neck and someone produced a pair of enormous earrings for her to clip on.

‘A swan’s neck is desirable in our girls. Yours will

do, just about. Take the stairs slowly and make an entrance.'

Maddy lifted the front of the gown. There were yards of brocade to lift. She was trying to look elegant as she drifted into the drawing room with the beautiful chandeliers and Louis XIV chairs, gold paint and elegantly swagged curtains. There was a mirror facing her and she remembered to straighten up like a swan, lift her neck and glide slowly, extending her back until she felt she was seven feet tall.

Remembering all those training sessions in Leeds at Marshfields, she stared ahead as if down a long corridor, trying to feel like a princess . . . Cinderella at the ball.

There was a prince of sorts waiting, watching her every move. He was not the handsome prince of her dreams but a middle-aged man with a moustache and dyed black hair. 'Turn, walk this way . . . name?' He'd forgotten her already.

'Madeleine,' she said, not deigning to break her pose. Haughty she must be.

'Well, Miss Madeleine, I think I can use you but I want to see no smiles, no attitude. I create the shape, the look. You are nothing. You will either inspire me or not. Where are you from?'

'Yorkshire, sir.'

'Where's that?' He turned to Hortense who shrugged her shoulders. 'No matter. You have something, but hair and make-up alone will not do. I want no tanning; keep out of the sun – smoke if you must – and punctuality. You've a lot to learn but you are fresh and young.

I can mould you . . . Now I am busy, off you go and wear some decent shoes next time. I want high heels. I like my girls as tall as guardsmen, proud and stiff in the back.'

'Yes, Mr Henry,' Maddy croaked, hardly able to believe this stroke of luck. The head of the couturier house had deigned to speak to her himself!

She didn't even dare to ask about money. Was she paid by the hour? How could she manage on piece-work? To have a place here, however humble, a place in a couture house in London, was a wonderful break. If only she could feel some joy in her success.

At night she'd lain awake on her makeshift sofa bed, worrying if she'd done the right thing. Greg had not come back and tried to change her mind. Even Gloria hadn't bothered to write to her. Could it really be possible that the loss of that baby was her own fault? That made her feel so sick and scared, all she could do was smoke cigarette after cigarette until she lay back and fell into a fitful sleep. Better to leave. Out of sight was out of mind, so they said.

Then she thought of all the shining moments she and Greg had shared, the cuddles, the kisses, the promises of a future together, all the things she'd given up in coming to London. She just had to succeed and make a future here, salvage something from the mess that was her life.

The Henry collection was top secret and only his most trusted workers knew the final style. It was down to fewer than a hundred garments from hundreds of sketches, designed over his dummy or favourite model.

Pieces were worked on separately to keep the secrets safe from prying eyes. Details of buttons, trimmings, lace had to pass his eagle eye. After weeks of thunder and lightning in the fitting rooms, tantrums as gowns were flung across the atelier floor in rage at a dropped stitch, Mr Henry was almost satisfied.

Now the deb season was back in full swing, there was a demand for couture presentation gowns and wedding dresses, cocktail gowns and theatre outfits.

'No one is born to a ball gown like my English girls,' he smiled, satisfied when the night of the fashion show at last arrived.

The moment of truth was upon the House of Raoul Henry. Would his designs be snapped up by eager buyers, wanting to reproduce them quickly for their customers, or would the orders be slow to arrive?

The gilt chairs were lined up in the salon, waiting for the invited guests to grace the House with their glittering presence. The season would soon be under way and a row of débutantes and their mothers would be eyeing the ball gowns for their coming-out parties and balls. Who would be there? The duchess . . . the marchioness and the American film star who thought Mr Henry was a genius, able to disguise her heavy bust and thick waist with the cut of his design?

Then there were the ladies of the press, eyeing up any new collections for their magazines and, of course, the buyers from department stores, who would purchase a sample to be unpicked, or a cotton toile, a mere sketch and pattern outline for a large fee. Nothing must be left to chance: not fittings, rehearsals nor last-minute alterations. No wonder nerves were frayed.

Each model must work like fury, slithering in and out of her gowns at speed to sparkle before the audience, whether she be Barbara Goalen, Jean Dawnay or the lovely Bettina: *la crème de la crème.* One of Mr Henry's troupe, Alannah, thought she was above the rest, notorious for getting to the rack of dresses hung high, grabbing the pole, and snatching the most glamorous gown for herself. She would make snide remarks from behind the screen about the others as if they couldn't hear. 'Why has the old man picked her for the finale? She's hardly been here five minutes!' she sneered, waving her talons in Maddy's direction. Her mushroom-black hat was already in place while she was sitting in a waspie-waist corselette and stockings.

'Bitch!' whispered Charmaine Blake, who'd taken Maddy under her wing. 'Take no notice of her. She's always bad-tempered. That one's in love with herself . . . She lives on cigarettes and black coffee before a show so her waist is smaller than anyone else's. Her breath is toxic. Watch your back, though. She'll steal your best exit if she thinks she can get away with it.'

Maddy's dress fell down on the ground just as she was about to make her exit, but Hortense smiled. 'That is good luck. Now the show is bound to please our customers . . .'

'Kick me down the steps, kick me down the steps, Charmaine!' Maddy whispered, knowing from her days at Marshfields that it was good luck to get a shove on your first exit. Serene on the surface but bubbling like a volcano underneath, Maddy fell into a trance as she stepped from the curtain to the catwalk . . . Don't forget the five points: glide, slide off the jacket, then trail the mink across the laps of the important customers in the front row, pirouette at the corners to show the swing of the skirt, pause, pose, look aloof. The customers in the front row were the most important guests to impress. One nod from them was worth twenty from the back.

They'd had a pep talk from Mr Henry. 'You are my girls,' he ordered, wiping a pink silk hanky across his brow. 'The gown is what is on show, not you. You don't wear it . . . it wears you. Do honour to the cloth, to the design. I don't want any *prima donnas* here,' he warned, looking straight at Alannah Bateman. 'If it goes well we will all be happy. If not, some of you will be out of work. It's as simple as that. So go forth, my beautiful swans, and glide, don't rush. Give them time to see what beauties I have created. Let them hear the rustle of silk and satin, swish those yards of tulle and lace. Let them feast their eyes. Wear the jewels like a queen, as if you were born to them. Stare ahead like thoroughbreds you are. The House of Raoul Henry expects . . . and Madeleine, don't forget, no smile from you. I want that disdainful look again. You must give them your disdain, a tinge of arrogance and sorrow.'

Maddy hadn't a clue what he was talking about so she turned to Charmaine, whispering, 'What look?'

'That faraway look you have in your eyes. You always look a little sad as if you might burst into tears any time. Just stare ahead, fix your eye on a spot on the opposite wall and go for it. You'll be fine.'

Do I look sad? she thought. Her intention was always to put everything together and not make a mistake. Just the mere thought of sitting on the train back to Leeds with her tail between her legs was her motivation.

'What are you waiting for? It's your exit now! Don't think about it. Just go!' Charmaine gave her a shove. 'You look gorgeous. Fancy some dinner after the show with my sister and me?'

Off Maddy sailed in a huge magenta ball gown with a diamond necklace slung around her neck at the last minute as if it was paste from Woolworths. What a life! What had she landed into? It was hard not to smile with satisfaction. If they could see me now . . . but all she could think about down that long catwalk was keeping one step in front of the other and trying not to trip.

If Gloria thought leaving Brooklyn Hall was the answer to her problems then she'd made a big mistake. Trust her to land under the tutelage of the one and only Avis Blunt, the erstwhile hostel wardress who had made their lives a misery at the Old Vic. St Felix's Preparatory School was out in the country in Nidderdale, a large stone mansion with what seemed like thousands of little boys in shorts hurtling themselves up the stairs into the dorms, noisy, with verminous heads that needed combing out after a right old infestation of nits.

The school was understaffed and the assistant

domestic bursar post she'd applied for consisted of being a general skivvy to all and sundry. But to come face to face with Miss Blunt on her first day was punishment enough. Why hadn't she been at the interview?

'Miss Gloria Conley, I thought it must be you. How could I forget that mop of hair?'

'Yes, Miss Blunt,' she answered. And I remember your rug too, Gloria thought, trying to look contrite and not giggle.

'I'm Mrs Partridge now,' she smiled. 'Mr Partridge is the deputy headmaster. I'm only helping out because we're a bit short of qualified staff, otherwise you, my dear, would not have got past the door. How are all the old things at the Brooklyn? Mr Belfield – did he ever make it back home after the war?'

Gloria shook her head, feeling disloyal to Mrs Plum in telling the truth.

'I thought not. Got more sense than to return to that nest of vipers. What a wearisome place that was, with all those vaccy scruffs. I don't suppose any of them stayed around?'

'Actually, my brother is farming up the dale,' Gloria replied in defiance.

'Horses for courses, my dear. He was not the sharpest pencil in the case, now was he? I don't suppose you could have found anything better than this sort of work,' she sneered. 'No starring roles in pantomime then? You always were the little show-off.'

Gloria wanted to smack her on the gob there and then, but walking out on her first day in post was not an option, not if she wanted a reference to go anywhere else. Nothing for it but to stick it out until she found something better closer to Harrogate town.

The bus route was a long way out of Harrogate. She had written to Greg's office, telling him of her change of position, hoping he'd reply, but he hadn't so far. She was glad now. Who would want to see her in this dump of a job? How could she have landed up working under 'The Rug'?

Served her right, she shrugged. It was punishment, of course, for what she'd done to Maddy, but only a temporary blip to her plans. All was fair in love and war, she kept saying to herself, but there was a bit of her deep inside that was uneasy with all the lies she had told – the part of her that had always been Maddy's friend, that recalled how Maddy had saved her so many times . . . but she shoved such misgivings to the back of her mind. Picking nits out of heads of wriggling hair was punishment enough, and she felt itchy all over.

This was time away to plan her next move, escape from the Brooklyn for a while, and Ken. What a relief to put all that smutty posing behind her. She must have been crazy to think it would ever come to anything. She'd managed to disappear from his radar screen but was stuck here for a term at least. It was going to be hell on earth to be out in the wilderness, knowing Greg was only a few miles away, licking his wounds, thinking nobody cared for him. She hoped it would be easy to find his office when the time came. And then she'd not be so easy to ignore.

*

Greg looked up at the sign above the builders' merchants with pride. He'd left subcontracting behind, got his own team together and had found an old scrap-yard, cleared it out, smartened it with prefabricated huts for offices and started trading to his own trade. Every penny he earned had been ploughed back into the business and now this was his kingdom.

He was back shovelling sand and cement, bagging up nails and slates, but they were his sand and cement, his gravel chippings, his lorries on the tarmac. When staff let him down he was happy to muck in and kick the backsides of any slackers. He knew the tricks, the fiddles lads got up to when unsupervised: borrowing tools, selling stuff on the black market, making out fairy-tale time sheets, moonlighting on other jobs with his materials, and he locked his yard with thick gates. It took one to know one, he smiled, and nobody was ever going to take advantage of him again.

The move had gone smoothly and he ought to be the happiest guy in Yorkshire but the success was bouncing off him like rain on slate. There was no one special to share his success with, except Charlie and the Afton family. He'd never go near the Foxups and the rally crowd in case he saw Maddy on someone else's arm, or go back to the Brooklyn. That part of his life was over. He'd gone soft in the head but no matter. He wanted to write to Mrs Plum and give her his good news, but pride wouldn't let him. He'd never return there until he could go back with his tail up, accompanied by his wife and two children and in the biggest saloon car he could find. He'd show them.

That would wipe the smile off Maddy Belfield's haughty face. He tried not to give her the satisfaction of a second thought but at night when he lay in his flat off Dragon Parade, staring up at the wallpaper and the plasterwork scrolls on the ceiling, he wondered just where he'd gone wrong.

When had she changed? Was it over the course of that one weekend? He just didn't understand any of it, but tough luck, he'd not waste time fathoming out the mysteries of a two-timing snob. There had to be someone else in the picture, some toffee-nosed git who could give her a better life. Her rejection stung him to the core. He'd thought they were soul mates. Never trust a woman would be his motto from now on. She must have found someone else and dumped him, got a better offer. That had to be the explanation.

Gloria would know everything. She'd already send him a newsy letter telling him about her new position at The Rug's school, of all places. Poor cow! He'd have to rescue her and take her out. In his eyes she was still a sweet kid, pretty enough – but he wasn't into pretty young schoolgirls, not any more.

The Harrogate boutiques were full of classy shop girls and waitresses, and he was going to sample the full menu. Once bitten twice shy and all that. His pride was wounded by Maddy and he'd not be so easy to fool next time around. He was going to play the field and not get trapped again.

*

When Ken Silverstone turned up at the front door of St Felix's School he was given short shrift once they realised he was not a prospective parent. The Rug sent him round to the back yard and called out to Gloria to get downstairs and see to this intruder at once.

'We don't allow staff to have followers or have them turning up at all hours demanding an audience! This is not the hostel. We know how all the girls came to a sticky end there, but never in my day! See to your business and then back to work.'

'Yes, Mrs Partridge!' Gloria was fuming at this unexpected visit. How had he found her address? She must've slipped up somewhere.

'What do you want?' she snapped at Ken, feeling foolish in her overalls and turban.

'That's no way to speak to your lover-boy,' said Ken.

'I told you it was off,' she retorted. The last thing she wanted was complications. Ken was part of her past, Bradford, and all that silly business was over.

'Not in my book, darling. I've brought you some lovely pictures. Didn't I promise you that I'd get you into some lovely mags, and I have?' He produced a parcel. 'Aren't you going to give me a cup of tea?'

'I can't. I'll look at these later,' she said.

'Meet me in the pub, the one in the village,' he ordered.

'I can't, not in the village. Girls don't go in them places. The Rug'll go spare.'

'Let's go for a spin then, for old times' sake.' He winked lasciviously.

'Please yourself, but I don't get off until nine. Everywhere will be shut.'

'We can sit in the car or,' he paused with a grin, 'I'll take you to a nice hotel and treat you to some dinner.'

'If you must, but I'm not staying over. All that is finished,' she said, not wanting to give him any encouragement.

'Of course, darling, whatever you say. I'll be waiting at the gates. I've missed our little sessions.'

'Well, I haven't. I've finished with all that!' Gloria insisted

'We'll see. Nine o'clock sharp. I'll be waiting.'

Gloria didn't know what to think. On the one hand, Ken's arrival made her feel uneasy. There was something in the way he'd hunted her out, something in the tone of his voice that worried her. Ken could always unsettle her. There was something about him now that set her teeth on edge; something exciting, uncertain, difficult to pinpoint. How could such an ugly-looking man twist her round his little finger? Heaven knew why. It was not as if he was handsome like Greg, or well-mannered, but on the other hand it would be good to dress up and get away from this prison for a night on the town.

She'd make him pay up and treat her right, she smiled, throwing his parcel on the bed and rushing back to her evening chores. She might even wear her precious silk stockings and new shoes tonight.

Later, when she was dressed in a jumper and her best skirt, she opened the envelope and glanced at the magazine. It wasn't one she recognised. It was called

Girls Galore and inside were pages of scantily dressed girls in provocative poses, the usual stuff, and then she saw herself, topless on the rug with her legs bent to hide her privates. How her heart was thudding at the sight of those pictures. She looked hard-faced and silly and not a bit glamorous.

Gloria threw the magazine across the room. I'll kill him for this! How dare he! These were private shots done for fun, not to be pored over by dirty men. Anyone could see them and recognise her. Bastard! He'd sold those shots behind her back. There was sweat on her brow, knowing that there were other shots he'd encouraged her to do, much worse than these. Oh, no! What had Ken done with them?

She ran down the drive to the gate in a lather of anger, thinking, Wait until I see you, Ken Silverstone. I'll kill you for this! He was standing by the gate, smoking, his trilby hat cocked at a jaunty angle.

'How could you?' she screamed, throwing the parcel at him.

'What's up now, darling?' said Ken.

'Don't you darling me! You sold those pictures and I want them burned!' Gloria threw a punch at him.

'I thought that's what we agreed,' laughed Ken. 'I did your portfolio, and the others were specials. Get in the car.'

'Give them back and don't sell any more!' she demanded, throwing the magazine on the car seat.

'I can't do that, darling.'

'Why not? I don't want you to sell them to anyone else. One magazine is bad enough.'

They drove in silence around the twisty lanes of Nidderdale but Gloria was too angry to look out of the window. Just when she had got her life on a new track, up pops Ken to spoil things. It was all going up a gumtree. She'd been flattered by Ken's enthusiasm at first, carried away by the thought of being famous, but nothing had come of it and then he'd persuaded to her to do things, dirty stuff she'd bitterly regretted the moment she left the studio.

'Promise me there'll be no more of them, Kenny,' she pleaded, hoping to appeal to his better nature. 'I don't want the world to see me like that. I'll get sacked if anyone finds out.'

'Don't worry, anyone who buys the magazine and sees you in it will want more, believe me. You're in good shape!'

'I don't care. It's not what I want now. Those shots were between us, you and me, for our pleasure, and I never thought you'd sell them.'

'Oh, come off it! Gloria. What shelf did you fall off? There's a ready market in the glamour pics. You were happy enough to do them. What's changed? Why are you going all prissy on me now?'

'I don't want to do them any more. I look dirty and common and cheap,' she said, trying to make him understand.

'That's easily sorted. We can change the setting, if you like, to velvet sofas, a mink coat, but it's your body the lads want to gawp at. You could be a star. Don't get so het up. Come on, here's a decent place. Let's have a drink here and talk this is all over.'

The hotel on the slope overlooking Harrogate was the grandest place Gloria had ever been to. It was the one where the famous writer, Agatha Christie, had disappeared to all those years ago under a false name. Ken had booked a room and dinner for two.

Gloria was much too nervous to settle down and enjoy her surroundings. 'I shouldn't be here,' she whispered. What if someone was reading the magazine and recognised her? Don't be silly, she thought. With her prim skirt and hat, she was safe enough, but she gulped down her sherry cocktail and whatever drinks Ken bought her until her legs were shaky. She picked at the meal and then staggered back to his room to collect the promise of the other photographs. As soon as they got upstairs, Ken shoved her through the door.

'Where are those negatives?' she pleaded, knowing full well he'd not have them, but she had to make a stand.

'Where do you think? Back in the studio. Relax and calm down. You've said your piece, so shut up and start being nice to me. If you're nice to me I'll do anything you say, darling.'

'You won't send any more of them off to the mags then?' she pleaded.

'Of course not, if you treat me right. Come here and be nice to me how I like it,' Ken smiled, pointing to the bed.

'None of that! I've got to go now or I'll be in trouble.' Gloria turned to the door but he grabbed her arm quickly.

'Forget your sodding job, come and show me you're still my girl.'

How stupid could she be to have got tiddly, alone in his room, miles from the school, with not even the bus fare to go home. He'd lured her here for one reason only and now she must please him one more time or else. The thought of not having those negatives made her go cold. She hated him but what else could she do?

Neon lights flashed in her head. I am my mother's daughter after all, she sighed, removing her hat and her jacket, her shoes and hairpins. There was only one way to placate his lust. If that was what it would take . . . She groaned as she sank to her knees and unbuttoned his trousers.

'That's better,' Ken said as they lay on the bed, illuminated by the lamplight. 'Better get you back to the barracks, I suppose, before the old dragon finds out.'

Gloria felt ashamed, confused and sick. This was not how the evening was supposed to end. 'You will give me back the negatives?' she pleaded. 'I've got to be sure.'

'Of course you have, love. Am I not a man of my word? I promised to make you a star and I have . . . the rest is up to you.'

'I know, I know, but it's getting late. Take me home. You'll send them in the post. Promise?'

'Of course, now I know where you are. It was naughty of you to run out on me like that. The posh bitch at the Brooklyn was very snooty. Good job I got round the old washerwoman and she spilled the beans. I'll bring them in person next time.'

'Next time?' Gloria gasped. 'There can't be a next time, Ken. I don't want to carry on like this. It's not fair on either of us. I'm starting a new life here.'

'I know you are, Gloria, you keep telling me. But there's lots of negatives, aren't there . . . or have you forgotten those close-ups we did with the mirror and Rita Mason?'

'Oh, no! Ken, please God . . . I was drunk.'

'Exactly, now the penny's dropping at long last. Every one of them will have to be earned out. You owe me that for all my investment in you.'

'But that's blackmail! Please, just give them to me. I'll pay you proper money for them. I'll find it somehow.'

'No!' he replied, and his voice was full of menace. 'I look on this as a repayment for lost future income. I am claiming back my investment outlay. Once a week should do it. We'll have a nice night out and lots of fun. You should know by now, Gloria, everything has its price.'

In the darkness, smelling the stale fumes of the car, feeling sick, Gloria fell silent, defeated and dirty. She was no better than all those tarts in Elijah Street – in fact worse, for she had brought all this on herself with her jealousy of Maddy's career, her stupid trust in Ken's promises. No one forced her to climb those stairs into his studio but her own vanity. Now she must pay and it was only what she deserved after all.

Hard as they struggled in the garden at Brooklyn Hall, it was getting so overgrown and battered with the wind and rain that Plum knew she was losing the will to keep it under control. She was staking up a line of herbaceous plants that were flopping badly in the border that Pleasance had refused to yield up to vegetables during the war.

None of her new permanent lodgers had shown any inclination to give a hand or walk her dogs. She'd had to get the Boy Scouts to do some bob-a-job work, but they didn't know a weed from a prize specimen so she'd hovered over them, pointing where to pull and where to stake. In fact, they'd got her so worked up and weary she decided to go to rake over the gravel before she blew a gasket and scared them off.

Gardening was such a chore when you had no one to share it with. Her new man, Mr Lock, who sorted out the vegetable allotment, would not deign to look at the 'fancy stuff', as he called it. So if she wanted cut flowers and sweet-smelling perennials, she'd just have to do it herself.

Plum loved her poppies, phlox, foxgloves, peonies, lupins, hebes and roses. They filled the house with scent and colour – even if there was only her to appreciate them since Gloria had left her in the lurch months ago.

She'd not replaced her with live-in help, just two dailies from Sowerthwaite who were efficient in their own way but had no initiative.

Gloria's letters were thinning out now, after that first bombshell about her being in Avis Blunt's employ! Poor Gloria was not enjoying her new position. There was no mention of Gregory either. In fact, everything sounded very subdued, which was not like her at all.

Plum had written to tell Gloria about Maddy's success in London, being taken on as a house model in a couture establishment, because she sensed Gloria and Maddy were not communicating much. With Greg now out of the scene, Maddy was out of touch with them all.

The best outing of the summer was a reunion with Totty Foxup. They met halfway for lunch in a hotel near Ripley, recognising each other immediately. They'd laughed and swopped stories, and for an afternoon Plum had felt like a skittish young gal again, not a rather weary middle-aged has-been, deserted by her husband. Totty was full of Bella's wedding and her hopes for grandchildren. Plum tried not to feel envious, and boasted about Maddy's success in London to keep her end up. On the drive home she thought how different their worlds were now. She going back to an empty house whilst Totty went home to Hugh and her family.

She was busy wondering how to engineer them all to meet up together when she bent over and missed one of the canes that was staking up the delphiniums in the border. It caught her right in the eyeball with a blinding pain. She'd not blinked in time.

'Damn and blast!' she cried out as the eye closed shut and she started to cry tears, blinded for a few seconds. She staggered back to the house to the medicine cabinet for the borax crystals and tried to blink it open properly, but it stayed shut. Then she remembered that there might be one of Maddy's old eye patches lurking in the back of a drawer. Rooting with her good eye, Plum searched until she found it in the all-sorts drawer of the big dresser in the kitchen amidst the marbles, recorders, broken china waiting to be repaired, drawing pins, paper and all the old paraphernalia of the evacuee days.

Fixing the patch over the eye, she stared down sadly at the bits and pieces of those busy days and wept more tears again. Don't be a sentimental fool! she sniffed, just get up and keep going. It's only a scratch.

Over the next few days, the stinging pain didn't let up and she thought she might have to call out Dr Armitage, the new doctor from Manchester who'd come to relieve Dr Gunn now that they had their free National Health Service. Then she thought the better of it. She was sure the poor young man was inundated with all the town's folk queuing for long-overdue treatments, not just tonics, but glasses and new teeth, or wanting their tonsils out.

It was when the other eye started to go blurry that Plum thought it might be sensible to see why nothing was healing. She walked down into town in the fresh air, feeling like Long John Silver in her black eye patch. Poor Maddy! Now she knew how it must have felt for her all those years ago.

Plum sat in the waiting room feeling like a fraud, until it was her turn to see the young man. Only he wasn't a newly qualified doctor. He was an ex-army medic about her own age, who looked at her patch and the blisteringly painful left eye with concern, peering into it with his light.

'What on earth made you think this would heal itself woman?' he snapped.

'It's only a scratch but it's so uncomfortable,' she sniffed.

'You've scratched your cornea and it's become infected and the infection has gone into your other eye, silly woman,' he said, in a very military tone.

'Don't you call me a silly woman!' she cried. 'I was only trying to sort out the garden.' Then she burst into tears.

'Let me take your temperature . . . rising, no doubt! It's the eye hospital for you now.' This man was used to giving orders.

'But that's in Bradford and I haven't got time. There's my lodgers to see to,' Plum protested, now feeling utterly wretched.

'Mrs Belfield, I'm sure your life is very important but if we want to save your eyesight you'd better get down there and get some treatment pretty damn quick, do I make myself plain?'

'Yes, Doctor,' she sniffled, feeling foolish. 'It's just I run a guesthouse alone. There's the horses and the dogs to see to.' What was she going to do if she couldn't see?

'Then close it for the duration. You look run down to me. This is no light matter.' His voice softened, seeing her distress. 'You know accidents sometimes happen when we are run down. My wife once dropped a garden fork on her toes in the herbaceous border. She was too busy to see to it and it turned nasty.'

'She's fine now, though?' Plum asked

'Sadly, she died three years ago, hence my change of venue,' he replied, not looking at her.

'I'm sorry I didn't mean . . .' Poor man, she thought. It must be harder for a man on his own, but he sounded a devil to live with.

'Your husband works away then?' It was his turn to ask the questions.

'We live apart,' she said calmly. 'I have a niece in London, but I can't bother her.'

'Why ever not? That's what families are for, to help each other out in a crisis.'

'I suppose I could ring her.'

'You do that – your eyesight is precious. You've wasted enough time already. I shall check to see you've gone.'

'Thank you, Dr Armitage,' Plum said, making for the door.

'Now, you get going, or I'll have to drive you there myself!' He laughed and she noticed what a wrinkled face and warm grey eyes he had. This man'd do well in Sowerthwaite. He was no fool and he'd soon give any time-wasters short shrift.

Now she'd have to get Bert Batty to drive her to hospital, all because she bent over a cane without paying attention. It could have poked her eye out but she'd not bother Maddy. Bringing her back from London was quite unnecessary, much as she'd love to hear all about her new life. She'd soldier on somehow.

*

The first Maddy knew of the accident was weeks later when she rang on spec and Grace Battersby answered the phone.

'Mrs Belfield's out at the eye hospital for a check-up,' said Grace. 'She gave herself a right sidewinder with a garden cane, proper nasty turn, but they gave her some new-fangled drugs to clear the infection. We've been telling her to take it easy but you know Mrs Plum. We can't keep up with her. The doctor's called in twice and found her out . . . he told her off good and proper. Nice chap is Dr Armitage – a widower, by all accounts. He's joined the cricket team and now she's doing teas, as if she hasn't enough to do. That's where she'll be once she gets home,' Grace chuckled.

'Should I come?' Maddy said, feeling guilty to have neglected her aunt over the past months.

'If she'd wanted to bother you, she'd have written. But she does worry me, so independent and allus on the go, can't sit still for a minute. He's given her a tonic to settle her down but she never takes it, says it makes her sleepy . . . I ask you! Happen you can ring later. It's grand having a proper phone line in, at last. I can order from the grocer and butcher and saves my legs. How's yer job doing, love?'

Maddy filled her in with all the glamorous details she could think of, the shows and the parties she'd been to, but the truth was she was homesick, pining for the hills and the grey stone walls, the smell of the horses, freshly mown hay and for the soft flat vowels of the North Country.

Sometimes this longing would catch her unawares.

Sometimes when she was sitting on a bus looking down at the busy crowds in Oxford Street, she thought of the haunting old folk song 'The Oak, the Ash and the Bonnie Ivy Tree'. She found she was humming it wistfully all the time.

It wasn't that she didn't love her London life. She now shared a little mews flat off Marble Arch with Charmaine Blake and her sister, Penny. It was a bit of a squash and took every penny she had, but it was fun. There were always gangs of their friends sitting on the floor listening to jazz records, students and old school friends. Sometimes they all took off down to the coast when they had free weekends, walking on the South Downs. The countryside was lush and balmy compared to Yorkshire, and made her yearn for the bleak grey hills of home.

When she glanced across the River Thames she could see scaffolding on concrete and smoking power stations. They were erecting the buildings for the new Festival of Britain site on the south bank of the River, which would open in the spring. It was true that London was a great place for the young, and it was to be the hub of all the exhibitions. The couture houses were busy vying with each other to make fashion for the festival and get their designs showcased in displays. It was all going to be so exciting.

After all the drab years and misery of war, here was something for the country to celebrate at last. Why did she feel so flat? Perhaps she had stayed away from the Brooklyn too long – maybe she would give Plum a surprise and turn up unannounced, make up for all her absences. But the very thought of returning there made her feel sick. Gloria's chilling words still rang in her ears. Was that terrible secret going to haunt her for the rest of her life? Would she ever find peace within? At the thought of anyone finding out her heart would pound with panic, making her feel shaky.

She rushed down the stairs into the street, took some deep breaths as she began to walk towards Regent's Park, towards green lawns and trees. The open air calmed her nerves. How could she go back and face her demons or hide her true feelings from Aunt Plum? Better just to stay put and invite her down for a visit. They could do some shows, a concert, a gallery and Maddy could show her aunt that she was happy down here in the city. Perhaps she could come for a holiday when the Festival of Britain was on, but that was ages yet. It would be good to spend time together like that.

Standing rigid for a fitting, daydreaming, she never thought about the old days, but nighttime was a different story. How she must have hurt Greg. There was a crowd of Charmaines's friends who took her out to parties and to dinner, but no one took her eye amongst the boys. She was never alone or bored, and Mr Henry was a demanding employer who expected total loyalty. She knew it could all end in a moment if he no longer found her an inspiration or needed her as one of his main clothes horses. If she put on an inch of fat he'd notice and sulk. Sometimes she starved for days, and her smoking was such a waste of money and made her cough, but it kept her from eating. She lived on coffee and toast. If Maddy went back to

Yorkshire, what with Grace's home baking, she'd not fit into anything on her return.

No, far better to stay put and invite Plum down in due course. She could have her room and Maddy would kip down on the sofa. Perhaps Plum would prefer a smart hotel. Charmaine wouldn't mind. She had a fiancé in the army. They had a place in the country and went there whenever he was on leave. It was a perfect arrangement. Maddy felt bad about neglecting Plum and resolved to ring her later and check everything was OK.

This self-imposed exile was a pain, and all because of something stupid done years ago. No, it wasn't stupid. It was wicked, according to Gloria. If only she could remember what happened, but try as she might, nothing came. There were snippets in dreams, but nothing else. It was like a great glass barrier between her and the rest of her life, a barrier she wanted to smash but didn't have the strength or courage to take a hatchet to it.

At least in London there were no reminders of her past to disturb her everyday life. Here, she was just La Madeleine, draped in silk and satin and jewels and wonderful creations like a prize racehorse in a trainer's stable, exercised and pampered and paraded in a paddock. But suddenly she imagined herself on Monty, hair flying in the wind tearing over the Dales at a gallop without a care in the world, and she wanted to weep.

Something was missing, something so important. If only she knew what it was, but it was all tied up with Sowerthwaite and the Brooklyn and her childhood. As she thought about her best friends tears rose up in her eyes; that faraway look of sorrow everyone liked to see.

'Ah, there it is again,' said Mr Henry. 'You are beautiful in black like our Lady of Sorrows.'

Maddy stood there, draped in black silk and stuck with pins, trying not to move, trying not to weep. This was not how it was meant to be at all.

Gloria stopped on the forecourt of Byrne the Builders office in Harrogate with her suitcase at her feet, hoping that she'd found the right place and praying that Greg would be on site. She stood in her gaberdine mac and black beret. It was raining and it had been a long walk from the bus stop. But Greg was her last hope since she'd been sacked last night.

There she was, after one of Ken's demanding visits, feeling cheap and tired, climbing in through the little side window into the scullery that Doreen always left unlocked so they could come and go of a night. She was halfway in the room, bottom in the air, when a torch flashed, startling her, blinding her for a moment. She knew she was done for when she saw Mr and Mrs Partridge standing there. Next morning she was for the chop.

'You're on your way to becoming a first-class tart, young lady! Like mother like daughter, as I recall. Don't deny it,' said Mrs Partridge, peering down her spectacles.

It was just like the old days with The Rug on the warpath, her wig all of a quiver.

'We caught you red-handed, yet another example

of moral lassitude from you girls. The war has a lot to answer for, allowing such antics. We don't want domestics setting a bad example to our boys.' The Rug was barking from her high horse, looking down on her as if she was muck, and Gloria saw red.

'Don't you speak of my mother, you old bitch! What I do in my private time out of this prison is my business!' It all rattled out like bullets from a gun. 'You can stick this job where the sun don't shine!'

'Get out at once, and don't think of asking for a reference. I always knew you were trouble. You'll come to a sticky end, my girl, if you carry on like this.'

'With pleasure, you old bat! I pity the poor little buggers having to do time in this Dotheboys Hall. You know, we had a right old party when you left the Old Vic.'

Gloria was determined to have the last word, storming off full of righteous indignation. This move had been a mistake, and Ken turning up and pestering her just made it worse. But in the cold reality of dawn she'd sobered up, knowing she had no job, nowhere to sleep and very little cash in her purse.

For a second she even thought about apologising to The Rug and her priggish husband, but not about going back to Ken in Bradford. After all those awful sessions in the hotel room lately, she still hadn't got all her negatives and she hated him for what he wanted from her. What a fool she'd been! How had she ever thought him a decent bloke or an artist? He was making money out of her stupidity and she hated him.

At least if she left she could shake him off good and

proper, disappear with no forwarding address and this time he would never find her. There was only one person she knew nearby, and Greg wouldn't see her short. This was her big chance now to claim him for herself. There would be no Maddy to queer her pitch, but she'd have to make him believe her sob story. He was her only chance to get out of this mess.

The forecourt of Byrne's was lined with expensive cars, and there was a young girl eyeing her up through the office window. Gloria stood there all of a dither, not sure what to do next, but then it came to her. Do something dramatic . . . The office girl stood up just as she collapsed in a heap over her case in a faint.

'Hold on, love . . . Mr Byrne! There's a lass here on the floor. She looks done in. Come on, love, inside. Can you lean on me? I'll fetch your case . . . Mr Byrne!' Her voice was shaking. 'Now, you hold on to me.'

Gloria found herself in the foyer of smart brick building with big glass windows. She was led to a chair by a large desk. Suddenly a dark shadow towered over her.

'Gloria? Whatever is the matter? What are you doing here?' Her knight in white armour was here at last.

'Oh, thank goodness I've found you.'

'It's OK, Hilary, I'll see to this. I know the lady.' Greg kneeled down, patting her hand. 'Whatever's up?'

'I'm in trouble, Greg. I am so glad to see you,' she gabbled breathlessly.

'I had to come here, there's no one else. It's that school I'm working at. I had to leave. The Rug was there and she picked on me. She remembered me as a vaccy and I couldn't take any more, so I left, and now I've got no job, no work. I just couldn't bear it another day. I'm so sorry to burden you with all of this. I did write to you,' Gloria burst into floods of tears, believing her own version of events – well, almost.

'Yes, I know you did, love, but I lost the letter and address. I'm sorry. Hilary! A cup of tea with lots of sugar in it, there's a good lass. You've had a bad shock.'

Gloria melted into those blue eyes and smiled wanly. 'I don't want to burden you but if you could see your way . . . There must be places in Harrogate that need chambermaids, waitresses. I'll do anything but don't send me back. Please don't make me go back!'

'Don't worry,' whispered Greg. 'You won't have to go back to that old cow. Happen you should have stayed with Mrs Plum. Have you heard from her?'

'Not really, Greg, not since Maddy left . . . I do think she was awful to you and I couldn't stand by and stomach how cruel she was. I just felt it was the right time to leave.'

'You did right then,' he added. 'We'll think of something. Your clothes are soaking and you look so peaky – but I like your hair cut all short.' He grinned, turning her insides out. Gloria made sure to remove her coat so he could see her pretty blouse and prim skirt and the knitted cardigan she'd made in the winter. She wanted to look plain and neat and sensible, old-fashioned enough for Greg to want to protect.

She sat sipping tea in the office until it was dinnertime and Greg took her to a nice corner café with chequered cloths for a fish-and-chip dinner.

'I've been thinking, Gloria. You remember Charlie, Charlie Afton? His mother might be able to give you a room. She's a kind soul and if she couldn't help, she'd know someone who could.'

'But I've no references,' she simpered.

'Don't you worry. I'm well in with Beattie Afton. She'll take you on my word.'

'Oh, Greg, how can I thank you?' Gloria gave him one of her winning smiles. 'We always looked up to you in the hostel. You've done so well for yourself . . . Got yourself hitched up yet?' she asked, winking, her heart in her mouth in case he was spoken for.

'Nah! No time for wedding bells, me . . . not after . . . well, you know. There's a business to run and rallies to drive. I'm not ready to get kicked in the teeth again!'

'You do right,' said Gloria, looking concerned. 'She didn't deserve you.'

'What about you and the photographer . . . in Bradford, was it?' he said, changing the subject.

'I sent him packing. We were never suited, him and me,' she replied.

'You and me both. There's lots of time yet before settling down to pipe and slippers,' he laughed, but his eyes looked sad.

'No strings then,' she smiled, her heart jumping with glee. Round one to her.

The Afton parents were Methodists, teetotal and strict, but they welcomed her warmly. They lived in a great stone villa between Leeds and Harrogate. Beattie Afton sat on so many committees and on the board of the Temperance Hotel that served teetotal commercial travellers, preachers and ramblers. They were always looking for domestic help, and on Mrs Afton's recommendation Gloria was soon taken on as a chambermaid-cum-waitress-cum-dogsbody. The manager and his wife were a stern couple called the Huntleys.

As in all jobs, there were the usual humdrum duties, like changing linen, cleaning and making herself useful. Mostly the clients were respectable, sober and kept their hands to themselves but she had to watch out for Mr Huntley when he cornered her.

Sometimes there were singsongs on Sunday nights, and Gloria sat down to join them with her loud clear voice, making her a popular addition to their makeshift choir. But the biggest joy of the job was that it wasn't far from Greg's office and he took to popping in as a friend of the family with Charlie and the Aftons. Once when she was coerced into singing a solo she saw him eyeing her up with interest.

The rallying took up most of Greg's spare time. He and Charlie were car mad. She made an effort to go and watch them if there were stages nearby. It was hard to look keen, standing in the cold wet mud in old boots and macs, cheering them on as they splashed past. Soaked and encrusted with mud wasn't the greatest way to spend a Saturday afternoon but later, when she finished serving teas, they called for her and took her with them back to a public house, miles from the town, where the rally drivers let off steam with a group of girls who eyed them as their own property.

One afternoon they were all dancing around but

Gloria felt out of it as she wearing her work clothes. The smart girlfriends wore slacks and short fur coats, pretty bootees and silk headscarves, but in the evenings they often arrived in tight-fitting dresses with full skirts and high-heeled court shoes, hanging around the drivers, eyeing up the talent, ignoring her. She was definitely not one of them.

As she sat watching the others dancing until it was her turn, Greg came across. 'Fancy a spin around the floor?' he said, pulling her into the crowd.

'I wish I looked like them over there,' she sighed, nodding in the direction of the pretty girls in wide skirts. 'I don't have much in the fancy line.'

To her astonishment Greg pulled out his wallet. 'Go and buy something to cheer yourself up, then. You've worked hard: time for a little reward. You deserve a treat.'

Gloria tried not to whip away the notes but hesitated until he shoved them in her hand. 'Thanks, you really are a gentleman.'

There was just time to flee and catch the dress shops before they closed. She found a lacy blouse and a pretty dirndl skirt. This was progress. She smiled a foxy smile. No longer was Greg thinking about her as Maddy's side kick but as poor Gloria who needed taking in hand.

Greg was weakening and she must make sure she pulled out all the stops to make him sweeten to her even more. It was like they were playing parts in a play. He was the rescuing Prince to her Cinderella, and she must make sure the slippers fitted when the time came.

For the first time in her life, Gloria felt safe, clean,

cocooned by the kindness of strangers who accepted her as this sweet undemanding unfortunate who'd been a childhood friend of Greg's and needed some Christian charity. She was repaying them with hard work and loyalty, but she'd no interest in the churchy side of things, nor had Greg any connections there except as Charlie's friend.

By the looks of things, making money was his first and only love for the moment. It soothed his broken pride but Maddy's reign was in the past and soon it would be time for Gloria to make her own move.

Three months later, Greg was late for the rally time trial in the forest. They'd had one of those weeks at work when nothing had gone quite right: late deliveries, a builder going bust owing them hundreds of pounds, and Greg's best chippy poached by a rival firm. Now it was pouring down on top of slushy ice and he was late. He'd souped up the engine but they were still trying to get to grips with it. This was another Saturday afternoon trial, where they had to plot and battle with map references and driving tests on public roads.

There was a race to the forest but there were roads closed off and no proper signs, just chalk marks on trees. Then came a reversing test that had to be done at speed. Everything had to be timed to the second but Greg's mind was not on the job for once. To win they must combine being fast on the road and faster and accurate on the driving tests.

His forte was to lean out of the side of the car and

reverse accurately with some hard braking. 'Back! Back!' yelled Charlie, but this time he made a right Horlicks of it and holed the petrol tank, spilling fluid everywhere.

'Damn and blast it!' Greg exploded with frustration. Charlie wasn't being much help.

'Greg, calm down. It's only a car; you didn't roll! We can soon fix it later. Your mind's just not on the job, is it?'

'Is it that obvious? I'm sorry, so much trouble at t'mill to mull over. Sorry . . .'

'I think that little Miss Conley is distracting you. I saw you both at the dance the other night. She's a little pocket Venus, is that one. You could do far worse . . . She's hard-working, respectable, not one of those awful tarts you've been chasing down the pub, all lipstick and heaving bosoms.' Charlie laughed, seeing Greg flush.

But she is not Madeleine, Greg sighed to himself, bending down to examine the damage. It was Maddy's face that haunted his dreams, Maddy's long legs and slender shape that entranced him. Gloria was pretty enough, simple to please, she busied herself helping Mrs Afton after Sunday teas. Nothing was too much trouble for her to do, and the Aftons were pleased with her. He knew she fancied him but she was waiting for him to make the first move and he liked that.

Yet Gloria was like him, a reject, a misfit in a strange town, but in need of protection. She made him laugh when they danced, and teased him. She was like a pretty doll dressed up, and fun to have on his arm. He was treating her like bone china, but Greg guessed she was more pot mug than porcelain, tough and serviceable for everyday use.

Maddy was bone china, and you only brought that out for Sunday best; decorative, delicate, but kept for show in a glass cabinet. Maddy had made her choice and turned him down. So be it. Perhaps Charlie was right. If he settled down with anyone, he could do far worse. With Gloria he'd be sure of an honest, no-nonsense bargain. She would work hard in the home, bring up his kids and see to his every need. In turn, he would be generous and they'd make a fine family home together. If she was a bit rough round the edges, they could keep her family background under wraps. She was no worse than he was; a workhouse boy. He'd no room to be snobby.

They were cart horses, the both of them, not fancy thoroughbreds, but cart horses got there in the end, steady away, strong, and they lasted longer.

The rally that afternoon might have been a disaster, but tonight he was taking Gloria to see the new film at the Regal. He thought about the box still sitting in his tallboy drawer with the Fattorini label. Gloria would jump at such a label. She'd open her arms to him and he'd enjoy teaching her the joys of sex.

No, he might not be love struck or head over heels this time round, but he knew a good bargain when he saw it. He could do far worse than propose to Gloria Conley.

He was lonely and a man needed regular sex. He was ready to make a go of things and she had nothing better on the horizon. He could give it a try, nothing lost there. Together they'd make a good team and show the world that vaccies were as good as anyone else in making their dreams come true.

19

1951

Plum sat facing forward in the compartment on the early morning train from Scarperton Junction. She was on her way to meet Maddy at King's Cross and was dressed in her best linen summer suit and straw hat – nothing but the best for this visit. She was going to see the Festival of Britain, which King George VI had opened in May.

It had taken so much planning just to get a few days off. Grace Battersby was doing the evening meal for the half-boarders, and Stephen Armitage had promised to give the dogs a good run round Sowerthwaite, and Sally from the vicarage would be exercising the horses.

She smiled, thinking about how her life had changed since she'd scratched her cornea and met Dr Armitage. He'd been most attentive, and they'd started to meet to play bridge at one of Dilly Baslow's bridge suppers. He'd walked her back home and they'd met for longer walks. Suddenly Sowerthwaite had taken on a whole new brightness. The two of them met in church and sat on the Roof Repair Committee. He'd even got tickets for a concert in Leeds Town Hall where they met up with Totty and her husband, and had heard the Liverpool Philharmonic playing Beethoven's Violin Concerto. It was a long drive home and they chatted fifteen to the dozen all the way back, like school kids on the bus.

The summer seemed brighter, the sky bluer, trees greener now.

There was hope and tenderness in his kiss and his concern. Plum finally felt womanly and wanted, after years of despair in the chilly frost of divorce. Plum knew Maddy would understand and be happy for her, but she wanted to spend a little time with her niece, just to see how she was getting on in London. Her letters were still brief and snappy, telling Plum nothing much that she didn't already know.

Maddy was still living with Charmaine and her sister – still hard up, still at the House of Raoul Henry, with 'Haughty Henry', as she called her boss. A day out together would do them both good. She wanted to tell Maddy all about Stephen in person, her glad tidings of joy that she'd found a loving man at long last.

Stephen made her realise how cold and wooden was her first marriage to Gerald. How sad that she'd wasted all those years pretending that he'd loved her. It had been a useful marriage of convenience for him. There'd been little tenderness in his lovemaking, little attention to those details that Stephen just took for granted, like ringing home to see if she was busy. Once he'd even cooked her a meal, very basic but tasty, just to prove that he wasn't hopeless in the kitchen.

Love is in the details, she smiled to herself. When she returned he'd be at the station to greet her with the dogs. He would ring to see if she'd arrived safely. For the first time in decades she felt cherished, and she hugged the word around her like a soft woolly blanket. Just when she was feeling redundant, no evacuees, no Maddy to care for, Stephen had bounced into her life. What had she done to deserve such good fortune?

She read a magazine and a newspaper from cover to cover, dozed and gazed out of the window. Soon the green fields turned into houses and back gardens, and then to tall buildings, and the train came to a halt in the city.

There was Maddy, waiting at the barrier, looking so pale and wan in her elegant two-piece, a lilac suit with a black trim and hat made out of straw. She always looked good in mourning colours, Plum thought.

'Maddy, darling, at long last! You look *très chic*. Haughty Henry must be doing very well.'

'If only,' laughed Maddy, taking her arm. 'You're on time and I've got so much planned. I hope your feet are up to it.' She examined Plum's sensible brogue lace-ups with a smile.

'Better than yours will be, young lady. At my age, comfort comes first. I can walk for miles in these old coal barges but look at your court shoes, such high-heels!'

'Don't worry, I've got sandals in my bag. It's going

to be hot . . . Oh, Plum, I'm so glad you're here. Let's get the tube to the Tate. You must see the Henry Moore exhibition and then we'll stop for coffee and buy a souvenir programme and choose what bits we see first tomorrow. We're going to have such a wonderful time!'

Gloria awoke, seeing Greg silhouetted naked by the window of the hotel behind Park Lane. He was long, lean, his buttocks rounded, his shoulders broad. She smiled to herself and sighed. Now he's all mine, mine, mine. She couldn't believe how quickly it had all happened. One minute she was little Miss Nobody, skivvying at the Temperance Hotel and now she was Mrs Gregory Byrne, on the up.

He'd proposed out of the blue one night, after a dance. They'd not so much as kissed before they'd rushed to the registry office, dragging in Charlie and Hilary as witnesses. It was all done and dusted in a flash with no fuss, no expense, no flashy wedding. She'd been too shocked to kick up a fuss about a white church wedding – better to strike while the iron was hot.

But who cared when this ruby flashed in the sunlight on her ring finger? Now they were on honeymoon in London for a whole week of dinners and shows. They'd walked the soles off their shoes on the hot pavements. Everything she'd wished for was coming true. This was the life!

Gregory was attentive, protective, initiating her into foreplay and sex as if she was a virgin, and she played the innocent, revving him up with a few little tricks of her own, as if she'd discovered them all by herself.

'Is this nice?' she whispered, and he groaned with pleasure.

'Do it to me, then,' she commanded, and he obliged, and she cried out with shouts that pleasured him even more.

Every night they raced back after work just to lie together and share this bliss.

'You're a wild one,' Greg said. 'A natural . . . It must be all that red hair.'

'Do it again, then,' she challenged him, and he did.

How different he was from Ken, with his devious tactics and dirty tricks. Greg was her slave and she adored his handsome body, the way his hair flopped over his brow when it wasn't Brylcreemed. At last she was safe, secure. Nothing could touch her now that she was married. Ken would never find her. Maddy's days were long gone. Everything was perfect.

'What shall we do today?' Greg asked.

'Stay in bed,' Gloria grinned.

'It's too bright a day to waste. Let's do what we intended and go to the Festival of Britain.'

'It'll be boring, all that queuing . . . come back to bed. It's so soft.'

'We have to see the Festival. I've been reading all about it. It'll be good for business. I want to see the new building materials. Then we can go on the funfair at Battersea. I'll treat you to a special lunch. There'll be something for both of us. We can't miss the Great Exhibition; there's a transport show.'

'I thought we'd agreed – no business on our

honeymoon. Trust you to want to see cars,' Gloria pouted. 'I shall be bored.'

'No you won't. Think of all the famous people you'll bump into there – film stars all dressed up. Wear your pretty wedding suit and hat and I'll show you off to them,' he cajoled her.

That was the trouble with Greg. It was business first, her second, along with his rally cars. He had all these enthusiasms, always reading and planning ahead, but she'd put a stop to that at bedtime. Who needed pages when she was ready and willing to entertain him? She threw a slipper at him.

'Ouch! You devil woman!' He turned and grinned, and she opened her arms to him again and he jumped on her.

'Ouch! You're heavy!' she snapped.

'Serves you right!'

'Where do you want to start first, Aunt Plum?' asked Maddy, examining the map of the South Bank Festival site in their souvenir programme. It was a fine June morning and the day was their own. Tomorrow she would be working at one of the fabric and textile design shows, representing the best of British designers. Although Mr Henry was a refugee from fascism, part French and part Hungarian, his best work was coming from his atelier workshop close to Cavendish Square.

Maddy looked up at the enormity of all the modern buildings set amongst the bombed ruins of Lambeth, the site rising like a concrete giant with flags flying and banners. It made her heart just burst with pride to see all the new buildings. Plum insisted on being country comfortable in her sensible shoes, floral dress and hand-knitted cardigan, standing and staring alongside her.

'You choose first,' she smiled, gazing at this strange Lion and Unicorn pavilion with its undulating roof. 'That looks just like a corrugated iron roof to me.'

'It says it's made of oak and lamella on the roof, whatever that it is,' Maddy read from the programme. 'What's lamella?'

'Don't ask me. Let's find the People's Pavilion and the Dome of Discovery. Oh, look up there. There's the Skylon Tower . . . come on!' Plum was racing ahead in front of her.

'Hold your horses, I'm supposed to be the young one here,' Maddy laughed, trying to catch her up. It was still quiet, but the crowds would be thronging the avenue soon. So there was time to stop and stare at the Epstein's *Youth Advancing* sculpture.

'Wow!' said Plum. 'What do you make of that?'

'Not sure,' replied Maddy. 'I like my sculptures sculptured, if you know what I mean, but it's interesting and so strong.'

'Philistine!'

It was lovely to have Plum's company. She was a good egg, full of Yorkshire common sense. Taking her to see the Henry Moore sculptures had been a great success. She had done her homework and prepared for her visit with diligence. It was more like a school outing in the olden days at Palgrave House School.

By the time they'd walked around for two hours,

queued for the toilets, shuffled around exhibitions, waited for the toucans to pop out of the Guinness clock, the women's feet were swelling and they were ready to collapse into the nearest café in the Homes and Gardens Pavilion with its wonderful mural dominating the food hall.

'Can I take it you won't be wanting the funfair?' said Maddy, with a grin. This was turning out to be a lovely outing.

Plum raised her brows. 'I didn't think the site would be so huge, so grand. I'm whacked. If you want to wander off for a while, just let me be. I'll be fine. I'd like to browse in the Homes and Gardens exhibits. We can meet up by the Skylon Tower if you like, about two thirty?'

Maddy nodded. There was so much to see that interested her. It wouldn't do any harm to split up for a while.

Greg couldn't wait to explore the Transport Pavilion but Gloria hung back, sucking on her Neapolitan wafer, which had cost three shillings! Her face was a picture, with chocolate, strawberry and vanilla ice cream in a smudge around her lips. She really was still a big kid at heart, a pretty redhead in an emerald-green candy-striped cotton dress and broad-brimmed picture hat with ankle straps on her high-heeled shoes. She'd never make it around the vast acres of the exhibition, but he daren't tell her that.

The site was like being on another planet, a scientific fantasy Wonderland – so much to see, and only one shot at it by all accounts. Gloria wouldn't come twice.

She loved the shops and restaurants and cinemas and making love. If he'd not known better he'd have wondered just what sort of things she had been up to with that Ken Silverstone, but had believed her assurances that their relationship was almost platonic.

There was something about her lovemaking that reminded him of some of the girls he'd had in the army. There was almost a desperation in her need to be desired and pleasured that puzzled him. It was something that he hadn't expected. Now she was pouting at the thought of doing the Science Pavilion. So he'd given in and done the Homes and Gardens displays, and they had given him food for thought.

'Look at that furniture!' Gloria pointed eagerly to the neat square lines of the furniture, the curve chairs and blond woods of contemporary designs. He'd never seen anything like it.

'We must get one of them lights,' she screamed, rushing over to examine the sticks of light that sprung out like a spray of flowers. It was all very stylish, but Greg preferred the old oak stuff he'd grown to love at the Brooklyn, though his customers would want such details in their modern homes.

'We could build that stone fireplace in our show house,' he enthused. 'York Stone bricks . . . I've got a good source for them. Everything is so modern and light . . .'

'And expensive,' added Gloria.

'If we're going to build new houses, then they must

have everything up to date,' he added, making for the fitted kitchen display. This was a grand exhibition.

'You carry on, love,' he said, hanging back. 'I'm going out for smoke and I want to chat to some of these businessmen. They might be on the look out for an outlet in Yorkshire. There's business to be had here. I'll meet you by the café. You do your women's stuff . . . in an hour?'

Gloria pointed to her watch and nodded. Greg was glad of a few minutes away from her incessant chatter. It had been a job to get her out of bed and into a taxi, but at last they'd found something to interest her and he promised her the funfair later to round off the visit. She could be tiring to be with when she got ideas fixed in her head, and stubborn with it. He had to keep finding new things to distract her. For one second he let comparisons with Maddy leach into his mind and then wished he hadn't. Gloria loved him and that was all that mattered now.

His mind was racing. He'd acquired some prime building land on the outskirts of Harrogate. These modern shapes were the future. They'd need a show house and he'd build that for themselves on the best plot. A new house would keep Gloria occupied, choosing furniture and fittings.

Gloria got bored so easily, even in London. They'd done the waxworks, the Tower but she was not interested in history or art or buildings or anything with wheels. That made her eyes glaze over into murky green ponds.

The more time he spent with his wife the more he

realised he didn't know her at all. She contradicted herself now and again, just little things, but had let slip that she'd been sacked from the school, not resigned. That wouldn't have bothered him much but why had she not been straight? Perhaps she was ashamed and scared.

The wedding had been a bit of rush, but that was his doing. He wanted no last-minute cold feet this time. He'd been disappointed that she'd not invited Sid, her brother, to their wedding, or asked Mrs Plum. Sid was doing his National Service, and Gloria refused to have any reminders of evacuee days either. She never mentioned Madeleine, for which he was grateful. He still couldn't stop that girl drifting through his dreams.

He hadn't intended to get wed so fast but it just seemed the right thing to do. He didn't want to hang about, and he had fancied Gloria, but he wasn't going to take advantage of her. When he got something into his sights he just went for it.

Greg found himself staring up at a huge stone sculpture: two giant figures facing each other – a strangely intimate and moving placing of human forms, sort of balanced. He'd never seen anything like it before. The programme said it was by Barbara Hepworth. His eye roamed over the shapes, trying to understand them. But he stood back, bumping into someone also contemplating it.

'I'm sorry!' He jumped back and came face to face with Maddy Belfield. 'Maddy!' he gasped.

'Greg!' She stared at him with those grey eyes. 'My God! What are you doing here?' she stammered, her cheeks flushed with genuine delight as he reached out his hand instinctively.

'Same as you,' he said, trying not to shiver as he touched her gloved hand. 'You look so . . .' He didn't know what to say. The very sight of her face stunned him; everything about her was so smart, so simple, so elegant. She was like a sculpture herself with soft curls around her face, the pretty purple dress falling to her calf, with a belt clinching her tiny waist. A rush of emotion flowed through him. 'Maddy! It's been such a long time . . . I heard you were in London. How are you doing?' He tried to sound cold and indifferent but he couldn't keep it up.

'I'm fine, busy, but I've got Aunt Plum staying here. I managed to lure her out of Yorkshire at long last!'

His eyes instinctively looked to the ring finger, under her white lace gloves. There was nothing there.

'Isn't this wonderful? So cheering, so hopeful . . . I feel so proud to be British, don't you? Have you come down for the day? I hear there're special trains bringing folk from all over the country. Oh, do come and meet Plum. She'll be so glad to see you.'

Greg stood in silence, just drinking her in. There was no time to explain as she took his arm and guided him back into the Pavilion, towards the café and the crowds queuing for seats as if all that had happened between them was some phantom of his imagination.

'Look who I picked up in the street!' Maddy almost pushed over the chairs in her rush to find Mrs Plum.

'My goodness me! Gregory, what a surprise! "Of all the gin joints in all the world . . ."' she mimicked the famous words from the film *Casablanca*. 'Sit down. Find another chair, Maddy. How lovely to see a known face in all these crowds. How are you?'

Greg ought to have spoken there and then and told them he wasn't alone, but the warmth of the welcome flooded over him like a wave of warm water, soothing him, reminding him of the old days at the Brooklyn. Once again he felt the granite in his heart melt into putty. This was his only family. Plum always made him feel special. Maddy was still his friend. Whatever tension there had been between them had long evaporated into genuine delight again. But Gloria ought to be here amongst them, sharing this special moment.

Suddenly he felt that granite again He didn't want to share this with her, not just yet. If all had gone well, these two would have been his family now, his wife and her aunt, but he didn't want to break the moment by telling them he'd married Gloria. Why not? Why ever not?

He knew why. He was ashamed of his new wife and it felt like a terrible betrayal even to think it. In those fleeting seconds of recognition he felt sweaty and moved to leave. 'I'd better go. I'm supposed to be meeting someone.'

'But you've only just got here. There's so much to catch up on,' said Mrs Plum, unaware of his panic. 'Don't go. Find your friend to meet us.'

He should've said it there and then, but his lips stuck together, and his tongue went dry.

*

It was Gloria who saw them chatting in a huddle from her seat by the door. A shaft of sunlight, bathed their heads; smiling, laughing as if she didn't exist. How dare they ignore her?

Why was Greg smiling and waving his hands about, his cheeks beaming with delight! Then he glanced at his watch. He looked anxious. This was awful.

She'd got bored with all the furnishings and stuff – teapots, fancy goods, bed linen – and you couldn't buy any of it, just take leaflets about suppliers. She'd come to the café early to rest her feet, to kick off her ankle straps, which were digging into her swollen feet.

Maddy still looked a million dollars in her fancy clothes. Even Plum had made an effort. Maddy never took her eyes off her husband. What a pretty scene. Time to spoil the party, Gloria smiled, striding across the room, trying to look relaxed.

'Oh, there you are, Greg, love! What a surprise! Plum . . . Maddy? Well, what a co-incidence. I've never seen owt like it, have you? We're so glad we came, aren't we, darling?' She sat down, took off her gloves and flashed her rings so everyone could see.

It was Plum who noticed first. 'Gloria! You're married to Greg!'

'Of course!' Gloria grinned. 'We're on our honeymoon, aren't we?'

'How delightful . . . congratulations to both of you,' Plum continued.

Maddy nodded and jumped up. 'I'll get you some more tea.'

'No, I'll do it,' said Greg nearly knocking his chair

over. Clumsy boy! Gloria knew he hadn't told them and she was furious.

'I was working near Harrogate, we bumped into each other again, and the rest, as they say, is history.' She grabbed his arm in a show of coupledom.

'You dark horses,' added Mrs Plum. 'I'd have loved to have sent you a telegram and present, if I'd known.'

'We didn't want a fuss. Greg is so busy with his business. We were going to send a postcard to everyone from London, weren't we? That's why we came down, to get ideas from the Pavilion, to see all that Scandinavians' stuff. It's gorgeous, and the lighting – fancy having a kitchen with a built-in sink, oven and fridge. Greg wants to do the Transport and then we're off to Battersea Funfair.'

No one was saying much and Maddy's face was a picture. She was tight-lipped and cool, trying so hard not to look put out, the jealous cow! This news had popped her balloon and no mistake. Anyone could see she was still carrying a torch for Greg after all these years. This was one glorious moment of victory. He was hers now but she'd try to be generous in her triumph.

'I suppose you're still doing the mannequin shows?' she asked, knowing full well that Maddy was now one of the best in the business.

Plum stepped in quickly. 'She's doing a big show tomorrow, part of the Festival of Britain in fashion.'

'We'd better be on our way,' offered Greg, slurping his tea and looking awkward. 'So nice to see you both again.' Everyone stood up.

'But at least when you get home, please come and have some tea. I'd love to give you a little something for your wedding, and we'd all like to see the pictures! I can't believe how we all bumped into each other so many miles from home. Isn't it strange?'

'Come on, Gloria, we need to get on if you want to see the Grotto and the Tree Walk,' ordered Greg. He couldn't get out of there fast enough.

'I'd like to see those too . . . Let's all go together,' said Mrs Plum. 'It'll be fun, like old times. Is it far?'

Maddy followed behind, feeling sick, sad and as if living in some strange dream. It was as if the sun had gone in and now everything was grey and flat. Seeing Greg like that brought everything to the surface, all those emotions she'd held down since she'd stormed out of his life. It was such a shock to see Gloria wearing him like a trophy was on her arm. She didn't understand. What had happened to Ken?

Greg appeared older, his eyes creased, and he'd scarcely looked in her direction. Why had he not bothered to tell them about Gloria being his wife when they met by the statue? He should have warned her what was coming. Not that it ought to matter now, but it did. No wonder he couldn't look her in the eye when Gloria arrived.

They were all grown-ups now, and he had made his choice because she'd let him go. Why shouldn't her friend step into the breach?

Then a terrible suspicion crept out of the shadows into her mind. All that advice Gloria had dished out . . .

Surely not? She was her friend, surely she wouldn't do such a thing deliberately – make Maddy give him up for her own ends? Greg was not some prize to be fought over. He was flesh and blood and a good man. No, they must have met by chance long after she'd let him go. Good luck to them.

It was all over now and they lived in different worlds The pain of this would pass. She'd never have to meet up with them again. There were plenty of beaux down south. Some of the other models went out with racing drivers, actors, peers, Members of Parliament. Once, when she complained to them about their wages, Alannah had the cheek to laugh in her face, 'Don't be a simpleton. We're not expected to live off these wages, darling. All of us have other patrons, don't we?' There was no response from the *cabine*.

'Speak for yourself,' Charmaine snapped. 'Not everyone has a sugar daddy to rent them a flat like you!'

'But she's pretty enough to find other means of support, surely. Madeleine's no different from any of us,' Alannah sniffed. 'No one gets rich on the pittance Scrooge hands out after a show.'

The meaning of it had shocked Maddy. She was not that type of girl, no matter what had happened in the past! When she gave herself in marriage it would be to a man who made her arms ache, her heart thud, her eyes brim with pride and love for who he was, not what he had. It would be to a man like Greg.There was always that terrible secret at the back of her mind, gnawing away at her sense of her own value. In hiding her labour from Dr Gunn, had she caused the death of her own baby in some way? If she had, she wasn't fit ever to be a mother. If only she could remember what had happened that night, but what if Gloria hadn't been straight with her? Had she planned this all along? No . . . this was her own jealous heart talking now.

But it was time that she was told where little Dieter was buried. Gloria owed her that, at least. It was terrible to feel so suspicious around her once good friend. They'd been so out of touch lately and now she knew why. Gloria held the key to her happiness – if only they could talk over things again so she could get it straight in her mind what had happened to his little body. Then she'd be free to get on with her own life again.

For everyone's sake, now she must put on a brave face and welcome them back to Brooklyn. But not yet, not until she could get used to the idea of Greg being married to Gloria. She couldn't bear to see them together again until she could sort out her own feelings

They all parted company before going to the funfair. The lights flickering across the South Bank were like beacons in the dark, those special up-lights coming from the pavement, torching their path that everyone was talking about, underlighting the statues and fountains and some of the buildings. It was eerie but magical. In the half-light Maddy could hide her despair in a bubble of chatter and false bonhomie.

She shook their hands and wished them well, not giving Gloria the satisfaction of showing her distress.

'I'll get you tickets for the show tomorrow,' she offered, hoping against hope they'd refuse, but Greg was quick to step in.

'We've got tickets for a musical tomorrow, then it's home James for us. It was lovely to see you both, though, and I promise we'll keep in touch.'

They were all making promises they wouldn't keep, all of it so polite, so false and so empty. It was a relief to see them into the taxi.

'You never know what a day can bring,' said Plum on the way home. 'I thought you handled that very tactfully, darling,' as a hand reached out to her in the dark. That one motherly gesture opened the floodgates of pain and Maddy felt the tears stinging down her cheeks.

Plum had guessed something of her anguish, even though she didn't know the half of it. But it was enough for Maddy just to know that she still had one loyal friend in the world, one who was more like a mother than an aunt.

The next evening, Greg didn't hear a word of the musical and sat staring into the darkness in turmoil. The shock of meeting Maddy and Plum numbed him still. When would he ever get Maddy Belfield out of his hair? He thought he'd got over her rejection but one smile and she'd reeled him in again on an invisible line. He'd made a terrible mistake in marrying Gloria, poor girl. He'd rushed in for all the wrong reasons. What he'd felt for her was at first concern and then lust, nothing more. Maddy didn't have to say or do anything to melt the ice around his heart. She was just Maddy, his friend once upon a time, but, more than his soul mate, the love of his life. What had gone wrong between them? He'd never understand. Now it was all too late to mend. He'd made his choice and he must play fair by Gloria, give her all the toys that would make her happy. They'd be fine, given a bit of space between them, a bit of give and take.

'You don't always get what you want,' he'd heard Mr Afton say in a sermon. 'You get what you need,' and he'd been glad enough of her body in bed.

The look of gratitude in her eyes when he'd found her digs and a job, when he placed a ruby ring on her finger, was genuine enough. There'd be plenty more of that with the new show house, and when kiddies came along. They'd want for nothing. It would do. It would have to do. There was nothing else he could give her.

She wasn't Maddy and never could be, but he'd try to make up for that one irredeemable fact for the rest of his life.

Part Four

20

November 1956

Maddy listened with concern to the World Service – first the British collapse at Suez and then Hungary. The uprising in Hungary that had gone so well at first was now turning nasty, and the Russian tanks were on the streets of Budapest. Students were dying and the crowds were helpless against such terror. Pleas for help from the West went unheeded and she thought of poor Mr Henry, who would be in a dreadful mood. Everyone in the atelier knew he still had relatives in that country and was concerned for his niece and nephew's safety.

At times like this she yearned to be safe among people she loved – not stuck in a hotel in the South of France, out of touch.

The last time she'd been back to Yorkshire properly was over nine months ago, when Plum and Steve got married in Scarperton registry office, with a blessing in St Peter's church. How proud she was to be the maid of honour.

Plum wore a velvet two-piece, the colour of autumn leaves, with little mink cuffs and collar. They'd looked so happy, and Maddy was so envious, but Plum deserved every ounce of happiness.

She'd brought Julian Shaw, the actor, as her escort. They'd been lovers on and off, but it had petered out because she was too busy and he was pushing for a film career in Hollywood. There'd been others, but no one special enough to tear her away from busy photo-shoots and fittings.

Yet standing on that windswept parapet at Cap de Ferrat, as she was looking out in the weak winter sunshine to a turquoise sea, posing for the camera and trying to appear insouciant, there'd been a strange moment of clarity like a voice inside her head, pinging in her ear like crystal glass.

What on earth are you doing here, Madeleine, when people your age are dying in the streets? Go home, do something useful . . .

It wasn't the first time she'd heard this nagging. It had begun when she stopped enjoying her work, when she realised there were gaps that needed filling and an emptiness inside her that being on parade didn't fill, when she found herself restless and tired of London. It was a kind of schoolmarmish voice, bending her ear. *Stop messing about and do something useful. It's time to pay back for all you've been given.* It almost sounded like the voice of Pleasance Belfield, her grandmother, or was it Granny Mills from Chadley, with her rich Lancashire burr? She knew what it was like to be bombed out, her whole world blown to smithereens. She'd had to face life alone in a strange place. That was what was happening now to children all over the world and here she was, prancing around half naked, shivering and trying to concentrate. What could she do to help? Sending money to the appeal seemed too easy . . .

'Madeleine . . . Wake up! Madeleine!' She stood in a trance, unable to concentrate. 'Maddy Belfield, what's got into you today?'

It was at that precise moment that she knew her modelling career was over. One minute she was primping and preening, the next she was packing up bags, flying back to Paris and on to London and King's Cross Station without a backward glance.

Everyone thought she was having a breakdown but she was making for home, for the hills of home, in time for Christmas. I've been away far too long, she thought.

Charmaine and Bella might think she was bonkers – it was not as if she'd made a fortune – but she didn't care. Being a fashion clothes horse had given her an entrée into all sorts of glamorous worlds, but it must end one day whether she liked it or not. She'd had a good innings. Better to go before she was pushed.

'Quit while you're ahead.' Old Mr Marshfield's words came to her aid. She'd seen enough older models, reduced to catalogue work, trying to hide their age with make-up. Maddy was only twenty-six and there were still some good years ahead, but it was time for her to do something else, far from footlights and dressing rooms.

The answer lay in the hills. That was all she knew. She'd make a pilgrimage to the old Victory Tree HQ and sort out her options.

Her face was stuck into the *Manchester Guardian* on the way home, reading about those poor kids fleeing across the border at night and the terrible fate of those who stayed on. If only there was something she could do to help. Perhaps talking things over with Plum and Steve might give her a solution.

They were still in the Brooklyn, holding the fort with the guesthouse, while Steve was busy with his medical practice. She was longing to see them both.

How kind Plum had been all those years ago when they'd met Greg and Gloria at the Festival of Britain. How silly she'd been to get so upset, but Plum had never pushed for an explanation for those tears.

Those two evacuees were never invited back to Sowerthwaite or to the wedding. They'd exchanged enough Christmas cards for her to know there was a child. It was a little girl called Bebe – one of Gloria's affectations, no doubt.

Greg's building empire now stretched across the West Riding and he'd raced in the RAC Rally. There was always a handwritten note in Plum's card from Greg, which was left around for Maddy to read.

She didn't think about Gloria much. There was no point. Their friendship had just petered out. They'd got nothing in common but Greg, and thinking about them together just made her angry and mean. Her courage failed when she thought about asking Gloria one more time about that awful night. It was all so long ago, another lifetime ago, and she never wanted to see either of them again.

She gazed out with anticipation as the train chuffed

its way north. She'd forgotten how green the land became when they left Leeds station, how the hills rose up, grey stone walls in all directions, farmsteads dotted about. It was all so beautiful in a rugged, comfortable sort of way.

Her London life was over and she was shedding it like a snakeskin. It had been a good experience but now she wanted another challenge. This was a big risk and a challenge, letting go of her career with no surety where the next one was coming from.

'Never go back,' someone once said, but she had to go back to find out who she was again. If only she could go back to being ten, dangling her legs from the Victory Tree, making wishes. Everything was so much simpler then. If only . . .

Plum was waiting at the station in their Morris Traveller estate, piling bags into the back. 'I've got your room ready. The dogs will go mad to see you. They're old now, but they'll expect a good walk up Simmonds Ridge before dusk. We'll have the best Christmas yet, with no guests! I'll put them all off. It's just us, family together. I want to know what's been happening. Your letters were intriguing. I can't believe you just walked away from all that glitz and glamour to Sowerthwaite.'

As they drove down the High Street Maddy saw the same familiar grey stone shops, the market square with its preaching cross, the cars and vans, the horse-drawn carts, the pubs and churches and pretty Christmas lights in shop windows. Sowerthwaite had grown prosperous since the war. A new housing estate had sprung up where once they used to play in fields. A swing park had been built for the children and the old school extended.

They passed the Old Vic. It was shuttered up and sad-looking.

'Do we still rent it out to the mill?' Maddy asked.

'I'm afraid not,' said Plum. 'The cotton mill's closing down, didn't I tell you? We've lost our lodgers there. Steve's solicitor friend, Barney Andrews, suggests we sell it off for housing to a builder. It would make a nice townhouse for someone, with such a big garden at the back. Now, you ought to meet him. He's very—'

'No matchmaking, Plum.'

'Forgive me, but the estate's really yours now and it's time you ought to know what it entails. I'm only caretaking until such times—'

'But Brooklyn is your home,' Maddy said, wanting to reassure her.

'And your home too. In fact, Stephen and I were only talking last night . . . but it can wait until you've had a walk, a bath and a good meal inside you. You're just skin and bone, young lady.'

'Models don't eat. We smoke, we drink, we pick at food – but not any more! I hope you've made a Christmas pudding and all the trimmings?'

'We'll have the full works, don't worry. Grace is seeing to that. We'll kill the fatted calf for the prodigal's return. Have no fear, you'll be as plump as a turkey by New Year if she has anything to do with it.'

'Jolly good!' Maddy laughed. It was marvellous to be home.

*

Plum was dreading the end of their wonderful welcome home dinner of roast pheasant casserole with juniper berries, followed by blackberry and apple cobbler and cream, and the best coffee she could order from York.

Maddy looked radiant in the candlelight in her thick stylish sweater dress, her hair wound up in a French pleat and her gold earrings flashing in the firelight. The strain had gone from her face, and that pinched tight look across her cheekbones was loosening. This was their first proper Christmas together for years but she feared she was going to have to spoil it all with some startling news. She was not sure how Maddy would react.

Maddy kept darting in and out of the house like a child, admiring the Christmas decorations in the hall, the festive banners, reading cards pinned up that they'd opened. The tree had been left for them to decorate together later. The box of decorations was all prepared, each bauble with its own story of who bought it or made it. It was a beloved tradition that neither of them wanted to miss.

Steve said that he'd break the news for her, but Plum insisted they both do it. Just as he was about to start, the phone rang and he was called out to a difficult birth on a farm up the Dale.

'Maddy, I've got some news. I'm not sure how to say this.'

'You're not ill, are you?' Maddy looked apprehensive.

'No, not at all. It's just that Steve's got a new opportunity, a wonderful chance,' Plum gulped.

'That's great. He's a good doctor. He's taking another practice?'

'No, in a hospital clinic, but it's in New Zealand . . . working with a friend he met in the war. They always promised they'd work together. You know he was in the Battle for Crete. They evaded capture with the help of these New Zealanders. They've kept in touch. He owes them his life and now he feels . . .'

She saw Maddy's face crumple. 'New Zealand! But it's the other side of the world!'

'I know, dear, but it's what he's always wanted.'

'So you must go with him, of course, but it's so far away, by ship.'

'Yes, but there are flights. I'll stay on until everything is sorted out. They've got a replacement in the practice here so he'll leave in the New Year and I'll follow, but not for ages yet.'

'How long?'

'I hope to leave at the end of March. We can find someone to help run the guesthouse. That's why you must speak to Barney. I'm sorry to land you right in it.' Plum reached out for her hand.

'Not half! I can't believe it. Oh, Plum, just when I thought everything was settled,' she replied, looking so woebegone.

'I'm sorry. Nothing ever stays the same, does it? I have to go. Finding Steve has been the best thing in my life – a little late perhaps, but I want to help him all I can,' Plum continued. Her face was alive with love and concern.

'Forget what I said, I'm only being selfish. You're

the only family I've got and it's hard to think of you being so far away. It's such a shock.' Maddy was trying not to cry.

'I know we've not seen each other for ages, Maddy, not since our wedding, but we can write to each other,' Plum replied.

'It's not the same, though, is it? I wish I hadn't stayed away so long . . .'

'You had your reasons, but no door shuts without another opening. I've always believed that. Look at how you all filled my life, you and the evacuees, when things were dire with Gerry. It was the making of me.'

'I was sorry to hear Uncle Gerald died so suddenly and, just like his mother, with a stroke. I should have gone to his funeral but I was abroad at the time.'

'Steve and I went out of respect for times past. Gerald was the last of the Belfield brothers; the only one to die in peacetime. End of an era,' Plum sighed. 'We met Daisy Abbott – not a bit like I imagined my rival would be. You know, I think we could've been friends . . . I felt sorry for her. So this is all yours now. I'm sorry to spring this on you but we must make it the best of Christmases. I'm scared too . . . I'm an old stick-in-the-mud at heart. Making a new life at my age is terrifying.'

'Oh, Plum, what will I do without you?' Maddy cried.

'You'll manage fine and dandy. Look on this as a great opportunity to sell up and move on yourself, if you want to,' Plum replied, trying not to blubber.

'Sell up Brooklyn?'

'Why, yes. There's nothing to interest you here, is there?'

'But this is my home . . . I can't sell it. Pleasance would turn in her grave and haunt me.'

'Well, you're free to do what you want now, Maddy, you're a big girl. It's an expensive item to keep up. It'll have to pay its way and the Old Vic needs sorting too. You'll rattle around in here like a pea in a drum. Speak to Barney, he's got some ideas.'

'But it's Christmas – I'm not going to think about any of it until after New Year. I shall take old Monty for a long hack over Simmonds Ridge and chew the cud if the weather holds. Your news takes some swallowing.'

'I knew you'd see the sense of it. We're going carol singing tonight with the choir and there's the school Nativity play tomorrow night. We'll do some last-minute shopping and get squiffy on damson gin. How's that for starters? If it's going to be our last Christmas here.'

'No, it's not . . . you'll be back. Brooklyn won't be Brooklyn without you . . . you must return. I'm not going to sell it.'

They were both in tears. It was time for Plum to play the trump card. 'Let's go and decorate the tree, you always loved doing that.'

The tree smelled of pine needles and ginger in the firelight. Out came all the wartime dough decorations: bells and angels, Santas and glass baubles, the shepherd's crook filled with long-forgotten chocolate drops, stars painted with glittery paint and tinsel angels, pretty glass lanterns and bells from another era. Neither spoke, but Plum saw the tears trickling down Maddy's face.

She had been cruel to be kind. Better to spoil her illusions now so they could get on with their new lives and new plans and really enjoy Christmas together without any secrets.

Maddy had chosen to return just when Plum was choosing a new life and she had no regrets about leaving with Steve. The girl was a woman, old enough to have lovers and admirers. She'd done her job, seen the girl right in dark times. Christmas brought out the child in everyone, and Maddy's worst Christmas had been here all those years ago. This one would be brilliant.

But now Plum was looking to her own life and love for a change. A man like Steve was such an unexpected bonus. She'd follow him to the ends of the earth and back. If only Maddy could find her match then she'd rest content.

She'd kept all those postcards from the Festival Exhibition, pictures of the Barbara Hepworth sculptures, in particular; those two figurines in harmony called *Contrapuntal*. She'd never forgotten the impact it had made on her. Life was a balancing act, and she'd finally found her other half in Stephen.

Maddy must make her own decisions about Brooklyn. It was a relief to be handing it over in one piece. It had felt like a burden for so long. Now, it was Maddy's turn to sort things out. She would have bags of energy to face this challenge.

Maddy rode out to the Ridge along the old Green Road, the drovers' road, and she had gates to open. It was frosty but still safe enough for the horse. She needed to think out everything after the shock of Plum's coming desertion.

Christmas was everything she hoped for, but it was tinged round the edges with panic every time she thought of the Armitages setting sail for a new life. Their news had kept her awake until dawn, worrying about how to sort out Brooklyn. She was angry at first, feeling dumped with the responsibility of it all, but she was a grown-up now, not a child. Time to face up to her duties.

Reluctantly she had discussed it over drinks at The Vicarage with their local solicitor, Barney Andrews, an earnest young man in tweeds, smoking a pipe, who listened intently and suggested they met in his offices over the Yorkshire Penny Bank to discuss it further in the New Year.

Maddy was in no mood for details. She wanted to shove it all to the back of her head, for her problems to just disappear. There was only one quick, easy solution and that was to sell the property.

'There's a big demand for gentleman's residences and Brooklyn's just the right size. Or we could sell it as a going concern, as a potential hotel or guesthouse. The Old Vic is ripe for development too. The market is buoyant after years of austerity and gloom. You're a very lucky girl!'

She'd flashed her steely eyes at him. He was not a year or two older than her. 'Thank you, young man,' she replied.

He'd blushed at the rebuke. 'You don't want to sell, do you?'

'Not if I can help it, but I'm not a hotelier and I can't live there like Lady Muck on my own. It'll have to earn its keep.' There had to be a way, but Barney hadn't come up with anything sensible.

It was market day in Sowerthwaite and the stalls filled the High Street, selling ironmongery, leather bags, fresh fish, toffees, nighties flapping from poles, fent bolts of cotton and woollen cloth, a watch repairer, fresh vegetables and fruit, shoppers gathering down the aisles, meeting up in cafés for hot tea and gossip. There was a bustle of sheep on their way to the pens, drovers bringing cattle for auction and farmers' wives setting up booths to sell their butter and cheese. Maddy bought a copy of the local *Gazette* and the *Manchester Guardian* and retired to Polly's Kettle Tearoom to read them in peace.

The *Gazette* was full of all the Christmas celebrations and New Year revels, country farming prices, balls, and grumbles about the upkeep of highways and gaslights flickering in the street.

In contrast, the *Guardian* was full of accounts of refugees pouring into the country from Europe with harrowing tales of escape. They were filling the displaced persons camps. Tidworth and Cannock, old prisoner-of-war camps, were turned over to hundreds of refugees who had nowhere to stay. The faces of women, looking exhausted and drawn, and holding terrified children, peered at her out of the paper. Here, they were all full of Christmas cheer, cosy, safe, warm in this Yorkshire pocket of peace and tranquillity. It wasn't right.

Maddy walked the long way home through the narrow alleyways, skirting the high stone walls until she found the gates to the Old Vic. There was the familiar figure of the beech tree, its arms outstretched, beckoning as it had done so many times when she was a kid.

She scrambled up the fraying rope ladder with care and plonked herself down on the boards of the tree house; her thinking house, she'd called it. It was one of those crisp winter mornings when the light was clear and chilly. The sky was blue and the smell of coal fires and wood smoke drifted from the houses nearby, the washing lines limp as there was no wind. The air was crisp on her cheeks.

Down the stone steps lay the Old Vic, empty, shuttered, damp and deserted. Once it had thronged with noisy kids, rows of smalls hanging on the line, Enid hanging out of the window, having a tantrum, and Plum gathering them up in a crocodile line as they walked reluctantly to Sunday school or to see the welfare nurse. Was it is a whole lifetime ago that it welcomed in refugees of war and terror and despair?

Then it came to her in a flash, and she grinned and clambered down from the tree house. She ran back down to the marketplace, to Barney's office, to a secretary who looked up startled at her flushed cheeks.

'Can I see him? Has he got another client in?'

'No, it's time for his coffee and biscuits,' the secretary said, plonking a tray on the desk.

'Give them to me, Miss Bird. I'll take it in,' Maddy offered, pushing her way through the door.

'Barney! It's Maddy Belfield, and I've had a wonderful idea!'

'Darling, you're not serious! You can't possibly take on all those people, these strangers, who don't speak English?'

Plum had never seen Maddy so excited, bursting with plans to turn the empty Old Vic into a hostel for Hungarian refugees.

'You will need planning permission. It's a crazy idea.'

'No, it's not. The camps are bursting at the seams. There's a local appeal going in Yorkshire. I've been on to them. If the Vic was good enough for evacuee children, it'll do for adults with families, and there's the Brooklyn too.'

'Oh, no! Maddy, think about it. What does Barney say?'

'He does what he's told. It's my money, and my contribution. There will be grants and expenses. It's about time Sowerthwaite woke up to what's happening in the world.'

'You'll need to be careful. There's bound to be a protest in the High Street. Neighbours don't like off-comers, strangers on their doorsteps. They don't understand,' Plum tried to argue, but it was no use.

'Oh, stuff the neighbours! It can't be any worse than when the vaccies came to town. People have heard the news and the Churches will give a hand.' Maddy gave her one of those hard stubborn Belfield glares. There was no shifting her.

'I hope you know what you're taking on.'

'You sound just like Grandma Pleasance. I bet she gave you a hard time when you took us all on?'

'She did!' Plum laughed. 'I must be getting old, as I can only see all the dangers. How appalling of me.'

'You have to admit it's a great idea.'

'It's a wonderful, kind, and a generous act, and I'm proud of you . . . Where's the buckets then? I suppose you want me to scrub the floor before I leave?'

'Now you're talking! The Vim is in the cupboard. It's going to be a busy afternoon.'

Plum felt proud of Maddy, seeing her so focused, her chin stuck out against all authorities. How she reminded her of her own battle to use the Old Vic all those years ago. Now she could pack with less of a heavy heart, knowing Maddy was occupied with a new challenge, eating like a horse and full of plans. If only she had someone to share it with. Perhaps in time Barney would be her consort. She pictured them going down the aisle and then she paused. Perhaps not . . .

'I hope you realise just what you're taking on, Miss Belfield, in offering your property for a hostel. Most of them don't speak any English. There won't be much work for them in the district. It's not good for them to live off charity,' said the billeting officer from the council, who sat across the mahogany desk, examining Maddy's application with a sniff.

'I've made enquiries. There's plenty of summer farm work and domestic work. There's the paper mill, and cotton and woollen mills close by. I'm sure we can find them all work,' she replied, waving her own list of arguments towards him.

'These are educated young people, not manual workers on the whole, but students and professionals with children. They've had a rough time and many thought they were going to America, not Britain. Have you thought about that?'

'Yes, I am aware of all this, Mr Potter, but we have a tradition of taking in people at the Brooklyn. My aunt, as you may recall, kept evacuees in the Old Vic for the duration of the war. I myself know what it's like to lose my family and home and be uprooted.' She gave him the famous Belfield intense glare.

'Yes, yes, of course, Miss Belfield. Your aunt gave us sterling service. It is a pity she's not available to chaperone this venture, though,' he countered.

'Why should I need a chaperone? I do have some staff of my own. The vicar will vouch for my respectability.'

'Oh, I didn't mean to suggest . . . but you are very young to take this upon yourself.' Mr Potter flushed, looking at the floor, not at her.

'Look, do you want this offer of accomodation or not?' Maddy snapped, having no patience with ditherers.

'If there are no local objections, I'm sure we will be able to come to an arrangement.'

'When?'

'We mustn't rush these matters, Miss Belfield.'

'Tell that to the poor sods who are camped in Butlin's like POWs!' she replied, sensing old Potter could be worn down by her persistence.

In the months that followed Plum's departure, Maddy had no time to bemoan her decision, but wondered what she'd let herself in for. There was the place to clean out, decorate, and rooms to furnish with cots and beds, which she begged and borrowed from sympathetic parishioners. There was the kitchen to service, the wash house and the copper boiler to set up, the stove to decoking. It was all very shabby, but once the fires were lit the rooms were homely enough.

The first Hungarian couple who came were Ernst and Elisabetta, with a small boy, Ferenc, who had such wonderful golden curls that he stopped the traffic on market day. Then there were Elsa and Anna, young sisters who crossed the border with just the clothes they stood up in.

The local authority insisted that they must be found work in mills, factories or domestic service. Every room was filled, and the attic bedrooms bursting with smoke and the chatter of Hungarian late into the night.

Soon, the Brooklyn piano was used to practice by a music student called Zoltan and his girlfriend, Maria, who sang haunting folk songs that made everyone cry. A man from Skipton came up to teach English and the young children were signed in to school, just like the evacuees had been. There were problems, fights, misunderstandings, complaints, but they soon settled down. Every time there was a theft in town the police were called to the Old Vic as routine, but by the summer of 1957 the Hungarians were no longer a novelty around the town.

Maddy had learned to be patient, polite and political

to get what she needed for her refugees, any way she could. She wrote to Raoul Henry, begging for support, and he sent bales of materials so that her girls were the best dressed in town and sold skirts and dresses to raise funds.

Some stayed only a week or so, but others stayed for months. Some were so shocked and silent and sullen that she thought she'd never get through the barrier that was round them like a bell jar.

Working in the old kitchen garden provided an interest. They tried to grow strange crops of peppers and vegetables, for variety and to remind them of home, which flummoxed Mr Hill, who was supervising their efforts. It gave some of the young men a purpose to their days, whilst others took to walking the hills in groups. Some got drunk in the pubs and made a nuisance of themselves, others soon latched on to local girls and started courting, but there was one girl who never mixed with the others and who seemed to go through the motions of living. She snapped at the girls in the kitchen and they left her alone. No one could get through to her, her English was poor, and her silence off-putting.

Maddy took her to the Brooklyn and away from the chatter of the Old Vic, sensing she needed to be away from the incessant company of the other refugees. On her first visit she stared at the house in disbelief.

'This is for you?'

Maddy nodded, ushering her through the door. Ava walked around each room, examining the paintings, the books, the photographs, shaking her head. 'It is not all for you?'

'And you and my friends.'

The girl went to her room and stayed there until the next morning. It was not going to be easy. Maddy knocked on the door in her jodhpurs and old jumper, encouraging Ava into the kitchen to eat. The girl followed her to the stables, fearful at first until she saw old Monty, his head half out of the door, eager to get some exercise.

Ava watched as Maddy saddled up and followed her out onto the hill track at a distance. Later, she watched how Monty was groomed and the next day she helped muck out and groom him and finally she smiled. Ava had found a friend.

There was something between the old horse and the girl that touched Maddy, a kinship and empathy she'd never seen before. Ava kept herself to herself, but with Monty she jabbered away, telling him all her secrets. Maddy was happy to leave him to melt the ice around the girl's heart.

There were a few refugees she was glad to see the back of – the ones who sneered at Brooklyn Hall as bourgeois and extravagant, but who wolfed down everything on offer without even a thank you.

The *Gazette* came and did a short article on the new occupant of Brooklyn Hall, and the *Yorkshire Post* picked up the idea and ran a feature on Madeleine, the ex-mannequin who single-handedly restored the hostel. It was all exaggerated nonsense and she hardly dared put her head over the doorstep, being a five-minute celebrity. But she received letters of congratulations with cheques enclosed and encouragement, as well as terrible condemnation and hateful abuse.

One fateful morning she went into the stable and found Monty in a terrible state, fitting, sweating and in need of emergency treatment. Anxiously she and Ava sat trying to calm the stricken beast, listening for the vet's wagon on the gravel.

When he came there was nothing he could do. Monty was suffering. He shook his head, ordered them out and shot the horse.

It was all so quick, so sudden, so unexpected. Maddy stood shivering but it was Ava who was inconsolable, shaking, screaming, running into the stable. 'No! No! You . . . No!' She threw herself at the startled vet in fury.

But Maddy couldn't console her or understand. In desperation she called in Zoltan, who could interpret her words. He sat with Ava, trying to translate why she was so distraught.

'She was in Budapest,' he said. 'The soldiers take her husband and shot him against the wall. Just like that . . . into the head, no mercy, no justice. Bang and he is gone.'

'Oh, no!' Maddy sat holding Ava, who was weeping and gesticulating wildly, Zoltan trying to keep up with her.

'She take baby and run away with other students down to the safe border. They walk many miles and her milk go but she find powder, but then baby is sick. There is no doctor and she carried him across into Austria in the woollen shawl but baby didn't move. It was sick.' He paused looking up at her, crying.

'I was there. I saw too. There was a little one wrapped in blue woollen shawl. We passed it down the line, one by one with the message he must be buried on Hungarian soil, like his father. But she not know where he is buried . . .'

Maddy cried. There were no words to offer comfort. She too had a baby who died that had no known grave. Where was little Dieter?

'I'm so sorry,' was all she could say. 'Tell Ava I too have suffered, but not like that.'

They had all suffered loss because of the war but now this. 'Thanks for translating, Zoltan. Monty was my friend but he'd had a good life. Poor Ava's husband never got that chance. Perhaps one day I can teach Ava to ride another horse, but not yet.'

Ava looked up, calmer, and held out her hand. The glass bell jar was shattered; Monty had seen to that. Now Ava could start living again, but this tragedy and loss stirred up all Maddy's own unexpressed guilt and grief again. She must find out about her own little baby. This mystery had gone on too long. Only when she heard the truth from Gloria would she ever start to live again.

21

Gloria was sitting at a breakfast bar trying to think up a present for Greg, when she saw the article in the *Yorkshire Post*.

'Look at this! You read it . . . Maddy's got herself in the news. She's opened up the Old Vic for refugees . . . look,' she said.

Greg was shoving toast in his mouth, whilst searching for his car keys. 'No time,' he said. 'Can't stop . . . must dash. I'll be late tonight. We've got a new site to view . . . Bye, Bebe!' He pecked his little daughter on the cheek and rushed out of the back door into the double garage.

Gloria slammed down the morning paper with a sigh. Once she'd taken Bebe to school, that would be her whole day until hometime. She looked around her kitchen with satisfaction. It had fitted cupboards and Formica surfaces, Marley tiles on the floor and a built-in washing machine, a pantry stocked with tins of meat, fruit and salmon. It was like something out of *Ideal Home*.

'Come on, Bebe,' she called to the little girl with a

mop of red curls, sitting in her expensive green school uniform. 'Where's your panama hat?' It was lovely to see the child looking so smart.

'I've got a tummy ache, Mummy. Do I have to go to school?'

'Again? Have you been to the toilet?' Gloria ignored Bebe's usual morning complaints. 'Hurry up!'

Gloria was the only wife in Sunnyside Drive to have her own car, a Triumph Herald with an open top, and a double garage. They had the corner plot with an acre of garden, an ornamental pond with a heron statue, a big swing and slide for Bebe, and a huge rockery in the front garden that Mr Taylor, the gardener, kept up to scratch.

Gloria grabbed her pink duster coat and straw hat as she might nip into Harrogate and do a recce round the shops, have lunch in Betty's and spin out the day until it was time to pick up Bebe again.

'Do I have another name?' asked Bebe in the car. It was strange seeing her own green eyes staring back at her.

'No, just Bebe. Why?'

'Belinda says it's a silly name, Bebe Byrne. Haven't I got another name?'

Gloria shook her head. Greg had wanted her to be Beatrice Prunella, and make Mrs Belfield her godmother for old-times' sake, but Gloria soon knocked that one on the head. Bebe was so feminine – short and different, to her thinking. It made Bebe stand out too. 'You tell Belinda Pike you're named after the famous actress Bebe Daniels. There's no one else in Yorkshire with your name.'

'Why couldn't I have been Susan or Carol?'

'Susans are two a penny, but you're special.' That seemed to shut her up. Bebe was so full of questions and into everything. She'd been a sickly baby and difficult to feed. Greg had wanted to try for a boy later but Gloria said she was never going through that agony again. She'd got herself fitted with a Dutch cap and made sure it was in on the few times they did make love.

As she sat in a café sipping coffee, she stared around at all the other well-heeled ladies in hats chattering to their friends. Why hadn't she got any chums like that? The mums at school were stand-offish, a posh bunch who kept together and ignored her. The girls in Sunnyside Drive were older and stick-in-the-muds: they were all into the WI, church and coffee mornings that she never got invited to.

Somehow she didn't fit in. Perhaps it was her expensive carpets and curtains, and modern G Plan teak sideboard and room dividers, table and chairs and velvet sofa, or the fact that she didn't do church or have family to visit. Greg was always off at weekends rallying. There was ballet class for Bebe and the occasional birthday party but not much of a social life. The Afton family gatherings didn't count. There was no smoking or drinking at their dos. A little part-time job might have been good, but Greg wouldn't hear of it.

'No wife of mine need go out to work. Bebe needs you to be around for her.'

The one chink in his tough armour was Bebe. Sometimes she felt as if their child was the only sun in his sky. Every time he went away he brought her back expensive dolls and clothes.

Now she was at school all Gloria's days were the same, at the weekend the routine was the same, and holidays were spent in hotels in Bournemouth, or else she took Bebe to stay near the farm where Sid was working in the Dales. She drove many miles out of her way to avoid Sowerthwaite, just in case she bumped into Maddy and her cronies. Sid was always glad to see them both but they lived in different worlds now.

They dutifully sent cards to Plum, and to old Mrs Batty at the Brooklyn. Fancy Mrs Plum going off to New Zealand. Maddy was now queen bee there. Sunnyside Drive was no match for Brooklyn Hall and Gloria was still jealous of her old friend, and had followed her career, perturbed why she should given it up to return north.

Gloria couldn't forget that look on Greg's face when she'd seen them in that café in London, all aglow with excitement. Once they'd got home he was on the phone every hour, working late, restless, checking his sites as if she hardly existed.

It wasn't as if they weren't content together. He made a great fuss of Bebe, but he was hardly at home, too busy making money. If only he'd spend more time with them. He was talking of them moving up again to a Victorian villa in town, one of the huge ones off the Ripon Road. 'It'll be closer to the shops,' he laughed. He seemed to think money was all she was after, but all she wanted now was his attention

They'd got every gadget you could wish for and yet

Gloria was fed up, dissatisfied, empty, and she didn't know why. Her days were always the same in a life of leisure her mam could have only dreamed of. They'd lost touch with each other years ago. She wanted no reminders of Marge Conley's life. No friends, no family, no job, Gloria had nothing to do but housework, and she had Mrs Handley to do that.

If only Greg would share things with her, take her with him on trips, surprise her once in a while, but he spent most of his spare time with his mechanic under that blessed rally car, tinkering until all hours while she sat in watching television: *Coronation Street. Emergency Ward 10*, *What's My Line*: anything to while away the evenings.

All her dreams were coming true. They'd never had it so good, and yet . . .

Gloria was lonely at times, bored and disappointed, and she'd still got to think of something for Greg's birthday. As she had headed towards the car park in town, she noticed a new photographic studio, The Yorkshire Portrait Gallery. There were some pretty shots of girls in party dresses with sashes, smiling from gilded frames, hand-tinted to show off the colours, and it gave her an idea.

She darted to the reception desk and made an appointment for one Saturday morning. This would be a surprise for Greg's birthday, gilt framed like a portrait to hang on the wall. But first Bebe would need something pretty to wear. She dashed back to Marshall and Snelgrove, snatching a selection of party dresses on approval so they could try things on in secret. She'd have her own hair set, a new dress and make-up on, and Greg would be delighted with such a novel present.

'I can't be thirty,' Greg sighed out loud. 'Where's the time gone? Making all this happen, he thought, staring at the forecourt where his beautiful red Jaguar sat in the sunshine. On the coat rack hung his Crombie overcoat, as the weather was still chilly. His oak desk, cluttered with bills and diaries, was solid and antique, and in a silver frame was a photo of Bebe as a baby.

He could still recall the thrill of holding her in his arms for the first time, red-faced, with a fluff of ginger hair. She flickered her eyes at him and he was lost, besotted, her slave. Every working hour was worth it just for her arms round him when he came home at night.

He'd snatched a glimpse of that article about Maddy in the *Post* when Gloria wasn't looking and had cut it out. It was locked in his desk drawer. Then memories of birthdays in the Old Vic came flooding back: up the tree, throwing balloons, and those wonderful parcels of stuff from America, with all those comics.

He was glad the hostel was still being used. Trust her to think up a scheme. He'd sent some cash to the Hungarian relief appeal straight away.

Sometimes he lingered late in the office, putting off the moment when he must leave for Sunnyside Drive and Gloria, who would be made up to the nines, waiting eagerly to dish up supper, all airs and graces. Poor girl, she spent money like there was no tomorrow on contemporary wallpaper, rugs, fancy standard lamps, and then she'd spoil the effect by putting wax flowers in the window when they'd got a garden full of plants.

He'd suggested she go to flower-arranging classes, but was given one of those pained looks he knew so well and changed the subject.

Was this it? Was this all there was to marriage: a gleaming house, a pretty child, net curtains, and sex on Saturday night if he was lucky? What could have happened to make life so predictable?

Sometimes he felt as if he'd been trapped by his own ambition and drive. He wanted a wife and family to care for, but when he turned into the driveway his heart sank with dismay. That was unfair of him; to be disloyal to Gloria who'd never done him any harm.

He knew when he married her he'd get a simple girl from a rough background, thrown on a train by a selfish mother. She'd pulled herself up by the ankle straps, made a cosy home, dressed smartly. There was nothing about her he didn't know. He'd rescued her when she was down and she'd been so loving to him.

They rushed into marriage too quickly, and Bebe was a honeymoon baby. Gloria had had a terrible delivery, the doctor said. If only there was a little lad to hand on the business to somehow. He didn't see Bebe as a managing director. Nothing was turning out as he planned.

It was late and dark, the last of the guys had left the storerooms. But someone had forgotten to put the light out in their cubbyhole, the makeshift den that smelled of sawdust, axle grease and Swarfega, dirty towels and manly sweat from oily dungarees. It was not a place he went to, unless invited. There were pint mugs of tea with rims of stale milk waiting to be washed, newspapers and girly mags; the usual male clutter.

On the wall was one of those calendars that came in brown paper envelopes, by courtesy of tyre companies, exhaust fitters and car accessory companies.

What was it this time? he smiled. The calendar was years old. Wasn't it bad luck to have one of those up on the wall, or was it bad luck to open next year's too early? He flicked over the pages, glancing through the pictures of the poor cows posing, arms aloft, bums and tits on show. Nothing was left to the imagination.

Imagine having to do that for a living, he thought, but he thumbed through it just the same. Some of the poses were a bit close to indecency – Miss May . . . Miss June . . . and then his eyes stuck to Miss October. There were a few dried leaves covering her complete nakedness, but her ginger pubes and glorious red hair were decorated with berries.

Greg's heart was thumping at the picture before him. It just couldn't be . . . Gloria must have a double, but that sexy, knowing look he recognised so well . . . His wife's face was staring up at him. It made him want to throw up. How could she have done this? It couldn't be his Gloria, it just couldn't. He tore the calendar off the wall, rammed it into his briefcase and headed for home via the Black Horse.

Bebe was staying up late to give her daddy the present. She was so excited and kept dashing to the window to see if the car was coming. Gloria kept looking at the clock, having made his favourite roast with all the trimmings, bought a fancy Victoria sponge cream cake, especially iced, and put candles on it. The parcel was wrapped in fancy paper, and the bird was getting dry in the oven.

Come on, come on, she thought, what's keeping you? Had he had an accident? But someone would have telephoned. It was not like Greg to be late for his own birthday party. It was a school day and Bebe would have to go to bed soon. Then she heard the roar of his Jaguar, and Bebe jumped on the sofa.

'He's here! Shall I hide?'

'Behind the sofa, quick, or he'll see!' laughed Gloria, relieved that the dinner was still salvageable.

She rushed to the door to greet him. The whisky fumes hit her as soon as it was opened.

'Happy Birthday, Greg! You're late; you know what day it is?'

'Of course I bloody do! Thirty years into my life sentence,' he snapped.

'Don't be like that . . . What's up? You're not that old,' she replied, trying to reassure him.

He brushed past and stomped into the kitchen in a strop.

'We've got the party all ready. Bebe's been helping me,' she added, seeing thunder on the horizon. What had gone wrong at work now?

'I hope she's in bed, that's all I can say.'

'No, she is . . . what is it? What's got into you?'

'This is what's got into me!' he yelled, producing the calendar, a grubby motor tyre annual calendar.

'Look at Miss October. Do you recognise anyone?' He shoved it into her face, dropping it on the floor, open. 'You cow, you deceitful cow.'

'Stop this . . . I don't understand.' Then she saw her face staring out from the floor, her body bedecked with leaves, and began to shake.

'It is you, isn't it?'

What could she say? 'I can explain it . . . It was a long time ago,' she whispered.

'I can see that. You must have been barely out of school, and it was hanging in the lads' den for anyone to see. The boss's wife naked for all to see like a tuppenny tart!'

'Greg, please, shush!' Gloria pointed to the sofa through the dividing doors.

'I'll not shut up. You made a right fool of me. I thought you were different from all the others. All that innocence was window dressing. This is Ken's work, isn't it? How many more are there floating around?'

'I don't know! Oh, please, Bebe will hear. She's listening.'

'No excuses. Better she knows what sort of mother she has. You're as bad as Marge. Blood will out. They always say redheads are hot for it!'

'Gregory, please, calm down. I was desperate. I thought I was doing catalogue work. I was young and silly, and Ken Silverstone persuaded me to do things for fun and then he started to blackmail me and I was scared. I did what he told me. That's why I left him. Please believe me, it's the truth.' She saw the look of hatred in his face and cowered from him.

'Get out of my sight! You wouldn't know the truth if it jumped up and bit you on the nose. Leave me alone!'

'Daddy?' Bebe poked her head up from behind the sofa. 'Happy Birthday. We bought you a present. Come and open it. It's a surprise.' The child looked at him, puzzled. 'Why are you so cross?'

'I don't feel like a birthday tonight, poppet. Perhaps tomorrow.'

'But I made this card all by myself. Daddy, don't be angry with Mummy. We want you to see our present.' Bebe took his hand and dragged him to the parcel.

Gloria quickly stepped in to hide it. 'Let Daddy wait until he feels better. We'll save it for another day, Bebe. Time to go to bed now, come on.' She had to avoid any more rows while the child was in the room.

'But you said I could stay up and I want Daddy to have his birthday.' Bebe was stamping her feet in a paddy of frustration.

'Oh, let me open the damn thing then!' Greg snarled, tearing at the paper.

'Now's not the right moment. Let's leave it, Greg,' Gloria pleaded but it was too late. He opened the cardboard to reveal the staged, posed portrait of Bebe and Gloria in all their finery, smiling in a gilded frame. Madonna and child it was not.

For a moment there was silence, and she hoped he'd be pleased, but Greg stared at it, and then with one roar of fury he put his fist right through the glass. 'Take it away!'

Bebe was howling but Gloria was strangely calm.

'Daddy's not well. He's upset. He didn't mean to frighten you, love. Better go upstairs now, up the wooden hill to dreamland.'

In one act of defiance she turned on her husband. 'How could you? That was so childish,' she said, but there was no response. He was too busy looking for something to wrap round his hand.

Bebe was distraught at the sight of blood.

'You can sleep in my bed tonight as a treat. Daddy will go in the spare room,' Gloria ordered.

Greg was not going to sleep in their bed tonight, not stinking of whisky and with his bloodied knuckles.

When she came downstairs to face his fury she heard the roar of the engine and the front door was open. It was a relief to know he'd gone to cool off. Tomorrow she would try to explain again and then he'd see things in a different light.

Greg sped down the drive. It was late and he was drunk, heading onto the moor road. It was a clear starlit night with frost listening on the tarmac. He wanted to drive into the hills and forget those images forged into his brain. He wanted to burn the engine until she smoked. He wanted to punish the metal, to test his own strength and stamina.

Speed and timing, the perfect harmony of mind and body and machine, this was the holy trinity of rallying. Not tonight, though. Now he just wanted to race into the wind and forget all the mess down there, lose himself in the pure act of driving this beauty. Faster and faster, he drove through the night as if in a trance.

This was the only way to release his fury, by taking it out on the metal, burning through the white-hot rage he was feeling.

He thought he was a man on top of the job but everything was built on shifting sand. How could he have been such a dunce? Gloria was never his princess, but now he knew her for little more than a common tart and in his rage he hated her for making a fool of him. He would not let her antics disturb his concentration. It was as if for the first time in years there was just him and speed. He smiled, thinking of his go-karts, jumping from that railway bridge, tearing around on a motor bike during the war. He was at his happiest when attached to wheels, not women. Wheels may puncture but they could be mended. The heart was not so easily repaired. Why were women so faithless, so deceitful? First Maddy, and now Gloria. Drive on . . . Don't think about that now . . . Drive on!

Nothing compared to the simplicity of speed. Nothing could reach him here, just one man and the open road. It was perfect, the engine was powering and he could go on like this, forgetting all the night's terrible revelations.

Then he saw the deer leap over the stone wall into his path and there was nothing he could do but pray.

It was Grace Battersby who saw the notice in the *Yorkshire Post*. 'That's not our Greg, is it?' She pointed to the News in Brief. '"Farmer saves rally enthusiast hit by deer. The managing director of Byrne the Builders and rally driver, Gregory Byrne, 30, of

Sunnyside Drive, in serious accident on the Pateley Bridge Road late last night." He always was a devil for speed,' Grace added. 'Don't look too good does it, Maddy?'

Maddy couldn't concentrate for the rest of the day, wondering what hospital he was in or whether he was in fact still alive. Was Gloria with him? How her heart ached to go to him. If only Plum were here they could go together, but to go on her own was not appropriate. Every time she paused, his face would come into her mind. She rang his office and a worried secretary said they were operating but Maddy didn't leave her name just in case. Speed was his weakness. She thought of the story of how his friends had carried him back in the old pram when he jumped from the railway bridge and that was the reason he was sent to the Old Vic as an 'awkward evacuee'.

What was he doing racing round the hills in the middle of the night? They'd not seen each other for six years but she could recall every detail of that meeting in London.

As long as Greg was in this world, he'd always have a piece of her heart. He'd been her friend, no matter what Gloria thought, and friends needed friends when they were in trouble.

She penned a brief note to Gloria and asked if she and Grace might be permitted to visit him in hospital. The reply, when it came, was equally terse, just the address and ward number of the local hospital, and that it was too soon for visitors. There was no mention of his progress.

Maddy replied saying she'd be in Harrogate and intended to go to the hospital. On the day of her intended visit, she dressed with care, not as a former mannequin but as a country lady in a dogtooth-checked suit and Hèrmes scarf. Grace was too busy to be spared, but they'd known that all along. This visit would be combined with shopping for provisions for Brooklyn Hall and extra sheets from the linen shop in Harrogate.

Her heart was thumping as she drove the Morris Traveller estate over the Pennines across Blubberhouses to Harrogate and the hospital.

This was all new territory to Maddy, the outskirts of town was Gloria's area. She knew visiting hours were strict, so it was important to be on time. The thought of coming face to face again with Gloria made her nervous, on top of worrying about Greg. What if he was unconscious, paralysed or worse? What if he didn't want to see her?

Gloria was waiting in the hospital entrance, white-faced in a smart suit and hat, but her make-up couldn't disguise pinched cheeks. There was a hunted wary look on her face when she saw Maddy had come alone.

'How is he? I'm not too late?' Maddy asked. 'What happened?'

'He'll live – but it's going to be a slow job. He smashed his pelvis and his leg. He might have to lose it but I'm afraid he's not fit to see anyone yet. Only family, of course.' She didn't look at Maddy as she spoke. Not a good start, but Maddy ignored the comment.

'But I'm an old friend. It might cheer him up to see another face.'

'So, you know better than the doctors then, do you?' Gloria snapped.

'You must be so worried and so tired, how is the little one coping?' said Maddy. Time to try a different tack.

'She's with the Aftons and not allowed to visit. Rules is rules. Perhaps it's for the best. Bebe will only get upset when she sees him all plastered up.'

'Is there anything I can do to help? I'm going to the shops later.'

'Can't keep away from the shops?' There was a hard edge to Gloria's comment.

'Nothing like that. Just sheets for the hostel.'

'So you're Little Miss Plum now, ministering to the needy. We read it in the papers. Charity begins at home, I say. You look well on it. Filled out a bit since I last saw you . . .'

'Gloria! It's not like that at all – we're only trying to help. Plum sends her love, by the way. I rang to tell her and she will write to Greg once we have his address. How did it happen . . . you haven't said?' Maddy was determined to find out more. 'If I can't visit let's go and have a cup of tea, we need to talk,' she said.

Gloria pointed to her blue car, climbed into the Triumph. 'Follow me,' she ordered, and they drove out to a tearoom near Ripley, parking side by side.

Maddy knew that this was about as close as she was going to get to seeing Greg now, and her heart sank. All this way for nothing, but she would glean as much news as she could and write to him. Gloria couldn't stop a letter.

They sat down like two matrons, removing gloves, eyeing each other up like strangers.

'Well, what really happened?' Maddy said. It was time for talking straight.

'We had a bit of a tiff. He drove off and hit this deer, rolled over and got trapped. It was late but Greg was always the lucky one. Some farmer came past and saw the mess and they got him out and over here quickly. He saved his life, but I never thought Bambi would make so much mess. You know how he likes to drive like a man possessed. He told everyone he was practising for the RAC Rally, but that's not true.'

They circled around each other, eyeing each other up over the tea cups.

'If there's anything I can do . . . I only want to help.'

'Oh, I know your game. You still fancy him, don't you? I saw you at the Festival, all over him like a rash. Have you no pride?'

Maddy flushed. 'What I feel or felt is none of your business. You didn't hesitate to jump into my shoes, did you? You were the one keen for me to let him go. One guess why. Can't I even be a friend to Greg now? What harm is there in that?'

'I'm . . .' Gloria hesitated, '. . . just jealous. You have a part of him I can never share. We've not been getting on lately . . . it's my fault. I let him down. There, are you satisfied? There's the truth of it. You know how he is when he gets mad; he takes out on the road. I drove him to it. Greg's a strait-laced bloke, straight up and down, black or white. He sees things his way. He likes his women high on a pedestal like porcelain vases, unblemished, no cracks and faults. I did summat stupid, like you did . . . but with photos. Greg found a calendar with me on it and he went mad. I got given what I gave you. I know that now: what comes round goes round, Maddy. Now it's my turn. I made a right mess of everything but I'm going to make it right again and I don't want you interfering.'

They eyed each other as they sipped their hot tea.

'I saw his face – when we met you on honeymoon. It crumpled when you left. I've never had him properly – his body, yes, but not his head. You will always be Miss High and Mighty to him. No matter what I do I can't measure up, even though he thinks you chucked him. But there's little Bebe to think of now.' Gloria paused. 'Go on, say it.'

'Say what?' Maddy replied, seeing fear in Gloria's eyes.

'I only got what I deserved . . . after what I did to you. They were lies I told you, lies I made up. If I tell you everything will you leave us alone?'

'Tell me what?' Maddy leaned forward, not believing what she was hearing.

'Your baby was born dead . . . it never breathed. I panicked. I made it all up.'

There was a deafening silence as Maddy drank in her words.

'And you let me go on believing I'd . . . ? How could you? You blackmailed me, burdened me with the fear that I might have neglected the baby. How could you?

I thought you were my friend. Why, Gloria?' Maddy leaned over, wanting to punch her stupid face.

'It was the only way to get what I wanted. Hadn't you noticed I fancied the pants off him? When you brought him back I was so . . . jealous. You've got everything, Maddy Belfield, handed to you on a plate. I was young and I thought, all's fair in love and war. I'm just like my mam after all. She'd told us lies to get shut of us . . . threw us on that train. She taught me to look after number one. I thought if I got Greg it would make up for everything.'

'And did it?'

'For a while, but then he found the smutty pictures and the look on his face . . .'

Maddy was too shocked to be sympathetic to this confession. 'Have you any idea what you've done to all of us?' she yelled, banging her cup on the table. The tearoom audience was silenced by the drama at table four.

'Oh, yes, I have now. I've got everything and nothing. What'll I do?'

'Don't ask me. You stole him for yourself and now you expect my pity? How you must have hated me, even when we were little. All those years you waited to pay me back for being a Belfield. I lost everything, or have you forgotten: my parents, my home, everything. How dare you? I trusted you. You were my friend and I was so ashamed of letting the family down. You knew I'd let him go, didn't you? I couldn't risk public shame. I thought you were my friend and all the time . . . Oh Gloria, what have you done? Well, now you have a beautiful home and a child, everything you wanted, and you expect me to feel sorry for you?'

The whole room was agog but Maddy didn't care.

Gloria turned round, embarrassed. 'It's a house full of toys, not a home. Greg's never in it,' she whispered.

'That's not my problem,' said Maddy, trying to contain her fury. 'Sort it out as best you can. I have my own life to live. It's not the life I'd have chosen, but each day has its own rewards.'

'So you don't want him back, then? I thought you'd come to steal him away now he doesn't want me. You can come again and see him, if you like,' Gloria smiled, softening as if everything between them was all right again.

How childish the woman in front of her was, Maddy thought, this cheap stranger with her rouged cheeks and fancy earrings. How dare she suggest such a thing? It was hard not to walk out there and then. Maddy put on her gloves, making to go.

'Oh, grow up, Gloria. Let's get this straight. You're his family now and I'm a stranger who will visit only by appointment. Why should I want him now? We can't just turn the clock back and make everything hunkydory. At least you had the decency to tell me that I'm not a murderer!'

'Hang on! I never said you were a murderer!'

'You said I'd caused the baby's death. It's tantamount to the same thing.'

'No, never. I just suggested perhaps . . . I had to make you let him go. You did the right thing, as I knew you would. You Belfields are so proper. We've been happy enough, Greg, me and little Bebe.'

'Have you? Is that why he drove out and nearly killed himself?' Maddy rose, knocking over her chair, wanting to be far away from those foxy eyes. 'Tell Greg I was asking after him, and Plum will write to him, but I've heard enough!'

Every eye in the room was on them now. Gloria was blushing.

'Sit down . . . sit down. How am I going to nurse him? What if he never walks again? What will it do to his business?' Gloria was whining, her eyes wide with fear.

'That's your problem, not mine. Get off your backside and support him. That's what real partners do in hard times. Take a lesson from some of my refugees. You should see what some of them are doing to help each other out, and they have nothing but each other. He's your problem, not mine.'

'Don't be bitter, Maddy,' Gloria said, putting on her gloves.

'How dare you? You tricked me and now you have to live with what you've done and so have I. For better or worse, in sickness or in health, like Mrs Plum did all those years of putting up with Uncle Gerald's cheating. At least she's found Steve, and they're such a team. Without their support I couldn't have opened up the hostel again. Find your own way through, Gloria – you're a big girl now. Get your friends to rally round.'

'I haven't got any real friends, just a few neighbours.'

'You do surprise me.'

'You were my forever friend,' Gloria sighed.

'And look how you treated me,' Maddy sneered.

'I'm sorry . . .'

'It's a bit late for apologies from you. We can't go back, not ever. You told me I was the cause of my baby's death. Wires crossed or not, how can I forgive you for that? At least you can tell me what really happened that night. Isn't it time we squared this off once and for all?' She stood waiting for the reply. 'No more lies.'

'The baby was born in a rush. It was too little, like a bird thrown out of the nest, glassy and still. I wrapped it in a teatowel and hid it. I was meaning to tell you but you were sleepy and sick, and I was scared. I wasn't thinking straight.' Gloria rose up to face her.

'How do you live with yourself? All these years and here's me thinking such terrible thoughts. It's been like carrying a rock on my back, the fear that because I didn't want this baby, it didn't go to term . . . I threw it out of myself. That's what I really feared. That I might do it again if I had another child.' Maddy could barely contain herself.

'I'm sorry. I just put it to the back of my head like you did. We both pretended it never happened. I didn't know what real fear was like until Ken did the dirty on me and trapped me in a corner. It was a filthy place to be . . . now I know. I'm sorry.'

'Words are easy to say. It's what we do that shows the person we are. We both have to live with our mistakes as best we can. Being your friend was one of mine.'

'But I didn't mean to . . . don't you see?'

'Oh, don't kid yourself. You must have envied me so much to tell me those lies. You took away my trust, my confidence. You ruined my chance of happiness . . . I have to go, I can't listen to any more of this.' Maddy rushed for the door.

'Don't go! Don't you want to know what I did with the little one?'

Gloria chased after Maddy as she ran for the Morris, but Maddy didn't stop to listen. If she turned round she might have killed the stupid woman.

'Go away. Go back to Greg,' she yelled from the car window. 'He needs you. You need his forgiveness, not mine. He's all yours now!'

'But, Maddy, I have to tell you where I . . .'

Maddy was beyond hearing as she sped out of the car park, leaving Gloria shouting into the wind.

22

Maddy drove across the moors in a daze, numb with shock after hearing Gloria's confession. Although it had taken such a weight off her mind, there was so much to take in. It was all too much. All of her grown-up life was spent trying to prove that she must make amends for her mistakes, that she must be the best mannequin, the best carer and the best hostess. That her best friend had betrayed her in such a way was unbelievable. 'Smile and smile and be a villain' – that was Gloria, reeling her in on a hook of deceit and subtle lies. What a fool I've been, Maddy wept. Poor Greg never stood a chance against such wiles.

Yet Gloria's actions had set her free to live out the rest of her life without that constraint. She would always yearn for that tiny mite, born too soon. What if he'd lived? What would her life be now? Would Plum have supported her or would she have had to give her baby away – the baby she'd never know, the baby who never lived but who was so much a part of her life, even now?

Perhaps being cushioned by training and education

and income she might have brought him up alone. How many other young mothers were there today in the world who didn't have her advantages? What agonies they must go through.

Make no mistake, the miscarriage had given her another chance and freed her to make a new life. But that terrible day would never be forgotten. His birthday was always marked and next year little Dieter would have been ten.

Would they have coped with the disgrace that his birth would have brought on the family? How would she feel knowing that her baby was out there in the world, not knowing her, living with adopted parents?

Her secret was safe. No one stared after her when she passed, whispering, 'That one had a baby out of wedlock.' Being an unmarried mother was a stigma that lasted a lifetime in Sowerthwaite.

Maddy drove on towards Skipton, looking down towards the grey town. Nearly home, she sighed. When would she ever get Greg out of her mind? She prayed he'd make a safe recovery. But she wasn't going back there ever. That part of her life was over.

The hostel would be emptying soon. There wasn't enough work in the town and many of the refugees came for a few weeks' rest in the country and then moved on. What new use could it be put to now? It was a shame to leave it furnished and gathering dust. If only there was someone she could share all this with, someone who would understand and advise, but that person was living on the other side of the world. Maybe it was about time she told Aunt Plum the whole truth. Perhaps it might help if she wrote it all down?

There was a germ of an idea growing in her mind but it would take guts and a brass neck to make it happen. Plum was the only person in the world who would give her permission to make it a reality.

In the weeks following the accident, Gloria went about her routines like an automaton, cleaning the house from top to bottom regardless that she employed a cleaner, visiting Greg dutifully, taking Bebe to the pictures and out for treats; anything to get away from the confusion in her head.

Everything was churning up inside. She couldn't blot out those terrible images of her lying on that rug, opening her legs like a slut. How had she done these things? Why had she told such lies to Maddy? Who was this Gloria, this bitch, this whore? She didn't recognise herself any more.

At first she blamed Mam, poor feckless Marge, who fumbled through life chasing one fella after another. Gloria didn't even know if she was dead or alive, and she didn't care. What was wrong with them?

Mothers were supposed to nurse their kids through bad times and worry over them. They knew you from the day you were born and encouraged you to grow a kind heart. But Marge had taught her only to lie and deceive, abandon people only to pick them up when it suited her. Then she blamed the war for separating them into another world – a world so different from

Elijah Street – where she'd seen how the other half lived. Going to Leeds was hate at first sight.

In some ways she'd been an orphan like Greg all her life. Sid had found his way in the countryside and she'd pinned her hopes on Greg making her life easy and safe. Now, nothing was safe, with no husband and no friends. For the first time in her life she'd taken a hard look inside and didn't like what she saw. She must face the awful truth that it was payback time. The only person to blame in all this was her stupid insecure self. She had tried to bridge the social gulf between herself and Maddy. She had used Greg to further this end. Maddy had tried her hardest to be her true friend, as best she could.

She couldn't help being a Belfield, just as it wasn't Gloria's own fault that she was born to Marge Conley. The difference hadn't really mattered until she'd got it into her head to try to be Maddy. Wanting everything she had was pointless in the end. It had cost her her husband's respect and her only chum.

Maddy was right to feel betrayed. Now Gloria had lost that friendship for ever. She was alone and if Greg left her she'd have to find work, something that fitted in with Bebe. Surely it was not too late to build bridges with him, for Bebe's sake.

While he was an invalid perhaps she could help out in one of his other ventures, make herself useful. He could baby-sit when he was out of convalescence.

Greg was making slow progress. He'd been grateful for her visits but she never told him about Maddy's visit and collected his post at reception so she could check the handwriting. But nothing came. Even now she didn't trust them not to meet up again behind her back.

They'd not spoken of that row over the calendar since the accident. He'd apologised about the portrait and she'd had it reframed and put in his hospital room. Bebe sent him letters and drawings, and he followed the preparations for the RAC Rally in Hastings with great interest.

The Aftons were kind, and Gloria felt ashamed of all her meanness to them. Now she had to prove herself to everybody, stand on her own, show true grit and surprise them for once with her own enterprise.

She'd even gone so far as to try to trace Ken Silverstone. It took every bit of her courage to climb those studio steps in Bradford, but it was all shuttered.

The waitress in the pub next door looked her up and down when she made enquiries and said, 'I'd not go looking after him. You're throwing good money after bad, love. He did a stretch in gaol, I heard . . . Not seen him since. It's somebody else in there now; a tattoo artist.'

It was a relief to Gloria to know she wouldn't have to face him again. She felt such a rage inside. If she blamed her mother, she blamed Ken even more. He'd taken advantage of her silly pride, her gullibility and ignorance. Knitting catalogues, indeed! That devil had schmoozed her vanity and flattered her, making mincemeat of her with all his promises. He'd seen her weakness and used it for his own ends.

She'd fallen for the whole kit and caboodle. Nothing in life was without its price and, boy, was she paying for her stupidity. If she ever met him again, she'd kill him! In the films, wronged women like her bought guns and shot their lovers dead. Poor Ruth Ellis got hanged for shooting hers, but now Gloria understood how a woman could do that in rage. She'd seen that same fury in Maddy's eyes. What have I done? she asked herself. She felt sick.

Gloria didn't want anything else to do with that sort of life again. She wanted to give Greg a big surprise and show him she was going to stop taking their life for granted. When he got better she'd pull her weight and make amends. It mustn't be too late to save their marriage.

There was an advertisement in the *Yorkshire Post* that took her eye, for the opening of a brand-new night-club and dining club in Scarperton. Greg had shares in that investment. They were looking for a manageress of smart appearance, with catering experience. It would be good to get involved and keep an eye on the place for him. She could sit in on interviews so they got the right class of girl. This was a chance to show that Gloria Byrne could get something right for once, help him in his business. Things were looking up.

Greg sat among the clutter of toys and jigsaws, trying to find a comfortable position for his leg. Everything was healing, but slowly. He'd got crutches to hobble around on. No chance of any driving yet, since his concentration was shot and he felt like a useless cripple.

Gloria was being nice to him, feeding him proper meals, being attentive to his every need, but there was an invisible wall between them. They whispered over the parapet at each other, not wanting to stir things, like polite strangers. He was glad when Charlie visited, bringing news of his garages and the rally season, but Greg couldn't enthuse. He felt trapped by injury, by disability, and shamed that he was dependent to the point that his wrists were so weak sometimes he needed help to unbutton his flies. Everything was an effort, even though he was officially on the mend. He'd never race again, though. The muscles in his right leg were wasted beyond repair.

The days were long, trying to read business accounts. He got a driver to ride him round all his sites just to let them know he was still on top of the job, but his head ached and he got impatient.

At home there was nothing to live for except when Bebe came bounding in from school. He'd help her read, play ludo and jigsaws and spelling games. He felt like an old man. Then there were the pictures shooting into his eyes. He couldn't help them but when he looked up at Gloria, he saw only that naked calendar, and it wasn't fair. She was doing her best to make amends.

Much to his surprise she'd stepped in to take over the refurbishment of the Bamboo Club. It was not one of his better investments, being a little downmarket for his taste. They'd taken the top floor of an old warehouse and transformed it into a Hawaiian bar with a restaurant and fancy food. It was all very smart.

'You're not to go swanning around in a grass skirt,' he snapped at Gloria, as she busied herself around him.

'Don't be daft,' she smiled. 'I'll be wearing a cocktail dress, and we have a bar and a dancing area. It's all very sophisticated and you'll love it.'

'Sounds expensive. I'm not sure Scarperton can support something like that,' he replied, knowing they'd not been successful in property speculation there.

'Wait and see. It'll soon be the hot spot where businessmen take their clients. It's really exotic inside.'

'You don't have to do it,' he argued.

She didn't need to work. There was always a property to sell if his recovery slowed him down, but it was good to see her taking the initiative for once.

'Oh, yes I do, this is my chance to prove I'm not just a cracked ornament,' she offered, clearing away the tray on his lap with a sigh.

This is your chance to leave me, he thought meanly, a chance to find another rich sucker to sponge off. In his heart he sensed their marriage might be over. Everyone thought them the perfect couple but they had nothing in common, no shared interests, nothing but Bebe, and they kept up appearances for her sake alone.

Trapped indoors, he found himself looking out onto the garden with frustration. There were a few trees, a bare lawn, a clump of pampas grass, pleasant enough, but he found himself longing for grey stone walls, rough tracks, and most of all the hills. How he missed those Dales, the open roads, sheep grazing dotted like mushrooms over the green hills.

Here was a tame suburban landscape making him feel trapped like a budgie in a gilded cage. He thought of Sowerthwaite and Brooklyn Hall. Bebe would love to see all their childhood haunts. But the thought of Madeleine stopped him. He couldn't bear her to see the wreck of a man he'd become.

No use feeling sorry for himself when the accident was his own stupid fault. Be patient, he thought. Maybe it was time he put back what he had taken out of life. Lying in the hospital bed had made him notice those in there far worse off than him. All he ever worked for was more and more things. Was this the right example to set his daughter? Surely there was more to life than business?

Plum read Maddy's letter with amazement and disbelief, then slowly reread each section. It was like some film script.

Maddy had miscarried Dieter Schulte's baby when they'd not actually even had sex? Gloria had helped her deliver in the night . . . the night Pleasance died, then hidden the body? They'd fallen out – she didn't say why – oh yes, over Gregory. That made sense of so much at the Festival. Now Greg was injured, the Byrne marriage was in trouble . . . The hostel was closing but she had another brainwave.

What did they think of allowing it to be used for young unmarried mothers as a place of safety to prepare for motherhood and care for their babies?

Oh, Maddy! Do think carefully over this, Plum's heart cried out. You may have brave new ambitions but Sowerthwaite might not be ready for revolutionary ideas. There was bound to be opposition and protests, letters to the paper accusing them of encouraging immorality on their doorstep. Small minds were full of fear and suspicion.

If only I were nearer, Plum thought, but Steve's clinic was doing so well and this was such a beautiful country, and they were so happy together. All she could do would be to write letters and help with the funding.

Maddy might need to get some support from the local Church. If Plum wrote to Vera and Archie, and Audrey at the Mother's Union, or perhaps Steve wrote to the new doctor's practice . . . There would be all sorts of red tape over benefit books and maternity provision official inspections, but in principle it sounded a wonderful if bizarre enterprise. It could be a place where the girls could go with their babies in safety and seclusion and not be objects of ridicule and punishment.

To do it well, Maddy might have to use the Brooklyn, not the Old Vic. It was more private. How apt that would be now as a place of refuge. Maddy and her good causes: when was she ever going to find her own heart's desire and settle down?

There was no mention of any romance with Barney Andrews, the solicitor. He'd get a shock when she brought this scheme to his attention.

Plum wrote her reply with care.

'A word of caution, my darling. Think it all through and be prepared for trouble. Thank you for telling me all this: trusting me with all your troubles, using me like a rope to hang on to. I feel so honoured,' Plum wrote.

If any meaning could be made of the miseries of her own childlessness it was that she could now be a mother to her niece, the closest thing that Maddy would ever have since Dolly Belfield died. The poor girl had had to bear so much on her own. Surely it was time she found a little happiness for herself?

If the Bamboo Club wasn't quite the Cafe Royal, it was about as near as Scarperton would get to sophisticated nightlife. For a start the whole thing was on the top floor of a woollen mill warehouse on the wharf of the Leeds–Liverpool canal. It was in the centre of town, more back street than top end, but that didn't stop it being well patronised by the young ones out for a night on the town, for men's nights out, and commercial travellers on expense accounts, looking for some entertainment out of hours.

The black-tie rule soon faded, as did the Henry Fiske trio in favour of a jukebox, a visiting steel band and a jazz ensemble.

Phil Starkey, who managed it with his brother for the consortium, spared no expense with the décor but the entrance up the wooden stairs was still a bit cheap, covered as it was with visiting celebrity's photographs and film posters.

Charlie Afton drove Gloria to the club on the first night just to check it over for Greg. They'd made a fuss of him, giving him a special seat at the front for a cabaret singer, a girl called Marlene Mallon, who could belt out a song just like Alma Cogan.

They'd gone to town or a bit over the top on the Caribbean bar area, with high stools and a straw hut, lots of netting and shells, which were a devil to dust, but in the twilight of lamps and tables it all looked authentic – as authentic as Yorkshire could make it. Gloria kept tabs on all the details, making sure the hostesses took coats, set up drinks, found tables and generally looked decorative.

Sometimes they were open until dawn with a lock-in, and there was a taxi laid on to take the girls home. Sometimes when it was quiet they all had to help clean in the kitchen and pretend they were busy.

Greg was always asleep when Gloria let herself in, kicking off her high heels with relief and sponging off her make-up in the mirror. It was work of a sort, making sure the till receipts tallied. She was not at all convinced about the club's future and was concerned by the rickety stairs.

Television was killing trade. It wasn't like the old days, when pictures and dancing were the only entertainment. There were decent pubs in the town serving meals. Rock'n' roll was all the rage, not Victor Sylvester and Vera Lynn. Phil was talking of having speciality acts, conjurers, men-only nights, anything to bring the punters in.

The bar girls were younger than Gloria, single pretty things in tight skirts and frilly blouses. They looked on her as an older married woman and brought their troubles to Auntie Gloria as if she knew how to guide them.

'He's having a stripper in next Friday night,' whispered Betty as they were primping up tables. 'Some poor little scrubber from Bradford, poor cow – men-only night, but it'll be us as gets the bother when she's got them all worked up.'

Gloria felt a flush of concern at this news.

'Is it true?' she tackled Phil later. 'Stripping doesn't go with the Bamboo Club, does it?'

'We've got to liven things up and get more punters in,' he said.

'Why's everything shuttered up?' she asked, noticing that all the windows were boarded up.

'Keeps it all dark in the summer. I'm in charge here, you know,' he sniffed, sensing her disapproval.

'Have we had the safety brigade round lately?' she replied. She wanted to make it clear that she was not some slapper to be bossed about

'Soon . . . Don't worry, Mr Byrne's investment's safe. If we go bust, he can allus sell the mill on. We just need to move with the times, rock 'n' roll nights and bring the young ones in. It'll be a full house on Friday.'

'Don't worry, I'll be there, but it isn't quite what we imagined,' Gloria said, knowing if Greg knew there was a striptease she be in trouble. She didn't much like the smoky atmosphere or the heat, but she'd see it through a while longer until Greg was back on his feet again and running things. Then she'd jack it in.

Phil was cutting corners to make a profit. He was

only doing what others did when pushed. She'd have to stick it out and see how it went.

Greg was going out with Charlie, his first outing for weeks, so Bebe was sleeping at the Aftons'. It was good to see Greg smartened up, even if he was on crutches. Gloria pecked him on the cheek and headed off to the bright lights of Scarperton, dressed up as usual in her little black dress with the V-neck, and fishnet stockings and black courts. It was a warm dry night; they'd not had rain for weeks. There was a stiff breeze blowing as she drove across the hill into the town. It was not a night to be stuck indoors, but a job was a job.

Everything was normal – setting up the glasses, checking supplies, clearing away tab ends, menus at tables. They made snacks and easy-to-cook meals served with chips and beer and Coca-Cola, espresso coffees and spirits.

With the lights full on, Gloria noticed how shabby it all looked. How had she ever thought this was sophisticated? It was little more than an out-of-hours drinking den.

Then she saw the girl, a pinched little thing, heavily made up, dyed black hair wrapped in a scarf like a gypsy, not a bad figure. She looked continental: all bust and no bottom, with skinny legs, but so young. Not much more than sixteen or seventeen.

She trotted into the powder room with her gold-spangled costume over her arm but she was shivering.

'You OK?' Gloria asked, seeing her nervousness. 'You're the act tonight? You have done this before, haven't you?'

The girl nodded weakly. 'For my fella. It'll be all right.'

Trust Phil to get someone on the cheap, Gloria sighed to herself. 'But there's going to be a room full of rugger buggers baying for your blood if you don't do it right,' she added.

'I have to do it. It'll be right,' said the girl, popping a pill into her mouth. 'Got a bit of bellyache,' she smiled wanly.

That's all we need, a novice being led to the slaughter. Gloria didn't know why but she felt very protective of the kid. 'What's your name?'

'Joan, but I'm called Jules tonight. All spangles and jewels . . . get it? Can I change in here?'

The crowded bar was full of beefy rugger players, shouting and calling. It was not the usual crowd on a Friday night. They were all tanked up with beer before they arrived. There'd be brawling and scuffling.

Gloria followed the girl into the toilet, concerned. 'You've not come alone, have you?' she asked.

'Nah! Me fella brought me. He got me this gig, trained me up, and he'll be watching outside. If I do it right, there'll be more work and I need to work. I have a babby, one year old, she's with me mam. They don't know I'm doing this. They think I'm working down the pub. If they find out, Mam'll go spare.'

'You sure you want to do this?' Gloria persisted, sensing trouble. She'd be like a lamb to the slaughter if the kid got nervous and performed her act too quick.

'What's it got to do wi' you? There's nowt wrong with my body. I don't mind gawping punters. My fella will step in if they get cheeky.' Julie stared back at her with suspicion. 'Have you got a problem with it? It's none of your business so let me get sorted in my own time. Piss off!'

Gloria shrugged, leaving her to her fancy dress, opening the door with her shoulder into a sea of faces. It was just too smoky and fumy tonight, too noisy and too boisterous for her liking. When Julie made her entrance they'd go wild or boo her to death. Suddenly Gloria felt uneasy. There was a look on that kid's face. What had her fellow done to make her strip off against her will? This was no Gypsy Rose Lee in the making, no sophisticated burlesque act, but a sleazy, desperate attempt to please her man. What did that remind her of?

Then she saw him standing with Phil, leaning over the bar, and their eyes locked in recognition; as plump and self-satisfied as ever, his black hair slicked back. Ken Silverstone.

'Bloody hell! Gloria . . . fancy seeing you here, but then not so much of a surprise. Are you the second act? You're still a looker . . .' He assessed her up and down with relish.

'So little Jules in the back's your protégée, then? Why am I not surprised? Another little sucker fallen for your tricks,' she sneered. 'She's only a kid, Ken, but then you always did like 'em young and tasty and green as grass.'

'Now don't be bitter, love. We can't stay young for ever. You must be hard-pushed to be up at this time of night. What are you now, the barmaid?' He sniggered, but she wasn't having any of this

'Phil, this gentleman is troubling me,' she said, slapping an order on the bar. 'Will you take care of him or will I?'

'Shut up, you tart! I'm Jules's manager. I'll not take any cheek from this old scrubber. Why, I could tell you a thing or two about her that could make your pecker stand up and salute!' Ken laughed, seeing the look on her face.

'That's enough, sir. Mrs Byrne is one of the owners here,' said Phil, sensing trouble between them. Gloria's dander was up at the insult. She was shaking with fury, her flame-haired temper beyond control.

'We don't want your sort in this establishment,' she roared, grabbing the nearest tin tray and walloping Ken so hard he staggered back and knocked the table over. The kerosene lamp hit the dusty straw thatch, turning it quickly into flames.

It was all so quick. The soda siphon was useless against it, there was no time to quell the flames, and no one knew where the fire buckets were.

'Get everyone down the stairs and quick . . . Fire!' Phil tried to make his voice heard over the jazz band. 'Gloria, go and shut the bloody band up! We need water. Gloria, just snatch the mike. Do a drum roll, anything to get their attention!'

'Please vacate the building at once!' he shouted but only those round the bar took any notice.

Gloria made for the mike, but the drunks thought she was part of the act and shouted, 'Come on, lady . . . get them off!'

'Shurrup! There's a fire. Everyone out!' she shouted

until she was hoarse. 'It's all under control but go down the stairs . . . down the stairs in an orderly fashion. Don't rush. Has someone sent for the fire brigade?'

Phil was too busy trying to beat out the flames. The smoke was getting thicker, flames were licking up the walls and the smell was suffocating.

'Open the windows and let in some air!' someone cried, and Gloria felt her panic rising. The mill was an old brick building, tinder dry, and the fake paper flowers and netting were alight.

'I can't open the windows: they're all boarded up!' yelled Betty.

'Then get something to bash them with!'

Betty dashed for help.

The kitchen hand brought a cleaver and hacked at the window. The wood splintered and cracked. There was an opening out at last onto the old warehouse hoist and tackle that was hanging out like a flagpole over the canal.

The crowd were pushing down the stairs, held back by a funnel of smoke and darkness. Some poured bottles over their heads and tried to rush the flames; fifty people pushing and shoving, yelling, pushed back by fear, and the flames arching above their heads. Then Gloria remembered the kid getting changed in the lavatory behind the heavy door. She had to get Jules out of there in one piece . . .

Greg and Charlie were on their way to the Bamboo Club to give Gloria a surprise when they heard the clanging of fire engines in the street and smelled the smoke.

'What's going on? You go ahead, Charlie,' said Greg. 'See where it's at!'

They stopped a man covered in smoking clothes. 'Where's the fire, mate?'

'Bamboo Club's gone up in flames, down there!' he pointed, and Greg began to hobble, every inch of him hurting in the race to follow the fire engines.

There was a crowd gathered on the canal bank, looking up at the building.

'It's owd mill, afire from top to toe, by the looks of things!'

There were policemen running round, trying to find another entrance, but it was bricked up. The iron staircase didn't reach as far as the top storey. There was a furniture store on the first two floors and someone said, 'If yon stuff catches on . . .'

Greg was frantic. 'My wife's in there – can't we do something?' He tried to make for the entrance but Charlie held him back. 'The fire engines will get ladders. Don't you try to get up there. It's too steep. Let them do their job.'

'I'm going up.'

'Don't be daft. It's a fireball up the stairs. The draught will make it a deathtrap, but don't worry, look . . . there's some on the roof, look. The ladders'll bring them off.'

Greg looked up and saw the wharf hoist with the lads clinging on screaming, yelling edging over the end to drop themselves down into the canal. He counted six of them jumping into the murky water. There were others scrambling onto the roof, but slates gave way and the crowd screamed as a man fell down to the pavement. Someone rushed over and put her mac over his smashed body.

The firemen were struggling to get their turntable ladder to reach up high enough. It was all taking too long and bits of the roof were crumbling and cracking, but the hose pipes had arrived and were throwing canal water up as high as they could to get the blaze under control.

Greg was hoarse, screaming for Gloria, the billowing smoke was clouding everything, and they were being pushed back from the heat. All he could think about was Gloria trapped in that furnace. 'You've got to get them out!' He was willing her onto that hoist.

Charlie stood frozen, not knowing what to say. He gripped Greg's arm as he tried to get through the cordon. 'Let them do their job, Greg. Gloria's tough, she'll find a way.' All they could do was look up and pray.

'Come on, Jules, put the towel over your face,' panted Gloria, crawling on all fours 'and keep following me. It's not far. Come on, love, up to the door with the hoist. We can get out there but you've got to keep going.'

Jules was panicking, 'Don't leave me, don't go . . . What about my baby?'

'Don't talk, don't waste your breath, just crawl.' Gloria was pushing forward, surprised that some had curled up and gone to sleep on the floor. The fresher air in the toilet had filled the lungs with enough oxygen to keep going on. She'd wrapped soaked towels over their faces and clothes. Fire drill at St Felix's School had come in useful, for once. With the mask over their faces they might make it. She was not going to die in this inferno.

There was a pushing and shoving to get out, and she didn't want to think of what they must do when they got out the window. But they were going to get out of that building together, her and the poor kid in a sequined outfit, black-faced, tear-stained, half naked. There was no time to be prudish.

The roar of the flames grew, but there was a hiss of the water somewhere. It was smoke that was the killer, dense, choking stuff. This was the only way out.

Everyone was gathered by the window, bodies clinging to the hoist for dear life, too scared to budge or jump onto the blanket down below.

'You'll be all right, just go . . .'

'Let me through. Get them buggers off!' Ken Silverstone was shoving his way to the front but, strangely calm, Gloria stood her ground.

'Shut up! Ladies first. Let this kid go first!'

'Like hell! It's every man for himself. It was you as started this bloody fire.' He started pushing but a rugby player shoved him back into the darkness. 'You heard what the lady said. Wait your fucking turn!'

Gloria guided Julie out onto the hoist, gulping in the fresher air. She looked down with horror, trying to stay calm for the kid's sake. 'It's just a little jump into the canal.'

Jules was frozen with fear, looking down. 'I can't . . . I can't!'

'Yes, you can. Think about your baby. What's her name?'

'Lesley – Lesley Louise, and what's yourn?'

'I'm Gloria . . . Think about Lesley waking up and you've not been there. It's just a dip in the cut! Come on . . .'

'Why is that bitch holding us up? Get them off there,' Ken was choking. 'The smoke'll do us in. If she doesn't jump out, I'll shove them off myself. Get that bloody cow off the ledge . . .'

'Go to hell!' Gloria yelled back. 'Go back where you belong. We'll jump together, Jules . . . after three. Come on, you can do it for Lesley and my Bebe.' She paused. 'One, two . . . three.'

Greg saw two girls straddling the hoist. He hoped to God one of them was his wife. They were edging slowly like trapeze artists on the high wire, waiting for the ladder to reach them and grab them to safety. Then to his horror he saw them jump just as the old hoist cracked under the weight of the three men pushing behind them. There was a terrible scream from the crowd as they all tumbled into the air.

He saw them all diving feet first into the canal. Oh, Gloria, he prayed, hold on! 'Can someone help them?' he cried, but his limbs wouldn't move.

There was another splash and then another. Someone dived in to rescue them, hoping the water would have broken their fall. Greg clung to Charlie, full of relief and hope. The roar of the flames, the whirr of the fire engines, alarm bells clanging, screaming from the poor sods still trapped, drowned out his own desperate cries.

They were pushed back into the crowd so the ambulance men could deal with the burned and the injured. Greg searched the faces, blackened in tattered and torn party clothes. But there was no Gloria.

Then came the stretchers with blankets covering faces as more desperate revellers, jumped to their deaths and missed the canal, and still no sign of his wife.

'Come on, let's see if she jumped over there. It'll be fine,' said Charlie. 'Look, there's some on the canal bank.'

'I'm not budging until we find her. She's gone in the cut, she might drown.' Then they saw someone coughing and spluttering, and they rushed over with joy. 'Gloria, you made it!' But Greg looked down and saw it was the blackened face of a frightened girl in a sequined bathing costume shivering and coughing up.

'Where's Gloria? Where's my wife?'

The girl looked up at him, trying to fix her eyes to where the voice was coming from. 'Gloria saved my life. It were her what made me jump. Gloria, that's her . . .' Then the girl fainted.

He tugged at the sleeves of everyone who passed in desperation. 'Did you see my wife jumping? Gloria Byrne?'

'Down there, she jumped,' said someone, pointing to further down the tow path.

They were pumping out her lungs, her face soaked

with mud and slime. They were pumping, pumping in desperation.

'That's my wife!' Greg sobbed. 'Gloria, love, wake up.' He was on his knees now. 'We'll make a go of it, don't you worry. We're so proud of you. You just wake up for me.'

For a brief second her eyelids flickered and then she coughed and vomited. It was a good sign.

'Come on, love, it's Greg here, and Charlie's here. We'll take you home, you just wake up there. Squeeze my hand if you can hear me.' He knew she could hear him; her fingers were fluttering the response. Only then did he see the way her limbs were splayed out like a rag doll. She must have broken every bone in her body.

They put her in a side room next to the sister's office. Doctors pointed and prodded, cleaned her up, made her comfortable, but their faces said it all. There was never any hope. Greg sat with her night and day, willing her limbs to respond.

'I can't feel my legs, anything,' she whispered. Her lungs were full of smoke and they were giving her oxygen in a mask.

'Don't worry, the doctors can do marvellous things,' Greg replied, leaning over her. 'Look at me – how I bounced back all of a piece.' He was trying to cheer her up.

'I want to see Bebe . . . I don't care what they say, I have to see her. How's Jules?'

'Those flowers in the vase are from her family. You saved her life . . . the papers are full of it. Fame at last!'

Gloria closed her eyes and shook her head. 'How many died?'

'Nineteen, I'm afraid. Some got caught in the smoke – Phil and his brother. They found them curled up as if they were asleep, all together in a corner and not a mark on them.'

'Did Ken Silverstone make it then?' She hardly dare ask.

'I don't think so. What's he got to do with this?'

She saw the panic on his face. 'He brought that kid to do a striptease . . . little Jules. He tried to shove us off the edge. I wasn't having any of it. I kicked him back. He doesn't deserve to live. If he's gone then I'm glad.' Her voice was hardly audible, and it was a struggle to breathe.

'Don't waste your breath about him then. You've got so many cards and flowers. Your mam's on her way to see you . . . when you get better . . .'

'Don't talk soft. I can't breathe and there's such a pain in my chest. I can't move. I'm sorry. Oh, why do I always do the wrong things? I've let everybody down.'

She took some gulps and spoke again. 'Promise me you'll look after Bebe. I wouldn't have had the courage to jump without her. She's all that matters now . . . do tell her that, won't you?' She saw how Greg's eyes were full of tenderness and love.

'Don't tire yourself out. Stop fretting. Rest is what you need, and I'm so proud of you,' he whispered.

Why did she have to be on her last legs to have his undivided love? 'Shut up and listen. You've got to tell

Maddy something for me . . . It's important . . . just tell her "Under the Victory Tree". She'll know what that means . . . Under the Victory Tree . . . promise?'

It was good to get that off her mind before she got cosy again. It was funny how she kept drifting back to Sowerthwaite, kicking leaves, dancing down the Avenue. They'd been such happy times in their own way. What a pity she had to grow up and leave it all behind. The terrible stuff didn't matter any more; all those awful things that happened didn't make sense when she was in the middle of them, but now she understood when it was too late. But she'd done something good and saved a life. That sort of balanced it all out, she hoped . . . no matter.

She was tired, so tired and ready for a long, deep sleep. She hoped that Heaven would be like Saturday afternoons, dangling legs in the Victory Tree, sucking the biggest ice-cream cone money could buy and looking forward to going to the pictures with a friend.

Maddy read the account of the terrible fire at the Scarperton mill and the names of the victims with dismay.

'Naked striptease artiste saved by a manageress' was one of the more garish headlines. She wrote a careful letter of condolence to Greg and the child, but didn't attend the funeral. It would have been hypocritical to go when she'd been so livid with Gloria, but the anger was replaced now with such sadness.

Instead she took herself down to the Victory Tree

to post in a letter for old-times' sake. It was the only way she could think of to say goodbye.

I'm sorry you died in such a tragic way and I am glad you helped to save someone else's life. I don't understand you and never will. We could have been such great friends, and were for a while, but what I had and what you didn't got in the way somehow. We don't choose our family. I was blessed with love and support right from my first breath. You were not so lucky but you found it with Greg and let it go.

Wish I knew what you were thinking when you deceived me. When trust is gone friendship soon follows. I hope it troubled you but it's over and done now. You told me most of what I needed to know. You set me free.

I shall miss the fun and the mischief we had as kids. You always made things exciting fun. I was such a serious child. When things were very sad for me, you came to play and helped me forget. I shall miss your kindness when I had the eye operation, and you came to cheer me up. Why did it go so wrong?

I wish it all hadn't ended like this before we had a chance to understand each other. What matters is that you came so strong in the end. You could have saved your own skin, but you helped another mother on her way so while she and her child live, you'll never be forgotten.

For old-times' sake I'll post this into the tree as your forever friend. God keep you in his care now.

Love, Maddy

The tree would keep their secrets. Soon it would be shelter to other secrets, prams of babies watching the sky through its leaves, she hoped. More than ever now, Maddy was determined to make her plan come true. Plum had suggested the seclusion of the Brooklyn for the pregnant girls, but those who stayed on with their babies for a while would live in the town like normal mothers.

They formed a committee of worthies to support her application in secret. No one wanted to risk their public reputation in being seen to support immorality. Archie Murray, Barney Andrews and some of the women from the WI promised their support and went out on a limb to no avail.

'You're too young to hold the responsibility,' said the man from the council. 'We cannot approve anything official.'

'You need to be affiliated to one of the charities or a Church,' said another.

The Council for the Unmarried Mother and her Child suggested another way forward that bypassed all the red tape.

Why not open Brooklyn Hall and the Old Vic as private hostels, like guesthouses for special guests – convalescent guesthouses, open only to girls referred by doctors and almoners and probation officers? They would have to be run on a shoestring if there were no grants offered, but it just might work.

The Bamboo Club fire made Maddy inspect her properties for safety. They would need an iron staircase outside the hall. She may be young and inexperienced but she'd gather the wisest heads around her: welfare officers and midwives, clergymen, anyone in sympathy with her cause.

Barney Andrews had come on board with a useful suggestion to form a Board of Trustees. He was being extra attentive, but she ignored his mild flirtation. She'd no time for romance now. This was her cause, her baby, she thought wryly.

If life had taught her anything it was that she must make herself useful, leave her own stamp on all she'd been given, justify her existence and make her parents proud.

Only she, of all the committee, knew the shame, guilt and confusion of a young girl finding herself pregnant in an unforgiving world.

At the Brooklyn there would be choices made away from prying eyes, a safe haven for some that decided to brave it out and keep their babies. If Sowerthwaite didn't like it, well, tough! That was how it was going to be.

23

In the months following Gloria's death, Greg fought the nightmares with his bed sheets, the smell of acrid smoke waking him, the scorching heat burning his skin. In slow motion he kept seeing the silhouette of those girls edging onto the hoist, the crack of the joist and the figures falling into the black canal, the limp bodies on the tow path, and he woke up sweating and crying out, 'Gloria! I'm sorry . . .'

Each morning he got up only for the sake of Bebe, the precious daughter who was a daily reminder of his wife, with that glorious red hair and those bright eyes. When she was tired and cross she cried for her mummy and wouldn't be consoled, kicking and screaming until he soothed her with tales of her parents as little children.

'Tell me again about the Victory Tree?' she'd ask. They were reading Enid Blyton's *The Enchanted Wood*, with its story of the Faraway Tree and she got it into her head that it was real. 'Can we go and find the magic tree?'

'One day, when I can drive properly,' Greg promised.

‘I want to see it now. Uncle Charlie will drive us there,’ his daughter demanded, stamping her foot.

Greg had no energy to protest. It was as if his whole world had fallen apart in a few weeks. Nothing was as it once was: his wife, his rally hopes, his business, his agility, his health. He could hardly make a simple decision.

It was Charlie who suggested they take a holiday far away from recent memories to the Lakes or Wales. ‘It’s time you got away from these four walls,’ he said ‘Bebe needs to have some treats. Let’s ask her where she would like to go, let her decide, if you want, and perhaps we might catch sight of some stages of the RAC Rally if we plan our route carefully.’

Greg grinned. Trust Charlie to have an ulterior motive but he’d never been more in need of a friend in his life.

They drove south and then west through Wales, landing at the coast near Aberdovey, with its long beach, taking a cottage by the sea front, and ate fish and chips and freshly caught mackerel. They walked and talked for miles every day. Greg felt his legs strengthening with fresh air and exercise. It was then that he told Charlie all about Ken Silverstone and Gloria’s chequered past. Charlie listened and made encouraging noises but offered no comments at first.

It was later, over a pint of beer when Bebe was in bed, that Charlie laid into him.

‘The trouble with you, Mr Love ’em and leave ’em,’ he said, ‘is that you want every girl to be perfect. Up on that pedestal or down in the gutter. I saw you in

Germany, remember . . . poor Marthe? She adored you, not me, but you dismissed her because she'd had to sell herself to the highest bidder to put food on the table for her family. She could do no right in your eyes. You're a bit of a prude at heart. I've seen you in the dance hall, charming the pants off every lass, and then when they give in to you and don't measure up, you lose interest. I reckon the only one that got under your skin was young Maddy – and she dumped you first so you've sulked over her ever since.'

'That's not true!' Greg protested, but Charlie was determined to have his say.

'It may be the beer talking but poor Gloria never stood a chance. She tried so hard to be the ideal wife but she wasn't and never could be another Maddy Belfield. I don't think you've ever got over her.'

'Rubbish!' Greg snapped. 'What do you know?'

'Hear me out. What are friends for if they can't tell you the facts now and then? It must be hard being up on your pedestal; one wobble and off they go! What makes you so bloody perfect?'

Greg shook his head. 'You've got it all wrong there, mate. I just wanted someone better than me. I think men and girls should be different. We look to them to set an example.'

'Don't be so old-fashioned. What century are you living in?' said Charlie. 'It's one rule for us and another for them, according to you, Greg. We're all just human beings. Weakness and mistakes aren't the preserve of any one sex. We expect girls to close their legs while we spend all our time trying to open them and get up their skirts. It's not fair on them. It's two-faced nonsense.'

'Hark to Marge Proops! What's brought this on? I don't see you playing around much, do I? You sound like an old woman. What's it got to do with you?' Greg was back-footed by Charlie's outburst.

'My turn will come. She's out there somewhere,' said Charlie. 'I just haven't met her yet but I'll know her when she turns up. Poor sod will have to put up with my moods and my boring habits so I'll not be making an idol of her, chucking her away if she's not Miss Perfect. When you meet Mrs Right, I hope you'll learn sense from your mistakes.'

'You can forget that. I'm never getting wed again,' Greg snapped, peeved by Charlie's harsh words.

'Famous words. Think about Bebe – she needs a woman in the house.'

'I never had one and it didn't do me any harm.' Greg was going to argue his corner. What did Charlie know of being an orphan?

'Pull the other one! There was Mrs Plum Belfield, Maddy and Gloria, my mother. There's always been plenty of women in your life, but I'm not sure you ever appreciated any of them,' Charlie said.

'Why're you saying all this? Poor Gloria's hardly cold in her grave,' Greg snapped.

'Because it needs to be said. I'm your oldest mate. I owe you my life. I want you to find some peace and get back on the treadmill of life. Stop feeling sorry for yourself. Make some more profit. Perhaps when you're recovered I'll be free to find someone of my own.'

Greg was shocked at Charlie's frankness. He'd never spoken out before or challenged him. Had Charlie put his own life on hold since the accident just to nursemaid him?

As they strolled over the sand the next day, Greg felt the salt wind up his nostrils, and he smiled.

Dear old Charlie was a good mate. He was a friend who liked him even though he knew him, warts and all. Perhaps he was more right than Greg cared to think as he watched Bebe throwing pebbles on the beach, her jacket puffing out like a balloon. How was he going to advise her when she was older?

He loved her so much just as she was, a sad little lost girl who cried for her mummy in the night and was trying to be brave. But he couldn't be both mother and father to her. What about all that female stuff to come?

Spending the rest of his life as a monk didn't appeal either, but it was far too soon to think about any romance. Bebe was the most important thing in his life now.

'Bebe Byrne,' he yelled, 'how would you like to visit my magic tree?'

Maddy was fixing up the new twin tub in the wash house of the Old Vic Hostel. She'd begged it from an advert in the *Gazette* for a good cause. No questions were asked but now they had to fix the pipes and the whole place needed lime washing.

She was covered in plaster dust, wearing an old shirt and dungarees, and her hair wrapped up in a turban like the skivvy that she was.

Everything was being set up ready for the arrival of the first batch of mothers-to-be. Nappy washing in a machine would make life easier all round. She wanted everything to be welcoming and easy to run. They would have to start small and learn on the job, but she was looking forward to the challenge and hoped she wouldn't make too many mistakes.

It was a beautiful afternoon in late spring, with blossom on the apple trees and the beech leaves glistened in the sunshine. It was hard work cajoling friends and townsfolk into giving furniture, old prams, baby clothes, anything to fill cupboards. The most generous offers came from the council houses at the back of town. Her venture was the worst kept secret in town.

Bit by bit, her list of jobs was ticked off. Plum and Steve had sent such a generous cheque, the vicar had contacted the Church of England Children's Society, 'The Waifs and Strays', who sent a special almoner and adviser to help the mothers with their difficult decisions. All that was left was to wait for the first nervous arrivals and make them at home.

Maddy leaned against the tree to catch her breath and have a smoke. This tree was still her private thinking place. Suddenly there was a twitch of leaves and a pair of little legs dangled from the tree house, black patent leather shoes with ankle straps swinging. She was not alone. The curtain of leaves brushed aside to reveal a girl with bright copper curls and a pair of green eyes. It was like seeing a ghost.

'Hello . . . Is this the Faraway Tree, the magic tree?' squeaked the child of about five.

Maddy's heart leaped at the sight of little Miss Byrne. She'd have recognised that hair anywhere. 'We used to call it the V for Victory Tree . . . Yes, I suppose it's a magic tree,' she replied.

'My daddy and mummy used to play in here in the big war,' the child continued.

'And so did I,' Maddy smiled.

'You knew my mummy? She's in Heaven now with the angels.'

'If her name was Gloria, then, yes, I did know her. We were friends once upon a time.'

'Once upon a time we were all friends,' came a familiar voice from out of the shadows behind the gate. He'd been watching the encounter with interest. 'Hello, Maddy. Still hard at it, changing the world, I hear.'

'Greg!' Maddy blushed. She must look an absolute wreck. 'It's been a long time. And this little lady, I presume, is the famous Bebe. I've heard all about you.'

'I'm going to be a ballet dancer when I grow up,' Bebe smiled.

'Are you now? What's all this about a magic tree? You'd better tell me about it.'

'Daddy says you can make wishes in its branches and they'll come true. I've asked it to send Mummy back from Heaven.'

Maddy looked at Greg, who looked so much thinner and older, and now troubled by the child's words.

'I'm not sure it works that sort of magic, love,' he said, struggling to explain.

Maddy came to his rescue. 'When I was little like you, my mummy and daddy went to Heaven and I sat in the tree, just like you, making wishes. It didn't bring them back to me but it brought me friends to play with and lots of things to do.'

'Will it bring me a puppy, if I ask?'

'If it thinks it will help you, I'm sure it will,' she whispered, looking at Greg, who nodded with relief.

'How's your leg?' she asked, seeing his walking stick. 'I'm glad to see you're recovering. What a terrible year for you all. Grace and I have been thinking about you. I didn't come to the funeral but did Gloria tell you I came to visit you in hospital? But you were too ill . . .'

'Never too ill to see you.' He paused. 'No, she didn't. You heard about the fire . . . ?'

'Yes, it made all the papers in the country. What a dreadful thing to happen. The coroner said it was an unfortunate accident . . . I'm so sorry. Where are you staying?'

'Just passing through on our way to see Uncle Sid, but I promised Bebe I'd show her the Old Vic. What happened between you girls?' he said as he walked alongside her.

'It was a long time ago and not for a child's hearing, Greg. Have you got time for a snifter at the Brooklyn? You won't recognise the place.'

'I thought you'd never ask.' He smiled the old smile, and she felt the familiar magnetic pull to his side but drew back, flushing.

'Come on, Bebe. I'll race you up the Avenue like your mummy and me used to do.'

'Perhaps Miss Belfield will tell you the story about the trees.'

'Aunt Maddy sounds better . . .'

Suddenly it didn't matter that she looked a wreck or that the place was a tip. They were her guests and she'd show them round the rooms with pride. What would Greg make of her new venture? Would she ever explain why she was taking on this mammoth task? Not today, no . . . she smiled. It was just wonderful to see him alive and well, broken though he seemed now. Perhaps if she made him welcome he might come back again.

They sat in the kitchen, sipping tea, taking sideways glances at each other. She just couldn't believe he was sitting there. Bebe was being plied with ginger biscuits that she dunked in the hot tea with relish.

'I'm taking in special guests,' Maddy began. Better he knew the worst first. 'Young expectant mothers who have nowhere else to go . . . just for a few weeks until they are confined and then some of them will live in the Old Vic.'

'That's very brave,' he said, looking directly into her eyes. To her relief she saw compassion not disgust. 'I bet that took a bit of doing round here.'

'Times are changing,' she quipped. 'People have to make allowances for the unexpected.'

'I've learned that the hard way,' Greg replied, and he looked so sad and lost and tired she just wanted to take him in her arms and hug him. 'Now we'd better be off if we're to catch Sid before milking.'

'I'm so glad you called in for old times' sake.' They both rose and she felt herself trembling. This was it, the moment to let him go. They were two different people now. He wouldn't want to be involved in her world. They walked slowly to the hall way and the silence was so powerful.

Do I let him walk out of my life for ever or do I ask him back in? If I do, he must know some of the truth about me . . . What shall I do? This is the moment to find out. Help!

'So what do you think about my hostel? Have I shocked you?' she said, not looking at him as she spoke, trying to be breezy and businesslike.

Greg turned to her and smiled. 'You've taken a huge risk. I think you're mad but brave. I envy you your courage.'

Take a risk . . . courage . . . what did his reply mean? She smiled back.

'It's the Carnival Day soon. Do you think Bebe would like to come? There's a fair and parade, and it should be fun. They've started up again. She can come in fancy dress . . .' She cast out a line. Would he bite?

'We'd love to come. Give me the date, we'll be there, won't we, Bebe?'

Gloria's daughter was already running in and out of the trees. 'It's magic here . . .

Can we come again?'

They were halfway up the Dale on his way to see Sid Conley when Greg recalled Gloria's last words: 'Under the Victory Tree.' He'd promised to give this message to Maddy and somehow he'd forgotten.

That was the trouble: one sight of her and all the old yearnings came rushing back. Everything else went out of his mind and Gloria not dead a year. How could he even think of it? What was wrong with him? After the mess they've made of everything he couldn't risk another cock-up. Bebe was his first and only concern now.

How the Brooklyn had changed now it was set up like a hostel. The drawing room was a big sitting room. The old kitchen was now a dining kitchen. There were bedrooms set out with beds like a dormitory. Why ever was Maddy on this crusade? He didn't understand her – perhaps he never had. Better not to stir things up, better to stay away, and yet the Sowerthwaite Carnival sounded fun.

He stopped off for petrol at Brigg's Garage. It was just the same old ramshackle shed with pumps in the forecourt. It still looked like the blacksmith's forge it once must have been. His professional eye sized it up with interest.

Good spot on the crossroads, lots of through traffic on the way to the Lake District, a nice bit of land at the back, ripe for development. There was money in the Dales. Farmers had done well after the war. They needed new Land Rovers, tough jobs for a rough terrain. If he were old man Brigg, he'd want to expand and get a dealership and make a proper business out of it.

Greg laughed, remembering how keen he was to be their oily rag with his go-kart and his wheels, polishing the Belfields' Daimler, and his first try at the wheel of the car. How could he not be fond of this one-horse town?

'Look, Daddy used to work here.' He turned round but Bebe was fast asleep. As he looked around him his heart just skipped a beat, made a drum roll. It was grand to be back.

The day of Sowerthwaite Carnival dawned fine, with blue sky, and all the weather pundits were right for once. 'The weather glass is rising,' said old Mr Lock. 'It'll be a right grand day.'

Maddy and Grace had set the three pregnant girls at baking for the cream teas, making scones, sponge cakes and Yorkshire curd tarts. None of them had much of a clue, being addicted to Wagon Wheels and Mars Bars.

Maureen, the first to arrive, was going to have a go. Cherry was all fingers and thumbs, and poor Sandra kept bursting into tears.They were only frightened kids, but Maddy was determined to teach them a few basic skills while they were with her. She kept thinking of Plum and her puppy-training regime. 'What they need, Maddy, is routine and lots of firm love.' Just what Plum had given the evacuees all those years ago.

She was going to make sure they enjoyed their day out at the fair. If they all wore white gloves with their maternity dresses no one would notice them in the crowds. In fact she'd bought rings for them all just so they could be anonymous.

There was the usual bustle of comings and goings, cakes to be collected and delivered. In a loose moment she'd been persuaded to be one of the judges for the fancy-dress parade. Oh Lord, that would mean her dressing up old style, with a hat, a frock and the full slap on. Everyone dressed up for the Carnival.

While she was busy the girls would have to fend for themselves but she was worried she would offend half the town by choosing the wrong competitor in the fancy-dress parade.

Barney was alongside her, and the referee was going to be Archie Murray, the vicar, as usual. They'd been such champions of her cause.

She'd not heard another word from Greg since that unexpected visit, not even a letter. She didn't know whether he'd bother to come so far out of his way, but she was going to doll herself up with extra care in case he did. She still had some pride left about her appearance. Sowerthwaite expected the Lady of the Manor to grace the public occasion with a bit of swank: a mink stole in case of a stiff breeze, a cartwheel mushroom hat and high-heeled shoes, even on the mud bath that was the Fellings recreation ground.

She had to provide jams and preserves for the WI stall, cakes for the cake stall, a bottle of wine for the raffle, bric-a-brac for the white elephant stall, and be expected to purchase something from every table so as not to give offence.

Rumours about the goings-on at Brooklyn Hall were rife, but Maddy was determined to hold her head up high. What she was doing was right and it was giving her such a sense of satisfaction and purpose never found in being a mannequin.

All the best stuff from the Brooklyn from the olden days was stashed away in the attic now: portraits, fancy rugs and silver, none of it being appropriate for a mother and baby home.

They'd not had their first baby at the home yet, but Maureen was not far off her time to deliver. Then she'd be sent to the maternity unit at Scarperton. Maddy just hoped they'd get there on time and that she didn't deliver today of all days.

The procession gathered up in the town square, waiting for the silver band to assemble in their red blazers with gold braid. There was the usual lorryloads of floating Rose Queens visiting from nearby villages and towns: Hellifield, Settle, and the district beyond; a queue of decorated floats, lorries dressed up in sheets and paper roses with benches on which sat each local princess in wide evening dresses and velvet cloaks, tended by an assortment of bridesmaids with ringlets and bouquets in baskets, and pageboys in velvet trews with scuffed knees and runny noses.

After them came the parade floats: the rugby club, the Guides and Brownies, the youth club, who were doing Bill Haley and the Comets in a rock 'n' roll scene, the WI pageant float, the Townswomen's Guild, Pedlar's Dairy float, the Amateur Dramatic Society presenting their next play, wobbling on the lorry, vying with the Operatic Club with their costumes and noise. The procession was backed up right down the street, and behind them came the fancy-dress competitors of all ages, shapes and sizes. Then a parade of vintage cars and saloons, an old fire engine to the rear. The opener of the Carnival sat in an open-topped landau with the mayor in his regalia, and to her horror Maddy found the judges were expected to sit in the next open-topped coach on view as honoured guests.

It was only the second Carnival since the war. So there was a great splash of ceremony about the crowning of the Carnival Princess, who was Miss Stephanie Sidwell, picked out of a hat at the youth club dance.

For one day of the year all the community gathered together to parade and spend money for charity. Not that any of it would come Maddy's way. Her venture was still too new and daring and disapproved of to get much support. Most of the town just pretended the home wasn't there. Nobody talked to her about it. She was a Belfield, and for once it worked to her advantage. If she wanted to use the old manor house in such a venture it was up to her. It was her money she was risking.

Now and again something came through the post – anonymous donations with little lines of encouragement. But she was on her own with this one and it felt lonely at times. At the end of each day, she carried her worries up the stairs on her own but for today she wanted just to enjoy the Carnival like everyone else.

For once the Yorkshire sun blazed down on the assembled crowds.

'It's faired up right gradely,' said the mayor. 'But what's the hold-up now?'

They seemed to have been sitting around in the coach for hours, waiting for the band to strike up and the procession to begin.

'There's a hold-up – right at the front,' the message

went down the line. 'One of them lorries . . . stuck in the square and nothing can get round it.'

'Blood and sand! That's not a good start to the day,' said the mayor. 'Anyone for a pint?' He laughed, pointing to the Three Tuns pub across the road.

Gregory and Bebe fought their way through the pavement crowds to where the fancy-dress competitors were gathering.

'Don't leave me, Daddy,' Bebe cried, clinging on to his hand for dear life. She was dressed as Little Bo-Peep, with peek-a-boo bonnet, a long party dress and a shepherd's crook with a toy lamb under her arm. Mrs Afton had borrowed this costume from her granddaughter, but Bebe was unimpressed.

'It's a baby costume,' she whined. 'I wanted to be a nurse.'

'You will take what you're given, young lady,' Greg shouted at her. He was nervous about coming back, but he must give Maddy that message from Gloria. But how was he to find her among this throng?

They stood while the sun beat down, waiting for the procession to begin, waiting and waiting until everybody got hot and impatient. 'What's the hold-up?'

'First lorry's broken down . . . typical. Nothing can move until it starts. And it won't start.'

There were all sorts of noises, roarings and judderings. Greg dragged Bebe down the street. He could tell that they were doing the wrong things. Nobody had a clue.

'Want a hand, mate?' Greg asked, but he was ignored at first. 'Look, why don't you try . . . ?'

His fingers itched to get his hands under the bonnet. What he didn't know about setting up an engine wasn't worth knowing. 'Give it here,' he ordered. 'Will you mind my little girl?' He turned to a young mother holding a baby dressed as Red Riding Hood. His shirt-sleeves were soon rolled up and he twisted and turned knobs. 'I think this might be the problem,' he said. 'Try it again? . . . No . . . not that one, the other.' The mechanic beckoned him under the bonnet. They were sweating, covered in engine grease. The metal was hot, the sun reminding him of all those treks across France, fettling up army trucks.

'Try again.' Then the engine ignited smoothly and everyone cheered.

'Owe you a pint, guv,' said the lorry driver. 'If you ever need a job Brigg's your man.'

'Not Derek Brigg . . . Briggsy? I used to work for your dad as his oily rag . . . Greg Byrne. You'll remember me?'

'One of the vaccies! Blood and sand! We were in the same class. You always were one for engines. How do!'

'How's your dad?'

'Not good . . . terrible rheumatics. There's just me now. Our Alan didn't make it back from the Far East in the war.'

'I'm sorry, but we'll have that drink, Derek, on me. I'd like to talk to you a bit more about the garage, but not now or we'll get lynched. You'd better move on.'

*

The parade was off at long last. The band was getting everyone in the mood as slowly they edged their way past the church where they'd made an arch of branches and leaves, and down the High Street under all the red, white and blue bunting, turning into the recreation ground with a flourish. There was a sea of clapping, waving noisy customers all rushing to enter the field. The funfair loudspeaker was working for once and it was time to make their way to the judging area.

Maddy was dreading this, but each age group was pegged to a post. There was a novelty class, family group, boys, girls, toddlers; so many classes to judge from, and hundreds of children.

'Don't worry, they'll all get a consolation lollipop. Just pick the one who's made the most effort,' said the vicar, 'and watch out for the professionals. They turn up at every fête in the district. They hire costumes or send for the stuff from adverts. You know the sort of thing – HP Sauce, Heinz Baked Beans. Don't pick one of those. They're not locals.'

They judged the contestants as they paraded round the ring, cowboys, Indians, fairies, Humpty Dumpty, Long John Silver, a cracking crocodile or red dragon – it was hard to tell which – and then Maddy saw the red ringlets of a Bo-Peep and smiled. If Bebe Byrne was on show Greg wouldn't be far behind. Suddenly, her heart just danced. They'd come. He was here somewhere in the crowd, watching. Once this was over she'd be able to join them and take tea with them in the tent, do all the things a family did together on a day out.

The judges huddled together making lists, while the assembled princesses gathered on the platform for the crowning ceremony by the mayor and his wife.

The fancy-dress competitors were quickly dispersed to make room for the procession of visiting queens, and when Maddy looked round Bebe was gone and she was smothered in nylon dresses, with lace trims and petal girls excitedly watching for when it was their time to parade.

Then Sandra came running out of the crowd, 'Miss . . . Maureen started – she's wet herself!'

'Stay calm,' said Maddy, trying to look composed, glad that they were hidden behind the striped awning. 'I see, yes, well, where is she?'

'Over there, right under the tree in the shade.'

They mustn't make a fuss and draw attention to the girl. Maddy was thinking on her feet.

'We'd better get the St John Ambulance man over. Have you seen Mrs Battersby anywhere?'

'No, miss, but the ambulance went off with someone in it. I saw that. An old man collapsed.'

'I see,' Maddy said as she strode down to where Maureen was gathering a crowd – no ambulance, no midwife or doctor in sight. Perhaps her own car would suffice, but it was stuck in the garage and blocked in by parked vehicles outside the Avenue. The town was chock-a-block with visitors on such a lovely day.

'We've got to get her to Scarperton, but don't panic. Babies take hours to be born,' she said, thinking ten miles wasn't very far to go, and then a welcome face beamed at her.

'Maddy! There you are!' Greg was dragging Bebe, sucking a lollipop. 'We thought we'd lost you.'

'Greg, I'm busy,' she whispered. 'One of my ladies is starting in labour.'

'OK, right,' he said. 'Do you need any help?'

'Not sure,' said Maddy. 'This needs careful handling in a public place. Just the drama our critics will be waiting for. I don't want to draw attention to her.'

'Don't worry, leave it to me. Just point me out where she is.'

'Under the tree, Greg, but I'm not sure . . .' she cried, but he'd raced ahead. What was he playing at, shouting to the crowd around her?

'Give her some air. Give my wife some air!' he shouted to the crowds. The girl looked up at him in amazement. 'Come on, love, time we got you to the hospital quickly.'

Maureen looked up at his rugged face with astonishment.

'Miss Belfield, will you look after the little one while we make our way to my car?' He ordered as if he was a stranger.

It was better than the television drama *Emergency Ward 10*. Greg lifted up the staggering girl and escorted her down as the crowds parted like the Red Sea before Moses. 'Over here into the shade, it's not far,' he said, turning round to Maddy. 'How am I doing so far?'

'Brilliant!' Maddy said. Maureen was swallowed up in sympathy now her husband was here to guide her. No one recognised Greg from the old days. He'd carried it off like a trooper, with Bebe, unperturbed, following in tow like a dutiful sister-to-be.

They all drove very slowly to Scarperton General in his saloon and went to the maternity wing. When Maddy explained the situation Maureen was duly booked in as Mrs Maureen Smith.

'You can leave me here. I'd better wait. Go back and enjoy the rest of the Carnival. Bebe shouldn't miss the rest.'

'You sure?' She thought Greg looked relieved.

'Thanks for your support. You ought to join the drama group after that performance.' She patted his arm and waved them away, sad to see them go. That was that, then. At least they came. All dressed up and nowhere to go, poor Maddy was Jilly No-mates again, she sighed. It was going to be a long wait.

They sent her home hours later, content in the knowledge that the first Brooklyn baby was safely in his cot and both he and his mother were well. He was a beautiful little boy with a mop of dark hair.

Maddy took a taxi, driving through the streets still thronging with merrymakers, enjoying the dancing on the marketplace cobbles. There was a little band and the kids were dancing and running around.

When she drove up the Avenue, to her surprise Greg's car was still there, and Grace and the girls were having a crafty cigarette on the steps, waiting for her to return.

'It's a boy!' she yelled, looking at Sandra. 'One down, two to go . . .'

They all looked at each other with relief.

Later, Maddy sat with Greg, knowing Bebe was asleep upstairs out of earshot.

'Thanks for staying on. You needn't have done that.'

'Thanks for asking us. It's been a great day out. Poor kid was whacked. We went up to Sid's farm to see his new girlfriend, Ava. I gather she's another one of your good causes,' he laughed.

'One of the Hungarians. Yes, I knew they were seeing each other.'

'I don't understand you, Maddy. There's so much I just don't understand about all this doing good . . . What's it all about?' He gestured around the room and her hackles rose.

'It's not doing good, as you call it. It's about paying back.'

'For what?'

'Do you really want to know, Gregory Byrne?' she replied, knowing it was now or never. Why hold back now? Maddy took a deep breath, bent her head so he couldn't see her face and told him about Dieter, the baby, the miscarriage and how Gloria had rescued her and protected her.

'When we fell out later, it was about something quite different.' She was lying, not ready to discuss all of that. 'So there, you know why I have to help others in the same boat. This could have been me and I'll never forget that fact. Giving birth is the easy bit for Maureen – it's what comes after that will be so hard for them to bear, whichever way they decide to go. Now I expect you'll never want to see us again.'

'Why is that then?' He stared hard into her eyes, forcing her to stare back.

'Because I'm not the paragon of virtue you thought I was.'

'Gloria wasn't who I thought she was either,' he said, giving his version of what had happened with Ken and the calendar, and how sadly it had all ended. 'She tricked me into thinking she was his victim but I reckon she knew what she was doing all along,' he said.

'Oh, come on, Greg, we were all victims one way or another. Haven't you ever made a mistake?'

'Of course I have.'

'Remember the night you booked us into the hotel and I wouldn't even come inside. I was scared. I couldn't risk another mistake. If I'd confessed the real story you'd have run a mile from soiled goods. You said you "didn't want a slice of a cut loaf" so I kept silent and Gloria jumped into your arms. She'd always fancied you. She wanted you and she told me if I didn't move over she'd tell you anyway. That's why we parted company . . . over you – and look what good it did either of us!'

Greg sat there with his head on his hands. 'I'd no idea.'

'No, men usually don't have a clue. When there's a battle for custody, it's the women who decide your fate, I'm afraid. I didn't feel good enough for you. I had to say no. What if we'd gone ahead and married and you'd found out?'

'What a mess all this is. Charlie was right. I've been an absolute pig-headed fool. I thought there was one rule for us and another for you. When Gloria told me the truth about those photos. I stormed out, and that's when I crashed my car. She took that job to prove herself to me. She would still be alive if only . . . I have to live with all that.'

'If onlys . . . all of us have to live with regrets.'

'Did you and Gloria ever make it up?'

'How can friends trust each other after such an argument? That doesn't mean to say I'm not sorry she died like that. If only . . .'

'I know. I'm sorry, I've been such an idiot. My pride was hurt when you dumped me and when you went on to be such a success, I had to match you.'

'You've not done badly for yourself.'

'I'm ready for a change from bricks and mortar, to be honest. I was eyeing up old Brigg's Garage the other day. It's ripe for development. It would get Bebe away from Sunnyside Drive, away from that snotty school she hates. Gloria insisted she went to a private school. She did so want to be like you. I always said I'd come back one day but not like this . . . a cripple.'

'You're not a cripple. Be patient . . . healing takes time. After what you two have been through, I think a change is a great idea, but don't rush it. Bebe needs time to get used to the idea. I think a puppy would be a good idea, though. Just don't leave it so long before you visit us again,' Maddy laughed.

He looked at her and she knew she had a friend again.

'Is there anything I can do to help?'

'You could take me out of this mad house now and again,' she smiled.

'That's a deal,' he replied.

Greg smiled as he thought how it had started just as friendly visits, but both of them knew it was more than that. Greg felt at long last that he'd found the other half of himself after all these years apart, after so much misunderstanding and half-truths. She was his equal – more than his equal – but he was trying hard not to worship Maddy too much.

They found a little Collie puppy for Bebe and it was love at first sight between the two of them. Every weekend they seemed to gravitate back across the Pennines to the Dales for tea and toast in the Brooklyn kitchen.

There were always jobs for Greg to tackle: new shelves, repairing a drain, knocking up some benches. The girls came and went, and his presence sort of balanced things in the household. Bebe took all the babies in her stride.

It was a sad place sometimes when a girl left without her baby. Some were taken away at birth, while others clung on for a couple of weeks. The strain would be etched on Maddy's face after a tearful farewell. She and Greg often went to the pictures or out for a meal, just to relieve her tension.

One night they parked up on the top moor road just to look at the stars, his arm round her, sniffing the gorgeous smell of the woman he adored. Things were changing between them. He felt her tense up, trying to say something and holding back.

This was it, he thought. She was wanting them out of her life just when he was negotiating with the Brigg family to buy into their garage business with a view to bringing his business acumen to the fore. He had this brilliant idea for buying in specialist sports cars to tune up to rally standard. They'd be moving soon, and perhaps Maddy felt it was time he got on with his own life.

'What's the matter?' he said. 'You've been quiet all evening.'

'I've got a lot on my mind. I'm thinking of taking on a partner at the Brooklyn. You've seen how chaotic it can get. Some of the girls can be, to say the least, difficult and emotional. I need to get some extra support.'

'I see,' said Greg. It would need a saint to take on that lot, and not someone like Miss Blunt. 'Mrs Plum would've been the perfect choice if she were free.' He was trying to stay calm and polite. 'Had you anyone in mind or are you going to advertise in the *Yorkshire Post*?' he answered in all seriousness.

Maddy burst out laughing. 'Don't look so worried. There was someone I had in mind but it would have to be a permanent live-in post.'

'They can be difficult to fill . . . references and checks . . .' He was trying to be helpful, even though he felt sick.

'I've got a lifetime of references on this one,' she whispered as she leaned over to nibble his ear.

'Oh?' he replied, struggling to grasp the gist of this.

'Marry me!' she laughed, and stopped his mouth with a kiss.

*

Three months later, they lit the torches on the path to the church porch on a dark December Saturday afternoon. Bebe was dressed in a green velvet Victorian outfit straight out of her fairy-tale book, with a velvet muff. Bella and Charmaine were matrons of honour, wearing deep burgundy hues. Plum was so excited to be home at long last, drinking in the damp Yorkshire air for the first time in years. Here it had all begun and here it would continue, she smiled. Maddy was taking on a motherless child as she herself had done all those years ago. The two of them would nurture those frightened girls through their labours and dramas. Greg would be the rock that grounded her when things went wrong and tempers flew and Bebe cried for Gloria. She wished them all the luck in the world.

It was enough that her prayers were answered on that wintry afternoon. Maddy had found her true friend, her life's companion, and she deserved to be happy. Was it fate those two had met once before by the Hepworth sculpture? Greg was learning to make allowances for other people's mistakes. He was no angel and never would be, but it was never too late to learn that old adage that he who never made a mistake, never made anything. She should know, she'd made plenty herself.

What was lovely about this wedding was that so many friends from other parts of their lives came to wish them well: all the Foxups – Totty and Hugh, Bella and Alex – and the Pinkertons; Charlie Afton, the best man and his family and Brigg's Garage crowd. Even

Raoul Henry caused a stir when he turned up with the tallest blonde anyone had ever seen in Sowerthwaite. There were rumours she must be a man! There was Sid Conley with his new wife, Ava, the only other evacuee present. But the usual line-up of church ladies lined the back pews to give the outfits the once-over.

Maddy looked wonderful, wearing a sleek cream velvet cape edged with swan's-down round the hood, over a body-skimming shift so simple and luscious against her dark hair. Greg wore tails with aplomb. Was this the same lad with the scuffed knees and scabby elbows, whom Plum had entrusted to find her niece all those years ago? How strange, how wonderful life could be!

February 2000

The simple tree-planting ceremony is over at last. Maddy smiles as they put the finishing touches to the bench made from stumps of the old beech, a place to stop and rest a while for those who come to pay their respects to the fallen heroes.

She recalls how, on the night before their wedding, in the bustle of preparation and visitors arriving, Greg had taken Maddy aside. 'We need to talk. There's something I should have told you ages ago and I sort of forgot, or I sort of blanked it out from my mind . . . I don't know why.'

She can see them as if it were yesterday, huddled together in the bedroom, cuddled up among packing cases and tissue paper, with her bridal outfit hidden out of sight in the dressing room. They were both tearful, tired and excited, but this was important judging by the look on Greg's face.

'On the night Gloria died, she whispered something in my ear,' he said, 'I didn't get it all, but it was for you. I heard your name . . . "Tell Maddy, under the

Victory Tree." I think that's what she said. She made me promise to tell you, "under the Victory Tree". Do you know what that means?'

'Oh, yes, I do,' Maddy wept. At last, the truth with her dying breath; Gloria had given her the baby's precious burial ground. It was a wedding present no one would ever know but herself. Thank you, she prayed, knowing her new life could begin.

But it had taken over forty years for the old tree to yield up its secret at long last, after all those attempts to dig round its roots until she thought for years Gloria had held out on her once again.

The old beech tree had gathered up her baby and grown it into itself: how strange, how wonderful, and how right now to be putting those tiny remains back in just a simple ceremony; earth to earth; for what is soil but the compost of many plants and lives, chalk, bones, the dust of generations of long dead?

The interviews with the police were a formality. They were not taking any action on the remains. They were examined and tissue samples suggested a male foetus too premature to have survived, probably as a result of a miscarriage or abortion, perhaps around the time of the Hungarian refugees or earlier.

She could have spoken out but some things are best just left unspoken.

All this confessional stuff is all very well today but she was brought up to be discreet, to bear suffering and disappointment with dignity, in silence; one of the stiff-upper-lip generation. Perhaps it was wrong but it served well enough. Silence is golden, went the proverb.

She suggested the baby be reburied under the new tree in the Avenue and there were no objections so old bones will soon return to dust, the circle will be complete, what was lost now found. Who else does it concern?

Why should she have to tell her secrets? Some are just better left unspoken. Only Greg and Plum knew the truth of it and that's where it ends.

Little Dieter rests in the Avenues of Tears amongst his ancestors: the last of the Belfields.

Try as they might, she'd not produced another child of her own. It was something to do with her cervix being slack and her womb being tilted. Nowadays it wouldn't be a problem but then, well, some things are just not meant to be. So like Plum she'd been given another woman's child to nurture and cherish.

Soon Bebe would be arriving from London to start her new life at the Old Vic. In time Gloria and Greg's child and grandchildren would inherit the house and the Old Vic, and the Avenue of Tears would be ringing to the yells of Bebe's boys on mountain bikes, later with motor cycles and cars, bringing girls home to meet their mother. That was how it should be in an ever-changing circle of friends and family.

It is enough to know that the little lost baby was put to rest properly. Gloria had put him where only they knew, under the Victory Tree, the repository of all their childish secrets. Why had she not guessed this earlier? Perhaps because it needed time for her to appreciate this instinctive gesture.

Maddy sits on the varnished stump bench looking

up at the Brooklyn. Once there were blackout curtains and taped windows, Pleasance and the oldies creaking up the stairs. The house was in darkness for a while. Then there were those wartime Christmas lights and candles, evacuees in crocodiles marching up to the big house for treats and bun fights.

Over the stone portico hangs the storm lantern made by Ernst, their first Hungarian refugee, as a gift for his stay in the refuge. He made the bars at the high windows to stop toddlers falling out in the makeshift nursery when it was a mother and baby home.

Gladly now, young mothers can keep their babies – choices never open to her girls all those years ago – but suddenly in the seventies her services were no longer required.

Brooklyn, she smiles, my refuge, my home, was always a house with attitude. I have been truly blessed.

Maddy rises slowly, looking at the old house. It will go on surviving, reinventing itself, sheltering the next generation from the storms of life, but now it was time for tea. Greg will be hitting the cake tin while she's not in view.

She walks towards the lamp-lit windows and closes the door.

In Conversation with Leah Fleming

What inspired you to write *Orphans of War*?

When Foot and Mouth struck the Yorkshire Dales a few years ago, the livestock of our local farm was taken out and the footpaths closed so that for 18 months I couldn't turn left outside our gate to walk the dog.

On one of our alternative tours round the village the dog wandered into the grounds of an empty Georgian house that had once served as an evacuee hostel during the war. It had a large walled orchard, barns and gardens and I began to tingle with those magic words: "what if . . ."

So a whole novel grew from the frustration of one closed footpath and a nosey Collie!

The idea of the Victory Tree grew from having our own trees lopped and talking to the tree surgeons about what they discovered inside trunks. One off-the-cuff remark sparked a whole plotline into life.

I take my inspiration from the hills and landscape of the North Craven Dales. I like creating imaginary villages and houses. The name of Brooklyn Hall came from a hotel in Bolton close to where I lived which was the nearest bit of country at hand. I never went in, it but it felt a huge mysterious place to a small child.

The wartime atmosphere of the Dales during WWII is beautifully evoked and really makes the reader feel as if they are with Maddy, Plum and Gloria at Brooklyn House. How much research did you have to do for this, and did you use your own experiences (or that of your family) in the book?

The local history group in my area had already researched its story and interviewed the former Warden, the late Mrs

Frances Capstick and some of her former evacuees. This story has evolved from some of the anecdotes they shared with us. Most admitted that their wartime experiences have left many scars.

How do you write? Do you have a routine?

I turn up at my desk every morning and keep to a strict regime, whether it is at home or abroad. I read and research in the afternoons and watch black and white movies for inspiration!

Which character do you feel most connected to and why?

The most complex character I feel connected to is Gloria. Her story is the most tragic. Her need to be accepted leads her into wrong choices from which there is no turning back but she redeems herself in the end.

Who are your favourite authors?

My favourite authors are those whose books take me into another world and another time and challenge me with their understanding of human nature. Douglas Kennedy does it for me every time.

What are you working on next?

Following the lives and loves of three evacuees took me into the world of 1950s fashion modelling, the Festival of Britain, the aftermath of the Hungarian revolution and the fate of unmarried mothers in the 1960s. This gave me an idea for my next novel: *Mothers and Daughters,* now a work in progress.